A
SUPERTHRILLER
TO REMEMBER!

For Dirk Pitt, raising the Titanic was one thing.
NIGHT PROBE! another thing. The consequences of raising a planeload of the deadliest
plague the world had ever known, something
else...

ICEBERG, THE MEDITERRANEAN CAPER,
RAISE THE TITANIC! have established Clive
Cussler as a novelist of enormous popularity.
With VIXEN 03 he demonstrates again his
superb mastery of the adventure novel.

VIXEN 03

A NOVEL BY
CLIVE CUSSLER

ABOUT THE AUTHOR

CLIVE CUSSLER lives the same sort of adventurous life as his hero, Dirk Pitt. Tramping the Southwest in search of gold mines, diving in isolated Rocky Mountain lakes for missing aircraft, heading an expedition to salvage John Paul Jones' ship, the *Bonhomme Richard*. Most recently Cussler discovered and excavated a sister ship to the *Monitor*, as well as finding artifacts from its famous nemesis the *Merrimack*. A noted collector of classic automobiles, Cussler lives in the foothills overlooking Denver, Colorado. Here he writes his bestselling thrillers: RAISE THE TITANIC!, ICEBERG, THE MEDITERRANEAN CAPER, VIXEN 03—and most recently, NIGHT PROBE!

15

They came with the rising sun. Somala counted at least thirty of them, clothed in the same type of field uniform he wore. He watched as they crept out of the bush like shadows and disappeared into the sugarcane.

He swept the acacia tree with his binoculars. The scout in the blind was gone. Probably slipped away to join his unit, Somala surmised. But who were they? None of the raiding force looked familiar to him. Could they be members of another insurgent movement? If so, why did they wear the distinctive black beret of the AAR?

Somala was sorely tempted to leave his hiding place inside the baobab tree and approach the intruders, but he thought better of it and remained motionless. He would watch and observe. Those were his orders, and he would obey them.

The Fawkes farm was slowly coming to life. The workers in the compound were beginning to spread out and commence their daily chores. Patrick Fawkes, Jr., passed through the electricity-wired gate and went off to the great stone barn, where he began tinkering with a tractor. The guards were changing at the gate, and the fellow who had manned the night shift was standing half in, half out of the enclosure, swapping small talk with his relief, when abruptly and silently he fell to the ground. Simultaneously, the other guard slumped and dropped.

Somala gaped in awe as a wave of raiders sprinted out of the sugarcane field in a loose skirmish line and advanced toward the house. Most were carrying Chinese CK-88 assault weapons, but two of their number knelt and aimed long-barreled rifles with scopes and silencers.

The CK-88s opened up and Fawkes Junior seemed to snap to attention as at least ten slugs ripped through his body. His hands splayed and clawed at empty air, and then he crumpled across the tractor's unhooded engine. The

thunder of the volley alerted Jenny and she ran to an upstairs window.

"Oh God, Mama!" she screamed. "There's soldiers in the
yard and they've shot Pat."

Myrna Fawkes grabbed the Holland & Holland and ran
to the front door. One look was all she needed to see that
the defenses had been breached. Already Africans in green
and brown mottled uniforms were surging through the
open gate left useless by the broken electrical circuit. She
slammed the door, threw the lock, and yelled up the stairs
to Jenny.

"Get on the radio and call the constable."

Then she calmly sat down, shoved two shells containing
double-O buckshot into the breech of the twelve-gauge,
and waited.

The crackle of the rifle fire suddenly increased and the
shrill cries of women and frightened children began coming
from the compound. Even the Fawkeses' prize cattle were
not spared. Myrna shut out the bellows of their dying
agony, choking off a dry sob at the waste of it all. She
lifted the twin barrels as the first attacker crashed his way
through the door.

He was the handsomest African Myrna had ever seen.
His features were distinctly Caucasian, and yet his skin
was nearly a perfect blue-black. He lifted his rifle as if to
smash out her brains with the butt and lunged across the
room. Myrna pulled both triggers and old Lucifer spat fire.

The blast at such close range nearly tore the African's
head off. His face dissolved in a spray of bone and red-
dish-gray tissue, and he jerked backward against the door
frame and melted to the floor, his torso quivering in spastic
pulsations.

Almost casually, as though she were at a skeet tourna-
ment, Myrna reloaded the gun. She had just snapped shut
the breech when two more men hurtled through the door.
Old Lucifer took the first squarely in the chest, dropping
him instantly. The other attacker leaped over his fallen
comrade's body, a move that threw Myrna's aim a trifle
low. The discharge from the other barrel hit her attacker
in the groin. He screamed, cast his weapon aside, and
clutched himself. He grunted incoherently and staggered
back outside to the veranda, pitching forward with his
booted feet still in the room.

Myrna reloaded again. A window shattered and holes

suddenly appeared in the wallpaper beside her chair. She felt no stabbing pain, no stinging sensation. She looked down. Blood was beginning to seep through the blue denim of her jeans.

A heavy booming sound erupted from upstairs and she knew Jenny was shooting down into the yard with the captain's .44 Magnum.

The next African was more cautious. He fired a quick burst around the door and waited before he entered. Not receiving any return fire, he became overconfident and ventured inside. The double-O buckshot blew away his left arm. For several moments he stared dazedly at the limb lying at his feet, the fingers still twitching. The blood pumped from his empty sleeve and spilled on the carpet. Still in a trance, the soldier slowly sank to his knees and knelt there, moaning softly as his life's fluids leaked away.

With one hand Myrna fumbled with Lucifer. Three bullets from her last assailant had shattered her right forearm and wrist. Awkwardly, she broke open the breech and ejected the spent shells. Her every movement seemed immersed in glue. The new shells slipped between her sweating fingers and fell past her reach.

"Mama?"

Myrna looked up. Jenny was standing in the middle of the stairway, the revolver hanging loosely in one hand, the front of her blouse soaked with crimson.

"Mama . . . I'm hurt."

Before Myrna could reply, another figure entered the room. Jenny tried to raise her gun. Her effort came slowly and too late. The newcomer fired first and she sagged and rolled down the stairs like a ragged, cast-off doll.

Myrna could only sit there and grip Lucifer. The loss of blood was sapping her energy and blurring her vision. She gazed vacantly at the man standing over her. Through the growing fog she could see him place the tip of the rifle an inch from her forehead.

"Forgive me," he said.

"Why?" she asked vaguely. "Why did you do this terrible thing?"

The cold dark eyes held no answer. For Myrna, the bougainvillea blossoms outside on the veranda exploded in a blaze of fuchsia and then blinked into blackness.

Somala walked among the dead, staring numbly at the faces forever frozen in shock and confusion. The raiders had ruthlessly killed nearly all the workers and their families in the compound. No more than a handful could have escaped into the bush. The feed in the barn and the equipment housed in the shed had been set on fire, and flames were already flickering orange fingers from the upstairs window of the Fawkes house.

How strange, Somala thought. The raiders policed the battleground and retrieved their own dead as quietly as ghosts. The movements had been efficient and deliberate. There was no hint of panic at the distant sound of the approaching helicopter units of the South African Defence Forces. The raiders simply melted into the surrounding brush as stealthily as they came.

Somala returned to the baobab tree for his gear and began trotting toward the township. His only thoughts were focused on rounding up the men of his section and reporting back to their camp across the Mozambique border. He did not look back at the dead strewn about the farm. He did not see the gathering vultures. Nor did he hear the shot from the gun whose bullet tore into the flesh of his back.

16

The drive from Pembroke back to Umkono was a total blank to Patrick Fawkes. His hands turned the wheel and his feet worked the pedals in stiff mechanical movements. His eyes were unblinking and glazed as he assaulted the steep grades and on blind instinct hurled the four-wheel-drive around the hairpin curves.

He had been in a small chemist's shop, buying Jenny's bath oil, when a sergeant from the Pembroke constabulary tracked him down and stammered out a sketchy outline of the tragedy. At first Fawkes refused to believe it. Only after he reached Shawn Francis, the Irish-born constable of Umkono, over the Bushmaster's mobile radio did he come to accept the worst.

"You'd better come home, Patrick," Francis's strained voice crackled over the speaker. The constable spared Fawkes the details, and Fawkes did not demand them.

The sun was still high when Fawkes came within sight of his farm. Little remained of the house. Only the fireplace and a section of the veranda still stood. The rest was no more than a pile of cinders. Across the yard, rubber tires on the tractors smoldered on their steel rims and emitted thick black smoke. The farm workers still lay where they'd fallen in the compound. Vultures were picking at the carcasses of his prize cattle.

Shawn Francis and several Defence Force soldiers were huddled around three forms lying under blankets when Fawkes braked to a stop in the yard. Francis came over to him as he leaped out of the mud-streaked Bushmaster. The constable's face was pale granite.

"God in hell!" cried Fawkes. He gazed into Francis's eyes, searching for a small ray of light. "My family. What of my family?"

Francis fought to get the words out, then gave up and dipped his head in the direction of the blanket-covered bodies. Fawkes pushed past him and stumbled across the

81

yard but was caught short by the stout arms of the constable, which suddenly encircled him about the chest.

"Leave them be, Patrick. I've already identified them."

"Dammit, Shawn, that's my family lying there."

"I beg you, my friend, do not look."

"Let me go. I must see for myself."

"No!" said Francis, grimly hanging on, knowing he was no match for Fawkes's massive strength. "Myrna and Jenny were badly burned in the fire. They're gone, Patrick. The loved ones you knew are no more. Remember them alive, not as they are in death."

Francis could feel the tenseness slowly drain from Fawkes's muscles and the constable loosened his hold.

"How did it happen?" asked Fawkes quietly.

"No way of describing in detail. All your workers have either been driven off or killed. There are no wounded to tell the tale."

"Somebody must know . . . must have seen . . ."

"We'll find a witness. One will turn up by morning. I promise."

The grim conversation halted while a helicopter whirled to the ground and the soldiers tenderly lifted the bodies of Myrna, Jenny, and Patrick Junior inside the cargo cabin and strapped them down. Fawkes made no move to go to them. He only stood there and watched with great sadness in his eyes as the helicopter lifted off and headed toward the mortuary in Umkono.

"Who is responsible?" Fawkes said to Francis. "Tell me who murdered my wife and children and my workers and burned my farm."

"One or two CK-eighty-eight plastic cartridges, the charred remains of an arm inside the house with a Chinese watch on the wrist, prints in the dirt from military-soled boots. Circumstantial as it is, the evidence points to the AAR."

"What do you mean, 'one or two cartridges'?" Fawkes snapped. "The bloody bastards should have left a whole mountain of them."

Francis made a helpless gesture with his hands. "Typical of an AAR raid. They always police the area right after an attack. Makes it tough to tag them with any hard evidence. They plead innocent to any international investigation of terrorism while pointing a hypocritical finger at the other liberation organizations. If it hadn't been for our Alsatian dogs, we never would have uncovered the spent shells or perhaps even the arm.

"The raiders' tracks come and go from the bush through the cane fields and up to the house. I figure they shot down the guards during a shift change, while the gate was open, breaking the electrical charge. Pat Junior was killed over by that burnt-out tractor. Myrna and Jenny were lying a few feet apart in the parlor. All had been mercifully shot. Patrick, for what little comfort it's worth, there was no indication of rape or mutilation."

Constable Francis paused to take a drink from a canteen. He offered it to Fawkes, who simply shook his head.

"Take a swig, Patrick. It's whisky."

Fawkes refused again.

"My office received a distress message over the radio from Jenny. She said that Pat had been shot and that men in bush fatigues were attacking the farm. She and Myrna must have put up one hell of a fight. We found four separate bloodstains in the yard behind the house. And you can see for yourself that what's left of the veranda floor is filled with bloody trails. Jenny's last words were, 'Good Lord, they're shooting the children in the compound.'

"We assembled our forces and came on as quickly as the whirlybirds could get us here. Thirteen minutes was all it took. By then everything was ablaze and the raiders had vanished. Two platoons and a helicopter are tracking them through the bush now."

"My people," murmured Fawkes, pointing at the still figures sprawled around the compound. "We can't leave them lying here for the vultures."

"Your neighbor Brian Vogel is coming with his workers to bury them. They should be here any time. Until then, my men will keep the scavengers away."

Fawkes was like a man wandering lost in a dream as he walked up the steps to the veranda. He could not yet grasp the immensity of the tragedy. He still half expected to see his three loved ones standing framed by the bougainvillea. And his mind very nearly formed a picture of them as they were, waving happily to him when he left for Pembroke.

The veranda was painted in gore. Puddled streaks traveled from the smoking embers down the steps to the yard, where they abruptly ended. It looked to Fawkes as if three or maybe four bodies had been dragged from the house before it was torched. The blood had coagulated and turned crusty under the afternoon sun. Fat iridescent flies hummed and waded about the trails in swarms.

Fawkes leaned against the lattice and felt the first uncontrollable tremor of shock. The house he had built for his family was nothing but blackened, grotesque ruins incongruously heaped in the middle of the trimmed lawn and the beds of gladiola and fire lilies that stood virtually unmarked. Even the memory of how it had looked was beginning to twist and distort. He sank down on the steps and covered his face with his hands.

He was still sitting there half an hour later when Constable Francis came over and gently nudged him.

"Come, Patrick, let me take you to my place. There is nothing to be gained by staying here."

Francis led the unresisting Fawkes to the Bushmaster and tenderly deposited him in the passenger's seat.

As the vehicle passed through the gate, Fawkes stared straight ahead, did not look back. He knew he would never see or set foot on his farm again.

Washington, D.C.—November 1988

Steiger's superiors at the Pentagon sat on his report of the discovery of Vixen 03 for nearly two months before summoning him to Washington. To Steiger it was like sitting in the audience of a staged nightmare. He felt more like a hostile witness than a key investigator.

Even with the evidence before their eyes, in the form of videotape, General Ernest Burgdorf, chief of Air Force Safety, and General John O'Keefe, aid to the Joint Chiefs of Staff, expressed doubts over the sunken aircraft's importance, and argued that nothing was to be gained by bringing it to light except sensationalistic play from the news media. Steiger sat stunned.

"But their families," he protested. "It would be criminal not to notify the crew's families that the bodies have been found."

"Come to your senses, Colonel. What good would dredging up old memories do them? The crew's parents are probably long since dead. Wives have remarried. Children raised by new fathers. Let all concerned go about their present lives in peace."

"There's still the cargo," Steiger said. "The possibility exists that Vixen 03's cargo included nuclear warheads."

"We've been all through that," snapped O'Keefe. "A thorough computer search through military-storehouse records confirmed that there are no missing warheads. Every piece of atomic hardware beginning with the bomb dropped on Hiroshima can be accounted for."

"Are you also aware, sir, that nuclear material was, and is still, shipped in stainless-steel canisters?"

"And did it also occur to you, Colonel," said Burgdorf, "that the canisters you *say* you found might be empty?"

Steiger sagged in his chair, beaten. He might as well have been debating with the wind. They were treating him like an overimaginative child who claimed he'd seen an elephant in a Minnesota cornfield.

"And if that actually is the same aircraft that was supposed to have vanished over the Pacific," added Burgdorf, "I think it best to let sleeping dogs lie."

"Sir?"

"The grim reasons behind the aircraft's tremendous course differential may not be something the Air Force wishes to publicize. Consider the probabilities. To fly a thousand miles in the opposite direction takes either the total malfunction of at least five different instrument systems aided by the blind stupidity of the crew, a navigator who lost his marbles, or a plot by the entire crew to steal the airplane, for what purpose God only knows."

"But somebody must have authorized the flight orders," said Steiger, puzzled.

"Somebody did," said O'Keefe. "The original orders were issued at Travis Air Force Base, in California, by a Colonel Michael Irwin."

Steiger looked at the general skeptically. "Flight orders are seldom kept on file more than a few months. How is it possible the ones in question were retained for over thirty years?"

O'Keefe shrugged. "Don't ask me how, Colonel. Take my word for it: Vixen 03's last flight plan turned up in old files at the Travis administration office."

"And the orders I found in the wreckage?"

"Accept the inevitable," said Burgdorf. "The papers you pulled out of that Colorado lake were too far gone to decipher with any degree of accuracy. You simply read something into them that wasn't there."

"As far as I'm concerned," O'Keefe said resolutely, "the explanation for Vixen 03's course deviation is a dead issue." He turned to Burgdorf. "You agree, General?"

"I do."

O'Keefe stared at Steiger. "Do you have anything else you'd like to put before us, Colonel?"

Steiger's superiors sat and waited for him to reply. He knew no words worth uttering. He had reached a dead end.

The implication dangled over his head like a suspended sword. Either Abe Steiger forgot all about Vixen 03 or his Air Force career would come to a premature halt.

The President stood on the putting green behind the White House and stiffly swatted a dozen balls toward the cup only five feet away. None dropped in, further proving to him that golf was not his game. He could understand the competitive challenge of tennis or handball or even a fast run of pool, but why one would choose to compete against one's own handicap escaped him.

"Now I can die content, for I have seen everything."

The President straightened and looked into the grinning face of Timothy March, his Secretary of Defense.

"It all goes to prove how much time I have on my hands now that I'm a lame-duck president."

March, a short, dumpy man who detested any sort of physical exertion, walked onto the green. "You should be happy with the election. Your party and your man won."

"Nobody ever really wins an election," the President grunted. "What's on your mind, Tim?"

"Thought you might like to know I've clamped the lid on that old aircraft found in the Rockies."

"Probably a wise move."

"A baffling affair," said March. "Except for those doctored flight plans in Air Force files, there is no trace of the crew's true mission."

"So be it," said the President, finally knocking a ball into the cup. "Let's leave it lie. If Eisenhower buried the answers during his administration, far be it from me to open a can of worms during mine."

"I suggest we remove the remains of the crew for a military burial. We owe them that."

"Okay, but absolutely no publicity."

"I'll make that clear to the Air Force officer in charge."

The President tossed the putter to a Secret Service man who lurked nearby and motioned for March to accompany him to the Executive Offices.

"What's your best educated guess, Tim? What do you really think Ike was trying to cover up back in 1954?"

"That question has kept me staring at the ceiling the past few nights," said March. "I don't have the foggiest idea."

Steiger shouldered his way past the lunchtime crowd waiting for tables at the Cottonwood Inn and entered the bar. Pitt waved from a rear booth and motioned for the cocktail waitress in almost the same gesture. Steiger slipped into a seat across from Pitt as the waitress, seductively attired in an abbreviated colonial costume, arched her blossoming breasts over the table.

"A martini on the rocks," said Steiger, eyeing the mounds. "On second thought, make that a double. It's been one of those mornings."

Pitt held up a nearly empty glass. "Another salty dog."

"Christ," moaned Steiger. "How can you stand those things?"

"I hear they're good for cutting down weight," Pitt answered. "The enzymes from the grapefruit juice cancel out the calories in the vodka."

"Sounds like an old wives' tale. Besides, why bother? You don't have an ounce of fat on you anywhere."

"See?" Pitt laughed. "They really work."

The humor was contagious. For the first time that day Steiger felt like laughing. But soon after the drinks arrived his expression clouded again, and he sat there silently, toying with his glass without touching its contents.

"Don't tell me," said Pitt, reading the colonel's dour thoughts, "your friends at the Pentagon shot you down?"

Steiger nodded slowly. "They dissected every sentence of my report and flushed the pieces into the Washington sewer system."

"Are you serious?"

"They wanted none of it."

"What about the canisters and the fifth skeleton?"

"They claim the canisters are empty. As to your theory on Loren Smith's father, I didn't even bring it up. I saw little reason to stoke the fires of their already flaming skepticism."

"Then you're off the investigation."

"I am if I wish to retire a general."

"They leaned on you?"

"They didn't have to. It was written in their eyes."

"What happens now?"

Steiger looked at Pitt steadily. "I was hoping you might go it alone."

Their eyes locked.

Pieter De Vaal closed the report folder on the Fawkes-farm massacre. His face was drawn and tired as he looked up. "I'm still shocked by this dreadful tragedy. It was so senseless."

Fawkes remained impassive. He sat across the desk from the Defence Minister and tamped the tobacco in his old pipe. The room fell silent; only the muted noise of Pretoria's traffic seeped through the large windows overlooking Burger Park.

At last De Vaal slipped the folder into a drawer and avoided Fawkes's eyes as he spoke. "I regret that our patrols failed to catch the savages who were responsible."

"Only one man was responsible," said Fawkes grimly. "The men who slaughtered my family were acting under his orders."

"I know what you are thinking, Captain Fawkes, but we have no proof that Lusana was behind this."

"I'm satisfied he was."

"What can I say? Even if we knew for certain, he is beyond our borders. There is no way we can touch him."

"I can touch him."

"How?"

"By volunteering to lead your Operation Wild Rose."

De Vaal could sense the vengeful hate that seethed within Patrick Fawkes. The Defence Minister rose to his feet and stood at the window, gazing over the sea of jacaranda trees that quilted the city. "I sympathize with your feelings, Captain. However, the answer is no."

"But why, man?"

"Wild Rose is a monstrous concept. If the operation failed, the consequences would prove disastrous to our government."

Fawkes rapped his pipe on the Minister's desk, snapping the stem. "No, dammit! My farm was only the opening thrust. Lusana and his bloody mob have got to be stopped before the whole country runs red."

"The risks far outweigh the possible benefits."

"I won't fail," Fawkes said coldly.

De Vaal looked like a man torn apart by his conscience. He paced the room nervously, then stopped and stared down at Fawkes. "I cannot promise to evacuate you successfully when the times comes. And the Defence Ministry will, of course, deny any association with the venture if you are uncovered."

"Understood." Fawkes heaved a great sigh of relief. Then a thought occurred to him. "The train, Minister. How was it you traveled from the operating room in a Durban hospital to the Pembroke rail yard so quickly?"

For the first time, De Vaal smiled. "A simple ruse. I went in the front door of the hospital and out the back. An ambulance carried me to the Heidriek Air Base, where I took a military jet to an airstrip near Pembroke. The train belongs to our President. I merely borrowed it for a few hours while it was traveling to a scheduled overhaul."

"But why the complicated illusion?"

"I often find it necessary to cloud my movements," De Vaal answered. "And, I think you'll agree, Operation Wild Rose is not exactly a product we want to advertise."

"I see your point."

"And you, Captain Fawkes. Can you drop from sight without prodding suspicious minds?"

Fawkes nodded solemnly. "I've left Umkono under a cloud of grief. My friends and neighbors think I've returned to Scotland."

"All right, then." De Vaal moved behind his desk, wrote on a slip of paper, and passed it across to Fawkes. "Here is the address of a hotel ten miles south of the city. Check into a room and wait for the necessary papers and instructions to get the ball rolling. As of this moment, the government of South Africa considers you dead." He relaxed his shoulders. "God help us now."

"God? No, I don't think so." An evil light began to dance in Fawkes's eyes. "I sincerely doubt he'd want any part of it."

On the floor below the Minister's office Colonel Zeegler sat alone in an operations room and paced back and forth in front of a large table stacked with glossy photographs.

For the first time in his military career he was totally baffled. The raid on the Fawkes farm had an aura of intrigue about it that did not fit the usual terrorist scheme. It was accomplished with too much precision and sophistication for the AAR. Besides, it was not Lusana's style. Granted, he might order the deaths of white soldiers, but he would never condone the murders of Fawkes's Bantu workers, especially the women and children. That part ran counter to the insurgent leader's known strategy.

"Who, then?" Zeegler mused aloud.

Certainly not black units of the South African Defence Forces. That would have been impossible without Zeegler's knowledge.

He stopped and shuffled the photographs taken by a team of investigators after the raid. No witnesses were ever found and none of the raiders caught. It was too perfect in execution, too completely free of flaws.

The slightest clue to the attackers' identities eluded him. But his years of experience told him it was there, obscured in the background.

Like a surgeon examining X rays in preparation for a delicate operation, Zeegler picked up a magnifying glass and for the twentieth time began scrutinizing each photograph.

22

The Air Malawi jet from Lourenço Marquês, Mozambique, touched down and taxied to the terminal of Pretoria's airport. A few moments after the whine of the engines had faded away, the boarding ramp was extended, and the passengers nodded their good-byes to the pretty African stewardess and made their way toward the terminal.

Major Thomas Machita followed the other travelers, and when his turn came, he handed his falsified Mozambique passport to the immigration official.

The white South African studied the passport photo and the name, George Yariko, beneath it and smiled sagaciously. "That makes three trips to Pretoria in the last month, Mr. Yariko." He nodded at the courier briefcase chained to Machita's wrist. "Instructions to your consul seem to be running hot and heavy, as of late."

Machita shrugged. "If my foreign department doesn't send me to our consulate in Pretoria, they send me to a consulate somewhere else. No offense intended, sir, but I'd prefer a Paris or London delivery."

The official motioned him toward the exit. "I look forward to seeing you again," he said with mock courtesy. "Have an enjoyable stay."

Machita smiled, showing every tooth, and casually made his way through the terminal to the taxi stand outside. He waved his free hand at the first cab heading a long line. The driver acknowledged him and started his engine. But suddenly, before he could pull up to his fare, another cab swung out from the rear of the line, cut in, and skidded to a stop in front of Machita amid a cacophony of angry shouting and horn honking from the outraged cabbies awaiting their rightful rotation.

Machita found the performance amusing. He threw the bag into the backseat and followed it. "The Mozambique Consulate," he said to the aggressive driver.

The cabby merely tipped his cap, set the meter, and

steered into traffic. Machita leaned back and idly watched
the scenery. He unlocked the wrist chain and threw it into
the brief case. The Mozambique consul, friendly to the
AAR cause, allowed Machita and his operatives to come
and go under the guise of diplomatic couriers. After a
proper length of time spent enjoying the Consulate's hospitality, they then retired to an inconspicuous hotel and
went about their business of espionage.

Something in the back of Machita's brain blinked a
warning signal. He sat up and studied the landscape. The
driver was not taking a direct route to the Consulate; instead, the cab's hood ornament was pointed toward the
bustling downtown business section of Pretoria.

Machita tapped the driver on the shoulder. "I am not a
tourist to be gouged, my friend. I suggest you take the
nearest shortcut to my destination if you expect to get
paid."

His only reply was an indifferent shrug. After a few
more minutes of weaving through the busy traffic pattern,
the driver turned into the underground parking lot of a
large department store. Machita needed no extrasensory
perception to detect the trap. His tongue swelled like a dry
sponge and he could hear his heart begin to pound. He
carefully clicked open the briefcase snaps and slipped out
a Mauser .38 automatic.

At the lowest level of the parking lot the driver eased
the cab into an empty space against the wall farthest
from the entrance tunnel and stopped. Then he turned
around and found the barrel of Machita's gun caressing the
tip of his nose.

It was the first chance Machita had had to observe the
cabby's face. The smooth dark skin and facial features
were those of an Indian, a race that numbered more
than half a million in South Africa. The man smiled a
genuine relaxed smile. There was none of the uneasiness
about him that Machita expected.

"I think we can dispense with the theatrics, Major Machita," said the cabby. "You are in no danger."

Machita's gun hand held steady. He did not dare turn
to scan the parking area for the army of heavily armed
men he was sure were there. "Whatever happens, you die
with me," he said.

"You are an emotional man," the driver remarked. "Stu-

pid, actually. It bodes ill for a man of your occupation to
react like an adolescent caught robbing a sweets shop."

"Can the fat talk, man," Machita snapped. "What's the
gig?"

The driver laughed. "Spoken like the true American
black that you are. Luke Sampson, of Los Angeles; alias
Charlie Le Mat, of Chicago; alias Major Thomas Machita, of the AAR; and God only knows how many others."

A chill gripped Machita. His mind hunted frantically for
answers, answers to who the cabby was and how he knew
so much about him. "You are mistaken. My name is
Yariko, George Yariko."

"Whatever comforts you," the cabby said. "However,
you'll pardon me if I find it more expedient to conduct my
conversation with Major Machita."

"Who are you?"

"For an intelligence man, your powers of perception
are woefully lacking." The voice altered subtly into an English now tinged with an Afrikaans accent. "We have met
twice before."

Machita slowly lowered the gun. "Emma?"

"Ah, the haze lifts."

Machita expelled a great sigh of relief and put the gun
back in the briefcase. "How in hell did you know I was
arriving on that particular flight?"

"A crystal ball," said Emma, obviously not willing to
share his secrets.

Machita stared at the man in the driver's seat, taking in
every minute detail of the face, the smooth, unblemished
skin. There wasn't the slightest resemblance to the gar-
dener and the café waiter who had claimed to be Emma
on the two previous occasions they'd met.

"I was hoping you'd contact me, but I hadn't expected
you quite this soon."

"I have come up with something I think Hiram Lusana
will find interesting."

"How much this time?" asked Machita dryly.

There was no hesitation. "Two million United States
dollars."

Machita grimaced. "There's no information worth that
cost."

"I haven't time to argue the point," said Emma. He
passed Machita a small envelope. "This contains a brief de-

scription of a highly classified bit of anti-AAR strategy known as Operation Wild Rose. The material inside explains the concept and the purpose behind the plan. Give it to Lusana. If, after examining it, he agrees to my price, I shall deliver the entire plan."

The envelope went in the briefcase, on top of the wrist chain and the Mauser. "It will be in the general's hands by tomorrow evening," promised Machita.

"Excellent. Now then, I will drive you to the Consulate."

"There is one more thing."

Emma looked over his shoulder at the major. "You have my attention."

"The general wishes to know who attacked the Fawkes farm in Natal."

Emma's dark eyes locked on Machita's speculatively. "Your general has a strange sense of humor. Evidence left at the scene tied your benevolent AAR to the massacre."

"The AAR is innocent. We must have the truth."

Emma shrugged affirmatively. "All right, I will look into it."

Then he shifted the cab into reverse and backed out of the parking space. Eight minutes later he dropped Machita off at the Mozambique Consulate.

"A last bit of advice, Major."

Machita leaned down to the driver's window. "What is it?"

"A good operative never takes the first taxi offered to him. Always pick out the second or third in line. You stay out of trouble that way."

Properly rebuked, Machita stood on the curb and watched the cab until it was swallowed by the swarming traffic of Pretoria.

The rays of the late-afternoon sun crept over the balcony railing and probed the languid form stretched outside one of the more expensive suites of the New Stanley Hotel in Nairobi, Kenya.

Felicia Collins wore a colorfully patterned bra and matching Kongo skirt over the bottom half of her bikini. She rolled over on her side, lit a cigarette, and considered her actions of the past few days. Granted, she had slept with a varied lot of men over the years. That part didn't bother her. Her first time had been with a sixteen-year-old cousin when she was only fourteen herself. At best, it was an experience dimmed by the passage of time. Then came at least ten other men by the time she was twenty. Most of the names were long forgotten and the faces vague and indistinct.

The lovers who had climbed in and out of her bed during the years when she was struggling as an aspiring vocalist formed a continuous montage of recording-company executives, disc jockeys, musicians, and composers. Most had in some way contributed to her rise to the top. With the sudden crest of success came Hollywood and a whole new orgy of high living.

Faces, she thought. How strange that she couldn't remember their shapes and features. And yet the bedrooms and their decors stood out vividly. The feel of the mattress, the design on the wallpaper, the fixtures in the adjoining bathroom, were still etched in her mind along with the different types of beams and plaster she had recorded on the ceilings.

As with many women, sex to Felicia was not necessarily exalted above other forms of entertainment. There were uncounted times she'd wished she had curled up with a good novel instead. Already Hiram Lusana's face was blurring into obscurity along with all the rest.

At first she hated Daggat, hated the very idea that he could turn her on. She had insulted him at every opportunity, and yet he had remained courteous. Nothing she could say or do angered him. God, it is maddening, she thought. She almost wished he would demean her as a slave so that her hatred would be justified, but it was not to be. Frederick Daggat was too shrewd. He played her gently, cautiously, as would a fisherman in the knowledge he had a record fish on the line.

The balcony door slid open and Daggat stepped outside. Felicia sat up and removed her sunglasses as his shadow fell across her body.

"Were you dozing?"

She offered him a fluid smile. "Just daydreaming."

"It's beginning to get cool. You'd better come inside."

He took her hand and pulled her to her feet. She gazed at him mischievously for a moment and then unclasped the bikini's bra and pushed her bare breasts against his chest. "There is still time to make love before dinner."

It was a tease and they both knew it. Since they had left Lusana's camp together, she had responded to his sexual manipulations with all the abandon of a robot. It was a part she had never played before.

"Why?" he asked simply.

Her expressive coffee eyes studied him. "Why?"

"Why did you leave Lusana and come with me? I am not a man whose looks turn women's heads. I've looked at this ugly face of mine in the mirror every day for forty years and I'm not about to kid myself into thinking I'm superstar material. You did not have to behave like a bartered cow, Felicia. Lusana didn't own you; nor do I, and I suspect no man ever will. You could have told us both to go to hell and yet you came with me willingly, too willingly. Why?"

She felt her stomach tingle as her nostrils detected his strong male scent, and she took his face in her hands. "I suppose I jumped from Hiram's bed into yours merely to prove that if he didn't need me, I could just as easily do without him."

"A perfectly human reaction."

She kissed him on the chin. "Forgive me, Frederick. In a sense, Hiram and I both used you: he to gain your goodwill for congressional support, and I in an adolescent game to make him jealous."

He smiled. "This is one time in my life that I can honestly say I'm happy I was taken advantage of."

She took him by the hand and led him into the bedroom and expertly undressed him. "This time," she said, her voice low, "I'm going to show you the real Felicia Collins."

It was well past eight o'clock when they finally released each other. She was far stronger than Daggat had believed possible. There was no plumbing the depths of her passion. He lay in bed for several minutes, listening to her humming in the shower. Then he wearily rose and pulled on a short kimono, sat down at a desk littered with important-looking documents, and began sorting through them.

Felicia padded from the bathroom and slipped on a belted wrap dress in a red and white zebra print. She approved of what she saw reflected in the full-length mirror. Her figure was slim and solid; the vitality that flowed through her lithe muscles overshadowed the soreness that was there from the vigorous exertions of early evening. Thirty-two years old and still damned provocative, she decided. There were still a few good years left before she could allow her agent to accept matronly roles for her, unless, of course, a producer offered a blockbuster script and a hefty percentage of the net.

"Do you think he can win?" Daggat asked, interrupting her reverie.

"I beg your pardon."

"I asked you if Lusana can defeat the South African Defence Forces."

"I'm hardly one to offer a valid prediction on the outcome of the revolution," Felicia said. "My part in the AAR was simply that of a fund raiser."

He grinned. "Not to mention providing entertainment to the troops, particularly generals."

"A fringe benefit," she said, and laughed.

"You haven't answered the question."

She shook her head. "Even with an army of one million men, Hiram could never hope to defeat the whites in a knockdown, drag-out conflict. The French and the Americans lost in Vietnam for the same reason the majority government fell in Rhodesia: guerrillas fighting under the cover of heavy jungle have all the advantages. Unfortunately for the black cause, eighty percent of South Africa is arid, open country, better suited for armored and air warfare."

"Then, what's his angle?"

"Hiram is counting on worldwide popular support and economic sanctions to strangle the white ruling class into submission."

Daggat rested his chin on his huge hands. "Is he a communist?"

Felicia tilted her head back and laughed. "Hell, Hiram made his fortune as a capitalist. He's too ingrained with making money to embrace the Reds."

"Then how do you explain his Vietnamese advisers and the free supplies from China?"

"The old P. T. Barnum sucker routine. The Vietnamese are so revolution happy they'd air-freight guerrilla-warfare specialists into the Florida swamps if someone sent them an invitation. As for Chinese generosity, after getting booted out of eight different African nations in as many years, they'll kiss anybody's ass to keep a toehold on the continent."

"He could be miring himself in quicksand without realizing it."

"You underestimate Hiram," said Felicia. "He'll send the Asians packing the minute they've outlived their usefulness to the AAR."

"Easier said than done."

"He knows what he's doing. Take my word for it. Hiram Lusana will be sitting in the Prime Minister's office in Cape Town nine months from now."

"He has a schedule?" Daggat asked incredulously.

"To the day."

Slowly Daggat picked up the papers on the desk and shuffled them neatly into a stack.

"Pack your things."

Felicia's neatly plucked brows raised. "We're leaving Nairobi?"

"We're flying to Washington."

She was taken aback by his sudden air of authority. "Why should I return stateside with you?"

"You have nothing better to do. Besides, arriving home on the arm of a respected congressman after shacking for a year with a known radical revolutionary might go a long way in restoring your image in the eyes of your fans."

Outwardly Felicia pouted. But Daggat's logic made sense. Her record sales had fallen off and calls from producers had taken a noticeable downward turn. It was time, she quickly deduced, to put her career back on its track.

"I'll be ready in half an hour," she said.

Daggat nodded and smiled. An edge of excitement began to form inside him. If, as Felicia indicated, Lusana was the odds-on favorite to become South Africa's first black leader, Daggat, by championing a winning cause on Capitol Hill, could assure himself of immense congressional stature and voter respect. It was worth the gamble. And if he was careful, and chose his words and programs cleverly, he might . . . just might . . . stand a shot at the vice-presidency, the major stepping-stone to his ultimate goal.

Lusana brought his hand up to eye level and then snapped the rod forward with a deft wrist action. The small wad of cheese clung to the hook, plopped daintily into the river, and then sank out of sight. The fish were there. Lusana's instincts began to vibrate in anticipation. He stood thigh deep amid the shadows of the trees leaning over the bank and slowly reeled in the line.

On his eighth cast he had a strike, a hard, splashing strike that nearly tore the rod from his relaxed grip. He had hooked a tiger fish, an Old World relative of the ferocious piranha of the South American Amazon. He gave the fish its head and eased out more line. He had little choice; the rod was nearly bent double. Then, abruptly, before the battle had a chance to warm up, the tiger fish circled a sunken tree stump, broke the line, and escaped.

"I did not think it possible that anyone could entice a tiger fish with a bit of cheese," said Colonel Jumana. He was sitting on the ground, his back resting against a tree. He held the envelope containing the brief outline of Operation Wild Rose in his hand.

"The bait is irrelevant if the prey is hungry," said Lusana. He waded back to shore and began tying a new leader to his line.

Jumana rolled on his side and scanned the landscape to see if Lusana's security guards were properly stationed and alert. It was a wasted gesture. No soldiers served with greater fervor and loyalty. They were lean and hard, picked by Lusana personally, not so much for their fearlessness and rugged physiques as for their intelligence. They stood poised in the underbrush, their weapons held in determined, steady hands.

Lusana turned to resume his casting. "What do you make of it?" he asked.

Jumana stared at the envelope and twisted his face in a skeptical expression.

115

"A rip-off. A two-million-dollar rip-off."

"You don't buy it, then?"

"No, sir. Frankly, I do not." Jumana rose to his feet and brushed off his combat uniform. "I think this Emma has fed Major Machita cheap bits and pieces as a buildup for the big score." He shook his head. "This report tells us nothing. It only indicates that the whites are going to launch a major terrorist strike somewhere in the world with a group of blacks posing as AAR followers. The South Africans are not so stupid as to risk international repercussions on such an absurd ploy."

Lusana cast his line. "But suppose—just suppose— Prime Minister Koertsmann has seen the handwriting on the wall. He might be tempted to take a desperate gamble, a last throw of the dice."

"But how?" asked Jumana. "Where?"

"The answers to those questions, my friend, come only with two million Yankee dollars."

"I still only see this Operation Wild Rose as a swindle."

"Actually, the scheme smacks of genius," Lusana continued. "If the strike involved heavy casualties, the nation that was the victim would then be provoked into turning their sympathies away from our cause and voting arms and aid for Koertsmann's government."

"The questions are unending," said Jumana. "What nation is singled out as the target?"

"The United States is my guess."

Jumana threw the envelope to the ground. "Ignore this stupid deception, my General. Put the money to better use. Heed my proposal for a series of raids to throw fear into the hearts of the whites."

Jumana was met with a steely stare. "You know my feelings on butchery."

Jumana pushed ahead. "A thousand hit-and-run assaults on cities, villages, and farms, from one end of the country to the other, would put us in Pretoria by Christmas."

"We will continue to conduct a sophisticated war," Lusana said coldly. "We will not act like primitive rabble."

"In Africa it is often necessary to drive the people with an iron hand. They seldom know what is best for them."

"Tell me, Colonel; I'm always willing to learn: who knows what's best for the African people?"

Jumana's face purpled with controlled anger. "Africans know what is best for Africans."

Lusana ignored the slur against his American blood. He could sense the impulses swirling in Jumana: the hatred of all things foreign; the driving ambition and the newly discovered luxury of power mingled with a distrust of modern ways; an almost childlike acceptance of bloodthirsty savagery. Lusana began to wonder if he hadn't made an enormous error in appointing Jumana to a high level of command.

Before Lusana could focus on the problems that might arise between them, the soft padding sound of feet emanated from beyond the lip of the riverbank.

The security guards tensed and then relaxed as Major Machita dog-trotted down the path into view. He came to a halt in front of Lusana and saluted.

"One of my agents has just arrived from Pretoria with Emma's report on the Fawkes-farm raid."

"What did he uncover?"

"Emma says he was unable to find evidence the Defence Forces had a hand in it."

Lusana looked thoughtful. "So it's back to the opening play."

"It seems incredible that a force can murder nearly fifty people and go unidentified," said Machita.

"Could Emma have lied?"

"Possibly. But he would have no reason for doing so."

Lusana did not answer. He turned his attention back to the fish. His line whispered over the running water. Machita looked questioningly at Jumana, but the colonel avoided his gaze. Machita stood there confused for a moment, wondering what had caused the atmosphere of tension that hovered over his two superiors. After a long uneasy silence he nodded at the envelope.

"You've reached a decision concerning Operation Wild Rose, General?"

"I have," Lusana answered as he reeled the line in.

Machita remained silent, waiting.

"I intend to pay Emma his thirty pieces of silver for the rest of the plan," Lusana finally said.

Jumana raged. "No, it is a fraud! Even you, my General, are not entitled to throw our army's funds away stupidly."

Machita caught his breath and tensed. The colonel had overstepped his rank. And yet Lusana kept his back to the shore and nonchalantly went about his fishing. "I'll remind you," he said over his shoulder with quiet authority, "the lion's share of our treasury came from me. What is mine I can take back or I can use as I please."

Jumana clenched his hands in tight knots and the cords in his neck stood out. He made a move toward the water's edge, his lips drawn back over his teeth. Then, suddenly, as if a circuit breaker somewhere in his gray matter had overloaded and clicked off, all expression of rage vanished, and he smiled. His words came casually, but with an undercurrent of bitterness.

"I apologize for my remarks. I am overtired."

Machita decided then and there that the colonel was a danger that bore watching. He could see that Jumana would never fully accept the position of number-two man.

"Forget it," said Lusana. "The important thing now is to lay our hands on Wild Rose."

"I will make arrangements for the exchange," said Machita.

"You will do more than that," Lusana said, facing the shore again. "You will create a plan to make the payoff. Then you will kill Emma."

Jumana's mouth hung open. "You never intended to give away the two million dollars?" he sputtered.

Lusana grinned. "Of course not. If you had been patient, you could have spared us your juvenile outburst."

Jumana made no reply. There was nothing he could say. He widened his smile and shrugged. It was then Machita caught the imperceptible shift of the eyes. Jumana was not looking directly at Lusana; his vision was aimed at a spot in the river ten feet upstream from the general.

"Guards!" Machita screamed, pointing frantically. "The river! Fire! For God's sake, fire!"

The security men's reaction time measured less than two seconds. Their shots exploded in Machita's ears and the water erupted a few feet from Lusana in a hundred shattered geysers.

Twenty feet of hideous brown scale burst through the surface and rolled over and over, its tail thrashing crazily as the bullets thudded into the thick hide like hail. Then the firing ceased and the great reptile made one more convulsive revolution and sank beneath the surface.

Lusana stood in his wading boots, his eyes wide, his body stunned into immobility. He stared dazedly into the clear water at the hulk of the crocodile, now gracefully tumbling along the riverbed in the current.

On the bank, Machita trembled, not so much at Lusana's narrow escape as at the satanic expression on Jumana's Neanderthal-shaped face.

The bastard had known, Machita thought. He had known the instant the crocodile slithered off the far bank and homed in on the general, and yet he had said nothing.

the land. Already resigned and to much of events a
minor matter as at the instant expression on the Parade's
meaningful stage later.

The bastard had known, Mitchell thought. He had
known, the bastard's forever. Mitchell all that it, He'd
made sure, in her thoughts, and set his soul and culture.

Chesapeake Bay, U.S.A.—
October 1988

It was two hours before dawn when Patrick Fawkes paid the cabdriver and walked up to the floodlit gate of the Forbes Marine Scrap & Salvage Company. A uniformed guard turned from a portable TV set and yawned as Fawkes passed a small folder through the arched window of the gatehouse. The guard scrutinized the signatures and compared the photograph with the man before him. Then he passed it back.

"Welcome to America, Captain. My employers have been expecting you."

"Is she here?" Fawkes asked impatiently.

"Tied up to the east dock," replied the guard, shoving a Xerox copy of a map of the salvage area through the window. "Mind your step. Since the energy rationing, the yard's night lights have been shut off. It's darker than Hades out there." As Fawkes passed under the giant derricks toward the dock, a wind swept in off the bay and carried a heavy odor to his nostrils: the pungent perfume of the waterfront. He inhaled the mingled aromas of diesel oil, tar, and salt water. It never failed to revive his spirits.

He came to the dock and glanced about for signs of human activity. The night crew had long since gone home. Only a seagull, perched on a wooden piling, returned Fawkes's gaze out of one beady eye.

After another hundred yards, Fawkes stopped at a huge spectral shape that loomed in the darkness beside the pier. Then he took the gangplank, stepped onto the seemingly endless deck, and unerringly made his way through the steel labyrinth to the bridge.

Later, as the sun crept over the eastern side of the bay, the mutilated shabbiness of the ship became manifest. But the peeling paint, the acres of rust, and the jagged torch marks of the salvage crew stood unseen in Fawkes's eyes. Like a father with a hideously disfigured daughter, he saw only her beauty.

"Aye, you're a bonny ship," he shouted across the silent decks. "You're gonna do just fine."

3

SALVAGE

Although it seemed as though his head had barely hit the pillow, Hiram Lusana had been asleep for seven hours when he was roused by the knock at his door. The wristwatch on the bed table read six o'clock. He cursed, rubbed the sleep from his coffee-brown eyes, and sat up.

"Come in."

The knock came again.

"I said, Come in," he grunted loudly.

Captain John Mukuta entered the room and stood stiffly at attention. "Sorry to wake you, sir, but section fourteen has just returned from its reconnaissance of Umkono."

"So what's the emergency? I can study their report later."

Mukuta's eyes remained fixed on a spot on the wall. "The patrol experienced trouble. The section leader was shot and lies critically wounded in the hospital. He insists on reporting to you and no one else."

"Who is he?"

"His name is Marcus Somala."

"Somala?" Lusana's brow knitted. He got out of bed. "Tell him I'm coming."

The captain saluted and left, softly closing the door behind him, pretending not to have noticed the second shape curled beneath the satin sheets.

Lusana reached over and pulled away the top sheet. Felicia Collins slept like a statue. Her short Afro hair gleamed in the half light and her lips were puffy and parted. Her skin was the color of cocoa and her conical breasts, with their dark, full nipples, heaved with each deep breath.

He smiled and left the sheet off. Still half asleep, he weaved into the bathroom and splashed handfuls of cold water on his face. The eyes that stared back from the mirror were streaked with red. The face around them was lined and haggard from a night heavily laced with liquor and sex. He tenderly patted the battle-worn features with a towel, returned to the bedroom, and dressed.

Lusana was a small, wiry man, medium boned and lighter skinned than any man in the army of Africans he commanded. "American tan" is what they called it behind his back. And yet any remarks about his color or his off-hand stateside manner were not uttered out of disrespect. His men looked up to him with a primitive sort of awe of the supernatural. He had the air of assurance that most lightweight fighters have in their early careers; some might call it an air of arrogance. He took a last fond look at Felicia, sighed, and walked across the camp to the hospital.

The Chinese doctor was pessimistic.

"The bullet entered from the rear, tore away half his lung, shattered a rib, and exited below the left breast. It is a miracle the man is still alive."

"Can he talk?" Lusana asked.

"Yes, but each word drains his strength."

"How long—"

"—has he to live?"

Lusana nodded.

"Marcus Somala has an incredibly strong constitution," the doctor said. "But I doubt if he can last out the day."

"Can you give him something to stimulate his senses, if even for only a few minutes?"

The doctor looked thoughtful. "I suppose speeding up the inevitable will not matter." He turned and murmured instructions to a nurse, who left the room.

Lusana looked down at Somala. The section leader's face was drawn and his chest rose shallowly with spasmodic breaths. A maze of plastic tubing hung from a rack above the bed and ran into his nose and arms. A large surgical dressing was taped across his chest.

The nurse returned and carefully handed the doctor a hypodermic. He inserted the needle and pushed evenly on the plunger. In a few moments Somala's eyes fluttered half open, and he moaned.

Lusana silently motioned to the doctor and his nurse and they withdrew to the hall and closed the door.

He leaned over the bed. "Somala, this is Hiram Lusana. Do you understand me?"

Somala's whispered voice came out hoarse but with a

trace of emotion. "I do not see well, my General. Is it really you?"

Lusana took Somala's hand and gripped it tightly. "Yes, my brave warrior. I have come to hear your report."

The man on the bed smiled thinly, and then a haunting, questioning look came into his eyes. "Why . . . why did you not trust me, my General?"

"Trust you?"

"Why did you not tell me you were sending men to raid the Fawkes farm?"

Lusana was shaken. "Describe what you saw. Describe everything. Leave out nothing."

Twenty minutes later, exhausted by the effort, Marcus Somala lapsed back into unconsciousness. By noon he was dead.

Patrick Fawkes stood alone and shoveled the molasses-like clay soil over the coffins of his family. His clothes were soaked through by a light rain and his own sweat. It had been his wish to dig the common grave and fill it himself. The burial services were long over and his friends and neighbors had departed, leaving him to his grievous task.

At last he patted smooth the last shovelful, stood back, and looked down. The headstone had not arrived yet, and the mound seemed stark and forlorn among the older grave sites that had been blanketed by grass and edged with rows of neatly kept flowers. He fell to his knees and reached into a pocket of his discarded coat. His hand came out with a fistful of bougainvillea petals. These he sprinkled over the damp earth.

Fawkes let the grief flow. He wept until after the sun dipped below the horizon. He wept until his eyes could no longer produce tears.

His mind traveled back twelve years and ran off images like a movie projector. He saw Myrna and the kids in the little cottage near Aberdeen on the North Sea. He saw the looks of surprise and happiness in their faces when he told them they were all packing up and heading to Natal to start a farm. He saw how sickly white skinned Jenny and Pat Junior were beside the other school children of Umkono, and how quickly they became tanned and robust. He saw Myrna begrudgingly leaving Scotland to alter her life-style totally, and then coming to love Africa even more than he.

"You'll never make a good farmer until you flush the salt water out of your veins," she used to tell him.

Her voice seemed so clear to him that he could not accept the fact that she lay beneath the ground he knelt on, never to see the daylight again. He was alone now and the thought left him lost. When a woman loses a man, he recalled hearing somewhere, she picks up her life as

before and perseveres. But when a man loses a woman, he
dies by half.

He forced the once-happy scenes from his mind and
tried to conjure the shadowy figure of a man. The face had
no distinct features, because it was the face of a man
Fawkes had never seen: the face of Hiram Lusana.

Fawkes's grief was suddenly engulfed by a tidal surge
of cold hatred. He balled his fists and beat them against
the wet ground until his emotions finally drained away.
Then he gave a great sigh and neatly arranged the bougainvillea petals so that they spelled out Myrna's and the
children's names.

Then he rose unsteadily to his feet, and he knew what he
had to do.

Lusana sat at the head of an oval conference table, his eyes pensive, his hands toying with a ball-point pen. He looked at the ever-smiling Colonel Duc Phon Lo, chief military adviser to the AAR, then at the officers sitting in tense formation in the chairs beside him.

"Some bloodthirsty idiot takes it into his head to knock over the farm of the most respected citizen of Natal, and you all sit here looking as innocent as Zulu virgins." He paused a moment, searching their faces. "Come, come, gentlemen. Let's stop playing games. Who was behind it?"

Lo bowed his head and spread his hands on the table. His almond eyes and closely cropped straight hair made him seem out of place among the others. He spoke slowly and enunciated each word precisely.

"You have my word, General, no one under your command was responsible. I have studied the exact placement of every section during the time of the attack. None of them, except for the one Somala led, was within two hundred kilometers of Umkono."

"Then how do you explain it?"

"I cannot."

Lusana's gaze lingered on Lo, appraising the Asian's expression. Satisfied that he saw nothing devious in the permanently etched smile, he turned and surveyed the other men at the table.

To his right sat Major Thomas Machita, his chief intelligence analyst. Next to him was Colonel Randolph Jumana, his second-in-command. Opposite them were Lo and Colonel Oliver Makeir, coordinator of AAR propaganda programs.

"Any theories on the subject?" Lusana asked.

Jumana straightened a sheaf of papers for the tenth time and avoided Lusana's gaze. "What if Somala imagined the Fawkes raid? Perhaps he saw it during a fit of delirium; or, then again, perhaps he made it up."

Frowning, Lusana shook his head in irritation. "You forget, Colonel, I was the one who took Somala's report. He was a damn good man. The best section leader we had. He was not delirious and he had no reason to create a fairy tale, knowing he was about to die."

"There is no doubt that the raid took place," said Makeir. "The South African papers and television newscasts have given it heavy play. Their stories all check with what Somala told the general here, except the government Defence Forces have yet to come up with any reliable witnesses who can provide a description of the attacking troops. We were fortunate that Somala was able to return from his mission and describe in detail what he saw before he died."

"Did he see who shot him?" asked Jumana.

"He was hit in the back at great distance," answered Lusana, "probably by a sniper. The poor devil managed to crawl three miles to the area he assigned the rest of his scouting party. They performed what first aid they could and then beat a track back to our camp."

Thomas Machita shook his head in utter incomprehension. "None of it tallies. I doubt that other liberation movements would dress up and masquerade as AAR soldiers."

"On the other hand," said Makeir, "maybe they staged the raid to cast blame on us and take the heat off themselves."

"I am in close contact with my countrymen who are advising your brother revolutionaries," said Colonel Lo. "They are all as angry as disturbed hornets. No one gained by the assault on the Fawkes farm. If anything, it has stiffened the resolve of the whites, the Indians, the coloreds, and many blacks, as well, to stand firm against outside intervention."

Lusana rested his chin on clasped hands. "Okay, if they didn't do it, and we know *we* didn't do it, who does that leave as a prime suspect?"

"South African whites," Lo answered simply.

Every eye focused on the Vietnamese adviser. Lusana stared into the inscrutable eyes. "Perhaps you'd care to repeat the statement."

"I am merely suggesting that someone in the South African government may have ordered the murder of the Fawkes family and their field workers."

They all stared at him wordlessly for several moments. Finally Machita broke the silence.

"I fail to see a purpose."

"Nor I," Lo said, and shrugged. "But consider this. Who else would have the resources to equip a group of commandos in arms and uniforms that are identical to our own? Also, and most important, does it not strike you, gentlemen, as odd that even though the attacking group retreated within the sound of Defence Force helicopters, none of them was tracked down. It is a fact of guerrilla life that we require a minimum of one hour to insure even a moderate chance of a successful escape. Less than ten minutes' head start on a force using helicopters and dogs is suicide."

"You make an intriguing case," Lusana said, his fingers drumming the table. "I don't for one minute accept it as valid. However, it won't hurt to run a check." He turned to Machita. "Do you have a trusted informer in the Defence Ministry?"

"Someone highly placed," answered Machita. "Costs us a pretty penny, but his information is thoroughly reliable. Odd sort, though; he never appears in the same place twice under the same guise."

"You make him sound like some kind of mystic," said Jumana.

"Perhaps he is," conceded Machita. "Emma materializes when we least expect him."

"Emma?"

"His code name."

"Either the man has a warped sense of humor or he's a transvestite," said Lusana.

"I cannot say, General."

"How do you contact him?"

"We don't. He reaches us only when he has useful information to sell."

Jumana's face clouded. "What guarantee have we that he isn't feeding us falsified documents?"

"To date, everything he passed us from the Ministry has checked out one hundred percent."

Lusana looked at Machita. "You'll see to it, then?"

Machita nodded. "I'll fly to Pretoria myself and await Emma's next appearance. If anyone can clear up the mystery, it will be him."

20

The African Army of Revolution's camp was not really a camp at all; rather, it was a headquarters in what was once a small university for the Portuguese when they ruled Mozambique. A new university for the nation's black citizens had since risen from the heart of a new city torn from the northern interior, on Lake Malawi.

The converted campus made an ideal base for Lusana's army: dormitories for the troops, cafeterias turned mess halls, sporting facilities now utilized for combat instruction, comfortable quarters for the officers, a newly decorated ballroom for social events.

Democratic congressman Frederick Daggat, one of New Jersey's three black congressmen, was impressed. He'd half expected a typical revolutionary movement run by tribesmen armed with Soviet rockets, dressed in drab Chinese uniforms, and spouting inane, overused Marxist clichés. Instead he was pleased to discover an organization run on the lines of an American oil corporation. Lusana and his officers came off more like business executives than guerrillas.

Everything at the cocktail party went strictly according to New York protocol. Even the hostess, Felicia Collins, would have done a midtown Manhattan party proud.

Daggat caught her eyes and she excused herself from an admiring group of Somalian legislators. She came over and laid her hand on his arm.

"Enjoying yourself, Congressman?"

"Very much."

"Hiram and I had hoped you could stay over until the weekend."

"Regrettably, I must be in Nairobi for a meeting with the Kenya Educational Council tomorrow afternoon."

"I hope your quarters are satisfactory. We're a little off the beaten track for a Hilton Hotel franchise."

"I must admit, Mr. Lusana's hospitality is far more than I bargained for."

Daggat looked down at her. Tonight was the first time he had actually seen Felicia Collins up close. Celebrity, singer with three gold records, actress with two Emmys and an Oscar for a difficult role as a black suffragette in the motion picture *Road of Poppies*. She was every bit as ravishing as she appeared on screen.

Felicia stood cool and poised in green crepe de chine evening pajamas. The small strapless top tied at the waist and the matching pants gave a diaphanous hint of her shapely legs. She wore her hair in a chic short African cut.

"Hiram is on the threshold of greatness, you know."

He smiled at her high-toned statement. "I imagine the same might have been said once of Attila the Hun."

"I can easily see why Washington correspondents crowd your press conferences, Congressman." Her hand remained on his arm. "Your tongue stabs."

"I believe they refer to it as 'Daggat's shaft.'"

"The better to screw the white establishment with, perhaps?"

He took her hand and exerted an increasing pressure until there was a tiny widening of her huge mahogany eyes. "Tell me, Ms. Collins, what brings a beautiful and renowned black entertainer to the jungle?"

"The same thing that brings the black *enfant terrible* of the United States Congress," she countered. "To help a man who is fighting to advance our race."

"I'm more inclined to believe Hiram Lusana is fighting to advance his private bank account."

Felicia smiled derisively. "You disappoint me, Congressman. If you'd bothered to do your homework, you'd know that is simply not true."

Daggat stiffened. The gauntlet had been thrown.

He released her hand and moved until his face was only a few inches from hers. "With half the world watching the African nations, waiting and wondering when they are going to get their circus act together and remove the last bastion of white supremacy, who should appear like a messiah from the wilderness, offering a proverb for every occasion, but none other than your friendly international drug smuggler Hiram Lusana. Like a revelation in the night, he unloads his thriving operation and takes up the cause of the poor foul-smelling black rabble of South Africa.

"Reinforced now by gullible black opinion and touted by

a world press hungry for a personality, any personality, handsome Hiram suddenly finds his smiling face on the covers of no fewer than fourteen magazines with a combined circulation of over sixty million. Thus the sun shines down from heaven and Hiram Lusana is adored by Bible beaters everywhere for his devout piety; foreign state departments vie for his presence at parties; he demands and receives fabulous fees on the lecture circuit; and suckers like you, Ms. Collins, from the entertainment world, kiss his ass and scratch for a percentage of the box-office limelight."

Anger flared in Felicia's lovely features. "You're being deliberately offensive."

"Nakedly honest, perhaps." Daggat paused and enjoyed Felicia's uneasiness for a moment. "And what do you think will happen if Lusana should win his war and the white racist government in South Africa surrenders? Will he, like Cincinnatus, renounce his generalship and return to the plow? Not likely. There is little doubt in my mind that he'll proclaim himself president and launch a virtual dictatorship. Then, with the enormous resources of Africa's most advanced country in his pocket, he'll shift the grand crusade into reverse and either by force or by subterfuge gobble up the weaker black nations."

"You're blind," she said harshly. "Hiram guides his life by high morals. I find it unthinkable that he would ever consider selling out his ideals for personal gain."

Felicia did not see the caution in Daggat's eyes. "I can prove it, Ms. Collins, and all it will cost you—financially, that is—if you lose is one Yankee dollar."

"You're fishing in a barren lake, Congressman. You obviously do not know the general."

"Bet me."

She thought a moment and then looked up. "You're on."

Daggat bowed gallantly and escorted her to where Lusana was talking tactics with an officer of the Mozambique Army. Lusana broke off his conversation at their approach and greeted them. "Ah, my two fellow Americans. I see you've met."

"May I talk with you and Ms. Collins alone for a moment, General?" asked Daggat.

"Why, yes, of course."

Lusana excused himself from the Army officer and led the way into a small study comfortably furnished in an Afro-modern motif.

"Very nice," said Daggat.

"My favorite style of decor." Lusana motioned them to sit down. "And why not? Is it not based on our ancestral native designs?"

"Personally, I prefer the new Egyptian creations," said an indifferent Daggat.

"What is it you wish to discuss?" asked Lusana.

Daggat came straight to the point. "If I may be frank, General, the only reason you put on this dog and pony show tonight was in the hope of conning me into exerting my influence with the House Foreign Affairs Committee on behalf of the AAR. Agreed?"

Lusana could not conceal a cornered look, but he remembered to be courteous. "My apologies, Congressman. I did not mean to be so obvious. Yes, I did hope to persuade you to lend your support to our cause. But a con job? No way. I am not fool enough to attempt to stuff cotton in the ears of a man with your reputation for shrewdness."

"So much for preliminaries. What's in it for me?"

Lusana stared at Daggat with fascination. Such directness was hardly what he'd expected. His plans called for a more circuitous seduction. Now he was caught off guard. An out-and-out request for graft left him stunned. He decided to play coy in order to gain time to think.

"I miss your point, Congressman."

"No big deal, really. If you want me on your team, it's going to cost you."

"I still don't understand."

"Cut the jive, General. You and I came from the same gutter. We haven't shoved aside poverty and discrimination to get where we are without picking up any smarts along the way."

Lusana turned away and slowly, meticulously lit a cigarette. "Do you wish me to open the negotiations with an offer for your services?"

"That won't be necessary. I already have a . . . ah . . . figure in mind."

"Please name it."

A smile lifted the corner of Daggat's lips. "Ms. Collins."

Lusana looked up, puzzled. "And a very comely figure at that. But I fail to see what she—"

"You give me Felicia Collins and I'll see to it my committee votes favorably on funding an arms program for your revolution."

Felicia leaped to her feet, her mahogany eyes ablaze. "I don't believe this."

"Consider it as a small sacrifice on behalf of a noble crusade," said Daggat sarcastically.

"Hiram, for God's sake," she snapped, "tell this turkey to pack up and ship out."

Lusana did not reply immediately. He gazed down at his lap and brushed off an imaginary piece of lint from a razor-creased pant leg. Finally he spoke in a soft voice. "I'm sorry, Felicia, but I can't allow sentimental feelings to enter into this."

"What crap!" She stared at him, her expression devoid of belief. "You're both mad, raving mad, if you think you can pass me around like a bowl of grits."

Lusana rose and came over and brushed his lips across her forehead.

"Do not hate me." He faced Daggat. "Congressman, enjoy your spoils."

Then he walked from the room.

For a long moment Felicia stood there, her face a study in mixed hostility and confusion; then understanding came and her eyes filled with tears. She made no protest, no gesture of resistance, as Daggat gently pulled her close and kissed her.

"You bastard," she whispered. "You rotten bastard. I hope you're satisfied."

"Not quite yet."

"You've won your pound of flesh. What more do you want?"

He pulled a handkerchief from his breast pocket and dabbed her misting eyes.

"You forget," he said, grinning sardonically. "You still owe me a dollar."

VIXEN 03

Clive Cussler

BANTAM BOOKS
TORONTO · NEW YORK · LONDON · SYDNEY

VIXEN 03
*A Bantam Book / in association with
Viking Penguin Inc.*

PRINTING HISTORY

*Viking edition originally published October 1978
Playboy Book Club edition September 1978
Preferred Choice Bookplan edition October 1978*

Bantam edition / October 1979

2nd printing .... October 1979	5th printing .. November 1979
3rd printing .... October 1979	6th printing ...... February 1980
4th printing .. November 1979	7th printing .... July 1981

*Bantam Books are published by Bantam Books, Inc. Its trade-
mark, consisting of the words "Bantam Books" and the por-
trayal of a bantam, is Registered in U.S. Patent and Trademark
Office and in other countries. Marca Registrada. Bantam
Books, Inc., 666 Fifth Avenue, New York, New York 10103.*

To the Alhambra High School Class of '49,
who finally held a reunion

Contents

Oblivion   ix

PART 1: VIXEN 03   xix

PART 2: OPERATION WILD ROSE   55

PART 3: SALVAGE   123

PART 4: NO RETURN TICKET   201

PART 5: THE IOWA   267

Fool's Mate   353

Omega   361

Oblivion

Buckley Field, Colorado—
January 1954

The Boeing C-97 Stratocruiser bore the look of a crypt.
Perhaps the image was bred by the cold winter night, or
perhaps it came from the gusting snow that was piling an
icy shroud on the wings and fuselage. The flickering lights
from the cockpit windshield and the fleeting shadows of
the maintenance crew served only to exaggerate the chilling scene.

Major Raymond Vylander, United States Air Force,
did not care for what he saw. He watched silently as the
fuel truck drove away and vanished into the stormy darkness. The loading ramp was dropped from the rear of the
great whalelike belly, and then the cargo doors slowly
swung closed, cutting off a rectangle of light that spilled
onto a heavy-duty forklift. He shifted his gaze slightly and
stared at the twin rows of white lights bordering the eleven-
thousand-foot Buckley Naval Air Station runway that
stretched across the plains of Colorado. Their ghostly
luminescence marched into the night and gradually faded
behind the curtain of falling snow.

He refocused his eyes and studied the weary face reflected in the windowpane. His cap was pushed carelessly
back, revealing a dense thicket of umber hair. His shoulders were hunched forward and he wore the taut look of a
hundred-meters runner poised for the starter's gun. His
transparent reflection, bleeding through the glass into that
of the aircraft in the background, caused him to shiver involuntarily. He closed his eyes, pushed the scene into the
far reaches of his mind, and refaced the room.

Admiral Walter Bass, who sat on the edge of a desk, neatly folded a meteorological chart, then patted his sweating forehead with a handkerchief and nodded at Vylander.

"The weather front is moving off the eastern slope of the Rockies. You should break out of the overcast somewhere over the Continental Divide."

"Providing I can get that big-assed bird off the ground."

"You'll do it."

"Lifting a heavy plane with a full fuel load and a cargo weighing seventy thousand pounds in the middle of a blizzard with a thirty-knot crosswind from a ground altitude of five thousand feet isn't exactly a garden-variety takeoff."

"Every factor has been carefully considered," Bass said coldly. "Your wheels should leave the earth with a margin of three thousand feet of runway to spare."

Vylander dropped into a chair like a deflated balloon. "Is it worth risking the necks of my crew, Admiral? Just what is so damned vital to the U.S. Navy that it has to drag an Air Force plane out in the middle of nowhere in the dead of night to haul some junk to an island in the Pacific Ocean?"

For a moment Bass's face flushed, and then it softened. When he spoke, it was gently, almost apologetically. "It's painfully simple, Major. That junk, as you call it, is a top-priority cargo destined for a highly classified test program. Since your Stratocruiser was the only heavy transport within a thousand miles that can do the job, the Air Force consented to put her on temporary loan to the Navy. They threw you and your crew into the bargain, and that's all there is to it."

Vylander shot Bass a penetrating stare. "I don't mean to sound insubordinate, Admiral, but that's not all, not by a long shot."

Bass walked around the desk and sat down. "You're to consider it a routine flight, nothing more."

"I'd appreciate it, sir, if you'd throw me a bone and enlighten me as to what's inside those canisters in my cargo cabin."

Bass avoided his eyes. "Sorry, it's highly classified material."

Vylander knew when he was licked. He swayed wearily to his feet, picked up the vinyl folder containing his flight plan and charts, and walked toward the door. Then he hesitated and turned. "In the event we have to ditch—"

"Don't! If an in-flight emergency develops," Bass said solemnly, "you ride her down into a nonpopulated area."

"That's asking too much."

"I'm not making a formal request; I'm giving an order! You and your crew are not to abandon the aircraft between here and your destination, regardless of how dire the circumstances."

Vylander's face clouded. "Then I guess that's it."

"There is one more thing."

"Which is?"

"Good luck," Bass said, his lips edging into a tight grin.

It was a grin Vylander didn't like, not one tiny bit. He pulled open the door and, without replying, walked out into the cold.

In the control cabin, slouched so far down that the back of his head rested a good foot below his headrest, Lieutenant Sam Gold, Vylander's copilot, preoccupied himself with a flight checklist while, behind him off to his left, Captain George Hoffman, the crew's navigator, fiddled with a plastic protractor. Neither man paid the slightest acknowledgment to Vylander as he stepped through the bulkhead door leading from the cargo cabin.

"Course plotted?" Vylander inquired of Hoffman.

"All the preliminary dirty work has been figured by the Navy experts. Can't say as I agree with their choice of scenic routes, though. They've got us flying over the most desolate country in the West."

A worried expression came over Vylander's face, which didn't go unnoticed by Hoffman. The major looked over his shoulder at the huge metal canisters strapped down in the cargo section and tried to summon up a vision of their contents.

His contemplation was interrupted by the Buster Keaton –deadpan face of Master Sergeant Joe Burns, the flight engineer, peering around the cabin door. "All buttoned up and ready for the wild blue yonder, Major."

Vylander nodded without taking his eyes off the sinister-looking canisters. "Okay, let's put this chamber of horrors on the road."

The first engine turned over and sputtered to life, followed quickly by the other three. Then the auxiliary-power unit was unplugged, the chocks holding the wheels were pulled, and Vylander began taxiing the overburdened aircraft toward the end of the main runway. The security guards and the maintenance crew turned away and scurried for the warmth of a nearby hangar as the prop wash lashed their backs.

Admiral Bass stood in the Buckley control tower and watched the Stratocruiser crawl like a pregnant bug across the snow-swept field. A phone was clutched in his hand and he spoke quietly into the receiver.

"You may inform the President that Vixen 03 is preparing for takeoff."

"When do you figure its estimated time of arrival?" asked the stern voice of Charles Wilson, Secretary of Defense, through the earpiece.

"Allowing for a fuel stop at Hickam Field, in Hawaii, Vixen 03 should touch down in the test area approximately 1400 hours Washington time."

"Ike has scheduled us for 0800 hours tomorrow. He insists on a detailed briefing of the upcoming experiments and a running report on Vixen 03's flight progress."

"I'll take off for Washington immediately."

"I don't have to paint you a picture, Admiral, of what would happen if that plane crashed in or near a major city."

Bass hesitated in what seemed a long and terrible silence. "Yes, Mr. Secretary, it would indeed be a nightmare none of us could live with."

"The manifold pressure and the torque read a shade low across the board," announced Sergeant Burns. He watched over the engineer's panel with the intensity of a ferret.

"Enough to abort?" Gold asked hopefully.

"Sorry, Lieutenant. Internal-combustion engines won't perform in the thin mountain air of Denver like they will at sea level. Considering the altitude, the gauge readings are par for the course."

Vylander gazed at the strip of asphalt ahead. The snowfall had lightened, and he could almost see the halfway marker. His heart began to throb a little faster, keeping time with the rapid beat of the windshield wipers. God, he thought to himself, it looks no bigger than a shuffleboard court. As if in a trance, he reached over and picked up his hand mike.

"Buckley Control, this is Vixen 03. Ready to roll. Over."

"She's all yours, Vixen 03," the familiar voice of Admiral Bass scratched through the headphones. "Save a big-chested native girl for me."

Vylander simply signed off, released the brakes, and shoved the four throttles against their stops.

The C-97 pushed her bulbous nose into the blowing snow and began her struggle down the long ribbon of pavement as Gold began calling out the increasing ground speed in a monotone.

"Fifty knots."

All too soon an illuminated sign with a large number 9 flashed by.

"Nine thousand feet to go," Gold droned. "Ground speed seventy."

The white runway lights blurred past the wing tips. The Stratocruiser lunged onward, the powerful Pratt-Whitney engines straining in their mounts, their four-bladed propellers clawing at the rarefied air. Vylander's hands were cemented to the wheel, his knuckles twisted white, his lips murmuring intermingled prayers and curses.

"One hundred knots . . . seven thousand feet left."

Burns's eyes never left his instrument panel, studying every twitch of the gauge needles, ready to detect the first signs of trouble. Hoffman could do nothing but sit there helplessly and watch the runway dissolve at what seemed to him an excessive rate of speed.

"One twenty-five."

Vylander was fighting the controls now, as the vicious crosswind attacked the control surfaces. A trickle of sweat rolled unnoticed down his left cheek and dropped into his lap. Grimly, he waited for some sign indicating that the craft was beginning to lighten, but it still felt as though a giant hand were pushing against the cabin's roof.

"One hundred thirty-five knots. Kiss the five-thousand-foot marker farewell."

"Lift baby, lift," Hoffman pleaded as Gold's readings began falling one on top of the other.

"One hundred forty-five knots. Three thousand feet left." He turned to Vylander. "We just passed the go, no-go point."

"So much for Admiral Bass's safety margin," Vylander muttered.

"Two thousand feet coming up. Ground speed one fifty-five."

Vylander could see the red lights at the end of the runway. It felt as though he were steering a rock. Gold kept glancing at him nervously, anticipating the movement of the elbows that meant the major had engaged the controls for the climb. Vylander sat still, as immovable as a sack of Portland cement.

"Oh God . . . the one-thousand-foot marker . . . going, going, gone."

Vylander gently eased back the control column. For almost three seconds, which seemed an eternity, nothing happened. But then with agonizing slowness the Stratocruiser slipped the ground and staggered aloft a scant fifty yards before the asphalt stopped.

"Gear up!" he said hoarsely.

There were a few uneasy moments until the landing gear thumped inside their wheel wells and Vylander could feel a slight increase in airspeed.

"Gear up and locked," said Gold.

The flaps were raised at four hundred feet and the men in the cabin expelled a great, collective sigh of relief as Vylander banked into a shallow turn to the northwest. The lights of Denver blinked beneath the port wing but quickly became lost as the overcast closed in. Vylander didn't relax fully until the airspeed crept over two hundred knots and the altimeter showed thirty-five hundred feet between the plane and the ground.

"Up, up and away," sighed Hoffman. "I don't mind admitting I had a couple of tiny doubts there for a while."

"Join the club," said Burns, grinning.

As soon as he broke through the clouds and leveled the Stratocruiser out at sixteen thousand feet on a westerly heading over the Rockies, Vylander motioned to Gold.

"Take her. I'm going to make a check aft."

Gold looked at him. The major did not normally relinquish the controls so early in the flight.

"Got her," Gold acknowledged, placing his hands on the yoke.

Vylander released his seat belt and shoulders harness and stepped into the cargo section, making sure the door to the cockpit was closed behind him.

He counted thirty-six of the gleaming stainless-steel canisters, firmly strapped to wooden blocks on the deck.

He began carefully checking the surface area of each canister. He searched for the usual stenciled military markings denoting weight, date of manufacture, inspector's initials, handling instructions. There were none.

After nearly fifteen minutes he was about to give up and return to the cockpit when he spotted a small aluminum plate that had fallen down between the blocks. It had an adhesive backing, and Vylander felt a tinge of smugness as he matched it to a sticky spot of stainless steel where it had once been bonded. He held the plate up to the dim cabin light and squinted at its smooth side. The tiny engraved marking confirmed his worst fear.

He stood for a time, staring at the little aluminum plate. Suddenly he was jolted out of his reverie by a lurch of the aircraft. He rushed across the cargo cabin and threw open the door to the cockpit.

It was filled with smoke.

"Oxygen masks!" Vylander shouted. He could barely make out the outlines of Hoffman and Burns. Gold was completely enveloped in the bluish haze. He groped his way to the pilot's seat and fumbled for his oxygen mask, wincing at the acrid smell of an electrical short circuit.

"Buckley Tower, this is Vixen 03," Gold was yelling into a microphone. "We have smoke in the cockpit. Request emergency-landing instructions. Over."

"Taking over the controls," said Vylander.

"She's yours." Gold's acceptance came without hesitation.

"Burns?"

"Sir?"

"What in hell's gone wrong?"

"Can't tell for sure with all this smoke, Major." Burns's voice sounded hollow under the oxygen mask. "It looks like a short in the area of the radio transmitter."

"Buckley Tower, this is Vixen 03," Gold persisted. "Please come in."

"It's no use, Lieutenant," Burns gasped. "They can't hear you. Nobody can hear you. The circuit breaker for the radio equipment won't stay set."

Vylander's eyes were watering so badly he could hardly see. "I'm bringing her around on a course back to Buckley," he announced calmly.

But before he could complete the hundred-and-eighty-degree turn, the C-97 started to vibrate abruptly in unison with a metallic ripping sound. The smoke disappeared as if by magic and a frigid blast of air tore into the small enclosure, assailing the men's exposed skin like a thousand wasps. The plane was shaking herself to pieces.

"Number-three engine threw a propeller blade!" Burns cried.

"Jesus Christ, it never rains . . . Shut down three!" snapped Vylander, "and feather what's left of the prop."

Gold's hands flew over the control panel, and soon the vibration ceased. His heart sinking, Vylander gingerly tested the controls. His breath quickened and a growing dread mushroomed inside him.

"The prop blade ripped through the fuselage," Hoffman reported. "There's a six-foot gash in the cargo-cabin wall. Cables and hydraulic lines are dangling all over."

"That explains where the smoke went," Gold said wryly. "It was sucked outside when we lost cabin pressure."

"It also explains why the ailerons and rudder won't respond," Vylander added. "We can go up and we can go down, but we can't turn and bank."

"Maybe we can slue her around by opening and closing the cowl flaps on engines one and four," Gold suggested. "At least enough to put us in the landing pattern at Buckley."

"We can't make Buckley," Vylander said. "Without number-three engine, we're losing altitude at the rate of nearly a hundred feet a minute. We're going to have to set her down in the Rockies."

His announcement was greeted with stunned silence. He could see the fear grow in his crew members' eyes, could almost smell it.

"My God," groaned Hoffman. "It can't be done. We'll ram the side of a mountain for sure."

"We've still got power and some measure of control," Vylander said. "And we're out of the overcast, so we can at least see where we're going."

"Thank heaven for small favors," grunted Burns.

"What's our heading?" asked Vylander.

"Two-two-seven southwest," answered Hoffman. "We've been thrown almost eighty degrees off our plotted course."

Vylander merely nodded. There was nothing more to say. He turned all his concentration to keeping the Stratocruiser on a lateral level. But there was no stopping the rapid descent. Even with full-power settings on the remaining three engines, there was no way the heavily laden plane could maintain altitude. He and Gold could only sit by impotently as they began a long glide earthward through the valleys surrounded by the fourteen-thousand-foot peaks of the Colorado Rockies.

Soon they could make out the trees poking through the snow coating the mountains. At 11,500 feet the jagged summits began rising above their wing tips. Gold flicked on the landing lights and strained his eyes through the windshield, searching for an open piece of ground. Hoffman and Burns sat frozen, tensed for the inevitable crash.

The altimeter needle dipped below the ten-thousand-foot mark. Ten thousand feet. It was a miracle they had made it so low; a miracle a wall of rock had not risen suddenly and blocked their glide path. Then, almost directly ahead, the trees parted and the landing lights revealed a flat, snow-covered field.

"A meadow!" Gold shouted. "A gorgeous, beautiful alpine meadow five degrees to starboard."

"I see it," acknowledged Vylander. He coaxed the slight course adjustment out of the Stratocruiser by jockeying the engine-cowl flaps and throttle settings.

There was no time for the formality of a checklist run-through. It was to be a do-or-die approach, textbook wheels-up landing. The sea of trees disappeared beneath the nose of the cockpit, and Gold cut off the ignition and electrical circuits as Vylander stalled the Stratocruiser a scant ten feet above the ground. The three remaining engines died and the great dark shadow below quickly rose and converged upon the falling fuselage.

The impact was far less brutal than any of them had a right to expect. The belly kissed the snow and bumped lightly, once, twice, and then settled down like a giant ski. How long the harrowing, uncontrolled ride continued Vylander could not tell. The short seconds passed like minutes. And then the fallen aircraft slid clumsily to a stop and there was a deep silence, deathly still and ominous.

Burns was the first to react.

"By God . . . we did it!" he murmured through trembling lips.

Gold stared ashen-faced into the windshield. His eyes saw only white. An impenetrable blanket of snow had been piled high against the glass. Slowly he turned to Vylander and opened his mouth to say something, but the words never came. They died in his throat.

A rumbling vibration suddenly shook the Stratocruiser, followed by a sharp crackling noise and the tortured screech of metal being bent and twisted.

The white outside the windows dissolved into a dense wall of cold blackness and then there was nothing—nothing at all.

At his Naval Headquarters office in Washington, Admiral Bass vacantly studied a map indicating Vixen 03's scheduled flight path. It was all there in his tired eyes, the deeply etched lines on his pale sunken cheeks, the weary slump of his shoulders. In the past four months Bass had aged far beyond his years. The desk phone rang and he picked it up.

"Admiral Bass?" came a familiar voice.

"Yes, Mr. President."

"Secretary Wilson tells me you wish to call off the search for Vixen 03."

"That's true," Bass said quietly. "I see no sense in prolonging the agony. Navy surface craft, Air Force search planes, and Army ground units have combed every inch of land and sea for fifty miles along either side of Vixen 03's plotted course."

"What's your opinion?"

"My guess is her remains are resting on the seabed of the Pacific Ocean," answered Bass.

"You feel she made it past the West Coast?"

"I do."

"Let us pray you're right, Admiral. God help us if she crashed on land."

"If she had, we'd have known by now," Bass said.

"Yes"—the President hesitated—"I guess we would at that." Another pause. "Close the file on Vixen 03. Bury it, and bury it deep."

"I'll see to it, Mr. President."

Bass set the receiver in its cradle and sank back in his chair, a defeated man at the end of a long and otherwise distinguished Navy career.

He stared at the map again. "Where?" he said aloud to himself. "Where are you? Where in hell did you go?"

The answer never came. No clue to the disappearance of the ill-fated Stratocruiser ever turned up. It was as though Major Vylander and his crew had flown into oblivion.

1

VIXEN 03

1

Colorado—September 1988

Dirk Pitt released his hold on sleep, yawned a deep, satisfying yawn, and absorbed his surroundings. It had been dark when he arrived at the mountain cabin and the flames in the great moss-rock fireplace along with the light from the pungent-smelling kerosene lamps had not illuminated the knotty-pine interior to its best advantage.

His vision sharpened on an old Seth Thomas clock clinging to one wall. He had set and wound the clock the previous night; it had seemed the thing to do. Next he focused on the massive cobwebbed head of an elk that stared down at him through dusty glass eyes. Slightly beyond the elk was a picture window that offered a breathtaking vista of the craggy Sawatch mountain range, deep in the Colorado Rockies.

As the last strands of sleep receded, Pitt found himself faced with his first decision of the day: whether to allow his eyes to bask in the majesty of the scenery or to feast them on the smoothly contoured body of Colorado congresswoman Loren Smith, who sat naked on a quilted rug, engrossed in yoga exercise.

Pitt discerningly opted for Congresswoman Smith.

She was sitting cross-legged, in the lotus position, leaning back and resting her elbows and head on the rug. The exposed nest between her thighs and the small tautened mounds on her chest, Pitt decided, put the granite summits of the Sawatch to shame.

"What do you call that unladylike contortion?" he asked.

"The Fish," she replied, without moving. "It's for firming up the bosom."

"Speaking as a man," Pitt said with mock pompousness, "I do not approve of rock-hard boobs."

"Would you prefer them limp and saggy?" Her violet eyes angled in his direction.

"Well . . . not exactly. But perhaps a little silicone here and a little silicone there . . ."

"That's the trouble with the masculine mind," she snapped, sitting up and brushing back her long cinnamon hair. "You think all women should have balloon-sized mammaries like those insipid drones on the centerfolds of chauvinist magazines."

"Wishing will make it so."

She threw him a pouting look. "Too bad. You'll have to make do with my thirty-four B-cuppers. They're all I've got."

He reached out, wrapped an iron arm around her torso, and dragged her half on, half off the bed. "Colossal or petite"—he leaned down and lightly kissed each nipple—"let no woman accuse Dirk Pitt of discrimination."

She arched up and bit his ear. "Four whole days alone together. No phones, no committee meetings, no cocktail parties, no aides to hassle me. It's almost too good to be true." Her hand crept under the covers and she caressed his stomach. "How about a little sport before breakfast?"

"Ah, the magic word."

She threw him a crooked smile. " 'Sport' or 'breakfast'?"

"What you said before, your yoga position." Pitt leaped out of bed, sending Loren sprawling backward onto her sculptured bottom. "Which way is the nearest lake?"

"Lake?"

"Sure." Pitt laughed at her confused expression. "Where there's a lake, there's fish. We can't waste the day dallying in bed when a juicy rainbow trout lies in breathless anticipation of biting a hook."

She tilted her head questioningly and looked up at him. He stood tall, over six foot three, his trim body tanned except for the white band around his hips. His shaggy black hair framed a face that seemed eternally grim and yet was capable of providing a smile that could warm a crowded room. He was not smiling now, but Loren knew Pitt well enough to read the mirth in the crinkles around his incredibly green eyes.

"You big conceited jock," she lashed out. "You're putting me on."

She launched herself off the floor, ramming her head into his stomach, shoving him backward onto the bed. She wasn't fooling herself for a second with her seemingly super strength. If Pitt hadn't relaxed and accepted her momentum, she would have bounced off him like a volleyball.

Before he could fake a protest, Loren climbed over his chest and straddled him, her hands pressing against his shoulders. He tensed himself, circled his hands behind her, and squeezed her soft cheek bottoms. She felt him grow beneath her and his heat seemed to radiate through her skin.

"Fishing," she said in a husky voice. "The only rod you know how to use doesn't have a reel."

They had breakfast at noon. Pitt showered and dressed and returned to the kitchen. Loren was bent over the sink, vigorously scrubbing a blackened pan. She wore an apron and nothing else. He stood in the doorway, watching her small breasts jiggle, taking his time about buttoning his shirt.

"I wonder what your constituency would say if they could see you now," he said.

"Screw my constituency," she said, grinning devilishly. "My private life is none of their damned business."

" 'Screw my constituency,' " Pitt repeated solemnly, gesturing as though he were taking notes. "Another entry in the scandalous life of little Loren Smith, congressional representative of Colorado's graft-ridden seventh district."

"You're not funny." She turned and threatened him with the dishpan. "There is no political hanky-panky in the seventh district, and I am the last one on Capitol Hill who can be accused of being on the take."

"Ah . . . but your sexual excesses. Think what journalistic hay the media might make out of that. I may even expose you myself and write a best-selling book."

"As long as I don't keep my lovers on office payroll or entertain them on my congressional expense account, I can't be touched."

"What about me?"

"You paid your half of the groceries, remember?" She dried the pan and set it in the cupboard.

"How can I build a business out of being kept," Pitt said sadly, "if I have a cheap screw for a mistress?"

She put her arms around his neck and kissed his chin. "The next time you pick up a horny girl at a Washington cocktail party, I suggest you demand an accounting of her financial assets."

Good lord, she recalled, that awful party thrown by the Secretary of Environment. She hated the Capital social scene. Unless a function was tied in to Colorado interests or one of her committee assignments, she usually went home after work to a mangy cat named Ichabod and whatever movie was playing on television.

Loren's eyes had been magnetically drawn to him as he stood in the flickering light of the lawn torches. She had stared brazenly while carrying on a partisan conversation with another Independent Party congressman, Morton Shaw, of Florida.

She felt a strange quickening of her pulse. That seldom happened and she wondered why it was happening now. He was not handsome, not in a Paul Newman sort of way, and yet there was a virile, no-nonsense aura about him that appealed to her. He was tall, and she preferred tall men.

He was alone, talking to no one, observing the people around him with a look of genuine interest rather than bored aloofness. When he became aware of Loren's stare, he simply stared back with a frank, appraising expression.

"Who is that wallflower over there in the shadows?" she asked Morton Shaw.

Shaw turned and gazed in the direction Loren indicated with a tilt of her head. His eyes blinked in recognition and he laughed. "Two years in Washington and you don't know who that is?"

"If I knew, I wouldn't ask," she said airily.

"His name is Pitt, Dirk Pitt. He's special-projects director for the National Underwater and Marine Agency. You know—he's the guy who headed up the *Titanic*'s salvage operation."

She felt stupid for not having made the connection. His picture and the story of the famous liner's successful resurrection had been headlined everywhere for weeks by the news media. So this was the man who had taken on the impossible and beaten the odds. She excused herself from Shaw and made her way through the crowd to Pitt.

"Mr. Pitt," she said. That was as far as she got. A breeze shifted the flames of the torches just then and the new angle caused a glinting reflection in Pitt's eyes. Loren felt a fever in her stomach that had come only once before, when she was very young and had a crush on a professional skier. She was thankful the dim light shaded the flush that must have tinted her cheeks.

"Mr. Pitt," she said again. She couldn't seem to get the right words out. He looked down at her, waiting. An introduction, you fool, she yelled inside her mind. Instead she blurted, "Now that you've raised the *Titanic,* what are you planning for your next project?"

"That's a pretty tough act to follow," he said, smiling warmly. "My next project, though, will be one with great personal satisfaction; one that I shall savor with great delight."

"And that is?"

"The seduction of Congresswoman Loren Smith."

Her eyes widened. "Are you joking?"

"I never regard sex with a ravishing politician lightly."

"You're cute. Did the opposition party put you up to this?"

Pitt did not reply. He took her by the hand and led her through the house, which was crammed with Washington's power elite, and escorted her outside, to his car. She followed without protest, out of curiosity more than obedience.

As he pulled the car into the tree-lined street, she finally asked, "Where are you taking me?"

"Step one"—he flashed a galvanizing smile—"we find an intimate little bar where we can relax and exchange our innermost desires."

"And step two?" she asked, her voice low.

"I take you for a hundred-mile-an-hour ride down Chesapeake Bay in a hydrofoil racing boat."

"Not this girl."

"I have this theory," Pitt continued. "Adventure and excitement never fail to transform gorgeous congresswomen into mad, insatiable beasts."

Afterward, as the sun's morning warmth fingered the

drifting boat, Loren would have been the last person on earth to dispute Pitt's seduction theory. She noted with sensuous satisfaction that his shoulders bore her teeth and claw marks to prove it.

Loren released her hold and pushed Pitt toward the front door of the cabin. "So much for fun and games. I've got a batch of correspondence to clear up before we can drive down to Denver for a shopping spree tomorrow. Why don't you go on a nature hike or something for a few hours. Later, I'll fix us a fattening dinner and we'll spend another perverted evening snuggling by the fire."

"I think I'm all perverted out," he said, stretching. "Besides, nature hikes are definitely not my bag."

"Go fishing, then."

He looked at her. "You never got around to telling me where."

"A quarter of a mile over the hill behind the cabin. Table Lake. Dad used to catch his limit of trout there all the time."

"Thanks to you"—he peered at her sternly—"I'm getting a late start."

"Tough."

"I didn't bring any fishing gear. Your dad leave any around?"

"Under the cabin, in the garage. He used to keep all his tackle down there. Keys to the door lock are on the mantel."

The lock was stiff from nonuse. Pitt spit on it and twisted the key as hard as he dared without breaking it. At last the tumblers gave and he squeaked the old twin doors open. After waiting a minute to adjust his eyes to the darkened enclosure, he stepped inside and looked around. There was a dusty workbench with its tools all neatly hanging in place. Cans of various sizes lined several shelves, some containing paint, some containing nails and assorted hardware.

Pitt soon found a fishing-tackle box under the bench. The pole took a little longer to find. He barely made one out in a dim corner of the garage. What seemed to be a piece of bulky equipment shrouded under a canvas drop cloth stood in his way. He couldn't quite reach the fishing pole, so he tried climbing over the obstruction. It shifted under his weight and he fell backward, clutching the drop cloth in a vain effort to catch his balance before both ended up on the dirt floor of the garage.

Pitt cursed, brushed himself off, and gazed at what barred him from an afternoon of fishing. A puzzled frown gripped his features. He knelt down and ran his hand over the two large objects he had accidentally uncovered. Then he rose and walked outside and called to Loren.

She appeared over the balcony. "What's your problem?"

"Come down here a minute."

Begrudgingly, she donned a soft beige trench coat and went downstairs. Pitt led her inside the garage and pointed. "Where did your father find those?"

She bent forward and squinted. "What are they?"

"The round yellow one is an aircraft oxygen tank. The other is a nose gear, complete with tires and wheels. Damned old, judging by the degree of corrosion and the grime."

"They're news to me."

"You must have noticed them before. Don't you ever use the garage?"

She shook her head. "Not since I ran for office. This is the first time I've been to Dad's cabin since he died in an accident three years ago."

"You ever hear of a plane crashing around here?" Pitt probed.

"No, but that doesn't mean it hasn't happened. I seldom see any neighbors, so I have little oportunity to catch up on local gossip."

"Which way?"

"Huh?"

"Your nearest neighbors. Where do they live?"

"Down the road, back toward town. First turnout to the left."

"What's their name?"

"Raferty. Lee and Maxine Raferty. He's a retired Navy man." Loren took Pitt's hand in hers and pressed tightly. "Why all the questions?"

"Curiosity, nothing more." He lifted her hand and kissed it. "I'll see you in time for that fattening dinner." Then he turned and began jogging down the road.

"Aren't you going fishing?" she called after him.

"Always hated the sport."

"Don't you want the Jeep?"

"The nature hike was your idea, remember?" he yelled over his shoulder.

Loren watched until Pitt disappeared through a clump of lodgepole pines before she shook her head at the incomprehensible whims of men and ran back inside the cabin to escape the early-fall chill.

2

Maxine Raferty had the look of the West about her. She was heavyset and wore a loose print dress, rimless glasses, and a net over her bluish-silver hair. She sat bundled up on the front porch of a cedar cabin, reading a paperback mystery. Lee Raferty, a string bean of a man, was down on his haunches, greasing the front-axle bearings of a battered old International flatbed truck, when Pitt trotted up and greeted them.

"Good afternoon."

Lee Raferty removed an unlit, well-chewed cigar stub from his mouth and nodded. "Hello there."

"Nice day for exercise," said Maxine, scrutinizing Pitt over the top of her book.

"The cool breeze helps," said Pitt.

The friendliness was there in their faces, but so was the backcountry wariness of strangers who trespassed, especially strangers who wore the look of the city. Lee wiped his hands on a greasy rag and approached Pitt.

"Can I help you with somethin'?"

"You can if you're Lee and Maxine Raferty."

That brought Maxine out of her chair. "We're the Rafertys."

"My name is Dirk Pitt. I'm a guest of Loren Smith, down the road."

The uneasy expressions were replaced with broad smiles. "Little Loren Smith. Of course," Maxine said, beaming. "We're all pretty proud of her around these parts, what with her representing us in Washington and all."

"I thought perhaps you might give me some information concerning the area."

"Be glad to," replied Lee.

"Don't stand there like a tree," Maxine said to her husband. "Get the man something to drink. He looks thirsty."

"Sure, how about a beer?"

"Sounds good," Pitt said, smiling.

9

Maxine opened the front door and hustled Pitt through. "You'll stay for lunch." It was more a command than a request and Pitt had no out but to shrug in acquiescence.

The living room of the house had a high-beamed ceiling with a bedroom loft. The decor was an expensive conglomeration of art deco furnishings. Pitt felt as though he had stepped back into the nineteen thirties. Lee scurried into the kitchen and quickly returned with two opened beers. Pitt couldn't help noticing there were no labels on the bottles.

"Hope you like home brew," said Lee. "Took me four years to get just the right blend between too sweet and too bitter. Runs about eight percent alcohol by volume."

Pitt savored the taste. It was different from what he expected. If he hadn't detected a slight trace of yeast, he would have pronounced the taste fit for commercial sale.

Maxine set the table and waved for them to come around She set out a large bowl of potato salad, a pot of baked beans, and a platter of thinly sliced rounds of meat. Lee replaced the rapidly emptied beer bottles with two fresh ones and started passing the plates.

The potato salad was hearty with just the right amount of tartness. The baked beans were thick with honey. Pitt did not recognize the meat or its taste, but found it delicious. In spite of the fact that he had eaten with Loren only an hour before, the aroma of the home-cooked meal inspired him to put it away like a farmhand.

"You folks lived here long?" Pitt asked between mouthfuls.

"We used to vacation in the Sawatch as far back as the late fifties," said Lee. "Moved here after I retired from the Navy. I was a deep-water diver. Got a bad case of the bends and took an early discharge. Let's see, that must have been in the summer of seventy-one."

"Seventy," Maxine said, correcting him.

Lee Raferty winked at Pitt. "Max never forgets anything."

"Know of any wrecked aircraft, say within a ten-mile radius?"

"I don't recollect any." Lee looked at his wife. "How 'bout it, Max?"

"Honest to Pete, Lee, where's your mind? Don't you remember that poor doctor and his family that was all

killed when their plane crashed behind Diamond? . . .
How's the beans, Mr. Pitt?"

"Excellent," Pitt said. "Is Diamond a town near here?"

"Used to be. Now it's only a crossroads and a dude
ranch."

"I recall now," Lee said, reaching for seconds on the
meat. "It was one of them little single-engine jobs. Burned
to a crisp. Nothin' left. Took the sheriff's department
over a week to identify the remains."

"Happened in April of seventy-four," Maxine said.

"I'm interested in a much larger plane," Pitt explained
patiently. "An airliner. Probably came down thirty or
forty years ago."

Maxine twisted her round face and stared unseeing at
the ceiling. Finally she shook her head. "No, can't say as
I ever heard of any air disaster of that magnitude. At least
not around these parts."

"Why do you ask, Mr. Pitt?" Lee asked.

"I found some old aircraft parts in Miss Smith's garage.
Her father must have put them there. I thought perhaps
he found them somewhere nearby in the mountains."

"Charlie Smith," Maxine said wistfully. "God rest his
soul. He used to dream up more schemes to get rich than
an unemployed embezzler on welfare."

"Most likely bought them parts from some surplus store
in Denver so's he could build another one of his nonwork-
ing contraptions."

"I get the impression Loren's father was a frustrated inventor."

"Poor old Charlie was that." Lee laughed. "I remember
the time he tried to build an automatic fishing-pole caster.
Damned thing threw the lure everywhere but in the
water."

"Why do you say 'poor old Charlie'?"

A sorrowful expression came over Maxine's face. "I
guess because of the horrible way he died. Didn't Loren
tell you about it?"

"Only that it was three years ago."

Lee motioned to Pitt's nearly empty bottle. "Like another beer?"

"No thanks; this is fine."

"The truth of the matter is," Lee said, "Charlie blew
up."

"Blew up?"

"Dynamite, I guess. Nobody never knew for sure. About all they ever found they could recognize was one boot and a thumb."

"Sheriff's report said it was another one of Charlie's inventions gone wrong," Maxine added.

"I still say bullshit!" Lee grunted.

"Shame on you." Maxine shot her husband a puritanical stare.

"That's the way I feel about it. Charlie knew more about explosives than any man alive. He used to be an Army demolitions expert. Why, hell, he defused bombs and artillery shells all across Europe in World War Two."

"Don't pay any attention to him," said Maxine haughtily. "Lee has it in his head Charles was murdered. Ridiculous. Charlie Smith didn't have an enemy in the world. His death was an accident pure and simple."

"Everyone's entitled to an opinion," Lee said.

"Some dessert, Mr. Pitt?" asked Maxine. "I made some apple turnovers."

"I can't manage another bite, thank you."

"And you, Lee?"

"I'm not hungry anymore," Raferty grumbled.

"Don't feel bad, Mr. Raferty," Pitt said consolingly. "It seems my imagination got the best of me also. Finding pieces of an aircraft in the middle of the mountains . . . I naturally thought they came from a crash site."

"Men can be such children sometimes." Max gave Pitt a little-girl smile. "I hope you enjoyed your lunch."

"Fit for a gourmet," Pitt said.

"I should have cooked the Rocky Mountain oysters a little longer, though. They were a bit on the rare side. Didn't you think so, Lee?"

"Tasted okay to me."

"Rocky Mountain oysters?" asked Pitt.

"Yes, you know," said Maxine. "The fried bull testicles."

"You did say 'testicles.' "

"Lee insists I serve them at least two times a week."

"Beats hell out of meat loaf," Lee said, suddenly laughing.

"That's not all it beats hell out of," Pitt murmured, looking down at his stomach, wondering if the Rafertys stocked Alka-Seltzer, and sorry now he'd skipped the fishing.

the scene of light at the side in operation. "Now I know what it was."

Loren stood and shivered in the chill dairy. Dirty garage under the damn cabin. Twice reading a big deal over ... the ... He murmured. "You sell it you'd, the Lake ... he has a logical explanation for how this dieves junk and here. Dad probably picked it up at some garage sale."

"I'm not so sure," Pitt said.

3

At three o'clock in the morning Pitt was wide awake. As he lay in bed with Loren snuggled against him and stared through the picture windows at the silhouetted mountains, his mind was throwing images inside his skull like a kaleidoscope. The last piece of what had turned out to be a perfectly credible puzzle refused to fit in its slot. The sky was beginning to lighten in the east when Pitt eased out of bed, pulled on a pair of shorts, and quietly stepped outside.

Loren's old Jeep was sitting in the driveway. He reached in, took a flashlight from the glove compartment, and entered the garage. He pulled the drop cloth aside and studied the oxygen tank. Its shape was cylindrical, measuring, Pitt guessed, slighty more than one yard in length by eighteen inches in diameter. Its surface was scratched and dented, but it was the condition of the fittings that attracted his interest. After several minutes he turned his attention to the nose gear.

The twin wheels were joined by a common axle that was attached at their hubs like the head of a *T* to the center shaft. The tires were doughnut shaped and their treads relatively unworn. They stood roughly three feet high and, amazingly, still contained air.

The garage door creaked. Pitt turned and watched Loren peek into the darkened cavern. He shined the light on her. She was wearing only a blue nylon peignoir. Her hair was tousled and her face reflected a mixture of fear and uncertainty.

"Is that you, Dirk?"

"No," he said, smiling in the dark. "It's your friendly mountain milkman."

She heaved a sigh of relief, came forward, and gripped his arm for security. "A comedian you're not. What are you doing down here, anyway?"

"Something bugged me about these things." He pointed

13

the beam of light at the aircraft fragments. "Now I know
what it was."

Loren stood and shivered in that dirty, dusty garage
beneath the silent cabin. "You're making a big deal over
nothing," she murmured. "You said it yourself: the Rafertys had a logical explanation for how this useless junk got
here. Dad probably picked it up at some salvage yard."

"I'm not so sure," Pitt said.

"He was always buying up old scrap," she argued. "Look
around you; the place is full of his weird, half-finished
inventions."

"Half finished, yes. But at least he built something from
the other trash. The oxygen tank and the nose gear he
never touched. Why?"

"Nothing mysterious about that. Dad most likely was
killed before he got around to them."

"Possibly."

"That's settled, then," she said firmly. "Let's get back
to bed before I freeze to death."

"Sorry, I'm not through here yet."

"What's left to see?"

"Call it a pebble in the shoe of logic," he said. "Look
here, at the fittings on the tank."

She leaned over his shoulder. "They're broken. What
did you expect."

"If this was removed from an obsolete aircraft at a salvage yard, the mounting brackets and the fittings to the
lines would have been disconnected with wrenches or
cut with either a torch or heavy shears. These were twisted
and wrenched apart by great force. Same goes for the nose
gear. The strut was bent and severed just below the hydraulic shock absorber. Strange thing, though: the break
did not happen all at once. You can see that most of the
ragged edge is weathered and corroded, while a small
section at the top still has a new look to it. Seems as if
the main damage and the final break occurred years
apart."

"So what does all that prove?"

"Nothing earth shattering. But it does indicate that these
pieces did not come from an aircraft-salvage yard or a surplus store."

"Now are you satisfied?"

"Not entirely." He easily lifted the oxygen tank, carried it outside, and deposited it in the Jeep. "I can't manage the nose gear by myself. You'll have to give me a hand."

"What are you up to?"

"You said we were driving down the mountains into Denver for a shopping spree."

"So?"

"So while you're buying out the town, I'll haul this stuff over to Stapleton Airport and find somebody who can identify the aircraft it came from."

"Pitt," she said, "you're not a Sherlock Holmes. Why go to all this trouble?"

"Something to do. I'm bored. You've got your congressional mail to keep you busy. I'm tired of talking to trees all day."

"You have my undivided attention nights."

"Man cannot live by sex alone."

She watched in mute fascination as he scrounged two long boards and propped them on the lowered tailgate of the Jeep.

"Ready?" he asked.

"I'm not exactly dressed for the occasion," she said, a chill in her voice and goose bumps on her skin.

"Then take off that thing so you won't get it dirty."

As if in a dream, she hung her peignoir on a nail, mystified as to why women instinctively indulge men in their juvenile idiosyncrasies. Then the two of them—Pitt in his shorts, Congresswoman Loren Smith in the nude—heaved and grunted the dusty nose gear up the makeshift ramp into the back of the Jeep.

While Pitt chained up the tailgate, Loren stood in the dawn's early light and gazed down at the dirt and grease smudged across her thighs and stomach and wondered what it was that possessed her to take a mad lover.

4

Harvey Dolan, principal maintenance inspector for the Air Carrier District Office of the FAA, lifted his glasses to the light and, detecting no smears, clamped them on a pyramid-shaped nose.

"Found them in the mountains, you say?"

"About thirty miles northwest of Leadville, in the Sawatch range," Pitt answered. He had to speak loudly to be heard above the roar of the forklift that was carrying the nose gear and oxygen tank from the Jeep through the huge, yawning door of the FAA inspection hangar.

"Not much to go on," said Dolan.

"But you can offer an educated guess."

Dolan shrugged noncommittally. "You might compare it to a policeman who's found a small lost child wandering the streets. The cop can see it's a boy with two arms and two legs, approximately two years old. The kid's clothes are J. C. Penney, and his shoes are Buster Browns. He says his first name is Joey, but he doesn't know his surname, address, or phone number. We're in the same boat, Mr. Pitt, as that cop."

"Could you translate your analogue into factual detail?" Pitt asked, smiling.

"Please observe," Dolan said with a professional flourish. He produced a ball-point pen from a breast pocket and probed it about like a pointer. "We have before us the frontal landing gear of an aircraft, an aircraft that weighed in the neighborhood of seventy or eighty thousand pounds. It was a propeller-driven craft, because the tires were not constructed for the stresses of a high-speed jet landing. Also, the strut design is of a type that has not been built since the nineteen fifties. Therefore, its age is somewhere between thirty and forty-five years. The tires came from Goodyear and the wheels from Rantoul Engineering, in Chicago. As to the make of the aircraft and its owner, however, I'm afraid there isn't too much to go on."

17

"So it ends here," Pitt said.

"You throw in the towel too early," said Dolan. "There is a perfectly legible serial number on the strut. If we can determine the type of ship this particular nose-gear model was designed for, then it becomes a simple matter of tracing the strut's number through the manufacturer and establishing the parent aircraft."

"You make it sound easy."

"Any other fragments?"

"Only what you see."

"How did you come to bring them here?"

"I figured that if anybody could identify them, it would be the Federal Aviation Administration."

"Putting us on the spot, huh?" Dolan said, grinning.

"No malice intended," Pitt said, grinning back.

"Not much to go on," Dolan said, "but you never can tell; we might get lucky."

He made a thumbs-down motion toward a spot circled with red paint on the concrete floor. The forklift operator nodded and lowered the pallet holding the parts. Then he wheeled the forklift backward, cut a ninety-degree right turn, and clanked off toward another corner of the hangar.

Dolan picked up the oxygen tank, turned it over in his hands in the manner of a connoisseur admiring a Grecian vase, and then set it down. "No way in hell to trace this," he said flatly. "Standardized tanks like this are still produced by several manufacturers for any one of twenty different aircraft models."

Dolan began to warm to his task. He got down on his knees and examined every square inch of the nose gear. At one point he had Pitt help him roll it to a new position. Five minutes went by and he didn't utter a word.

Pitt finally broke the silence. "Does it tell you anything?"

"A great deal." Dolan straightened up. "But not, unfortunately, the jackpot answer."

"The odds favor the proverbial wild-goose chase," said Pitt. "I don't feel right putting you to all this trouble."

"Nonsense," Dolan assured him. "This is what John Q. Public pays me for. The FAA has dozens of missing aircraft on file whose fates have never been solved. Any time we have an opportunity to mark a case closed, we jump at it."

"How do we go about laying our fingers on the make of aircraft?"

"Ordinarily I'd call in research technicians from our engineering division. But I think I'll take a stab in the dark and try a shortcut. Phil Devine, maintenance chief over at United Airlines, is a walking encyclopedia on aircraft. If anyone can tell us at a glance, he can."

"He's that good?" asked Pitt.

"Take my word for it," Dolan said with a knowing smile. "He's that good."

"A photographer you ain't. Your lighting is lousy."

A nonfiltered cigarette dangled from the lips of Phil Devine as he studied the Polaroid pictures Dolan had taken of the nose gear. Devine was a W. C. Fields–type character—heavy through the middle, with a slow, whining voice.

"I didn't come here for an art review," replied Dolan. "Can you put a make on the gear or not?"

"It looks vaguely familiar, kind of like the assembly off an old B-twenty-nine."

"That's not good enough."

"What do you expect from a bunch of fuzzy pictures —an absolute, irrefutable ID?"

"I had hoped for something like that, yes," Dolan replied, unruffled.

Pitt was beginning to wonder if he was about to referee a fight. Devine read the uneasy look in his eyes.

"Relax, Mr. Pitt," he said, and smiled. "Harvey and I have a standing rule: we're never civil to each other during working hours. However, as soon as five o'clock rolls around, we cut the hard-assing and go out and have a beer together."

"Which I usually pay for," Dolan injected dryly.

"You government guys are in a better position to moonlight," Devine fired back.

"About the nose gear . . ." Pitt said, probing quietly.

"Oh yeah, I think I might dig up something." Devine rose heavily from behind his desk and opened a closet filled from floor to ceiling with thick black-vinyl-bound books. "Old maintenance manuals." he explained. "I'm probably the only nut in commercial aviation who hangs on to them." He went directly to one volume buried among the mass and began thumbing through its pages. After a minute he found what he was looking for and passed the open book across the desk. "That close enough for you?"

Pitt and Dolan leaned forward and examined an exploded-view line drawing of a nose-gear assembly.

"The wheel castings, parts, and dimensions"—Dolan tapped the page with his finger—"they're one and the same."

"What aircraft?" asked Pitt.

"Boeing Stratocruiser," answered Devine. "Actually I wasn't that far off when I guessed a B-twenty-nine. The Stratocruiser was based on the bomber's design. The Air Force version was designated a C-ninety-seven."

Pitt turned to the front of the manual and found a picture of the plane in flight. A strange-looking aircraft: its two-deck fuselage had the configuration of a great double-bellied whale.

"I recall seeing these as a boy," Pitt said. "Pan American used them."

"So did United," said Devine. "We flew them on the Hawaii run. She was a damned fine airplane."

"Now what?" Pitt turned to Dolan.

"Now I send the nose gear's serial number to Boeing, in Seattle, along with a request to match it with the parent aircraft. I'll also make a call to the National Transportation Safety Board in Washington, who will tell me if they show any lost commercial Stratocruisers over the continental United States."

"And if one turns up missing?"

"The FAA will launch an official investigation into the mystery," Dolan said. "And then we'll see what turns up."

5

Pitt spent the next two days in a chartered helicopter, crisscrossing the mountains in ever-widening search-grid patterns. Twice he and the pilot spotted crash sites, but they turned out to be marked and known wrecks. After several hours in the air—his buttocks numb from sitting, the rest of his body exhausted from the engine's vibration and from the buffeting by surging drafts and crosswinds— he was genuinely thankful when Loren's cabin came into view and the pilot set the copter down in a nearby meadow.

The skids sank into the soft brown grass and the blades ceased their thump and idled to a stop. Pitt unclasped his safety belt, opened the door, and climbed out, luxuriating in a series of muscle stretches.

"Same time tomorrow, Mr. Pitt?" The pilot had an Oklahoma twang, and a short-cropped haircut to go with it.

Pitt nodded. "We'll angle south and try the lower end of the valley."

"You figuring on skipping the slopes above timberline?"

"If a plane crashed in the open, it wouldn't go missing for thirty years."

"You can never tell. I remember an Air Force jet trainer that smacked the side of a mountain down in the San Juans. The impact caused an avalanche and the plane's debris was buried. The victims are still under the rock."

"I suppose that's a remote possibility," Pitt said wearily.

"If you want my opinion, sir, that's the only possibility." The pilot paused to blow his nose. "A small, light plane might fall through the trees and become hidden till eternity, but not a four-engine airliner. No way pine and aspen could conceal wreckage that size. And even if it did happen, some hunter would have surely stumbled on it by now."

"I'm open to any theory that pans out," said Pitt. Out of the corner of his eye he saw Loren running across the meadow from the cabin. He slammed the door and waved off the pilot, turning and not bothering to look back as the engine whined into life. The craft lifted and droned over the tops of the surrounding trees.

Loren leaped into his arms, breathless from her dash in the thin air. She looked alive and vibrant in tight white slacks and red turtleneck sweater. Her elegantly molded face seemed to glow in the late-afternoon sun, the slanted light heightening the effect by tinting her skin to gold. He twirled her around and pressed his tongue through her lips, staring into a pair of liquid violet eyes that stared right back. It never failed to amuse Pitt that Loren forever kept her eyes open when kissing or making love, claiming that she didn't want to miss anything.

At last she came up for air and pushed him away, wrinkling her nose. "Whew, you stink."

"Sorry about that, but sitting behind the plastic bubble of a helicopter all day is like dehydrating in a greenhouse."

"You don't have to make excuses. There's something about a masculine musk smell that turns women on. Of course, the fact that you also reek of gas and oil doesn't help any."

"Then I shall immediately pass Go and proceed to the shower."

She glanced at her watch. "Later. If we hurry, you might still catch him."

"Catch who?"

"Harvey Dolan. He called."

"How? You have no telephone."

"All I know is a forest ranger came by and said you were supposed to call Dolan at his office. It was important."

"Where do we find a phone?"

"Where else? The Rafertys'."

Lee was in town, but Maxine was only too happy to show Pitt to the telephone. She sat him down at an old-fashioned rolltop desk and handed him the receiver. The operator was efficient, and in less than ten seconds Dolan was on the other end of the line.

"Where in hell do you get off calling me collect?" he grumbled.

"The government can afford it," Pitt said. "How did you get word to me?"

"The citizen-band radio in my car. I bounced a signal from the public-communications satellite to a ranger station in the White River National Forest and asked them to relay the message."

"What have you got?"

"Some good news and some not-so-good news."

"Lay it on me in that order."

"The good news is, I heard from Boeing. The nose gear was installed as original equipment on air-frame number 75403. The not-so-good news is, that particular aircraft went to the military."

"Then the Air Force got her."

"It looks that way. At any rate, the National Transportation Safety Board has no record of a missing commercial Stratocruiser. I'm afraid that's as far as I can take it. From here on in, if you wish to pursue your investigation as a private citizen, you'll have to go through the military. Their air safety is out of our jurisdiction."

"I'll do that," Pitt replied. "If nothing else, to settle any fantasies I have about ghostly aircraft."

"I hoped you'd say something like that," said Dolan. "So I took the liberty of sending a request—in your name, of course—for the current status of Boeing 75403 to the Inspector General for Safety at Norton Air Force Base, in California. A Colonel Abe Steiger will contact you as soon as he finds something."

"This Steiger, what's his function?"

"Basically he's my military counterpart. He conducts investigations into the causes of Air Force flying accidents in the Western region."

"Then we'll soon have the answer to the riddle."

"It would seem so."

"What's your opinion, Dolan?" Pitt asked. "Your honest opinion."

"Well . . ." Dolan began cautiously. "I won't lie to you, Pitt. Personally, I think your missing aircraft will turn up in the records of some wheeler-dealer who trades in government-surplus salvage."

"And I thought we had the beginnings of a beautiful friendship."

"You wanted the truth. I gave it to you."

"Seriously, Harvey, I'm grateful for all your help. Next time I come to Denver, I'll pop for lunch."

"I never turn down a free feed."

"Good. I'll look forward to it."

"Before you hang up"—Dolan took a deep breath—"if I'm right, and there's a down-to-earth reason for the nose gear being in Miss Smith's garage, what then?"

"I have this strange feeling that isn't the case," Pitt replied.

Dolan set the receiver back in its cradle, sat and stared at it. A strange chill crept up his back and turned his skin to gooseflesh. Pitt's voice had sounded as though it came from a tomb.

6

Loren cleared away the supper dishes and carried a tray with two mugs of steaming coffee out to the balcony. Pitt was sitting tilted back in a chair with his feet propped on the railing. Despite the cool September-evening air, he wore a short-sleeved sweater.

"Coffee?" Loren asked.

As if in a trance, he turned and looked up at her. "What?" Then, murmuring, "I'm sorry, I didn't hear you come out."

The violet eyes studied him. "You're like a man possessed," she said suddenly, without quite knowing why.

"Could be I'm going psycho," he said, smiling faintly. "I'm beginning to see aircraft wreckage in my every thought."

She passed him one cup and cradled the other in her hands, soaking up its warmth. "That stupid old junk of Dad's. That's all you've had on your mind since we've been here. You've blown its significance out of all proportion."

"I can't make any sense out of it either." He paused and sipped the coffee. "Call it the Pitt curse; I can't drop a problem until I find a workable solution." He turned toward her. "Does that sound odd?"

"I suppose some people are compelled to find answers to the unknown."

He continued to speak in an introspective way. "This isn't the first time I've had a strong intuitive feeling about something."

"Are you always right?"

He shrugged and grinned. "To be honest, my ratio of success is about one in five."

"And if it is proven that Dad's salvage did not come off an airplane that crashed near here, what then?"

"Then I forget it and reenter the mundane world of practicality."

A kind of stillness settled upon them and Loren came over and sank into his lap, trying to absorb his body heat in the cool breeze that drifted down from the mountains.

"We still have twelve more hours before we board a plane back to Washington. I don't want anything to spoil our last night alone. Please, let's go in now and go to bed."

Pitt smiled and kissed her eyes tenderly. He balanced her weight in both arms and rose from the chair, lifting her as easily as he would a large stuffed doll. Then he carried her inside the cabin.

He wisely decided that now was not the time to tell her that she would be returning to the nation's capital alone, that he would stay behind and continue his search.

7

Two evenings later, a subdued Pitt sat at the cabin's dining table and scrutinized a spread of topographical maps. He leaned back in the chair and rubbed his eyes. All he had to show for his effort was a distraught girl friend and a hefty bill from the company that had rented him the helicopter.

The sound of feet thudded up the stairs to the front balcony, and soon a head that was completely shaved and a face with friendly hazel eyes and an enormous Kaiser Wilhelm mustache peered through the window in the Dutch door.

"Hello, the house," hailed the voice that seemed to come from a pair of size-twelve boots.

"Come in," Pitt answered without rising.

The man's body was squat and barrel-chested and must have sagged the scales, Pitt judged, at close to two hundred twenty pounds. The stranger shoved out a beefy hand.

"You must be Pitt."

"Yes, I'm Pitt."

"Good. I found you on the first try. I was afraid of taking a wrong turn in the dark. I'm Abe Steiger."

"Colonel Steiger?"

"Forget the title. As you can see, I came dressed like an old pack rat."

"I hardly expected you to answer my inquiry in person. A letter would have done just as well."

Steiger gave a wide grin. "The fact of the matter is, I wasn't about to let the price of a stamp cheat me out of a prospecting trip."

"A prospecting trip?"

"I'm killing two birds with the same stone, so to speak. One, I'm scheduled to speak next week at Chanute Air Force Base, in Illinois, on aircraft safety. Two, you're sitting in the heart of Colorado mining country, and since

I have a raving fetish for prospecting, I took the liberty of stopping over in hopes of getting in a little gold panning before continuing on to my lecture."

"You're more than welcome to bunk with me. I'm baching it at the moment anyway."

"Mr. Pitt, I accept your hospitality."

"Did you bring any luggage?"

"Outside, in a rented car."

"Bring it in and I'll fix some coffee." Then, as an afterthought, "Would you like some supper?"

"Thanks, but I had a bite with Harvey Dolan before I drove up."

"You saw the nose gear, then."

Steiger nodded and produced an old leather briefcase. He unzipped the sides and passed Pitt a stapled folder. "The status report on Air Force Boeing C-ninety-seven, number 75403, commanded by a Major Vylander. You might as well go over it while I unpack. If you have any questions, just holler."

After Steiger was settled in a spare bedroom, he joined Pitt at the table. "Does that resolve your curiosity?"

Pitt looked up over the folder. "This report states that 03 vanished over the Pacific during a routine flight between California and Hawaii during January of 1954."

"That's what Air Force records show."

"How do you explain the presence of the nose gear here in Colorado?"

"No great mystery. Sometime during the aircraft's service life the gear assembly was probably replaced with a new one. It's not an uncommon occurrence. The mechanics found a flaw in the structure. A hard landing cracked the strut. Perhaps it was damaged while being towed. There are a dozen different reasons that would require a replacement."

"Do the maintenance records show a replacement?"

"No, they do not."

"Isn't that a bit peculiar?"

"Irregular, maybe, but not peculiar. Air Force maintenance personnel are noted for their skill at mechanical repair, not for administrative bookkeeping."

"This also states that no traces of the aircraft or its crew ever turned up."

"I'll concede a puzzler on that score. The records indicate the search was an extensive one, much larger than the normal air-sea rescue procedures called for by the book. And yet, combined units of the Air Force and Navy drew a big fat zero." Steiger nodded thanks as Pitt handed him a steaming cup of coffee. "However, these things happen. Our files are crammed with aircraft that have flown into oblivion."

" 'Flown into oblivion.' That's very poetic." There was no concealing the cynicism in Pitt's voice.

Steiger ignored the tone and sipped at his coffee. "To an air-safety investigator, every unsolved crash is a thorn in the flesh. We're like doctors who occasionally lose a patient on the operating table. The ones that get away keep us awake nights."

"And 03?" asked Pitt evenly. "Does that one keep you awake?"

"You're asking me about an accident that occurred when I was four years old. I can't relate to it. As far as I'm concerned, Mr. Pitt, and as far as the Air Force is concerned, the disappearance of 03 is a closed book. She's lying on the bottom of the sea for all eternity and the secret behind the tragedy lies with her."

Pitt looked at Steiger for a moment, then refilled the man's coffee cup. "You're wrong, Colonel Steiger, dead wrong. There is an answer and it's not three thousand miles from here."

After breakfast Pitt and Steiger went their separate ways—Pitt to probe a deep ravine that had been too narrow for the helicopter to enter, Steiger to find a stream in which to pan gold. The weather was crisp. A few soft clouds hovered over the mountaintops and the temperature stood in the low sixties.

It was past noon when Pitt climbed out of the ravine and headed back toward the cabin. He took a faintly marked trail that meandered through the trees and came out on the shore of Table Lake. A mile along the waterline he met a stream that emptied out of the lake, and he followed it until he ran into Steiger.

The colonel was contentedly sitting on a flat rock in the middle of the current, swishing a large metal pan around in the water.

"Any luck?" Pitt yelled.

Steiger turned around, waved, and began wading toward the bank. "I won't be making any deposits at Fort

Knox. I'll be lucky if I can scrounge half a gram." He gave Pitt a friendly but skeptical look. "How about you? Find what you were looking for?"

"A wasted trip," Pitt replied. "But an invigorating hike."

Steiger offered him a cigarette. Pitt declined.

"You know," Steiger said, lighting up, "you're a classic study of a stubborn man."

"So I've been told," Pitt said, and laughed.

Steiger sat down and inhaled deeply and let the smoke trickle between his lips as he spoke. "Now, take me: I'm a bona fide quitter, but only on the matters that don't really count," he said. "Crossword puzzles, dull books, household projects, hooked rugs—I never finish any of them. I figure, without all that mental stress, I'll live ten years longer."

"A pity you can't quit smoking."

"Touché," Steiger said.

Just then two teenagers, a boy and a girl, wearing down vests and standing on a makeshift raft, rounded a bend in the stream and drifted past. They were laughing with adolescent abandon, totally oblivious of the men on the bank. Pitt and Steiger watched them in silence until they disappeared downstream.

"Now, there is the life," said Steiger. "I used to go rafting down the Sacramento River when I was a kid. Did you ever try it?"

Pitt did not hear the question. He stood gazing intently at the spot where the boy and the girl became lost to view. His facial expression transformed from deep thoughtfulness to sudden enlightenment.

"What's with you?" Steiger asked. "You look as though you've seen God."

"It was socking me in the face all this time and I ignored it," Pitt murmured.

"Ignored what?"

"It just goes to prove the toughest problems fall by the simplest solutions."

"You haven't answered my question."

"The oxygen tank and the nose gear," Pitt said. "I know where they came from."

Steiger only looked at Pitt, his eyes clouded with skepticism.

"What I'm getting at," Pitt continued, "is that we've been overlooking the one quality they share."

"I fail to see the connection," said Steiger. "When installed in the aircraft, they work under two entirely different flow systems, one gas and the other hydraulic."

"Yes, but take them off the aircraft and they both have one characteristic in common."

"Which is?"

Pitt gazed at Steiger and smiled and smiled. Then he spoke the magic words.

"They float."

8

Alongside most sleek executive jets, the Catlin M-200 came off like a flying toad. Also slower in flight, it had one redeeming quality that was unmatched by any other airplane its size: the Catlin was designed to land and take off in impossible places with cargo loads twice its own weight.

The sun gleamed on the aquamarine color scheme adorning the plane's fuselage as the pilot expertly banked the craft and settled it onto the narrow asphalt strip of the Lake County airport outside Leadville. It came to an abrupt halt with nearly two thousand feet to spare and then turned and taxied toward the area where Pitt and Steiger waited. As it neared, the letters NUMA could be clearly distinguished on the side. The Catlin rolled to a stop, the engines were shut down, and a minute later the pilot climbed down and approached the two men.

"Thanks a lot, buddy," he said, and grimaced at Pitt.

"For what, a carefree all-expenses-paid vacation in the Rockies?"

"No, for prodding me out of the sack with a madcap redhead in the middle of the night to assemble a cargo and fly it out here from Washington."

Pitt turned to Steiger. "Colonel Abe Steiger, may I present Al Giordino, my sometimes able assistant and always chief bellyacher, of the National Underwater and Marine Agency."

Giordino and Steiger sized each other up like two professional fighters. Except for Steiger's cleanly shaved head and Semitic features, and Giordino's mischievous Italian grin and curly mop of black hair, they could have passed for brothers. They were built exactly alike: same height, same weight, even the muscles that fought to escape their clothing seemed poured from the same mold. Giordino extended his hand.

33

"Colonel, I hope you and I never get mad at each other."

"The feeling is mutual," Steiger said, smiling warmly.

"Did you bring the equipment I specified?" asked Pitt.

Giordino nodded. "It took some conniving. If the admiral finds out about your little back-door project, he'll throw one of his renowned temper tantrums."

"Admiral?" Steiger queried. "I don't see how the Navy enters into this."

"They don't," Pitt answered. "Admiral James Sandecker, retired, happens to be Chief Director of NUMA. He has this Scrooge hangup: he frowns on clandestine expenditures by the hired help that aren't included in the agency's fiscal budget."

Steiger's eyebrows rose with sudden realization. "Are you saying that you had Giordino take a government aircraft at government expense halfway across the country without authorization, not to mention a stolen cargo of equipment?"

"Something like that, yes."

"We're really quite good at it," Giordino said, deadpan.

"Saves enormous time," said Pitt unconcernedly. "Bureaucratic red tape can be such a bore."

"This is incredible," said Steiger softly. "I'll probably be court-martialed as an accomplice."

"Not if we get away with it," Pitt said. "Now then, if you two will untie the cargo, I'll back the Jeep up to the airplane." With that he walked toward the parking lot.

Steiger watched him for a moment and then turned to Giordino. "Have you known him long?"

"Since the first grade. I was the class bully. When Dirk moved into the neighborhood and showed up for his first day at school, I worked him over pretty good."

"You showed him who was boss?"

"Not exactly." Giordino reached up and opened the cargo door. "After I bloodied his nose and blackened one eye, he got up off the ground and kicked me in the crotch. I walked lopsided for a week."

"You make him sound devious."

"Let's just say that Pitt has a ton of balls, the brains to go with them, and an uncanny knack for knocking the shit out of any obstacle, man made or otherwise, that gets in his way. He is a soft touch for kids and animals, and helps little old ladies up escalators. To my knowledge, he's never stolen a dime in his life nor used his sly talents for personal gain. Beyond all that, he's one helluva guy."

"Do you think he might have gone too far this time?"

"You mean his stock in a nonexistent aircraft?"

Steiger nodded.

"If Pitt tells you there's a Santa Claus, hang your stocking on the mantel, because you better believe it."

Pitt crouched on his knees in an aluminum rowboat and fine-tuned the TV monitor. Steiger sat toward the bow and struggled with the oars. Giordino was in another boat, about twenty feet forward, nearly hidden behind a pile of battery-powered transmitters. As he rowed, he kept a wary eye on the cable that crept over the stern and disappeared into the water. At the other end was a TV camera enclosed in a watertight case.

"Wake me when a good horror movie comes on," Giordino said, yawning, across the water.

"Keep rowing," Steiger grunted. "I'm beginning to gain on you."

Pitt did not join in the idle banter. His concentration was focused on the screen. A frigid afternoon breeze rolled down the mountain slopes and turned the glassy surface of the lake into a mild chop, making it difficult for Giordino's and Steiger's aching arms to keep the two boats on an even course.

Since early morning the only objects that had strayed past the monitor were scattered mounds of rocks embedded in the muddy bottom, rotting remains of long-dead trees whose leafless branches seemed to clutch at the passing camera, and a few startled rainbow trout who gave the intruding camera a respectable berth.

"Wouldn't it have been easier to conduct a search with scuba equipment?" Steiger said, cutting into Pitt's fixed scrutiny.

Pitt rubbed his strained eyes with the palms of his hands. "TV is far more efficient. Also, the lake is two hundred feet deep in spots. A diver's bottom time at that depth is measured in mere minutes. Add to that the fact that fifty feet beneath the surface the water turns almost to freezing and you have one damned uncomfortable situation. A man would be lucky if his body could withstand the cold more than ten minutes."

"And if we find something?"

"Then I'll put on a wet suit and go over the side for a look-see, but not one second before."

Something materialized on the monitor and Pitt leaned forward for a closer look, shielding the outside light with a black cloth.

"I think we just picked up Giordino's horror movie," he said.

"What is it?" Steiger demanded excitedly.

"Looks like an old log cabin."

"A log cabin?"

"See for yourself."

Steiger bent around Pitt's shoulder and gazed at the screen. The camera, one hundred forty feet below the boats, relayed through the icy water a picture of what seemed to be a distorted structure. The sun's wavering light through the choppy surface and the hazy visibility at that depth combined to give it a ghostlike image.

"How in the world did that get there?" asked a bewildered Steiger.

"No great secret," said Pitt. "Table Lake is man made. The state dammed up the stream that flows through this valley in 1945. An abandoned lumber mill that stood near the old streambed was submerged when the water rose. The cabin we see must have been one of the old bunkhouses."

Giordino rowed back for a look. "All that's missing is a 'for sale' sign."

"Amazingly well preserved," murmured Steiger.

"Thanks to the near-freezing fresh water," Pitt added. Then, "So much for the local tourist attraction. Shall we continue?"

"How much longer?" Giordino asked him. "I could use some liquid nourishment, preferably the kind that comes out of a bottle."

"It'll be dark in a couple of hours," said Steiger. "I make a motion we call it a day."

"You win my vote," Giordino looked across at Pitt. "How about it, Captain Bligh? Shall I reel in the camera?"

"No, keep it dangling. We'll troll it back to the dock."

Giordino awkwardly turned his boat a hundred eighty degrees and began pulling for home.

"I think your theory has about shot its wad," said Steiger. "We've been over the center of the lake twice and all we have to show for it is a bundle of sore muscles and a picture of a tumbledown shack. Face the inevitable, Pitt: there's nothing of interest in this lake but fish." Steiger paused and nodded at the television equipment. "And speaking of the denizens of the deep—what a fisherman wouldn't give to own a rig like this."

Pitt looked up at Steiger thoughtfully. "Al, make for the old man on your left who's casting on the shore."

Giordino twisted around and noted the direction Pitt indicated. He nodded silently and altered his course. Steiger followed suit.

A few more minutes' rowing brought the boats within hailing distance of an elderly angler who was expertly laying a fly beside a massive boulder that protruded from the lake's surface. He looked up and tipped his fly-festooned hat at Pitt's greeting.

"Having any luck?"

"That's not very original," Steiger mumbled.

"Business is a mite slow today," answered the angler.

"Do you fish Table Lake often?"

"Off and on for twenty-two years."

"Can you tell me what part of the lake eats the most bait?"

"Come again?"

"Is there a section of Table Lake where fishermen frequently lose their lures?"

"Over toward the dam there's a submerged log that does a pretty good job of it."

"What depth?"

"Eight, maybe twelve feet."

"I'm looking for a spot that's deeper, much deeper," said Pitt.

The old angler thought a moment. "Up toward the big marsh at the north end of the lake there's this big hole. Lost two of my best spinners in it last summer while trolling deep. A lot of the big fish swim deep during hot weather. I don't recommend trying your luck there, though. Not unless you own part interest in a tackle shop."

"Much obliged for your help," Pitt said, and waved. "Good luck!"

"Same to you," said the old angler. He went back to his casting and within a few moments his pole arched with a strong bite.

"You heard, Al?"

Giordino looked longingly at the dock and then at the lake's north end, a quarter of a mile away. Resigning himself to the chore, he raised the camera to keep it from creeping into the lake bed and then adjusted his gloves and took up the oars again. Steiger gave Pitt a four-letter stare but raised the white flag.

A half hour of fighting a gusting cross chop passed with agonizing slowness. Steiger and Giordino went about their labor in silence; Giordino on blind faith in Pitt's judgment, Steiger because he was damned if he'd let Giordino outendure him. Pitt stayed glued to the monitor, every so often calling out depth adjustments to Giordino.

The bottom of Table Lake began to rise the closer to the marsh they rowed. Then, abruptly, the salt and weed began dropping away, and the water darkened. They halted to lower the camera and then resumed the stroke.

They had moved only a few yards when a curved object edged onto the screen. The form was not sharply defined; nor did it have a natural contour.

"Stop rowing!" Pitt ordered tersely.

Steiger slumped on his seat, grateful for the break, but Giordino looked piercingly across the narrow distance separating the two boats. He'd heard that tone of voice from Pitt before.

Down in the cold depths the camera slowly drifted closer to the object materializing on the monitor. Pitt sat as though turned to oak as a large white star on a dark-blue background crept into his view. He waited for the camera to continue its probe, the inside of his mouth as dry as Kansas dust.

Giordino had rowed over and was holding the two boats together. Steiger became aware of the tension, raised his head, and looked inquiringly at Pitt.

"You got something?"

"An aircraft with military markings," Pitt said, controlling the excitement he felt.

Steiger crawled astern and peered unbelievingly into the monitor. The camera had floated over the wing and was now falling back along the fuselage. A square port came into view as above it the words MILITARY AIR TRANSPORT SERVICE marched by.

"Sweet Jesus!" Giordino gasped. "A MATS transport."

"Can you tell what model?" Steiger asked feverishly.

Pitt shook his head. "Not yet. The camera angle missed the more easily identifiable engines and nose section. It came across the left wing tip and, as you can see, is now moving toward the tail."

"The serial number should be painted on the vertical stabilizer," Steiger said softly, as though in prayer.

They sat absorbed as the unearthly scene unfolded below. The plane had settled deeply in the mud. The fuselage had cracked open aft of the wings, the tail section twisted on a slight angle.

Giordino gently dipped his oars and towed the camera on a new course, correcting its viewing field. The resolution was so clear that they could almost make out the flush rivets in the aluminum skin. It was all so strange and incongruous. It was difficult for them to accept the image the television equipment relayed to their eyes.

Then they held their breaths as the stenciled serial number on the vertical stabilizer began entering from stage right. Pitt zoomed in the camera lens ever so slightly so there would be no mistaking the aircraft's identification. First a 7, then a 5, and a 4, followed by 03. For a moment Steiger stared at Pitt; the shattering effect of what he now knew to be true but was unable to accept turned his eyes as glazed as those of a somnambulist.

"My God, it's 03. But that's impossible."

"What you see is what you get," said Pitt.

Giordino reached over and shook Pitt's hand. "Never a doubt, partner."

"Your confidence in me is duly noted," Pitt said.

"Where do we go from here?"

"Drop a marker buoy over the side and we'll call it a day. Tomorrow morning we'll go down and see what we can find inside the wreck."

Steiger sat there, shaking his head and repeating, "It's not supposed to be here. . . . It's not supposed to be here."

Pitt smiled. "Apparently the good colonel refuses to trust his own eyes."

"It's not that," Giordino said. "Steiger has this psychological problem."

"Problem?"

"Yeah, he doesn't believe in Santa Claus."

In spite of the chilling morning air, Pitt was sweating inside the wet suit. He checked his breathing regulator, gave the thumbs-up sign to Giordino, and dropped over the side of the boat.

The icy water, surging between his skin and the interior lining of his three-sixteenths-inch-thick neoprene suit, felt like an electric shock. He hung suspended just below the surface for several moments, suffering the stabbing agony, waiting for his body heat to warm the entrapped water layer. When the temperature became bearable, he cleared his ears and kicked his fins, descending into an eerie world where wind and air were unknown. The line from the marker buoy angled off into the beckoning depths and he swam along beside it.

The bottom seemed to rise up and meet him. His right fin trailed through the mud before he leveled off, creating a gray cloud that mushroomed like smoke from an oil-tank explosion.

Pitt checked the depth gauge on his wrist. It read one hundred forty feet. That meant approximately ten minutes' bottom time without worrying about decompression.

His primary enemy was the water temperature. The icy pressure would drastically affect his concentration and performance. His body heat would soon be drained by the cold, pushing his endurance beyond its borders and into the realm of excessive fatigue.

Visibility was no more than eight feet, but that factor did not hinder him. The marker buoy had missed the sunken plane by mere inches and he had but to extend a hand and touch the metal surface. Pitt had wondered what sensations would course through him. He was certain fear and apprehension would raise their tentacles. But they did not appear. Instead, he felt a strange sense of accomplishment. It was as though he'd come to the end of a long and exhausting journey.

He swam over the engines, the blades of their propellers gracefully bent backward, like the curled petals of an iris, the finned cylinder heads never to feel the heat of combustion again. He swam past the windows of the cockpit. The glass was still intact but coated with slime, cutting off any view of the interior.

Pitt noted that he had used up nearly two minutes of his bottom time. He quickly kicked around to the shattered opening of the main fuselage, squeezed through, and switched on his dive light.

The first things his eyes distinguished in the somber gloom were large silver canisters. Their tie-down straps had broken in the crash and they lay jumbled about the cargo-cabin floor. Carefully he snaked in and around them and glided through the open door to the control cabin.

There were four skeletons sitting in their assigned seats, held in their grotesque positions by nylon seat belts. The navigator's bony fingers were still clenched; the one at the engineer's panel leaned backward, its skull cocked to one side.

Pitt moved forward, more than a touch of fear and revulsion in his chest. The bubbles from his air regulator cascaded upward and mingled in one corner of the cockpit's ceiling. What made the scene all the more unearthly was the fact that although the flesh of the bodies was gone, the clothes remained. The icy-cold water had held back the rotting process over the decades, and the crew sat as properly uniformed as at the instant they had all died.

The copilot sat stiffly upright, his jaws open in what Pitt imagined to be a ghostly scream. The pilot drooped forward, his head almost touching the instrument panel. A small metal plate protruded from his breast pocket, and Pitt gently retrieved it, pushing the small rectangle up one of the sleeves of his wet suit. A vinyl folder hung from a pocket next to the pilot's seat, and Pitt took that also.

A glance at his watch told him his time was up. He didn't need an engraved invitation to head for the surface and the friendly rays of the sun. The cold was beginning to seep into his blood and mist his mind. He could have sworn the skeletons had all turned and were staring at him through the empty sockets of their skulls.

He hurriedly backed out of the cockpit and turned around when space permitted in the cargo cabin. It was then he spied a skeletal foot behind one of the canisters. The body that belonged to the foot was secured by straps to several of the cargo tie-down rings. Unlike the remains of the crew forward, this one still had remnants of flesh adhering to its bones.

Pitt fought the bile rising in his throat and studied more closely what was once a living, breathing man. The uniform was not Air Force blue but rather a khaki similar to the old Army issue. He went through the pockets, but they were bare.

An alarm began to go off in his head. His arms and legs were losing all feeling and turning stiff from the relentless cold, and his movements came as though he were immersed in syrup. If he did not get some warmth to his body soon, the ancient aircraft would claim another victim. His mind was fogged and for a brief moment he felt the sharp knife of panic as he became confused and lost his sense of direction. Then he spotted his air bubbles, trailing from the cargo cabin and ascending toward the surface.

With great relief he turned from the skeleton and followed the bubbles into open water. Ten feet from the surface he could see the bottom of the boat as it wavered in the refracted light like an object in a surrealistic film. He could even make out Giordino's seemingly disembodied head peering over one side.

He barely had the strength to reach out and grasp an oar. The combined muscles of Giordino and Steiger then hoisted him into the boat as effortlessly as if he were a small child.

"Help me get this wet suit off him," Giordino ordered.

"My God, he's turned blue."

"Another five minutes down there and he would have entered hypothermia."

"Hypothermia?" asked Steiger, stripping off Pitt's jacket.

"Profound body-heat loss," explained Giordino. "I've known divers who died from it."

"I am not . . . repeat . . . am not ready for a coroner's slab," Pitt managed between shivers.

The wet suit was peeled off and they rubbed Pitt vigorously with towels and wrapped him in heavy wool blankets. The feeling slowly came back to his limbs and the warm sun added to his sensual comfort by penetrating his skin. He sipped hot coffee from a Thermos jug, knowing its rejuvenating benefits were more psychological than physiological.

"You were a fool," Giordino said, more out of concern than anger. "You damned near killed yourself by staying down too long. The water must be near freezing at that depth."

"What did you find down there?" Steiger asked anxiously.

Pitt sat up, pushing the last of the fog from his head. "A folder. I had a folder."

Giordino held it up. "You still do. It was clutched in your left hand like a vise."

"And a small metal plate?"

"I have it," said Steiger. "It fell out of your sleeve."

Pitt relaxed against the side of the boat and took another swallow of the steaming coffee. "The cargo cabin is filled with large canisters—stainless steel, judging by the negligible degree of corrosion. What they contain is anybody's guess. There were no markings on them."

"How are they shaped?" asked Giordino.

"Cylindrical."

Steiger looked thoughtful. "I can't imagine what kind of military cargo would call for the protection of stainless-steel canisters." Then his mind shifted gear and he looked at Pitt piercingly. "What of the crew? Was there any sign of the crew?"

"What's left of them is still strapped in their seats."

Giordino gently pried open one end of the vinyl folder. "The papers may be readable. I think I can separate and dry them back at the cabin."

"Probably the flight plan," said Steiger. "A few of the old die-hard Air Force pilots still prefer that particular type of folder to the newer, plastic ones for holding their paperwork."

"Maybe it will tell us what the crew was doing that far off course."

"I for one hope so," said Steiger. "I want all the facts in hand and the mystery neatly gift wrapped before I drop it on a desk at the Pentagon."

"Ah . . . Steiger."

The colonel looked at Pitt questioningly.

"I hate to bear tidings that will screw up your well-laid plans, but there's more than meets the eye concerning the enigma of Air Force 03—much more."

"We've found the wreck intact, haven't we?" Steiger fought to keep his voice down. He was not to be denied a moment of triumph. "The answers lie only a few yards away. Now it's only a matter of salvaging the remains from the lake. What else is there?"

"A rather unpleasant dilemma none of us counted on."

"What dilemma?"

"I'm afraid," Pitt said quietly, "that we also have a murder on our hands."

10

Giordino spread the contents of the folder on the kitchen table. There were six sheets in all. The small aluminum plate Pitt had found in the pocket of the pilot was simmering in a solution Giordino had concocted to bring out the traces of etching in the metal.

Pitt and Steiger stood before a crackling fire and sipped coffee. The fireplace was built of native rock; its heat warmed the entire room.

"You realize the enormous consequences of what you're suggesting?" Steiger asked. "You're conjuring up a serious crime out of thin air, without a shred of evidence. . . ."

"Stick it in your ear," Pitt said. "You act as though I'm accusing the entire United States Air Force of murder. I am accusing no one. Granted, the evidence is circumstantial, but I'll stake my life's savings that a forensic pathologist will bear me out. The skeleton in the cargo hold did not die thirty-four years ago with the original crew."

"How can you be sure?"

"Several items don't jibe. To begin with, our unaccounted-for passenger still has flesh on his bones. The others were stripped clean decades ago. This indicates, to me at least, that he died long after the crash. Also, he was tied hand and foot to the cargo tie-down rings. With a little imagination you could almost envision the earmarks for an old-fashioned gangland slaying."

"You're beginning to wax melodramatic."

"The whole scene reeks of it. One mystery ties illogically to another."

"Okay, let's take what we know to be true," said Steiger. "The aircraft with serial number 75403 exists not where it is supposed to. But nonetheless it exists.

"And I think we can safely assume the original crew sits down there in the wreck," Steiger continued. "As to the extra body, perhaps the report neglected to mention

47

his status. He might have been a last-minute assignment: a backup engineer or even a mechanic who strapped himself to the cargo rings just before the crash."

"Then how do you justify a difference in uniform? He was wearing khakis, not Air Force blues."

"I can't answer that anymore than you can say for certain that he was murdered long after the crash."

"There lies the catch," Pitt said evenly. "I've got a solid idea who our uninvited guest is. And if I'm right, his demise by person or persons unknown becomes a fundamental certainty."

Steiger's eyebrows raised. "I'm listening," he murmured. "Who do you have in mind?"

"The man who built this cabin. His name was Charlie Smith, Congresswoman Loren Smith's father."

Steiger sat there silently for a few moments, digesting the enormity of Pitt's statement. Finally he said, "What proof can you offer?"

"Quite literally bits and pieces. I have it on good authority that Charlie Smith's obituary says that he was blown to smithereens in an explosion of his own making. All that was ever found were a boot and one thumb. A nice touch, don't you think? Very neat and precise. I must keep it in mind the next time I want to do somebody in. Set off a blast, then as soon as the dust settles throw a recognizable piece of footwear and a slice of the victim's most identifiable anatomy at the edge of the smoking crater. Friends later identify the boot and the sheriff's department can't miss with a positive ID once they pull a print from the thumb. In the meantime I've buried the rest of the body where hopefully it will never be found. My victim's death goes down as an accident and I go merrily on my way."

"You're telling me the skeleton in the aircraft was missing a boot and a thumb?"

Pitt merely nodded an affirmative.

At half past nine Giordino was ready. He started by lecturing Pitt and Steiger as he would a class of high-school chemistry students. "As you can see, after more than three decades of submersion, the vinyl cover, because it's inorganic, is virtually as good as new, but the paper inside has nearly returned to pulp. Originally the contents were mimeographed—a common process prior to the miracle of Xerox. The ink, I'm sorry to say, has all but disappeared, and no laboratory on earth can bring it back, even under supermagnification. Three of the sheets are hopeless cases. Nothing vaguely legible remains. The fourth looks like it might have contained weather information. A few words here and there refer to winds, altitudes, and atmospheric temperatures. The only sentence I can partially decipher says 'Skies clearing beyond Western slopes.' "

" 'Western slopes' indicating the Colorado Rockies," said Pitt.

Steiger's hands gripped the edge of the table. "Christ, do you have any idea what that means?"

"It means 03's flight didn't originate from California, as stated in the report," said Pitt. "Her departure point must have been east of here if the crew was concerned about weather conditions over the Continental Divide."

"So much for data sheet number four," said Giordino. "Now then, compared to the rest, sheet five is a veritable treasure trove of information. Here we can faintly make out several word combinations, including the names of two crew members. Many of the letters are missing, but with a bit of elementary deduction we can figure the meanings. Look here, for instance."

Giordino pointed to the sheet of paper, and the other two leaned in closer.

A rc ft omm nd r: Ma   ay on V l nde

"Now, we fill in the blanks," Giordino continued, "and we come up with 'Aircraft commander: Major Raymond Vylander.' "

"And here's the combination," said Pitt, pointing. "This spells out the name and rank of the flight engineer."

"Joseph Burns," Giordino acknowledged. "In the lines that follow, the missing characters are too numerous to guess their intent. Then, this." Giordino pointed farther down on the paper.

ode n me: ix n 03

"Classified call sign," injected Pitt. "Every aircraft on a security flight is given one. Usually a noun followed by the last two digits of the aircraft's number." Steiger fixed Pitt with a look of genuine respect. "How would you know that?"

"Picked it up somewhere," Pitt said, shrugging it off.

Giordino traced over the blank areas. "So now we have 'Code name: *something* 03.' "

"What nouns have 'ix' in the middle of them?" Steiger mused.

"Chances are, the missing letter after *x* is *e* or *o*."

"How about 'Nixon'?" Giordino suggested.

"I seriously doubt that a mere transport plane would be named after a vice-president," Pitt said. " 'Vixen 03' seems closer to the mark."

"Vixen 03," Steiger repeated softly. "That's as good a shot as any."

"Moving right along," said Giordino. "Our final decipherable scrap on the fifth sheet is 'E-blank-A, Rongelo 060 blank.' "

" 'Estimated time of arrival, six in the morning at Rongelo,' " Steiger translated, his expression still incredulous. "Where in hell is that? Vixen 03 was scheduled to land in Hawaii."

"I only calls 'em the way I sees 'em," said Giordino.

"What about the sixth sheet?" Pitt asked.

"Pretty slim pickings. All gibberish except for a date and a security classification near the bottom. See for yourself."

```
   rdersd te  anu ry 2 ,  954
Aut or z d  y:   r   lt r B   s
TO   SE R T COD     1A
```

Steiger hovered over the indefinite wording. "First line reads 'Orders dated January, sometime between the twentieth and twenty-ninth, 1954.' "

Pitt said, "The second line looks like 'Authorized by,' but the officer's name is lost. The rank of general fits, though."

"Then comes 'Top-secret code one-A,' " said Giordino. "You can't get a classified rating any higher than that."

"I think it's safe to assume," said Pitt, "that someone in the upper echelons of either the Pentagon or the White House, or both, released a misleading accident report on Vixen 03 as a cover-up."

"In my years with the Air Force I've never heard of such an act. Why instigate a flagrant lie over an ordinary aircraft on a routine flight?"

"Face facts, Colonel. Vixen 03 was no ordinary aircraft. The report states the flight originated at Travis Air Force Base, near San Francisco, and was scheduled to land at Hickam Field, in Hawaii. We now know the crew was heading for a destination named Rongelo."

Giordino scratched his head. "I can't recall ever hearing of a place called Rongelo."

"Nor I," said Pitt. "But we can settle that mystery as soon as we lay our hands on a world atlas."

"So what have we got?" asked Steiger.

"Not much," admitted Pitt. "Only that during the latter part of January, 1954, a C-ninety-seven took off from a point either in the eastern or midwestern section of the United States on a top-secret flight. But something went wrong over Colorado. A mechanical malfunction that forced the crew to ditch the plane in the worst terrain imaginable. They got lucky, or so they thought. Miraculously avoiding smashing into a mountainside, Vylander found an open clearing and lined up the Stratocruiser for an emergency landing. But what they couldn't see—remember, it was January, and the ground was undoubtedly covered with snow—was in grim reality a lake frozen over with ice."

"So when the aircraft's momentum slowed and its weight settled," said Steiger vacantly, "the ice parted and she fell through."

"Exactly. The tidal surge of water into the broken ship and the staggering shock of the cold overwhelmed the crew before they had a chance to react, and they drowned in their seats. No one witnessed the crash, the water refroze over the grave, and all traces of the tragedy were neatly erased. The ensuing search discovered nothing and Vixen 03 was later concealed behind a phony accident report and conveniently forgotten."

"You've written an interesting plot," said Giordino, "and it plays well. But where does Charlie Smith come into the story?"

"He must have hooked the oxygen tank while fishing. Possessing an inquisitive mind, he probably dragged the area and wrenched the already broken nose gear loose from the wreckage."

"The expression on his face must have been priceless when the gear popped to the surface," Giordino said, smiling.

"Even if I accept Smith's murder," said Steiger, "I fail to see a motive."

Pitt raised his eyes and looked at Steiger. "There is always a motive for taking a man's life."

"The cargo," Giordino blurted, incredulous at his own realization. "It was a highly classified flight. It stands to reason that whatever Vixen 03 was transporting was worth a great deal to somebody. Worth enough to kill for."

Steiger shook his head. "If the cargo is so valuable, why wasn't it salvaged by Smith or his supposed killer? According to Pitt here, it's still down there."

"And sealed tight," Pitt added. "As near as I could tell, the canisters have never been opened."

Giordino cleared his throat. "Next question."

"Shoot."

"What's inside the canisters?"

"You had to ask," said Pitt. "Well, one conjecture bears consideration. Take an aircraft carrying cylindrical canisters on a secret mission somewhere in the Pacific Ocean in January of 1954—"

"Of course," interrupted Giordino. "Nuclear-bomb tests were being held at Bikini at that time."

Steiger rose to his feet and stood motionlessly. "Are you implying that Vixen 03 was transporting nuclear warheads?"

"I am not implying anything," Pitt said casually. "I am merely offering a possibility, and an intriguing one at that. Why else would the Air Force put the lid on a missing plane and throw up a smoke screen of misleading information to cloud the disappearance? Why else would a flight crew risk almost certain death to ride down a crippled aircraft in the mountains instead of taking to their parachutes and allowing it to crash, perhaps in or near a populated area?"

"There's one vital point that sinks your theory: the government would have never given up searching for a lost cargo of nuclear warheads."

"I admit you have me there. It does seem odd that enough destruction to obliterate half the country would be left to litter the environment."

Suddenly Steiger wrinkled his nose. "What is that god-awful stench?"

Giordino hurriedly rose and moved over to the stove. "I think the metal tag is done."

"What are you boiling it in?"

"A combination of vinegar and baking soda. They're all I could find that would do the trick."

"Are you sure it will bring out the etching?"

"Couldn't say. I'm not a chemist. Won't hurt it, though."

Steiger threw up his hands in exasperation and turned to Pitt. "I knew I should have saved this stuff for professional lab technicians."

Giordino calmly ignored Steiger's remark and delicately lifted the plate out of the boiling water with two forks and patted it dry with a dish towel. Then he held it up to the light, turning it at different angles.

"What do you see?" Pitt asked.

Giordino set the small aluminum plate down on the table in front of them. He inhaled deeply, his features taking on a grave expression.

"A symbol," he said tensely. "The symbol for radioactivity."

2

OPERATION WILD ROSE

11

Natal, South Africa—October 1988

To the casual eye the great trunk of the dead baobab tree looked like one of a thousand others spread about the northeast coastal plain of Natal Province, South Africa. There was no way of telling why it had died or how long ago. It stood in a kind of grotesque beauty, its leafless branches clutching at an azure sky with gnarled, woody fingers while its rotting bark crumbled into a medicinal-smelling humus on the ground. There was, however, one startling difference that set this dead baobab tree apart from the others: its trunk was hollowed out and a man crouched inside, intently peering through a small aperture with a pair of binoculars.

It was an ideal hiding place, blueprinted from some long-forgotten manual on guerrilla warfare. Marcus Somala, section leader of the African Army of Revolution, was proud of his handiwork. Two hours was all it had taken him the previous night to scoop out the spongy core of the tree and stealthily scatter the debris deep within the encircling brush. Once comfortably settled inside, he did not have to wait long for his concealment to pass its first test.

Shortly after dawn a black field-worker from the farm that Somala was observing wandered by, hesitated, and then relieved himself against the baobab. Somala watched, smiling inwardly. He felt an impulse to slip the blade of his long curved Moroccan knife out the sight hole and slice off the worker's penis. The impulse was to Somala an amusing one, nothing more. He did not indulge himself with stupid actions. He was a professional soldier and a dedicated revolutionist, a seasoned veteran of nearly a

57

hundred raids. He was proud to serve in the front line of the crusade to eradicate the last vestige of the Anglo cancer from the African continent.

Ten days had passed since he led his ten-man section team from their base camp in Mozambique over the border into Natal. They had moved only at night, skirting the known paths of the police security patrols and hiding in the bushveld from the helicopters of the South African Defence Force. It had been a grueling trek. The October spring in the Southern Hemisphere was unusually cool, and the underbrush seemed eternally clammy from constant rains.

When at last they had reached the small farming township of Umkono, Somala stationed his men according to the plan given him by his Vietnamese adviser. Each man was to scout a farm or military facility for five days, gathering information for future raids. Somala had assigned the Fawkes farm to himself.

After the field-worker had ambled off to begin his day's labor, Somala refocused his binoculars and scanned the Fawkes spread. The majority of the cleared acreage, waging a constant battle against the encroaching sea of surrounding bush and grassland, was planted in sugarcane. The remainder was mostly pasture for small herds of beef and dairy cattle with a bit of tea and tobacco thrown in. There was also a garden plot behind the main house, containing vegetables for the personal consumption of the Fawkes family.

A stone barn was used to store the cattle feed and crop fertilizers. It stood apart from a huge shed that covered the trucks and farm equipment. A quarter of a mile beyond, situated beside a meandering stream, was a compound that housed a community of what Somala guessed to be nearly fifty workers and their families, along with their cattle and goats.

The Fawkes house—more of an estate, actually—dominated the crest of a hill and was neatly landscaped by rows of gladiola and fire lilies edging a closely cropped lawn. The picturesque scene was spoiled by a ten-foot chain-link fence topped by several strands of barbed wire that guarded the house on all four sides.

Somala studied the barrier closely. It was a stout fence. The support poles were thick and were no doubt buried deep in encased concrete. Nothing short of a tank could penetrate that mesh, he calculated. He shifted his glasses until a solidly muscled man with a repeating rifle strapped to a shoulder came into view. The guard leaned casually against a small wooden shelter that stood next to a gate. Guards could be surprised and easily disposed of, Somala mused, but it was the thin lines leading from the fence to the basement of the house that diluted his confidence. He didn't require the presence of an electrical engineer to tell him the fence was connected to a generator. He could only speculate as to the strength of the voltage that surged invisibly through the chain link. He noted also that one of the wires led into the guard's shelter. That meant a switch had to be thrown by a guard whenever the gate was opened, and this was the Achilles' heel of the Fawkes defense.

Pleased at his discovery, Somala settled down inside his blind and watched and waited.

12

Captain Patrick McKenzie Fawkes, Royal Navy retired, paced the floor of his veranda with the same intensity he had once exhibited on the deck of a ship when approaching home port. He was a giant of a man, standing a shade over six feet six in his bare feet and supporting a frame that exceeded two hundred eighty pounds. His eyes were somber gray, tinted dark as the water of the North Sea under a November storm. Every sand-colored strand of hair was brushed neatly in place, as were the whitening filaments of his King George V beard. Fawkes might have passed for an Aberdeen sea captain, which is exactly what he was before becoming a Natal farmer.

"Two days!" he exclaimed in a booming Scots accent. "I canna afford to take two days away from the farm. It's inhuman; aye, that's what it is, inhuman." Miraculously, the tea in the cup he waved refused to slop over the brim.

"If the Minister of Defence personally asked to meet with you, the least you can do is oblige."

"But damn, woman, he does not know what he's asking." Fawkes shook his head. "We're in the midst of clearing new acreage. That prize bull I purchased in Durban last month is due to arrive tomorrow. The tractors need maintenance. No, I canna go."

"You'd best be getting the four-wheel-drive warmed up." Myrna Fawkes laid down her needlework and gazed up at her husband. "I've already packed your things and made a lunch to keep you in a good humor until you meet the Minister's train at Pembroke."

Fawkes towered over his wife and scowled. It was a wasted gesture. In twenty-five years she had yet to buckle before him. Out of stubbornness he tried a new tack.

"It would be negligent of me to leave you and the kids alone, what with all them damned heathen terrorists sneak-

61

ing through the brush and murdering God-fearing Christians right and left."

"Aren't you confusing an insurgency with a holy war?"

"Why, just the other day," Fawkes pushed on, "a farmer and his missus was ambushed over at Umoro."

"Umoro is eighty miles away," his wife said matter-of-factly.

"It could happen here just as well."

"You *will* go to Pembroke and you *will* visit with the Defence Minister." The words that came from the woman seemed chiseled in stone. "I have better things to do than sit around on the veranda all morning and palaver with you, Patrick Fawkes. Now get on your way, and stay out of them Pembroke saloons."

Myrna Fawkes was not a woman to ignore. Though she was lean and tiny, she possessed the toughness of two good men. Fawkes seldom knew her when she wasn't dressed in one of his outsized khaki shirts and blue jeans tucked into midcalf boots. She could do almost anything he could do: deliver a calf, ramrod their army of native workers, repair a hundred and one different pieces of mechanical hardware, nurse the sick and injured women and children in the compound, cook like a French chef. Strangely, she had never learned to drive a car or ride a horse and made no bones about not caring to bother. She kept her sinewy body in shape by miles of everyday walking.

"Don't fret for us," she continued. "We have five armed guards. Jenny and Patrick Junior can both shoot the head off a mamba at fifty meters. I can call up the constable by radio in case of trouble. And don't forget the electrified fence. Even if guerrillas get through that, there's still old Lucifer to contend with." She motioned toward a Holland & Holland twelve-gauge shotgun that rested against the door frame.

Before Fawkes could grunt a last-ditch reply, his son and daughter drove up in a British Bushmaster and parked by the steps of the veranda.

"She's filled with petrol and ready to go, Captain," Patrick Junior shouted. He was two months past twenty and wore the face and slimness of his mother, but in height he loomed three inches over his father. His sister, a year younger, big boned and large breasted, smiled gaily from a face sprinkled with freckles.

"I'm all out of bath oil, Papa," Jenny said. "Will you please remember to pick me up some when you're in Pembroke?"

"Bath oil," Fawkes groaned. "It's a damned conspiracy. My whole life is one great conspiracy engineered by my own flesh and blood. You think you can get along without me? Then so be it. But in my log you're all a bloody lot of mutineers."

Kissed by a laughing Myrna and herded by his son and daughter, Fawkes reluctantly boarded the four-wheel-drive. As he waited for the guard to open the gate, he turned and looked back at the house. They were still standing on the steps of the veranda, framed by a lattice bursting with bougainvillea blossoms. The three of them waved and he waved back. And then he was shifting the Bushmaster through the gears as he swung onto the dirt road, pulling a small dust cloud behind.

Somala watched the captain's departure, closely noting the procedure of the guard as he turned the electricity off and on when opening and closing the gate. The motions were accomplished mechanically. That was good, Somala thought. The man was bored. So much the better if the time came for an assault.

He angled the binoculars toward the dense elephant grass smudged with thick clumps of shrub that made up the snaking boundaries of the farm. He almost missed it. He would have missed it if his eye hadn't caught a lightning-quick glint from the sun's reflection. His instinctive reaction was to blink and rub his eyes. Then he looked again.

Another black man was lying on a platform above the ground, partially obscured by the fernlike leaves of an acacia tree. Except for slightly younger features and a shade lighter skin, he could have passed for Somala. The intruder was dressed in identical camouflage combat fatigues and carried a Chinese CK-88 automatic rifle with cartridge bandolier—the standard issue of a soldier in the African Army of Revolution. To Somala it was like gazing into a distant mirror.

His thoughts were confused. The men of his section were all accounted for. He did not recognize this man. Had his Vietnamese advisory committee sent a spy to observe his scouting efficiency? Surely his loyalty to the

AAR was not in question. Then Somala experienced a creeping chill up the nape of his neck.

The other soldier was not watching Somala. He was staring through binoculars at the Fawkes house.

13

The dampness hung like a soggy blanket and kept the water from evaporating out of the potholes. Fawkes glanced at the clock in the dashboard; it read three thirty-five. In another hour he would reach Pembroke. He began to feel a growing urge for a healthy tot of whisky.

He passed a pair of black youngsters squatting in the ditch beside the road. He paid them no heed and did not see them as they leaped to their feet and began running in the Bushmaster's dusty wake. A hundred yards farther on the road narrowed. A swamp on the right side held a rotting bed of reeds. On the left a ravine fell more than a hundred feet to a muddy streambed. Directly ahead a boy of about sixteen stood in the middle of the road, one hand gripping a broad-bladed Zulu spear, the other hand supporting a raised rock.

Fawkes stopped abruptly. The boy held his ground and stared with an expression of grim determination at the bearded face behind the windshield. He wore ragged shorts and a soiled, torn T-shirt that had never seen soap. Fawkes rolled down his window and leaned out. He smiled and spoke in a low, friendly voice.

"If you have a mind to play Saint George and the dragon with me, boy, I suggest you reconsider."

Fawkes was answered by silence. Then he became aware of three images simultaneously, and his muscles tensed. There was the sight of gleaming safety-glass fragments that had been carelessly kicked into a rain-eroded rut. There were parallel tire marks that curved at the lip of the ravine. And the other, most tangible evidence of something dangerously wrong was the reflection in the side mirror of the two boys charging toward his rear. One, a fat, lumbering youth, was pointing an old bolt-action rifle. The other swung a rusty machete above his head.

My God, Fawkes's mind flashed. *I'm being ambushed by schoolchildren.*

His only weapon was the hunting knife in the glove compartment. His family had hustled him on his way so quickly that he had forgotten to pack his favorite .44 Magnum revolver.

Wasting no time by cursing his laxity, he crammed the Bushmaster in reverse and mashed down on the gas. The tires bit and jerked the four-wheel-drive backward, missing the boy carrying the machete but clipping the one with the gun, sending him spinning into the swamp. Fawkes then braked and shoved the gearshift into first and spun wheels toward the boy who stood poised to throw both spear and rock.

There was no hint of fear in the black teenager's eyes as he rooted his bare feet and pitched both arms in unison. At first Fawkes thought the boy's aim was high; he heard the spear clatter and ricochet off the roof. Then the windshield dissolved in a hail of glittering slivers and the rock was in the front seat, beside him. Fawkes felt the glass particles slice his face, but the only thing he remembered afterward was the cold look of hatred in his assailant's eyes.

The impact lifted the boy off his feet like an elastic doll and flung him under the front wheels. Fawkes stomped on the brake pedal but succeeded only in making the injuries worse. The locked tires bounced and skidded over pliant flesh, tearing skin from sinew.

Fawkes eased from behind the wheel and cautiously walked back. The boy was dead, his skull crushed nearly flat, his skinny legs mangled chunks of crimson. The fat boy with the gun lay half in the algae-coated swamp water, half on the sloping bank. His head had been wrenched backward until it touched his spine. There was no sight of his companion; he had vanished into the swamp.

Fawkes picked up the rifle. The breech was open and a cartridge was jammed in the receiver. He pried it out and studied the problem. The reason the fat boy had not fired was that the rifle *could* not. The firing pin was too badly bent. Fawkes threw the old gun as hard as he could into the deepest part of the mire, watching it splash and gurgle out of sight.

A small lorry lay upside down in the ravine. Two bodies sprawled from the gaping, twisted doors. A man and a woman, brutally mutilated, were shrouded in swarms of flies.

It was obvious the three African boys had stoned the unsuspecting travelers, wounding the driver and sending the lorry hurtling into the ravine, where they had hacked to death the trapped survivors. Then, flushed and over-confident with their easy victory, they had settled down to await their next victim.

"Stupid kids," he muttered amid the stillness of death. "Damn stupid kids."

Like a marathon runner who had dropped out of the race a mile from the finish, Fawkes ached with exhaustion and regret. Slowly he returned to the Bushmaster, sopping with a handkerchief the trickles of blood that ran down his cheek. He reached inside the door, set the frequency dial on the mobile radio, and hailed the Pembroke con-stable. When he finished his report, he stood and cursed and tossed poorly aimed stones at the arriving vultures.

14

"He's late," Pieter De Vaal, Minister of the South African Defence Forces, said in Afrikaans. He lifted the window of the coach and leaned out, searching the road bordering the railroad siding. His words were directed at a tall, slender man with compelling blue eyes and dressed in the uniform of an Army colonel.

"If Patrick Fawkes is late," the colonel said, swirling the drink in his hand, "there must be a good reason for it."

De Vaal turned from the open window and brushed both hands through a thicket of gray wavy hair. He looked more like a professor of ancient languages than like the iron-willed head of the second largest military power on the continent. Not that he had exactly inherited a plum job. De Vaal was the fifth defense minister in seven years. His predecessor had lasted less than five months.

"Typical English performance," he said impatiently. "An Englander lives only for gin, the queen, and a practiced air of indifference. They cannot be relied upon."

"If you so much as even imply to his face that he is English, Herr Minister, Fawkes will become most uncooperative." Colonel Joris Zeegler downed his drink and poured another. "Fawkes is a Scotsman. I respectfully suggest, sir, that you try not to forget that."

De Vaal made no show of anger at Zeegler's insubordinate tone. He regarded advice from his intelligence chief seriously. It was no secret within the Ministry that De Vaal's success in smashing the advances by outside terrorists and suppressing local uprisings was due largely to the ingenious infiltration of the insurgent organizations by Zeegler's highly trained operatives.

"Englander, Scotsman—I would prefer dealing with an Afrikaner."

"I agree," said Zeegler. "But Fawkes is the best qualified to offer an opinion on the project. A month-long computer search of experienced military personnel proved that." He opened a file folder. "Twenty-five years Royal Navy. Fifteen of them in ship's engineering. Two years captain of HMS *Audacious*. Final time in service spent as engineering director of the Grimsby Royal Navy Shipyard. Purchased a farm in northern Natal and retired there eleven years ago."

"And what does your computer make of the fact that he coddles his Bantu workers?"

"I must admit that offering his blacks and coloreds shares of his farm profits is the gesture of a liberal. But there can be no denying Fawkes has built up the finest estate in northern Natal in an extremely short length of time. His people are loyal beyond belief. Woe to the radical who tries to stir up trouble on the Fawkes farm."

De Vaal was in the midst of formulating another pessimistic statement when there was a knock on the door. A young officer entered and came to attention.

"Forgive the interruption, Herr Minister, but Captain Fawkes has arrived."

"Show him in," De Vaal said.

Fawkes ducked his head under the low doorway and entered. De Vaal stared up at him in silence. He had not expected someone of such proportions, nor someone whose face was freshly cut in a dozen places. He extended his hand.

"Captain Fawkes, this is indeed a pleasure," De Vaal said in Afrikaans. "It was good of you to make the trip."

Fawkes crushed De Vaal's hand within his. "Sorry, sir, but I do not speak your language."

De Vaal smoothly slipped into English. "Forgive me," he said with a faint smile. "I forget that you Eng—ah—Scotsmen do not take to strange tongues."

"We're just dunderheaded, I guess."

"Pardon me for saying so, Captain, but you look as though you shaved with a branch of thorns."

"I encountered an ambush. Bloody little devils broke my windshield. I would have stopped at the local hospital, but I was running late for our meeting."

De Vaal took Fawkes by the arm and steered him to a chair. "I think we had better get a drink in you. Joris, will you do the honors? Captain Fawkes, this is Colonel Joris Zeegler, director of Internal South African Defence."

Zeegler nodded and held up a bottle. "I take it you prefer whisky, Captain?"

"Aye, that I do, Colonel."

De Vaal stepped over to the door and opened it. "Lieutenant Anders, inform Dr. Steedt that we have a patient for him. I suspect you will find him in his compartment, dozing." He closed the door and faced the room. "First things first. Now then, Captain, while we await the good doctor, perhaps you will be kind enough to provide us with a detailed report of your ambush."

The doctor came and went, grumbling good-naturedly over the rhinoceros hide Fawkes called skin. Except for two wounds that called for three stitches each, the doctor left the rest unbandaged. "Lucky for you those scratch marks don't match fingernail tracks, or you'd have a tough time explaining them to your wife," he joked as he snapped shut his bag.

"You're certain the attack was not organized?" Zeegler asked after the doctor departed.

"Not likely," Fawkes replied. "They were only ragged bush kids. God only knows what devil inspired them to go on a killing spree."

"I am afraid your run-in with bloodthirsty juveniles is not an isolated occurrence," De Vaal said softly.

Zeegler nodded in agreement. "Your story, Captain, fits the same crude modus operandi, if you will, of at least twenty other attacks in the last two months."

"If you want my opinion," Fawkes snorted, "that damned AAR is in back of it."

"Indirectly, the blame can be laid on the African Army of Revolution's doorstep." Zeegler drew on a pencil-thin cigar.

"Half the black boys between the ages of twelve to eighteen from here to Cape Town would give their testicles to become an AAR soldier," De Vaal injected. "You might call it a form of hero worship."

"You have to give the devil his due," said Zeegler. "Hiram Lusana is every bit as shrewd a psychologist as he is a propagandist and a tactician."

"Aye," Fawkes said, looking over at the colonel. "I've heard a great deal about that bastard. How did he come to be leader of the AAR?"

"Self-imposed. He's an American black. Seems he made

a vast sum of money in international drug smuggling. But
wealth was not enough. He entertained dreams of power
and grandeur. So he sold out his business to a French
syndicate and came to Africa and began organizing and
equipping his own army of liberation."

"Seems a staggering undertaking for only one man,"
said Fawkes, "even a wealthy one."

"Not so staggering when you have help, and lots of it,"
Zeegler explained. "The Chinese supply his arms and the
Vietnamese train his men. Fortunately, our security forces
are able to keep them in a state of almost constant rout."

"But our government will surely fall if we are sub-
jected to a prolonged economic blockade," added De Vaal.
"Lusana's game plan is to fight a clean war by the book.
No terrorism, no killing of innocent women and children.
His forces thus far have attacked only military installations. Then, by playing benevolent savior, he can gain
total moral and financial support from the United States,
Europe, and the Third World powers. Once he achieves
these goals he can exert his newly acquired influence to
close off all our economic dealings with the outside world.
Then the end of White South Africa is only a matter of
weeks."

"Is there no way to contain Lusana?" asked Fawkes.

De Vaal's bushy eyebrows rose. "There is one possibility, provided you give it your blessing."

Fawkes stared at the Minister, his expression one of bewilderment. "I'm only a beached sailor and a farmer. I
know nothing about insurgent warfare. Of what use
can I be to the Ministry of Defence?"

De Vaal did not answer but simply passed Fawkes a
leather-bound book about the size of a thin bookkeeping
ledger.

"It's called Operation Wild Rose."

The lights of Pembroke blinked on one by one in the
evening dusk. A light rain had pelted the windows of the
coach, leaving a myriad of streaks down the dust-coated
glass. Fawkes's reading spectacles clung to his great nose
and magnified his eyes as they darted back and forth over
the pages without pause. He was so engrossed in what
he was reading he absentmindedly chewed on the stem of
a pipe that had long since burned out.

It was a few minutes past eight o'clock when he closed

the cover of Operation Wild Rose. He sat there for a long moment as though in contemplation. Finally he shook his head tiredly.

"I pray to God it never comes to this," he said quietly.

"I share your sentiments," said De Vaal. "But the time is fast approaching when our backs will be against the wall and Operation Wild Rose may well be our final hope of escaping annihilation."

"I still fail to see what you gentlemen want from me."

"Merely your opinion, Captain," said Zeegler. "We've made feasibility studies of the plan and know what the computers say about its chances of success. We're hoping your years of experience will supply the pros and cons as judged by a human."

"I can tell you the scheme is damn near impossible," said Fawkes. "And for my money you can add 'insane' as well. What you're proposing is terrorism at its worst."

"Exactly," agreed De Vaal. "By using a black hit-and-run force masquerading as members of the African Army of Revolution, we can swing international sympathy away from the blacks and to the white cause of South Africa."

"We must have the support of countries like the United States to survive," Zeegler explained.

"What happened in Rhodesia can happen here," De Vaal went on. "All private property, farms, stores, banks, seized and nationalized. Blacks and whites slaughtered in the streets, thousands exiled from the continent with barely the clothes on their backs. A new black communist-oriented government, a despotic, tribal dictatorship suppressing and exploiting their own people in virtual slavery. You can be certain, Captain Fawkes, that if and when our government topples, it will not be replaced by one with democratic majority rule in mind."

"We don't know for sure that that will happen here," said Fawkes. "And even if we could look into a crystal ball and predict the worst, it would not condone unleashing Operation Wild Rose."

"I'm not after a moral judgment," De Vaal said sternly. "You've stated the plan is impossible. I will accept that."

After Fawkes left, De Vaal poured himself another drink. "The captain was frank. I'll give that to him."

"He was also quite right," said Zeegler. "Wild Rose *is* terrorism at its worst."

"Perhaps," De Vaal muttered. "But what choice does one have when one is winning battles while losing the war?"

"I am not a grand strategist," Zeegler replied. "But I'm certain Operation Wild Rose is not the answer, Minister. I urge you to shelve it."

De Vaal considered Zeegler's words for several moments. "All right, Colonel. Gather all data pertaining to the operation and seal it in the Ministry vault with the other contingency plans."

"Yes, sir," said Zeegler," his relief obvious.

De Vaal contemplated the liquid in his glass. Then he looked up with a thoughtful expression.

"A pity, a great pity. It just might have worked."

Fawkes was drunk.

If a monstrous claw had reached down and plucked away the long mahogany bar of the Pembroke Hotel, he would have fallen flat on his bandaged face. Dimly, he saw that he was the only patron left in the room. He ordered another drink, noting in a mild sort of sadistic glee that it was long past closing time and the five-foot-five-inch bartender was uneasy about asking him to leave.

"Are you all right, sir?" the bartender probed cautiously.

"No, dammit!" Fawkes roared. "I feel bloody-well awful."

"Beggin' your pardon, but if it makes you feel so bad, why do you drink it?"

"It's not the whisky that turns my guts. It's Operation Wild Rose."

"Sir?"

Fawkes looked furtively around the room and then leaned across the bar. "What if I was to tell you I met with the Minister of Defence right down the street at the station, in his private railroad car, not more than three hours ago?"

A smug smile curled the bartender's lips. "The Minister must be one hell of a wizard, Mr. Fawkes."

"Wizard?"

"To be in two places at the same time."

"Make your point, man."

The bartender reached under a shelf and threw a newspaper on the bar in front of Fawkes. He pointed to an article on the front page and read aloud the caption.

" 'Defence Minister Pieter De Vaal enters Port Elizabeth Hospital for surgery.' "

"Impossible!"

"That's this evening's paper," said the bartender. "You have to admit—not only does the Minister have extraordinary powers of recuperation, but one fast train as well. Port Elizabeth is over a thousand kilometers to the south."

Fawkes snatched up the paper, shook the fuzziness from his vision, put on his glasses, and read the story. It was true. Clumsily, he threw a wad of bills at the bartender and staggered through the doorway, through the hotel lobby, and into the street.

When he reached the railroad station, it was deserted. The moon's light glinted on empty rails. De Vaal's train was gone.

"You want me to raise the aircraft from Table Lake?"

"Why not? My God, you salvaged the *Titanic* from thirteen thousand feet in the middle of the Atlantic. A Stratocruiser in a landlocked lake should be child's play for a man of your talents."

"Very flattering. But you forget, I'm not my own boss. Raising Vixen 03 will take a crew of twenty men, several truckloads of equipment, a minimum of two weeks, and a budget of nearly four hundred thousand dollars. I can't swing that on my own, and Admiral Sandecker would never give NUMA's blessing to a project that size without solid assurance of additional government funding."

"Then what about simply bringing up one of the canisters and Smith's remains for positive identification?"

"And find ourselves holding the proverbial bag?"

"It's worth a try," Steiger said, excitement rising in his tone. "You can fly back to Colorado tomorrow. In the meantime I'll authorize a contract to retrieve the crew's bodies. That will get you off the hook with the Pentagon and NUMA."

Pitt shook his head. "Sorry, but you'll have to take a rain check. Sandecker assigned me to oversee the raising of a Union ironclad that sank off the Georgia coast during the Civil War." He paused to check his watch. "I'm scheduled to board a flight for Savannah in six hours."

Steiger sighed and his shoulders sagged. "Perhaps you can give it a go at a later date."

"Wrap up the contract and keep it on ice. I'll sneak off to Colorado the first chance I get. That's a promise."

"Have you told Congresswoman Smith about her father yet?"

"Truthfully, I haven't had the guts."

"A nagging doubt you could be wrong?"

"That's part of it."

A vacant expression clouded Abe Steiger's face. "Jesus, what a mess." He downed the double martini in one throw and then stared at the glass sadly.

The waitress returned with menus and they ordered. Steiger absently watched her backside as she swayed into the kitchen. "Instead of sitting here, beating out my brains over an old mystery nobody cares about, I should be concentrating on getting back to California and the wife and kids."

"How many?"

"Kids? Eight, all told. Five boys and three girls."

"You must be Catholic."

Steiger smiled. "With a name like Abraham Levi Steiger? You've got to be kidding."

"By the way, you neglected to mention how the brass explained away Vixen 03's flight plan."

"General O'Keefe found the original. It didn't jibe with our analysis of the one from the wreck."

Pitt pondered a moment and then asked, "Do you have a Xerox copy I might borrow?"

"Of the flight plan?"

"Just the sixth page."

"Outside, locked in the trunk of my car. Why?"

"A shot in the dark," Pitt said. "I have this friend over at FBI who can't resist a good crossword puzzle."

"Must you really leave tonight?" Loren asked Pitt.

"I'm expected at a morning meeting to discuss salvage operations," he said from the bathroom, where he was loading his shaving kit.

"Damn," she said, pouting. "I might as well have an affair with a traveling salesman."

He entered the bedroom. "Come now, to you I'm nothing but a current toy."

"That's not so." She flung her arms around him. "Next to Phil Sawyer, you're my very favorite person."

Pitt looked at her. "Since when have you been seeing the President's press secretary?"

"When the stud is away, Loren will play."

"But good God! Phil Sawyer. He wears white shirts and talks like a thesaurus."

"He asked me to marry him."

"I may vomit."

She held him tightly. "Please, no sarcasm tonight."

"I regret I can't be more of an adoring lover to you, but I'm too damned selfish to commit myself. I'm not capable of giving the one hundred percent a woman like you needs."

"I'll settle for any percentage I can get."

He leaned down and kissed her on the throat. "You'd make Phil Sawyer a rotten wife."

27

Thomas Machita paid his admission and entered the grounds of the traveling amusement fair, one of many that sprang up on holidays around the South African countryside. It was Sunday and large groups of Bantu and their families lined up at the Ferris wheel, merry-go-round, and booth games. Machita made his way over to the ghost ride, according to Emma's telephone instructions.

He was undecided as to which tool he would employ to kill Emma. The razor blade taped to his left forearm left much to be desired. The tiny bit of steel was a close-in weapon, lethal only if he sliced his victim's jugular vein in an unguarded, discreet moment, an opportunity Machita considered quite remote in view of the sizable crowd around him.

Machita finally decided on the ice pick. He let out a satisfied sigh, as though he had solved a great scientific riddle. The pick was unobtrusively threaded among the strands of a basket clutched in his hands. The wooden handle had been removed, and in its place electrical tape had been wound several times around the needlelike shaft. A quick thrust between the ribs to the heart, or into an eye or an ear; if he could somehow ram the shaft into one of Emma's eustachian tubes, there would be little if any body fluid to tell the tale.

Machita tightened his grip on the basket that held both the ice pick and the two million dollars for the payoff. His turn came and he paid for a ticket and mounted the platform of the ghost ride. The couple ahead of him, a giggling man and his obese wife, snuggled their way into a small car that seated two. The attendant, an old, haggard-looking derelict who constantly sniffed at a runny nose, lowered a safety bar over their legs and shoved a large lever protruding from the floor. The car bounced forward on a track and rolled through two swinging doors. Soon, wom-

131

en's screams could be heard escaping from the darkened interior.

Machita entered the next car. He relaxed and became amused at the thought of the ride. Images of his childhood returned and he remembered cringing in a similar car during another ghost ride long ago as phosphorescent banshees lurched out of the blackness at him.

He did not observe the attendant as the lever was pushed; nor did he react immediately when the old man leaped agilely into the car with him and lowered the safety bar.

"I hope you enjoy the ride," said a voice that Machita knew to be Emma's.

Once again the mysterious informer had shrewdly capitalized on Machita's laxity. The odds favoring a clean kill had suddenly evaporated.

Emma's hands expertly frisked his clothing. "How very wise of you to come unarmed, my dear Major."

A score for our side, thought Machita, his hands casually holding the basket and shielding the ice pick. "Do you have Operation Wild Rose?" he asked, his tone official.

"Do you have the two million American dollars?" the shadowy figure beside him retorted.

Machita hesitated and unconsciously ducked as the car swung beneath a tall stack of barrels that fell over toward them, jerking to a stop bare inches from their heads.

"Here . . . in the basket."

Emma pulled an envelope from inside a dirty jacket. "Your boss will find this most interesting reading."

"If not vastly overpriced."

Machita was glancing through the documents in the envelope when a pair of grotesquely painted witches, fluoresced by ultraviolet light, leaped at the car and shrieked through hidden loudspeakers. Emma ignored the wax figures and opened the basket, studying the print on the currency under the purple illumination. The car rolled onward as the witches were pulled back into their recess by hidden springs and the tunnel plunged into darkness again.

Now! Machita thought. He snatched the ice pick from its hiding place and lunged at where he guessed Emma's right socket should be. But in that split second the car snapped into a sharp turn and an orange floodlight burst on a bearded Satan who menacingly brandished a pitchfork. It was enough to deflect Machita's aim. The pick missed Emma's eye and its tip became embedded in the skull, above the brow.

The stunned informer cried out, chopped Machita's hand away, and plucked the thin shaft from his head. Machita grabbed the razor blade taped to his forearm and swung it at Emma's throat in a sweeping backhand slash. But his wrist was smashed downward by the devil's pitchfork, snapping the bone.

The devil was genuine. He was one of Emma's accomplices. Machita countered by throwing open the safety bar and lashing out with his feet, catching the costumed man in the groin, feeling his heels sink deeply into soft flesh. Then the car swung back into blackness and the devil was left behind.

Machita whipped his body back to face Emma, but found the seat beside him empty. A brief stream of sunlight flashed several meters to the left of the car as a door was opened and closed. Emma had vanished out an exit, taking the basket of money with him.

28

"Gross stupidity," said Colonel Jumana with fiendish satisfaction. "You must pardon me for saying it, my General, but I told you so."

Lusana stared pensively out the window at a formation of men drilling on the parade grounds. "A mistake in judgment, Colonel, nothing more. We will not lose the war because we have lost two million dollars."

A sheepish Thomas Machita sat at the table, his face beaded with perspiration, staring vacantly at the cast covering his wrist. "There was no way of knowing—"

He stiffened as Jumana stormed to his feet, the colonel's face radiating pure anger as he snatched Emma's envelope and hurled it into Machita's face.

"No way of knowing you were being set up? You fool! There you sit, our glorious chief of intelligence, and you can't even kill a man in the dark. Then you add insult to injury by giving him two million dollars for an envelope containing operating procedures for military garbage removal."

"Enough!" snapped Lusana.

There was silence. Jumana took a deep breath, then slowly stepped backward to his chair. Anger seethed in his eyes. "Stupid mistakes," he said bitterly, "do not win wars of liberation."

"You make too much of it," Lusana said stonily. "You are a superb leader of men, Colonel Jumana, and a tiger in battle, but as with most professional soldiers, you are sadly lacking in administrative style."

"I beg you, my General, do not take your wrath out on me." Jumana pointed an accusing finger at Machita. "He is the one who deserves punishment."

A sense of frustration enveloped Lusana. Regardless of intelligence or education, the African mind retained an almost childlike innocence toward blame. Bloodsoaked rituals still inspired them with a higher sense of justice than did a serious conference across a table. Wearily, Lusana looked at Jumana.

"The mistake was mine. I alone am responsible. If I had not given Major Machita the order to kill Emma, Operation Wild Rose might be lying in front of us this minute. Without murder on his mind, I trust the major would have checked the contents of the envelope before he turned over the money."

"You still believe the plan to be valid?" Jumana asked incredulously.

"I do," Lusana said firmly. "Enough to warn the Americans when I fly to Washington next week to testify at the congressional hearings on aid to African nations."

"Your priorities are here," said Machita, his eyes expressing alarm. "I beg you, my General, send someone else."

"There is none better qualified," Lusana assured him. "I am still an American citizen with a number of high contacts who sympathize with our fight."

"Once you leave here, you will be in grave danger."

"We all deal in danger, do we not?" asked Lusana. "It is our comrade-in-arms." He turned to Jumana. "Colonel, you will be in command during my absence. I shall furnish you with explicit orders for the conduct of our operation. I expect you to see that they are carried out to the letter."

Jumana nodded.

A fear began to swell inside Machita, and he could not help wondering if Lusana was paving the road to his own downfall and releasing a tidal wave of blood that would soon surge across the whole of Africa.

29

Loren Smith rose from behind her desk and held out her hand as Frederick Daggat was ushered into her office. He smiled his best politician's smile. "I hope you'll forgive my intrusion . . . ah . . . Congresswoman."

Loren grasped his hand firmly. It never failed to amuse her to see a man stumble over her title. They never seemed to get the hang of saying "Congresswoman."

"I'm happy for the interruption," she said, motioning him toward a chair. To his surprise, she held out a box of cigars. He took one.

"This is indeed a treat. I hardly expected . . . do you mind if I light up?"

"Please do," she said, smiling. "I grant that it looks a bit incongruous for a woman to pass out cigars, but the practical value becomes apparent when you consider that my male visitors outnumber the females by twenty to one."

Daggat expelled a large blue cloud toward the ceiling and fired his first broadside. "You voted against my initial proposal to budget aid to the African Army of Revolution."

Loren nodded. She didn't speak, for she was waiting for Daggat to make his full pitch.

"The white government of South Africa is on the verge of self-destruction. The nation's enonomy has plummeted in the last few years. Its treasury is exhausted. The white minority have cruelly and ruthlessly treated the black majority as slaves far too long. For ten years, in the time since blacks took over the government in Rhodesia, Afrikaners have become hardened and completely merciless in their dealings with their Bantu citizens. Internal riots have taken over five thousand lives. This bloodbath must not continue any longer. Hiram Lusana's AAR is the only hope for peace. We must support it, both financially and militarily."

"I was under the impression that Hiram Lusana was a communist."

Daggat shook his head. "I'm afraid you labor under a misapprehension, Congresswoman Smith. I admit that Lusana allows the use of Vietnamese military advisers, but I can personally assure you that he is not and never has been a pawn of international communism."

"I'm glad to hear that." Loren's voice was toneless. In her mind Daggat was trying to sell a bill of goods and she was determined not to buy.

"Hiram Lusana is a man of high ideals," Daggat continued. "He does not permit the slaughter of innocent women and children. He does not condone indiscriminate bloodthirsty attacks on cities and villages, as do the other insurgent movements. His war is aimed strictly against government installations and military targets. I, for one, feel that Congress should back the leader who conducts his affairs with virtuous rationality."

"Come down off the cross, Congressman. You know it and I know it: Hiram Lusana is a rip-off artist. I've examined his FBI file. It reads like a biography of a Mafia hit man. Lusana spent half his life in prison for every crime from rape to assault, not to mention draft dodging and a plot to bomb the state capitol of Alabama. After an extremely lucrative armored-car robbery, he went into the dope-peddling business and made a fortune. Then he skipped the country to beat paying taxes. I think you'll agree he's not exactly an all-American hero."

"He was never legally charged with the armored-car holdup."

Loren shrugged. "Okay, we'll give him the benefit of the doubt on that one. But his other crimes hardly qualify him to lead a holy crusade to free the downtrodden masses."

"What's history is history," Daggat said, pressing on. "Regardless of his shady past, Lusana is still our only hope of providing a stable government after the blacks take over the South African Parliament. You cannot deny that it is in the best interests of Americans to claim him as a friend."

"Why back any side?"

Daggat's eyebrow shot up. "Do I detect a leaning toward isolationism?"

"Look what it got us in Rhodesia," continued Loren.

"Within a few months after our former secretary of state's ingenious plan to transfer white-minority rule to the black majority took effect, civil war broke out between the radical splinter factions and set the country's progress back ten years. Can you promise that we won't see a repeat performance when South Africa bows to the inevitable?"

Daggat did not like being forced into a corner by a woman, any woman. He came out of his chair and leaned across Loren's desk. "If you do not throw your support to my proposal and the bill for aid which I intend to submit to the House, then, dear Congresswoman Smith, I fear you will be digging a grave so big and so deep for your political career that you may never get out in time for the next election."

To Daggat's amazement and anger, Loren broke out in laughter. "Good God, this is rich. Are you actually threatening me?"

"Fail to come out in favor of African nationalism and I can promise you the loss of every black vote in your district."

"I don't believe this."

"You'd better, because you will also see rioting like you've never seen before in this country if we don't stand solidly behind Hiram Lusana and the African Army of Revolution."

"Where do you get your information?" Loren demanded.

"I'm black and I know."

"You're also full of shit," Loren said. "I've conferred with hundreds of blacks in my district. They're no different from any other American citizen. Each is concerned with high taxes, the rising costs of groceries and energy, the same as whites, Orientals, Indians, and Chicanos. You're only kidding yourself, Daggat, if you think our blacks give a damn about how African blacks mess up their countries. They don't, and for the simple reason that Africans don't give a damn about them."

"You are making a sad error."

"No, it is you who is making the error," snapped Loren. "You are stirring up trouble where it need not exist. The black race will find equal opportunity through education, just like everyone else. The Nisei did it after World War Two. When they returned from the internment camps, they worked in the Southern California fields to send their sons and daughters through UCLA and USC to become attorneys and doctors. They arrived. Now it's the blacks' turn. And they'll do it, too, provided they're not hindered by men like you, who rabble-rouse at every opportunity. Now I'll thank you to get the hell out of my office."

Daggat stared at her, his face a mask of anger. Then his lips cracked slowly into a grin. He held the cigar at arm's length and let it drop onto the carpet. Then he turned and stormed from the office.

"You look like a boy who just had his bicycle stolen," said Felicia Collins. She was sitting in one corner of Daggat's limousine, filing her long nails.

Daggat slid in beside her and motioned for the driver to move on. He stared stonily ahead, his face blank.

Felicia slipped the emery board back in her purse and waited, her eyes apprehensive. Finally she broke the silence. "I take it Loren Smith turned you down."

"The foulmouthed white bitch," he said, almost spat. "She thinks she can treat me like some nigger stud on a pre-Civil War plantation."

"What on earth are you talking about?" she asked, surprised. "I know Loren Smith. She hasn't got a prejudiced bone in her body."

Daggat turned. "You know her?"

"Loren and I were high-school classmates. We still get together from time to time." A hardness came over Felicia's face that had not been there before. "You have something evil on your crafty mind, Frederick. What is it?"

"I've got to have Congresswoman Smith's support if I am to push through my bill to send arms and aid to the AAR."

"Would you like me to talk to Loren? Lobby on Hiram's behalf?"

"That and more."

She tried to read his thoughts. "More?"

"I want you to get something on her. Something I can use to twist her to our way of thinking."

Felicia stared at him, stunned. "Blackmail Loren? You don't know what you're asking. I can't spy on a good friend. No way."

"Your choice is clear: a girlish school friendship in exchange for the freedom of millions of our brothers and sisters who are enslaved by a tyrannical government."

"And if I can't dig any dirt?" Felicia said, searching for an out. "It's no secret her political career is unblemished."

"Nobody is perfect."

"What would I look for?"

"Loren Smith is an attractive single woman. She must have a sex life."

"What if she does?" Felicia argued. "Every single girl has her share of love affairs. And as long as she has no husband, you can't manufacture a scandal out of adultery."

Daggat smiled. "How astute of you. We shall do exactly that—manufacture a scandal."

"Loren deserves better."

"If she throws her support to our cause, she needn't worry about her secrets going public."

Felicia bit her lip. "No, I will not stab a friend in the back. Besides, Hiram would never pardon such a malignity."

Daggat refused to play her game. "Indeed? You may have slept with the savior of Africa, but I doubt if you ever truly read the man beneath the skin. Look up his past sometime. Hiram Lusana makes Al Capone and Jesse James look like sissies. It gets thrown in my face every time I stand up for him." Then Daggat's eyes narrowed. "Aren't you forgetting how he literally sold you to me?"

"I haven't forgotten."

Felicia turned away and stared out the window.

Daggat squeezed her hand. "Don't worry," he said, smiling. "Nothing will happen that will leave any scars."

She raised his hand and kissed it, but she didn't believe his words, not for an instant.

30

Unlike her famous parent ship the *Monitor*, the *Chenago* was virtually unknown to all but a handful of naval historians. Commissioned during June of 1862 in New York, she was immediately ordered to join the Union fleet blockading the entrance to Savannah. The unfortunate *Chenago* never had a chance to fire her guns: an hour away from her assigned station she met a heavy sea and foundered, entombing her entire crew of forty-two men ninety feet below the waves.

Pitt sat in the conference room of the NUMA salvage ship *Visalia* and studied a stack of underwater photos taken by divers of the *Chenago*'s grave. Jack Folsom, the brawny salvagemaster, chewed a massive wad of gum and looked on, waiting for the inevitable questions.

Pitt didn't disappoint him.

"Is the hull still intact?"

Folsom shifted the gum. "No noticeable transverse cracks that we can tell. Can't see it all, of course, since seven feet of keel is under the seafloor and the interior is filled with a yard of sand. But I'm guessing that chances of a longitudinal break are slim. I'll lay odds that we can lift her in one piece."

"What method do you propose?"

"Dollinger variable air tanks," answered Folsom. "Sink them in pairs beside the hulk. Then attach and fill with air. Same basic principle that hoisted the old submarine *F-four* after she sank off Hawaii way back in 1915."

"You'll have to use suction pumps to remove the sand. The lighter she is, the less chance she'll pull apart. The thick iron plate seems to have stood up well, but the heavy oak planking behind has long since rotted away its strength."

"We can also remove the guns," said Folsom. "They're accessible."

Pitt examined a copy of the *Chenago*'s original designs.

143

The *Monitor*'s familiar shape contained just one circular gun turret, but the *Chenago* possessed two, one at each end of her hull. From within both turrets extended twin thirty-centimeter Dahlgren smoothbore cannon, weighing several tons apiece.

"The Dollinger tanks," said Pitt, suddenly thoughtful, "how efficient are they for lifting sunken aircraft?"

Folsom stopped in mid-chew and stared at Pitt. "How big?"

"A hundred and seventy or eighty thousand pounds, including cargo."

"How deep?"

"One hundred forty feet."

Pitt could almost hear the gears whirring in Folsom's brain. Finally the salvagemaster resumed chewing and said, "I'd recommend derricks."

"Derricks?"

"Two of them on stable platforms could easily lift that much weight," said Folsom. "Besides, an aircraft is a fragile piece of hardware. If you used the Dollinger tanks and they got the least bit out of synchronization during the lift, they could tear the plane apart." He paused and looked at Pitt questioningly. "Why all the hypothetical questions?"

Pitt smiled a pondering smile. "You never know when we might have to bring up an airplane."

Folsom shrugged. "So much for fantasy. Now then, getting back to the *Chenago* . . ."

Pitt's eyes intently followed the diagrams Folsom began drawing on a blackboard. The diving program, the air tanks, the ships on the surface, and the sunken ironclad all took shape in conjunction with Folsom's running commentary on the planned lift operation. To all appearances, Pitt seemed keenly interested, but nothing he saw was relayed to his memory cells; his mind was two thousand miles away, deep in a Colorado lake.

Just as Folsom was describing the proposed towing procedure once the wreck reached sunlight for the first time in 125 years, a *Visalia* crewman poked his head through the hatchway and gestured toward Pitt.

"There's a shore-to-ship call for you, sir."

Pitt nodded, reached behind him, and picked up a phone sitting on a bulkhead shelf.

"This is Pitt."

"You're harder to track down than the abominable snowman," said a voice through the background static.

"Who is this?"

"Talk about shabby treatment," said the voice sarcastically, "I slave over a messy desk until three in the morning doing you a favor and you don't even remember my name."

"I'm sorry, Paul," Pitt said, laughing, "but your voice sounds about two octaves higher over the radiophone."

Paul Buckner, a long time pal of Pitt's and an agent of the Federal Bureau of Investigation, lowered his pitch to his belt buckle. "There, is that any better?"

"Much. Got any answers for me?"

"Everything you asked for, and then some."

"I'm listening."

"Well, to start with, the rank of the man you think authorized the flight orders for Vixen 03 obviously was not correct."

"But 'General' was the only title that fit."

"Ain't necessarily so. The title was a seven-letter word. All that was readable was the fifth character, which was an *R*. Quite naturally, it was assumed that since Vixen 03 was an Air Force plane piloted by an Air Force crew, its flight orders could only be authorized by an Air Force officer."

"So tell me something I don't know."

"Okay, wiseass, I admit it threw me, too, particularly the part where a search through Air Force personnel files failed to find any name that matched up with the known characters of our mystery officer's name. Then it occurred to me: 'admiral' is also a seven letter word, and its fifth character is also an *R*."

Pitt felt as though the reigning heavyweight champion had suddenly rammed a right hand into his lower gut. "Admiral"—the word ricocheted through his mind. Nobody had thought to consider that an Air Force plane might have been carrying naval hardware. Then a sobering thought brought Pitt back to earth.

"A name?" he asked, almost afraid of the answer. "Were you able to come up with a name?"

"All very elementary for a prying mind like mine. The first name was easy. Six letters with three known, two blanks with *LT* followed by another blank and then an *R*.

That gave me 'Walter.' Now comes the *pièce de résistance:* the surname. Four letters beginning with *B* and ending with *S*. And, since 'Bullshit' didn't fit and I already had the guy's rank and first name, a computer search through Bureau files and Navy records quickly made a match: 'Admiral Walter Horatio Bass.' "

Pitt probed further. "If Bass was an admiral back in 1954, he must be either past eighty years old or dead—most likely dead."

"Pessimism will get you nowhere," said Buckner. "Bass was a whiz kid. I read his file. It's most impressive. He got his first star when he was still thirty-eight years old. For a while it looked like he was headed for Naval Chief of Staff. But then he must have pulled a no-no or mouthed off to a superior, because he was suddenly transferred and placed in command of a minor boondocks fleet base in the Indian Ocean, which is like being exiled to the Gobi Desert to an ambitious naval officer. He then retired in October of 1959. He'll be seventy-seven next December."

"Are you telling me Bass is still around?" asked Pitt.

"He's listed on the Navy's retirement rolls."

"How about an address?"

"Bass owns and operates a country inn just south of Lexington, Virginia, called Anchorage House. You know the kind—no pets or kids allowed. Fifteen rooms complete with antique plumbing and four-poster beds, all slept in by George Washington."

"Paul, I owe you one."

"Care to let me in on it?"

"Too early."

"You sure it's not some hanky-panky the Bureau should know about?"

"It's not in your jurisdiction."

"That figures."

"Thanks again."

"Okay, buddy. Write when you find work."

Pitt hung up the receiver and took a slow breath and grinned. Another veil of the enigma had been pulled aside. He decided not to contact Abe Steiger, not just yet. He looked up at Folsom.

"Can you cover for me over the weekend?"

Folsom grinned back. "Far be it from me to insinuate the boss isn't essential to the operation, but what the hell, I think we can muddle through the next forty-eight hours without your exalted presence. What you got cooking?"

"A thirty-four-year-old mystery," said Pitt. "I'm going to dig out the answers while relaxing in the peace and quiet of a quaint country inn."

Folsom peered at him for several seconds, and then, seeing nothing behind Pitt's green eyes, gave up and turned back to the blackboard.

31

On the morning flight into Richmond, Pitt looked like any one of a dozen other passengers who seemed to be dozing. His eyes were closed, but his mind was churning over the enigma of the plane in the lake. It was unlike the Air Force to sweep an accident under the rug, he thought. Under normal circumstances, a full-scale investigation would have been launched to determine why the crew had strayed so far off the charted course. Logical answers eluded him, and he opened his eyes when the Eastern Airlines jet touched down and began taxiing up to the terminal.

Pitt rented a car and drove through the Virginia countryside. The lovely, rolling landscape imparted mingled aromas of pine and fall rains. Just past noon he turned off Interstate Eighty-one and drove into Lexington. Not pausing to enjoy the quaint architecture of the town, he angled south on a narrow state highway. He soon came to a sign picturesquely out of place with the rural surroundings, designed with a nautical anchor welcoming guests and pointing up a gravel road toward the inn.

There was no one behind the desk and Pitt was reluctant to break the silence in the neat and meticulously dusted lobby. He was about to say the hell with it and hit the bell when a tall woman, almost as tall as he in her riding boots, entered carrying a high-backed chair. She looked to be in her early thirties and wore jeans and a matching denim blouse with a red bandana tied over her ash-blond hair. Her skin displayed almost no evidence of a summer tan but had the smoothness of a fashion model's. Something about her unruffled expression at abruptly noticing a stranger suggested to him a woman who was high bred, the kind who is taught to act reserved under any circumstances short of fire and earthquake.

"I'm sorry," she said, setting the chair down beside a

beautifully proportioned candle stand. "I didn't hear you drive up."

"That's an interesting chair," he said. "Shaker, isn't it?"

She looked at him approvingly. "Yes, made by Elder Henry Blinn, of Canterbury."

"You have many valuable pieces here."

"Admiral Bass, the owner, gets the credit for what you see." She moved behind the desk. "He's quite an authority on antique collecting, you know."

"I wasn't aware of that."

"Do you wish a room?"

"Yes, for tonight only."

"A pity you can't stay longer. A local stock theater opens in our barn the evening after next."

"I've a knack for poor timing," Pitt said, smiling.

Her return smile was thin and formal. She spun the register around for him and he signed it.

"Room fourteen. Up the stairs and three doors to your left, Mr. Pitt." She had read his name upside down as he signed it. "I'm Heidi Milligan. If you need anything, just push the buzzer by your door. I'll get the message sooner or later. I hope you won't mind carrying your own luggage up."

"I'll manage. Is the admiral handy? I'd like to talk to him about . . . about antiques."

She pointed through a double screen door at the end of the lobby. "You'll find him down by the duck pond, clearing away lily pads."

Pitt nodded and headed in the direction Heidi Milligan had indicated. The door opened onto a footpath that meandered down a gently sloping hill. Admiral Bass had wisely chosen not to landscape Anchorage House. The surrounding grounds had been left to nature and were covered with pines and late-blooming wildflowers. For a moment Pitt forgot his mission and soaked up the scenic quiet that hemmed in the trail to the pond.

He found an elderly man, in hip boots and brandishing a pitchfork, aggressively attacking a circular growth of water lilies about eight feet from shore. The admiral was a big man and he threw the tangled root stocks onto the bank with the ease of someone thirty years younger. He wore no hat under the Virginia sun and the sweat rolled free from his bald head and trickled off the ends of his nose and chin.

"Admiral Walter Bass?" Pitt said, hailing him.

The pitchfork stopped in mid-throw. "Yes, I'm Walter Bass."

"Sir, my name is Dirk Pitt, and I wonder if I might have a word with you?"

"Sure, go right ahead," said Bass, finishing the toss. "Pardon me if I keep after these damned weeds, but I want to clear out as much as I can before dinner. If I didn't do this at least twice a week before winter, they'd choke off the whole pond come spring."

Pitt stepped back as a flying wad of tuberous stems and heart-shaped leaves splattered at his feet. To him, at least, it was an awkward situation, and he wasn't sure how to handle it. The admiral's back was to him, and Pitt hesitated. He took a deep breath and plunged. "I'd like to ask you several questions concerning an aircraft with the code designation Vixen 03."

Bass kept at his labor without a pause, but the whitened knuckles around the handle of the pitchfork did not go unnoticed by Pitt.

"Vixen 03," he said, and shrugged. "Doesn't ring a bell. Should it?"

"It was a Military Air Transport Service plane that vanished back in 1954."

"That was a long time ago." Bass stared vacantly at the water. "No, I can't recall any connection with a MATS aircraft," he said finally. "Not surprising, though. I was a surface officer throughout my thirty years in the Navy. Heavy ordnance was my specialty."

"Do you recall ever meeting a major in the Air Force by the name of Vylander?"

"Vylander?" Bass shook his head. "Can't say as I have." Then he looked at Pitt speculatively. "What was your name again? Why are you asking me these questions?"

"My name is Dirk Pitt," he said again. "I'm with the National Underwater and Marine Agency. I found some old papers that stated you were the officer who authorized Vixen 03's flight orders."

"There must be a mistake."

"Perhaps," said Pitt. "Maybe the mystery will be cleared up when the wreck of the aircraft is raised and thoroughly inspected."

"I thought you said it vanished."

"I discovered the wreckage," Pitt answered.

Pitt studied Bass closely for any discernible reaction. There was none. He decided to leave the admiral alone to collect his thoughts.

"I'm sorry to have troubled you, Admiral. I must have gotten my signals mixed."

Pitt turned and began walking up the path back to the inn. He'd covered nearly fifty feet when Bass yelled after him.

"Mr. Pitt!"

Pitt turned. "Yes?"

"Are you staying at the inn?"

"Until tomorrow morning. Then I must be on my way."

The admiral nodded. When Pitt reached the pines bordering Anchorage House, he took another look toward the pond. Admiral Bass was calmly forking the lily pads onto the bank, as if their brief conversation had simply been about crops and the weather.

32

Pitt enjoyed a leisurely dinner with the other guests at the inn. The dining room had been designed in the style of an eighteenth-century country tavern, with old flintlock rifles, pewter drinking cups, and weathered farm implements hanging on the walls and rafters.

The food was about as homemade as any Pitt had ever tasted. He ate two helpings each of the fried chicken, brandied carrots, baked corn, and sweet potatoes, and barely had room for the three-inch-thick wedge of apple pie.

Heidi moved about the tables, serving coffee and making small talk with the guests. Pitt noted that most were of social-security age. Younger couples, he mused, probably found the peaceful serenity of a country inn boring. He finished an Irish coffee and stepped out onto the porch. A full moon rose in the east and turned the pines to silver. He eased into a vacant bentwood rocker and propped his feet on the porch railing and waited for Admiral Bass to make the next move.

The moon had arched overhead nearly twenty degrees when Heidi came out and wandered slowly in his direction. She stood in back of him for a moment and then said, "There is no moon so bright as a Virginia moon."

"You won't get an argument from me," said Pitt.

"Did you enjoy your dinner?"

"I'm afraid my eyes were bigger than my stomach. I gorged myself. My compliments to your chef. His down-home cooking style is poetry to the palate."

Heidi's smile went from friendly to beautiful in the glow of the moon. "*She'll* be happy to hear it."

Pitt made a helpless gesture. "A lifetime of chauvinistic tendencies is hard to suppress."

She settled her tightly packed bottom on the railing and faced him, her expression suddenly turning serious. "Tell me, Mr. Pitt, why did you come to Anchorage House?"

Pitt stopped rocking and stared squarely into her eyes. "Is this a survey to check the effectiveness of your advertising or are you just plain inquisitive?"

"I'm sorry, I didn't mean to pry, but Walter seemed very upset when he returned from the pond this evening. I thought that maybe—"

"You think it was because of something I said," Pitt said, finishing for her.

"I don't know."

"Are you related to the admiral?"

It was the magic question, for she began talking about herself. She was a lieutenant commander in the Navy; she was assigned to the Norfolk Navy Yard; she had enlisted out of Wellesley College and had eleven years to go to retirement; her ex-husband had been a colonel in the Marines and had ordered her about like a recruit; she'd had a hysterectomy, so no children; no, she was not related to the admiral; she had met him when he was a guest lecturer at a Naval College seminar, and she came down to Anchorage House whenever she could sneak off from her duties; she made no bones about the fact that she and Bass had a May-December affair going. Just when it was getting interesting, she stopped and peered at her watch.

"I'd better run along and see to the other guests." She smiled, and again that transformation. "If you get tired of just sitting, I suggest you take a stroll to the top of the rise beside the inn. You'll find a lovely view of the lights of Lexington."

Her tone, it seemed to Pitt, was more one of command than of suggestion.

Heidi had been only half right. The view from the rise was not only lovely: it was breathtaking. The moon illuminated the entire valley and the streetlights of the town twinkled like a distant galaxy. Pitt had been standing there only a minute when he became aware of a presence behind him.

"Admiral Bass?" he inquired casually.

"Please raise your hands and do not turn around," Bass ordered brusquely.

Pitt did as he was told.

Bass did not make a full body search but instead slipped out Pitt's wallet and beamed a flashlight on its contents.

After a few moments he clicked off the light and returned the wallet to Pitt's pocket.

"You may lower your hands, Mr. Pitt, and turn around if you wish."

"Any reason for the melodramatics?" Pitt tilted his head at the revolver poised in Bass's left hand.

"It seems you've exhumed an excessive amount of information about a subject that belongs buried. I had to be certain of your identity."

"Then you're satisfied that I'm who I say I am?"

"Yes, I called your boss at NUMA. Jim Sandecker served under my command in the Pacific during World War Two. He gave me an impressive list of your credentials. He also wanted to know what you were doing in Virginia when you were supposed to be on a salvage tender off the coast of Georgia."

"I've not made Admiral Sandecker privy to my findings."

"Which, as you claimed earlier, at the pond, were the remains of Vixen 03."

"She exists, Admiral. I've touched her."

Bass's eyes flashed with hostility. "You're not only bluffing, Mr. Pitt, but you're also lying. I demand to know why."

"My case is not built on lies," said Pitt evenly. "I have two other reputable witnesses and videotaped pictures as proof."

A look of incomprehension shadowed Bass's face. "Impossible! She disappeared over the ocean. We spent months searching for her and didn't find a trace."

"You looked in the wrong place, Admiral. Vixen 03 lies under a mountain lake in Colorado."

Bass's tough facade seemed to dissolve, and in the moonlight Pitt suddenly saw him as a tired, worn old man. The admiral lowered the pistol and swayed drunkenly toward a bench at the edge of the overlook. Pitt reached out a hand to steady him.

Bass nodded thanks and sank onto the bench. "I suppose it had to happen someday. I wasn't fool enough to think the secret could last forever." He looked up and clutched Pitt's arm. "The cargo. What of the cargo?"

"The canisters have broken their moorings, but otherwise they seemed reasonably intact."

"Thank God for that, at least," sighed Bass. "Colorado, you say. The Rocky Mountains. So Major Vylander and his crew never made it out of the state."

"The flight originated in Colorado?" asked Pitt.

"Buckley Field was Vixen 03's point of origin." He held his head in his hands. "What went wrong so early? They must have gone down shortly after takeoff."

"It looks as though they had mechanical problems and tried to ditch in the only open space they could find. It being winter, the lake was frozen over, and they were fooled into thinking they were coming down in a field. The weight of the aircraft then broke through the ice and sank in a deep section of the lake, deep enough so that after the ice melted in the spring, her outline could not be distinguished from the air."

"And all this time we thought . . ." Bass's voice trailed off and he sat there in silence. Finally he said softly, "Those canisters must be retrieved."

"Do they contain nuclear material?" Pitt asked.

"Nuclear material . . ." Bass repeated, his tone vague. "Is that what you think?"

"The date stated in Vixen 03's flight plan could have put her in the South Pacific in time for the Bikini H-bomb tests. I also found a metal tag on one of the crewmen, marked with the symbol for radioactivity."

"You misread the evidence, Mr. Pitt. True, the canisters were originally designed to house nuclear naval shells. But the night Vylander and his crew disappeared they were used for a far different purpose."

"It's been suggested they're empty."

Bass sat like a wax statue. "If only it were that simple," he murmured. "Unfortunately, there are other instruments of war besides the nuclear kind. You might say that Vixen 03 and her crew were carriers."

"Carriers?"

"A plague," said Bass. "The canisters contain the Doomsday organism."

33

An uneasy silence settled over the two men as Pitt digested the enormity of the admiral's revelation.

"I see by your expression you are shocked," said Bass.

"'Doomsday organism,'" Pitt repeated quietly. "It has a terrifying ring of finality about it."

"An apt description, I assure you," said Bass. "Technically speaking, it possessed an impressive-sounding biochemical name that was thirty letters long and quite unpronounceable. The military designation, though, was short and sweet. We simply called it 'QD,' short for 'quick death.'"

"You refer to this 'QD' in the past tense."

The admiral made a helpless gesture. "Force of habit. Until your discovery of Vixen 03, I thought none still existed."

"What exactly was it?"

"QD was the ultimate in sophisticated military weaponry. Thirty-five years ago a microbiologist by the name of Dr. John Vetterly chemically created an artificial form of life that in turn was capable of producing a disease strain that was and still is quite unknown. As simply as I can put it, a nondetectable, unidentifiable bacteriological agent able to incapacitate a living human or animal within seconds of exposure and disrupt the vital body functions, causing death three to five minutes later."

"Won't nerve gas accomplish the same thing?"

"Under ideal conditions, yes. But meteorological disturbances such as wind or storm or extreme temperatures can dilute the lethal dosage of a nerve or toxic agent when it's released over a wide area. An outbreak of QD, on the other hand, can ignore the weather and produce a localized plague that is extremely tenacious."

"But this is the twentieth century. Surely epidemics can be controlled?"

"If the microorganisms can be detected and identified,

then it's possible. Decontamination procedures, inoculations with serums and antibiotics, will in most cases slow down or halt a raging epidemic. But nothing on this earth could stop QD once it grabbed a toehold on a city."

"Then how did QD come to be loaded in an aircraft in the middle of the United States?" Pitt demanded.

"Elementary. The Rocky Mountain Arsenal outside of Denver was the nation's primary manufacturer of chemical and biological weapons for over twenty years."

Pitt remained silent and let the old man go on.

Bass looked out at the panorama below, but his eyes were unfocused. "March of fifty-four," he said, as long-buried events began unfolding in his mind. "The H-bomb was set to burst over Bikini. I was placed in command of the QD tests because Dr. Vetterly was funded by the Navy and I was an expert on naval ordnance. I thought it logical at the time to conduct experiments cloaked under the excitement of the nuclear explosion. While the world was concentrating on the main event, we conducted our tests on Rongelo Island, four hundred miles to the north-east, totally unnoticed."

"Rongelo," Pitt said slowly. "The destination of Vixen 03."

Bass nodded. "A raw, bleached knob of coral poking through the sea in the middle of nowhere. Even the birds shy away from it." Bass paused to shift his position on the bench. "I scheduled two series of tests. The first was an aerosol device that scattered a small amount of QD over the atoll. The second included the battleship *Wisconsin*. She was to lie back twenty miles and lob a warhead with QD from her main batteries. That test never took place."

"Major Vylander failed to deliver the goods," Pitt surmised.

"The contents of the canisters," Bass acknowledged. "Naval shells armed with QD."

"You could have ordered up another supply."

"I could," Bass agreed. "But the real reason I halted the test series was because of what we learned after the aerosol drop. The results were godawful and filled all who shared in the secret with a feeling of horror."

"You talk as though the island was devastated."

"Visually, nothing had changed," said Bass, his voice barely audible. "The white sand of the beach, the few palms, all was as it had been. The test animals we had placed on the island were all dead, of course. I insisted on a waiting period of two weeks to give any residual effects a chance to dissipate before permitting the scientists to examine the results first-hand. Dr. Vetterly and three of his assistants landed on the beach wearing full protective clothing and breathing apparatus. Seventeen minutes later, all were dead."

Pitt fought to preserve his balance. "How was it possible?"

"Dr. Vetterly had vastly underestimated his discovery. The potency of other lethal agents wears off after a time. Conversely, QD gains in strength. By what method it penetrated the scientists' protective gear we were never able to determine."

"Did you retrieve the bodies?"

"They still lie there," said Bass with sadness in his eyes. "You see, Mr. Pitt, the terrible power of QD is only half its malignity. QD's most frightening quality is its refusal to die. We later found that its bacillus forms superresistant spores, which are able to penetrate the ground—in Rongelo Island's case, the coral—and live out an astonishing lifespan."

"I find it incredible that after thirty-four years no one can safely go in and carry out Vetterly's remains."

There was a sickness in Bass's voice. "There is no way of pinpointing the exact date," he murmured, "but our best estimate indicated that man won't be able to step foot on Rongelo Island for another three hundred years."

34

Fawkes leaned over the ship's chart table, studying a set of blueprints, his hand making notations with a pencil. Two large men, well muscled, the faces beneath their hard hats tanned and thoughtful, stood on either side of him. "I want her gutted, every compartment, every scrap of unnecessary tubing and electrical conduits, even her bulkheads."

The man on Fawkes's left snorted derisively. "You've lost your gourd, Captain. Tear out the bulkheads and she'll break up in any sea rougher than a millpond."

"Dugan is right," said the other man. "You can't gut a vessel this size without losing her structural resistance to stress."

"Your objections are duly noted, gentlemen," Fawkes replied. "But in order for her to ride high, her draft must be cut by forty percent."

"I've never heard of gutting a sound ship just to raise her waterline," said Dugan. "What's the purpose of it all?"

"You can scrap the armor as well as the auxiliary machinery," Fawkes said, ignoring Dugan's question. "While you're about it, you can see to the removal of the turret masts."

"Come off it, Captain," snapped Lou Metz, the shipyard superintendent. "You're asking us to ruin what was once a damned fine ship."

"Aye, she was a fine ship," agreed Fawkes. "In my mind she still is. But time has passed her by. Your government sold her for scrap and the African Army of Revolution bought her for a very special undertaking."

"That's something else that rubs us wrong," said Dugan. "Busting our ass so's some bunch of nigger radicals can kill white people."

Fawkes laid down the pencil and fixed Dugan with a rigid stare. "I don't think you people quite realize the economics of the situation," he said. "What the AAR does

with the ship once it leaves your shipyard needn't concern
your racial philosophies. What counts is that they pay my
wages the same as they pay yours and those of your men,
who, if my memory serves me, number one hundred and
seventy. However, if you insist, I'll be happy to convey
your sentiments to the officials in charge of the AAR
treasury. I feel certain they can find another shipyard
that will prove more cooperative. And that would be a
pity, particularly since their contract is the only one on
your books at present. Without it, all one hundred and
seventy men on your crew would have to be laid off. I do
not think their families will take it kindly when they find
out your petty objections put their menfolk out of work."

Dugan and Metz exchanged angry, defeated looks.
Metz avoided Fawkes's eyes and gazed down sullenly at
the blueprints. "Okay, Captain, you're calling the shots."

There was a confidence born of long years of commanding men reflected in Fawkes's tight smile. "Thank you,
gentlemen. Now that we've cleared the air of any mis-
understandings, shall we continue?"

An hour later the two shipyard men left the bridge and
made their way down to the main deck of the ship. "I
can't believe I heard right," Metz mumbled numbly. "Did
that lead-brained Scotsman actually order us to remove
half the superstructure, the funnels, and the fore and aft
gun turrets and replace them all with plywood sheeting
painted gray?"

"That's what the man said," Dugan replied. "I guess
he figures by dumping all that weight he can lighten the
ship by fifteen thousand tons."

"But why replace everything with dummy structures?"

"Beats me. Maybe he and his black buddies expect to
bluff the South African Navy to death."

"And that's another thing," said Metz. "If you bought
a ship like this to use in foreign war, wouldn't you try and
keep the deal under wraps? My guess is that they're going
to blast Cape Town all to hell."

"With dummy guns, no less," grunted Dugan.

"I'd like to tell that overgrown bastard to take his contract and stuff it up his ass," Metz rasped.

"You can't deny he's got us by the balls." Dugan turned
and stared up at the shadowy figure behind the bridge
windows. "Do you think he's ripe for a straitjacket?"

"Nuts?"

"Yeah."

"Crazy like a coyote, maybe. He knows what he's doing, and that's what bugs the shit out of me."

"What do you suppose the AAR really has in mind once they get the ship to Africa?"

"I'll make book she never sees port," said Metz. "By the time we're through ripping her bowels out, she'll be so unstable she'll go belly up before she leaves Chesapeake Bay."

Dugan eased his buttocks onto a massive capstan. He looked down the length of the ship. Her great mass of steel seemed cold and malevolent; it was as though she were holding her breath, waiting for some silent command to unleash her awesome power.

"This whole act stinks," Dugan said finally. "I only hope to God we're not doing anything we'll regret."

Fawkes examined the markings on a well-creased set of navigation charts. First he computed the known velocity and fluctuations of the current, then the range of tidal conditions. Satisfied with the figures, he next traced a mile-by-mile course to his destination, memorizing every buoy, every beacon and channel marker, until he could picture them all in his mind's eye without confusion as to their exact sequence.

The task before him seemed impossible. Even with precise analysis of every obstacle and its successful conquest, there were still too many variables that had to be left to chance. There was no way he could predict the weather on a given day still weeks away. The odds of colliding with another ship also reared their numerical heads. These unknowns he did not take lightly, and yet the possibility that he might be found out and stopped was refused entrance into his mind. He had even steeled himself to ignore any second thoughts from De Vaal, who might order the mission to be scrapped.

At ten minutes to midnight Fawkes removed his glasses and rubbed his tired eyes. He took a small photo holder from his breast pocket and looked into the long-ago faces of his family. Then he sighed and propped the holder on a small packing crate set beside the cot he maintained in the control room of the ship. The first week he had slept in the captain's quarters, but the comfortable accommoda-

tions were gone now; furnishings, facilities, even the bulkheads that once enclosed the cabin, had been torched
away.

Fawkes undressed and slid his huge frame inside a
sleeping bag, taking a final look at the photo. Then he
clicked off the drop-cord light and became smothered in
the darkness of his loneliness and unrelenting hatred.

35

De Vaal rolled a cigarette between his slender fingers. "Will Fawkes meet his schedule, do you think?"

"One of my operatives reports that he is driving the shipyard workers like a sadist," replied Zeegler. "I cannot help but think the good captain will launch Wild Rose at the required time."

"What of his black crew?"

"They are under tight security on a cargo freighter moored off a remote island in the Azores." Zeegler sat down across from De Vaal before continuing. "When all is in readiness, the crew will be smuggled on board Fawkes's ship."

"Will they be familiar with the operation of the vessel?"

"Training is being conducted with mock-ups on the freighter. Each man will know his job when Fawkes casts off the mooring lines."

"What have the men been told?"

"They think they have been recruited to pick up the ship for sea trials and gunnery practice before sailing it to Cape Town."

De Vaal sat in concentration for a moment. "A pity we can't have Lusana as a passenger."

"The possibility exists," said Zeegler.

De Vaal looked up. "Are you serious?"

"My sources say he has left for the United States," Zeegler replied. "Trailing him through Africa and knowing his exact traveling schedule in advance is next to impossible. He can slip out of the continent virtually undetected at will. But he cannot slip in without showing himself. When he leaves the States, I will be waiting."

"Abduction." De Vaal said the word slowly, savoring each syllable. "The very bonus that would make Operation Wild Rose virtually foolproof."

36

The BEZA-Mozambique overseas airliner pivoted off the main runway onto a seldom-used taxi strip and dipped its nose as the pilot applied the brakes. The boarding hatch swung open and a baggage handler wearing white coveralls and a red baseball cap stepped from the evening darkness and attached an aluminum ladder to the fuselage. A figure stooped in the light streaming from the interior of the plane, dropped a large suitcase to the man on the ground, and climbed down after it. Then the hatch closed and the ladder was removed. The engines picked up their whine and the plane rolled off in the direction of the Dulles Airport international terminal.

No conversation was exchanged as the baggage handler passed the stranger a spare set of coveralls, which were quickly donned. They climbed aboard a small tractor that had four empty carrier carts attached to its rear hitch and steered a course to the maintenance section of the field. After a few minutes of dodging parked aircraft, the tractor pulled up to a floodlit gate. A guard leaned out at their approach and, upon recognizing the driver, stifled a yawn and waved them through. The baggage handler waved back and drove to the employees' parking lot, stopping beside a door held open by the chauffeur of a large dark-blue limousine. Still without a word, the man from the airplane stepped into the backseat of the car. The chauffeur took the suitcase, lifted it into the trunk, and the baggage handler drove his empty caravan back toward the cargo terminal.

It wasn't until the car entered the outskirts of Georgetown that Lusana relaxed and slipped out of the coveralls. In past years he would have entered the States like any other traveler coming from overseas. But those were the days before the South African Defence Ministry took him seriously. Lusana's fears of assassination were well founded. With a sense of relief he watched the chauffeur stop in front of a house whose downstairs windows were lit. At least someone was home.

The chauffeur carried his suitcase to the doorstep and silently departed. A faint murmur from the TV set came through the open windows. He pressed the bell.

The porch light came on, the door opened a crack, and a familiar voice said, "Who is it?"

He moved under the light so that it illuminated his face. "It's me, Felicia."

"Hiram?" Her voice was stunned.

"Yes."

The door opened slowly. She was dressed in a sheer and sexy chiffon peasant blouse and a long soft jersey skirt. A knotted bandana covered her hair. She stood motionless, her eyes searching his. She wanted to say something appropriately clever but her mind went blank. All she managed was, "Come in."

He stepped inside and set the suitcase down. "I thought you might be here," he said.

Her dark eyes quickly shifted from surprise to calm composure. "Your timing is right on the money. I just got back from Hollywood. I've cut a new album and auditioned for a part in a TV series."

"I'm happy all goes well for you."

She looked up into his face. "You never should have sent me away with Frederick."

"If it will make you feel any better, I've often regretted my hasty decision."

"I could go back with you to Africa."

He shook his head sadly. "Someday, maybe. Not now. You can do more for our cause here."

They turned in unison as Frederick Daggat, casually attired in a paisley-print bathrobe, appeared from the living room. "My God, General Lusana. I thought I recognized your voice." He looked down at the suitcase and his face clouded. "There was no advance word of your arrival. Has there been trouble?"

Lusana grinned wryly. "The world is not safe for revolutionaries. I thought it expedient to return to the Land of the Free as inconspicuously as possible."

"But surely the airlines . . . customs . . . someone must have announced your presence."

Lusana shook his head. "I sat in the pilot's cabin on the flight from Africa. Arrangements were made for me to leave the plane after landing and bypass the Dulles terminal."

"We have laws that frown on illegal entry."

"I am a citizen. What difference does it make?"

Daggat's expression softened. He placed his hands on Lusana's shoulders. "If there is any fuss, my staff will take care of it. You're here, and that's all that counts."

"But why all the subterfuge?" asked Felicia.

"For good reason." Lusana's voice was very cold. "My intelligence people have uncovered a sensitive piece of information that can prove highly embarrassing to the South African minority government."

"That's a serious charge," said Daggat.

"It's a serious threat," retorted Lusana.

Daggat's eyes registered a mixture of confusion and curiosity. He nodded toward the living room. "Come in and sit down, General. We have much to talk over."

"Every time I see you it's like looking at an old photograph. You never change."

Felicia returned Loren's admiring look. "Flattery from another woman is flattery indeed." She idly stirred the ice in her drink. "It's amazing how time evaporates. How long has it been—three, maybe four years?"

"The last inaugural ball."

"I remember," Felicia said, smiling. "We went to that little dive down by the river afterward and got smashed. You were with a tall, sad-looking dude with spaniel eyes."

"Congressman Louis Carnady. He was defeated in the next election."

"Poor Louis." Felicia lit a cigarette. "My date was Hiram Lusana."

"I know."

"We parted company only last month in Africa," Felicia said as if Loren had not spoken. "I wonder if my life has been one big downer, chasing after every liberal cause that pops on stage, taking up with any stud who promises to save the human race."

Loren motioned to the waiter to bring them two more drinks. "You can't blame yourself for believing in people."

"I haven't got a hell of a lot to show for it. Every crusade I've ever joined, I screwed up."

"I don't mean to pry, but did you and Lusana have personal differences, or was it political?"

"Strictly personal," Felicia said. She felt her chest tighten as Loren circled the bait. "I no longer mattered to him. His only love was his fight. I think at first, deep inside him, there was a feeling for me, but as the struggle expanded and his pressures grew, he became distant. I know now that he had taken all he ever wanted from me. It was as though I was as expendable as one of his soldiers on the battlefield."

Loren saw the tears start to come to Felicia's eyes. "How you must hate him."

Felicia looked up, surprised. "Hate Hiram? Oh no, you don't understand. I was unfair with him. I let my own desires stand between us. I should have been patient. Perhaps when his war to give majority rule to blacks in South Africa is won, he will look upon me differently."

"I wouldn't hold my breath if I were you. I know his history. Lusana uses people like the rest of us use toothpaste. He squeezes every dab and throws away the empties."

An angered frown crossed Felicia's face. "You only see in Hiram what you want to see. The good outweighs the bad."

Loren sighed and leaned back as the waiter brought their second round. "It's wrong for old friends to argue after being so long apart," she said softly. "Let's change the subject."

"I agree," Felicia said, her mood changing. "What about you, Loren? Are there any men in your life?"

"Two, at the moment."

Felicia laughed. "It's common Washington gossip: one is Phil Sawyer, the President's press secretary. Who's the other?"

"He's a director at NUMA. His name is Dirk Pitt."

"You serious about either one of them?"

"Phil is the sort you marry: loyal, true blue, sets you on a gilded pedestal and wants you to be the mother of his children."

Felicia made a face. "He sounds perfectly mundane. What about this Pitt?"

"Dirk? Sheer animal power. He makes no demands; he comes and goes like an alley cat. Dirk can never be truly owned by a woman, and yet he's always there when you need him. The lover who turns you on but won't stand still long enough for you to grow old with."

"He sounds more my type. Send him my way when the affair crashes." Felicia sipped at her drink. "It must be tricky, maintaining your political purity in front of the voters while seeing a lover on the side."

Loren's cheeks turned crimson. "It is difficult," she admitted. "I never was very good at intrigue."

"You could say to hell with what people think. Most women do these days."

"Most women are not members of Congress."

"The old double standard again. Congressmen can get away with anything as long as it doesn't show up on their expense account."

"Sad, but true," said Loren. "And in my case, I represent a district that is heavily rural. The voters still believe in the Sears catalogue, Coors' beer, and the Eleven Commandments."

"What's the eleventh?"

"Thy Congresswoman shalt not screw around if she expects to win the next election."

"Where do you and Pitt meet?"

"I can't take the chance of a male's being seen leaving my apartment along with the milkman, so we meet at his place or drive to some little out-of-the-way country inn."

"You make it sound like a bus-stop romance."

"As I said, it's difficult."

"I think I can eliminate all the bullshit for you."

Loren looked at Felicia quizzically. "How?"

Felicia fished in her purse and came up with a key. She pressed it into Loren's hand. "Here, take this. The address is taped to the top."

"What is it for?"

"A pad I leased over in Arlington. It's yours anytime you get horny."

"But what about you? I can't expect you to get lost on a moment's notice."

"You won't be imposing," Felicia said, smiling. "I'm the houseguest of a dude across town. No more protests. Okay?"

Loren studied the key. "God, I feel like a hooker."

Felicia reached over and folded Loren's hand over the key. "If just thinking about it gives you a deliciously obscene feeling, wait until you take a shot of the upstairs bedroom."

37

"What do you make of it?" asked Daggat. He was seated at his desk. Hiram Lusana stood across the room and leaned over a high-backed chair, his expression anxious.

Dale Jarvis, director of the National Security Agency, pondered a few moments before answering. He looked up with a friendly, almost fatherly face. His brown hair was streaked with gray and he wore it in a crew cut. He was dressed in a tweed suit and a large red bow tie beneath his Adam's apple drooped as though it were melting.

"My guess is that this Operation Wild Rose is a game."

"A game!" Lusana rasped. "That's crap!"

"Not really," Jarvis said calmly. "Every nation with a sophisticated military establishment has a department whose function is solely to dream up what is generally referred to in the trade as 'feasibility games.' Improbable schemes, *ultra crepidam,* beyond the depth or grasp of likelihood. Strategic and tactical studies invented to combat unforeseen events. Then shelved against the unlikely day they are dusted off and put into action."

"And that's your opinion of Wild Rose?" Lusana asked with a certain acidity.

"Without knowing all the details, yes," answered Jarvis. "I daresay the South African Defence Ministry has contingency plans for phony insurgent raids on half the nations of the globe."

"Do you really believe that?"

"I do," Jarvis said firmly. "Don't quote me, but nestled in some deep, dark crevasse of our own government you'll find some of the wildest scripts ever devised by man and computer; conspiracies to undermine every nation on the globe, including our Western friendlies; measures to plant nuclear bombs in the ghettos in case of mass uprisings by minorities; battle plots to counter invasions from Mexico and Canada. Not one in ten thousand will ever be utilized, but they're there, waiting, just in case."

"Insurance," said Daggat.

Jarvis nodded. "Insurance against the unthinkable."

"You mean that's all there is to it?" Lusana exploded angrily. "You're just going to write off Operation Wild Rose as an idiot's nightmare?"

"I'm afraid you've taken this thing far too seriously, General." Jarvis sat unmoved by Lusana's outburst. "You've got to face reality. As my grandfather was fond of saying, you've bought yourself a pig in a poke."

"I refuse to accept that," Lusana said stubbornly.

Jarvis casually removed his glasses and inserted them in their case. "You are, of course, free to ask for neutral opinions from other intelligence organizations, General, but I think I can safely say that Wild Rose will get pretty much the same reception wherever you present it."

"I demand you verify De Vaal's intent to set the operation in motion!" Lusana shouted.

Controlling his rising anger, Jarvis rose, buttoned his jacket, and faced Daggat. "Congressman, if you will excuse me, I must get back to my office."

"I understand," Daggat said. He came out from behind his desk and took Jarvis by the arm. "Let me show you to the elevator."

Jarvis nodded at Lusana, diplomatically forcing a friendly expression. "General?"

Lusana stood trembling, his hands clenched tightly, saying nothing. He turned and stared out a window.

As soon as they stepped into the elevator foyer, Daggat said to Jarvis, "I apologize for the general's erratic behavior. But you must understand the tremendous strain he has shouldered these past months. And then there was the long flight from Mozambique last night."

"Jet lag has been known to make men testy." Jarvis arched an eyebrow. "Or could it be he's suffering conscience pangs over his back-door entry."

Daggat moistened dry lips. "You know?"

Jarvis smiled amiably. "Routine. Don't worry, Congressman. Our job is to keep tabs on men like the general. The NSA is not in the business of prosecuting civil violations. What Immigration doesn't know in this case won't hurt them. A piece of advice, though. If I were you, I wouldn't let the general hang around Washington too long. Befriending a radical revolutionary might prove embarrassing to a man of your reputation."

"General Lusana is not a radical."

Jarvis shrugged, unimpressed. "That remains to be seen."

The red "down" light flashed above the elevator. Jarvis started to turn. "There is one more thing," said Daggat. "A favor."

The elevator bell rang and the doors parted. The interior was empty. "If I can," Jarvis said, his eyes shifting from Daggat to his only means of escape.

"Check out Operation Wild Rose. I'm not asking for a maximum effort from your people," Daggat hastened to add. "Only a few probes that may or may not confirm its validity."

The doors began to close. Jarvis held them open, one foot in, one foot still on the foyer floor. "I'll instigate an inquiry," he said. "But I warn you, Congressman, you may not like what we find."

Then the doors clunked shut and he was gone.

It was ten o'clock when Daggat came awake. He was in his office alone. His staff had long since left for home. He looked at his watch and figured he had dozed for nearly an hour. He rubbed his eyes and stretched as he vaguely heard the outer-office door open and close. He didn't bother to look up, thinking it was the cleaning crew. It was only after he failed to tune in the familiar sounds of wastebaskets being emptied and vacuum cleaners humming that he became aware of a strange presence.

Felicia Collins leaned languidly against the doorway, saying nothing, just staring at Daggat.

A thought triggered in the back of his mind and he rose and made an apologetic gesture. "I'm sorry, time slipped away from me. I completely forgot our dinner date."

"You're forgiven," she said.

He reached for his coat. "You must be starved."

"By the fourth martini, all hunger pangs disappeared." She peered around the office. "I figured you and Hiram were probably tied up in conference."

"I turned him over to the State Department this afternoon. They're giving him the usual lukewarm treatment reserved for fourth-class visiting dignitaries."

"Is it safe for him to be out in public?"

"I saw to it that he's provided with round-the-clock security."

"Then he's no longer our houseguest."

"No, he has a suite at the Mayflower, courtesy of the government."

Felicia stretched her opulent body and flowed into the room. "By the way, I met Loren Smith for lunch. She poured out her love life to me."

"She took the bait?"

"If you mean the key to your little hideaway in Arlington, the answer is yes."

He took her in his arms, his eyes gentle but smug with satisfaction. "You won't be sorry, Felicia. Only good can come from this."

"Try telling that to Loren Smith," she said, turning away.

He released her. "Did she mention any names?"

"I gather she's teasing Phil Sawyer into marriage while she's screwing some guy from NUMA on the side."

"Did she say who?"

"His name is Dirk Pitt."

Daggat's eyes widened. "You did say Dirk Pitt?"

Felicia nodded.

Daggat's mind raced to make a connection and then he had it. "Son of a bitch! It's perfect!"

"What are you talking about?"

"The revered senior senator from California, George Pitt. Didn't it occur to you? Congresswoman Holier-Than-Thou Smith is shacking with the senator's son."

Felicia shivered as her skin suddenly went cold. "For God's sake, Frederick, drop this stupid scheme of yours before it gets out of hand."

"I don't think so," Daggat said, smiling a sinister smile. "I do what I think best for the country."

"You mean you do what you think best for Frederick Daggat."

He took her by the arm and led her from the office. "When you have time to reconsider, you'll come to find that I was right." He turned off the lights. "Now then, let's grab some dinner, and afterward we'll prepare Loren Smith's love nest for her one and only visit."

38

Admiral James Sandecker was a short, feisty character with flaming red hair and plenty of gall. When his retirement from the Navy was forced upon him, he used his considerable congressional influence to connive his way into the job of chief director of the then-fledgling National Underwater and Marine Agency. It was a match that was ordained for success from the start. In seven short years Sandecker had taken an insignificant eighty-person agency and built it into a massive organization of five thousand scientists and employees supported by an annual budget that exceeded four hundred million dollars.

He was accused by his enemies of being a grandstander, of launching oceanic projects that garnered more publicity than scientific data. His supporters applauded his flair for making the field of oceanography as popular as space science. Whatever his assets or liabilities, Admiral Sandecker was as solidly entrenched at NUMA as J. Edgar Hoover had been at the FBI.

He drained the last swallow from a bottle of Seven-Up, sucked on the stub of a giant cigar, and looked into the unsmiling faces of Admiral Walter Bass, Colonel Abe Steiger, Al Giordino, and Dirk Pitt.

"The part I find hard to swallow," he continued, "is the total lack of interest on the part of the Pentagon. It would seem logical—to me, at any rate—that Colonel Steiger's report on the discovery of Vixen 03 complete with photos would have shocked the hell out of them. And yet the colonel has told us his superiors acted as though the whole episode was best dropped and forgotten."

"There is a bona fide reason behind their indifference," Bass answered impassively. "Generals O'Keefe and Burgdorf are ignorant of the link between Vixen 03 and the QD project because none is recorded."

"How can that be?"

"What was learned after the deaths of Dr. Vetterly and

his scientists motivated everyone who knew of QD's ghastly power to bury every scrap of evidence and erase all memories of its existence so that it could not be resurrected ever again."

"You mean you suppressed an entire defense project under the noses of the Joint Chiefs of Staff?" Sandecker said incredulously.

"By direct order from President Eisenhower I was to state in my reports to the Joint Chiefs that the experiment had backfired and the formulation of QD had died along with Dr. Vetterly."

"And they swallowed the story?"

"They had no reason not to," said Bass. "Besides the President, Secretary of Defense Wilson, and myself and a handful of scientists, no one else knew exactly what Vetterly had discovered. As far as the Joint Chiefs were concerned, the project was simply another low-budget experiment within the ugly realm of chemical-biological warfare. They suffered no qualms; nor did they ask embarrassing questions before writing it off as a failure."

"What was the purpose of circumventing the armed-forces power structure?"

"Eisenhower was an old soldier who abhorred mass-kill weapons." Bass seemed to shrivel in his chair while he collected his thoughts. "I am the last surviving member of the Quick Death Team," he continued slowly. "Unhappily, the secret will not die with me, as I had once hoped, because Mr. Pitt, here, accidentally discovered a long-lost source of the disease strain. I did not bare the facts then —nor will I now—to the men who run the Pentagon, for fear that they would consider recovering Vixen 03's cargo and storing it, in the name of national defense, against the day it might be unleashed against a future enemy."

"But surely if it came down to protecting our country . . ." Sandecker protested.

Bass shook his head. "I don't think you understand the true horror of the Quick Death organism, Admiral. Nothing known can impede its deadly effects. Allow me to cite an illustration: if five ounces of QD were delivered over Manhattan Island, the organism would seek out and kill ninety-eight percent of the population within four hours. And no one, gentlemen, no human, could set foot on the island for over three centuries. Future generations could only stand on the New Jersey shore and watch the once-mighty buildings erode and crumble over the bones of their former inhabitants."

The other men around the table paled; their blood ran cold. For a while no one spoke. They sat frozen, visualizing a city entombing three million corpses. It was Pitt who finally broke the uneasy silence.

"The people in Brooklyn and the Bronx—they would not be affected?"

"QD organisms spread in colonies. Strangely, they do not travel by human contact or by the wind. They tend to stay localized. Of course, if enough of the biological agent were delivered by aircraft or rockets, theoretically blanketing all of North America, the entire continent would become barren of all human life until the year 2300."

"Is there nothing that can kill QD?" asked Steiger.

"H-two-oh," answered Bass. "The organism can only exist in an atmosphere with a high gaseous-oxygen content. You might say it suffocates when immersed in water, just as we do."

"It strikes me as odd that Vetterly was the only one who knew how to produce it." This from Pitt.

Bass smiled thinly. "I would have never permitted one man to keep the critical data to himself."

"So you destroyed the doctor's records."

"I also falsified all orders and paperwork I could lay my hands on that related to the project, which included, by the way, the original flight plan of Vixen 03."

Steiger sat back and sighed with apparent relief. "At least that's one part of the puzzle that won't bug me any longer."

"But surely the project left tracks," Sandecker said speculatively.

"Skeletons still lie on Rongelo Island," said Pitt. "And what keeps unsuspecting fishermen or yachtsmen off its beaches?"

"I'll answer your question in reverse," said Bass. "First, all nautical charts of that area designate Rongelo Island as a dumping ground for hydrogen cyanide. The shores are also ringed with buoys warning of danger."

"Hydrogen cyanide," Giordino repeated. "Sounds like bad medicine."

"Truely. It is a blood agent that interferes with all respiration. In certain doses it causes almost immediate death. This is spelled out on the charts and in six languages on signs attached to the buoys." Bass paused and pulled out a handkerchief and patted the sweat that gleamed on his bald head. "Also, what few records that remain dealing with the QD project are lying deep in a Pentagon high-security vault that contains documents classified as FEO."

"FEO?"

"'Future eyes only,'" Bass explained. "Each file is sealed and marked with a date when it can be opened. Even the President lacks the power to examine a document's contents before the specified time. It has been referred to as the closet where our nation's skeletons are kept. The file on Amelia Earhart, UFOs, the truth behind the government's insistence on the swine-flu shots in the mid-seventies, political scandals that make the old Watergate stories seem like Boy Scout adventures. They're all there. The QD-project file, for example, cannot be opened until the year 2550. By then, President Eisenhower hoped, our descendants would fail to glean its true implications."

The other men in the NUMA conference room had never heard of the Future Eyes Only file, and they were astonished.

"I suppose the next obvious question," said Pitt, "is why, Admiral, are you taking us into your confidence?"

"I requested this meeting to clear the air on Vixen 03 because I find myself in the position of having to trust someone to recover the QD in the aircraft and destroy it."

"You're asking a great deal," Sandecker said. He relit another cigar and puffed it to life. "If the Pentagon gets wind of this, we could all be branded as traitors."

"A disagreeable possibility that cannot be overlooked," admitted Bass. "Our only comfort would be in knowing that public and moral opinion stand on our side."

"Somehow I've never quite been able to picture myself as a savior to mankind," Giordino mumbled.

Steiger looked steadily at Bass, perhaps seeing his Air Force career going up in smoke for the second time in as many weeks. "I get the feeling your choice of accomplices is backed by mad logic, Admiral. Myself, for instance—where do I fit in with the recovery of Vixen 03?"

Bass's tight smile loosened. "Believe it or not, Colonel, you're the critical man on the team. Your report alerted the Air Force to the existence of the aircraft. Fortunately, someone high in government found it inconvenient to pursue the matter further. Your job will be to see that any Pentagon interest remains negative."

There was understanding on Pitt's face now. "Okay, so Admiral Sandecker bankrolls the overall effort with NUMA resources while Giordino and I handle the actual salvage work. How do you intend to destroy QD's lethal properties once we raise the canisters?"

"We deep-six the warheads in the ocean," Bass replied without hesitation. "In time, as their exterior surface erodes, the water will neutralize the disease strain."

Pitt turned to Sandecker and found himself saying, "I can transfer Jack Folsom and his crew from the *Chenago* job and have them on site at Table Lake with all necessary equipment inside forty-eight hours."

Admiral Sandecker was a realist. His choice was clear. He had known Bass well enough not to write off the old man as an alarmist. Every head angled toward the fiery little director of NUMA. He seemed lost in the blue cigar smoke that curled to the ceiling. Then at last he nodded.

"All right, gentlemen, we go."

"Thank you, James," Bass said, obviously pleased. "I fully realize the gamble you're taking merely on the word of a rusty old sea dog."

"I'd say those were pretty good odds," Sandecker replied.

"A thought just occurred to me," Giordino cut in. "If water kills this QD stuff, why don't we simply leave it on the bottom of the lake?"

Bass shook his head solemnly. "No thank you. If you found it, so can someone else. It's far better we deposit it for eternity where no human will ever set eyes on it. I can only thank God the canisters have gone undiscovered all these years."

"Which brings up another matter," Pitt said, noting the sudden uneasy lowering of Giordino's and Steiger's eyes.

Sandecker flicked an ash into an abalone-shell tray. "What is that?"

"According to the original flight plan, Vixen 03 departed Buckley Field with a crew of four. Is that correct, Admiral Bass?"

Bass's expression went quizzical. "Yes, there were four."

"Perhaps I should have brought this up sooner," Pitt said, "but I was afraid of complicating the issue at hand."

"You're not the type to beat around the bush," Sandecker said impatiently. "What are you getting at?"

"The fifth skeleton."

"The fifth what?"

"When I dove on the wreckage, I found the bones of a fifth man tied to the floor of the cargo section."

Sandecker looked at Bass. "Have you any idea who he's talking about?"

Bass sat like a man who had been slapped in the face. "A ground maintenance man," he murmured vacantly. "One must have somehow been left on board when the plane took off."

"Won't wash," said Pitt. "Flesh was still evident. The remains haven't been immersed as long as the others."

"You said the canisters were still sealed," replied Bass, snatching at threads.

"Yes, sir, I saw no evidence of tampering," Pitt reassured him.

"My God, my God!" Bass held his hands to his face. "Someone besides ourselves knows about the aircraft."

"We can't be sure of that," said Steiger.

Bass lowered his hands and stared at Pitt through glazed eyes. "Bring her up, Mr. Pitt. For the sake of humanity, bring up Vixen 03 from the bottom of that lake—and do it quickly."

Pitt could not shake the feeling of dread as he left the meeting and passed through the main entrance of the NUMA building. The Washington night was heavy with humidity, the stickiness adding to his depression. He walked across the deserted parking lot and opened the door to his car. He was halfway behind the wheel before he noticed a small figure on the passenger seat.

Loren was asleep. She was cuddled in a ball and lost to the world. She wore a Grecian-style green dress and calf-skin boots under a long fur coat. Pitt leaned over and brushed the hair from her cheeks and gently shook her awake. Her eyes fluttered open and then locked on his. Her lips arched into a feline smile and her face looked strangely pale and young.

"Mmm. Fancy meeting you here."

He leaned over and kissed her. "Are you crazy? A luscious creature all alone in an empty Washington parking lot. It's a miracle you weren't assaulted and gang-banged."

She pushed him away and wrinkled her nose. "Ugh, you reek of stale cigars."

"Blame that on being cooped up with Admiral Sandecker for six hours." He settled back and started the car. "How did you track me down?"

"No great feat. I called your office to get your number in Savannah. Your secretary said you were already back in town, tied up in conference."

"Whatever possessed you to stake out my car?"

"I fought and lost an overwhelming urge to do something foolish and feminine." She kneaded the inside of his thigh. "Glad?"

"I cannot tell a lie," he said, grinning. "You come as a welcome relief after the last twenty-four hours."

"Welcome relief?" Loren faked a pout. "You really know how to charm a girl with flattery."

"We don't have much time," he said, turning serious. "I'm off again in the morning."

"I figured as much. That's why I've planned a nice surprise."

She snuggled closer and her hand worked its way up his thigh.

"I don't believe this," Pitt murmured in awe.

"Felicia hinted it was sexy, but I had no idea."

Pitt and Loren stood ankle deep in a crimson carpet, staring in fascination at a room whose four walls and ceilings were solidly paneled with gold-tinted mirrors. The only piece of furniture was a large circular bed raised on a platform and covered with red satin sheets. Illumination came from four spotlights embedded in the corners of the ceiling, emitting a soft blue light.

Loren stepped over to the raised bed and touched its gleaming pillows reverently, as though they were exquisite art objects. Pitt studied her reflection, multiplied into infinity, for several moments, and then he walked up behind her and deftly stripped off her clothes.

"Don't move," he said. "I want my eyes to devour a thousand naked Loren Smiths."

Her face flushed dark, her eyes riveted to the unending images of herself in the mirrors. "Lord," she whispered, "I feel as though I'm performing in front of a crowd." Then she tensed and said something blurred and murmurous as Pitt bent down and flicked his tongue in her navel.

The telephone's muted ring summoned Frederick Daggat from a sound sleep. Beside him Felicia moaned softly, rolled over, and continued sleeping. He groped for his wristwatch on the bedstand and focused his eyes on its luminous dial. It read four o'clock. He picked up the receiver.

"This is Daggat."

"Sam Jackson. I have the pictures."

"Any problems?"

"A breeze. You were right. I didn't have to shoot with infrared. They left the lights on. Can't say as I blame them—the room mirrored from top to bottom and all. High-speed film should bring out all the details you asked for. They put on quite a show. Too bad we didn't tape it."

"They didn't suspect?"

"How could they know one of the mirrored panels was two way? They were too busy to notice anything short of an earthquake. Just to play safe, I used a special noiseless camera."

"When can I expect to see the results?"

"By eight in the morning, if it's a dire emergency. I could use some sack time, though. Wait till early evening and I promise you eight-by-ten glossy prints fit for a gallery exhibit."

"Take your time and do it right," said Daggat. "I want every detail highlighted."

"You can count on it," Jackson said. "By the way, who's the foxy lady? She's a real tiger."

"That doesn't concern you, Jackson. Call me when you're ready. And remember, I'm only interested in the artistic positions."

"I get the message. Good night, Congressman."

39

Dale Jarvis was just getting ready to clear his desk and leave for the thirty-minute drive home to his wife and a traditional Friday supper of pork roast when there was a knock at the door and John Gossard, who headed up the agency's Africa Section, entered. Gossard had come to the NSA from the Army after the Vietnam war, where he had served as a specialist in guerrilla logistics. A quiet man with a cynical sense of humor, he walked with a limp caused by a rifle grenade whose shrapnel had severed his right foot. He was known as a heavy drinker, but also as a man who fulfilled all his section's requests for data in precise and abundant detail. His intelligence sources were the envy of the entire agency.

Jarvis spread his hands in an apologetic gesture. "John, chew my ass if you will; it completely slipped my mind. I had every intention of RSVPing your fishing-trip invitation."

"Can you make it?" Gossard asked. "McDermott and Sampson, over in Soviet Analysis, are going."

"I never turn down a chance to show those Kremlin guys how to catch the big ones."

"Good. The boat is reserved. We cast off from slip nine at the Plum Point Marina at five sharp, Sunday." Gossard set his briefcase on Jarvis's desk and opened it. "Incidentally, I had two motives for stopping by your sanctum sanctorum before heading home. The second is this." He dropped a folder in front of Jarvis. "I'll let you take it over the weekend, providing you promise not to shit-can it along with your old paperback spy novels."

Jarvis smiled. "Small chance of that. What've you got?"

"That data you asked for concerning a weird South African feasibility plan called Wild Rose."

Jarvis's brows raised. "That was fast work. I only put in the request this afternoon."

"The African Section does not allow the moss to grow," Gossard said, pontificating.

"Anything I need to know before reading it?"

"Nothing of any earth-shattering consequence. Pretty much as you suspected: a wild pipe dream."

"Then Hiram Lusana was telling the truth."

"Insofar as the plan actually exists," Gossard replied. "You'll especially enjoy the plot. The concept is intriguing as hell."

"You've piqued my curiosity. Just how do the South Africans posing as AAR blacks intend to carry out the raid?"

"Sorry," Gossard said, smiling devilishly. "That would be giving away the meat of the story."

Jarvis threw him a serious look. "Can you fully trust the quality of your source?"

"My source is genuine, all right. Strange sort of duck. Insists on going under the code name of Emma. We've never been able to establish an identity. His information is solid enough. He sells to anybody and everybody willing to pay."

"I gather you doled out a pretty penny for Operation Wild Rose," Jarvis said.

"Not really. It was included in a box with fifty other documents. We paid only ten thousand dollars for the lot."

As the photographs dropped from the dryer into a basket, Sam Jackson scooped them up and neatly jiggled their edges until they were straight and orderly. He was a tall, angular black man with braided hair, a youthful face, and long, slender hands. He passed Daggat the photos and pulled his apron off over his head.

"That's all she wrote."

"How many?" Daggat asked.

"About thirty that clearly show faces. I checked out the contact prints with a magnifying glass. All the rest were nothing shots."

"A shame they aren't in color."

"Next time, hang something besides those blue lights," said Jackson. "They might hype a sexy gig, but they sure ain't got what it takes to make sharp color transparencies."

Daggat carefully studied the eight-by-ten black-and-white-prints. He went through them a second time. The third time, he sifted out ten and put them inside a brief-case. The remaining twenty he handed to Jackson.

"Put these together with the negatives and contact prints in an envelope."

"You're taking them with you?"

"I think it best if I alone am responsible for their safe-keeping. Don't you agree?"

It was clear Jackson did not. He threw Daggat an un-easy look. "Hey, man, photographers aren't in the habit of giving up their negatives. You're not going to produce these for sale, are you? I don't mind shooting a private porno job for a good customer, but I'm not about to make a commer-cial living at it. Trouble with the fuzz I can do without."

Daggat closed upon Jackson until their faces were only inches apart. "I am not 'Hey, man,' " he said coldly. "I am United States Congressman Frederick Daggat. Do you get the message, brother?"

For a brief moment Jackson glared back. Then, slowly, he lowered his eyes and stared at the chemical stains on the linoleum floor. Daggat held all the cards, bankrolled by his congressional powers. The photographer had no choice but to fold.

"Suit yourself," he said.

Daggat nodded, and then, as if dismissing Jackson's ob-jections completely, casually smiled. "I'd appreciate it if you'd hurry things up. I have a lovely but anxious lady waiting in the car outside. She's the impatient type, if you know what I mean."

Jackson slid the negatives, contact prints, and eight-by-ten glossies into a large manila envelope and handed it to Daggat. "About my fee."

Daggat flipped him a hundred-dollar bill.

"But we agreed on five hundred," Jackson said.

"Consider your labors an unselfish act on behalf of your country," Daggat said as he walked to the door. Then he turned. "Oh, and one more thing: just so you won't be inconvenienced by unforeseen problems in the future, it might be a good idea to forget this whole episode. It never happened."

Jackson gave the only possible reply. "Whatever you say, Congressman."

Daggat nodded and left, closing the door quietly behind him.

"Turkey-shit son of a bitch!" Jackson hissed through clenched teeth as he removed another set of the photographs from a cabinet drawer.

"You're gonna get yours!"

Dale Jarvis's wife was used to his habit of reading in bed. She kissed him good-night, rolled into her customary fetal position, facing away from the beam of the lamp on his night table, and soon drifted asleep.

Settling himself in, Jarvis arranged two pillows behind his back, bent the high-intensity light to the proper angle, and pulled his Ben Franklin specs low on his nose. He propped the folder lent him by John Gossard on his raised knees and began reading. As he turned the pages, he jotted notes on a small pad. At two o'clock in the morning, he closed the folder on Operation Wild Rose.

He lay back and stared into nothingness for several minutes, considering whether to drop the folder back in Gossard's lap and forget about it or have the outlandish plan investigated. He decided to compromise.

Easing slowly out of bed so as not to disturb his wife, Jarvis padded to his den, where he picked up a telephone and expertly punched its touch system in the dark. His call was answered on the first ring.

"This is Jarvis. I want a rundown on the current status of all foreign and United States battleships. Yes, that's right—battleships. On my desk sometime tomorrow. Thank you. Good night."

Then he returned to bed, kissed his wife lightly on the cheek, and turned out the lamp.

40

The House Foreign Affairs subcommittee hearing on economic aid to African nations, chaired by Frederick Daggat, opened to a half-empty conference chamber and a platoon of bored reporters. Daggat was flanked by Democrat Earl Hunt, of Iowa, and Republican Roscoe Meyers, of Oregon. Loren Smith sat off by herself near one end of the table.

The hearing stretched into the afternoon as representatives of several African governments made their pitch for monetary aid. It was four o'clock when Hiram Lusana took his turn and sat down before the subcommittee. The chamber was crowded now. Photographers stood on seats, their flashbulbs stabbing the walls, while reporters began furiously scribbling on note pads or muttering into tape recorders. Lusana paid no attention to the commotion. He sat poised at the table, like a croupier who knew the odds were in his favor.

"General Lusana," said Daggat. "Welcome to our hearing. I think you know the procedures. This is purely a preliminary fact-finding session. You will be allowed twenty minutes to state your case, Afterward, the committee will put their inquiries to you. Our opinions and findings will later be reported to the House Foreign Affairs Committee as a whole."

"I understand," said Lusana.

"Mr. Chairman."

Daggat turned to Loren. "Yes, Congresswoman Smith."

"I must object to the appearance of General Lusana at this hearing on the grounds that he does not represent an established African government."

An undercurrent of murmurs swept the room.

"It is true," Lusana said, leveling his gaze at Loren, "I represent no established government. I do, however, represent the free soul of every black on the African continent."

"Eloquently put," said Loren. "But rules are rules."

"You cannot turn a deaf ear to the pleas of millions of my people over a technicality." Lusana sat immobile, his voice almost too soft for those in the back of the room to hear. "A man's most prized possession is his nationality. Without it he is nothing. In Africa we are in a fight to claim a nationality that rightfully belongs to us. I am here to beg for black dignity. I do not ask for money to buy arms. I do not ask for your soldiers to fight alongside ours. I plead only for the necessary funds to buy food and medical supplies for the thousands who have suffered in their war against inhumanity."

It was a masterful performance, but Loren was not suckered by it.

"You are a clever man, General. If I argue your appeal, I'd be condoning your presence at this hearing. My objection still stands."

Daggat made an imperceptible nod to one of his aides in the background and turned to Earl Hunt. "Congresswoman Smith's protest is duly noted. How say you, Congressman Hunt?"

While Daggat was polling Hunt and Roscoe Meyers for their opinions, his aide moved behind Loren and handed her a large white envelope.

"What is this?"

"I was told to tell you it is most urgent that you open the envelope now, ma'am." Then he hastily turned away and left the chamber through a side door.

Loren undid the unsealed flap of the envelope and eased out one of several eight-by-ten photographs. It had captured her naked body entwined with Pitt's in one of a wild series of orgiastic positions. Quickly, she shoved the photo back in the envelope, her face gone white, reflecting fear and disgust.

Daggat turned to her. "Congresswoman Smith, we seem to have a hung committee. Congressman Hunt and I agree that General Lusana should be heard. Congressman Meyers stands with you. As chairman of this hearing, may I prevail upon you in the interest of fair play to permit the general to speak his piece."

Loren felt the hairs on the back of her neck stiffen. Daggat was leering at her. It was all there in his expression: he was no stranger to the contents of the envelope. She struggled to contain the sickness that was rising in her throat, suddenly realizing that Felicia Collins had sold her out to Lusana's cause. Silently she cursed her stupidity in allowing herself to be set up as naively as a teenage runaway with a big-city pimp.

"Congresswoman Smith?" Daggat said, prompting her.

There was no out. Daggat controlled her now. She lowered her eyes and trembled.

"Mr. Chairman," she said in total defeat, "I withdraw my objection."

Barbara Gore, at forty-three, still cut the figure of a *Vogue* fashion model. She remained trim and had shapely legs, and her high-cheekboned features had yet to flesh with age. She had once had an affair with Dale Jarvis, but that had long since passed through the sexual phase, and now she was simply a good friend as well as his personal secretary.

She sat across from his desk, those beautiful legs crossed at an angle comfortable only to women and showy to the male eye. Jarvis, however, took no notice of them. He sat engrossed in dictation. After a while he abruptly broke off and began probing through a mountainous batch of highly classified reports.

"Perhaps if you tell me what it is you're looking for," Barbara said patiently, "I can help you."

"A status check on all existing battleships. I was promised delivery for today."

She sighed and reached into the pile and extracted a stapled sheaf of blue papers. "Been on your desk since eight this morning." There were times when Barbara was moved to exasperation over Jarvis's sloppy work habits, but she had long ago learned to accept his idiosyncrasies and flow with the tide.

"What does it say?"

"What do you want it to say?" she asked. "You haven't bothered to tell me what you're after."

"I want to buy a battleship, of course. Who has one for sale?"

Barbara shot him a dour expression and studied the blue papers. "I'm afraid you're out of luck. The Soviet Union has one left, which is used to train naval cadets. France has long since scrapped hers. Same with Great Britain, even though she still keeps one on the rolls for the sake of tradition."

"The United States?"

"Five of them have been preserved as memorials."

"What are their present locations?"

"They're enshrined in the states they were named after: *North Carolina, Texas, Alabama,* and *Massachusetts.*"

"You said five."

"The *Missouri* is maintained by the Navy in Bremerton, Washington. Oh, I almost forgot: the *Arizona* is still sentimentally kept on naval rolls as a commissioned ship."

Jarvis put his hands behind his head and stared at the ceiling. "I seem to recall the battlewagons *Wisconsin* and *Iowa* were tied up at the Philadelphia Navy Yard a few years back."

"Good memory," said Barbara. "According to the report, the *Wisconsin* went to the ship-breakers in 1984."

"And the *Iowa?*"

"Sold for scrap."

Jarvis rose and walked to the window. He looked out, hands in pockets, for several moments. Then he said, "The Wild Rose folder."

As if reading his thoughts, Barbara pointed to its cover. "I have it."

"Send it over to John Gossard in the Africa Section and tell him the operation made damn fine reading."

"Is that all?"

Jarvis turned. "Yes," he said pensively. "All things considered, that's all there was to it."

At the same moment, a small double-ender whaleboat dropped anchor a hundred yards off Walnut Point, Virginia, and swung slowly around until its bow split the incoming tide. Patrick Fawkes unfolded a worn old deck chair and erected it on the narrow stern deck, barely fitting the ends between the bulwarks. Next he propped a fishing pole against the helm and threw its hookless line over the side.

He had just opened a picnic basket and was lifting out a large wedge of Cheshire cheese and a bottle of Cutty Sark when a tub towing three heavily laden trash scows acknowledged him with a passing signal blast from its whistle. Fawkes waved back and braced his feet as the wash from the plodding vessels rocked his little whaleboat. Fawkes noted the time of the tug's passing in a notebook.

The battered deck chair creaked in protest as he lowered

his huge body onto its cushioned slats. Then he ate a cut of the Cheshire and took a swig from the bottle.

Every commercial ship or pleasure boat that passed by the seemingly drowsing fisherman was sketched into the notebook. The time of their appearance, heading, and speed were also recorded. One sighting interested Fawkes more than most. He kept a pair of binoculars trained on a Navy missile destroyer until it disappeared beyond the land point, carefully observing the empty missile mounts and the relaxed attitude of the deck crew.

Toward late evening a light shower began to splatter against the scarred and paint-cracked deck. Fawkes loved the rain. During storms at sea he'd often stood and faced their furies on his ship's bridge wing, later upbraiding his junior officers who preferred hot tea and the creature comforts of the control room. Even now, Fawkes ignored the shelter of a small cabin and elected to remain on deck, donning a slicker to protect his skin and clothes from the damp.

He felt good; the rain cleansed the air in his lungs, the thick richness of the cheese filled his belly, and the scotch made his veins fairly glow. He allowed his mind to roam free, and soon it began flashing images of his lost family. The smells of his farm in Natal came to his nostrils and the sound of Myrna's voice calling him to dinner sounded clear and distinct to his ears.

Four hours later he jerked his thoughts back to reality as the tug, its tow of scows now empty, came into view on a return heading. Quickly he stood and jotted down the number and position of the navigation lights. Then Fawkes weighed anchor, started the engine, and eased into the wake of the last scow in line as it slipped by.

41

The snow was falling heavily at Table Lake, Colorado, when the NUMA salvage divers, immune to the frigid water in their thermal suits, finished cutting away the wings and tail of Vixen 03. Then they manhandled two huge cradle slings under the mutilated fuselage.

Admiral Bass and Abe Steiger arrived, followed by an Air Force–blue truck carrying several shivering airmen of the Remains Identity and Recovery Team along with five coffins.

At ten A.M. everyone was assembled and Pitt waved his arms at the crane operators. Slowly the cables hanging from the floating derricks to beneath the wind-rippled surface of the lake tightened and quivered as the power-unit operators increased the tension. The derricks listed a few degrees with the strain and creaked at their bolted joints. Then, abruptly, as though a great weight had fallen from their unseen clutches, they straightened.

"She's broken free of the mud," Pitt announced.

In confirmation, Giordino, standing at his side, wearing radio earphones, nodded. "Divers report she is on her way up."

"Tell whoever is operating the cradle sling around the nose section to keep it low. We don't want the canisters spilling out of the hole in the tail."

Giordino relayed Pitt's orders through a tiny microphone attached to his headphones.

The freezing mountain air was heavy with tension; every man stood motionless, numb with anticipation, his eyes locked on the water between the derricks. The only sounds came from the exhaust of the lift engines. They were a hard-bitten salvage crew, and yet no matter how many wrecks they had reclaimed from the sea, the same old tentacles of excitement during a lift operation never failed to wring their emotions dry.

Admiral Bass found himself reliving that snowy night so many years ago. To him it seemed all but impossible to associate the image of Major Raymond Vylander in his memory with the fleshless bones he knew to be inside the wreck's cockpit. He moved closer to the water's edge until it lapped at his shoes, and he began to experience a burning sensation in his mid-chest and left shoulder.

Then the water under the cables swirled from blue to muddy brown, and the curved roof of Vixen 03 arched into the daylight for the first time in thirty-four years. The once-shiny aluminum skin had corroded to a whitish gray and was streaked by slimy bottom weed. As the cranes lifted her higher into the air, the silt-laden water cascaded from the open wound at the rear of the fuselage.

The blue and yellow insignia that ran across the top of the fuselage appeared surprisingly sharp, and the words MILITARY AIR TRANSPORT SERVICE were still quite legible. Vixen 03 no longer resembled an airplane. It was easier to picture her as a huge dead whale whose fins and tail had been clipped. The severed and twisted control cables, electrical wiring, and hydraulic lines dangling from the gaping wounds could be imagined as entrails.

Abe Steiger was the first to break the hushed quiet.

"Odds are that's the cause of her crash," he said, pointing at the gash in the cargo cabin just aft of the cockpit. "She must have thrown a prop blade."

Bass stared at the ominous evidence, making no comment. The pain in his chest became more intense. With great force of will he put it from his mind while unconsciously massaging the ache on the inside of his left arm. He tried to peer through the plane's windshield glass, but the years of accumulated silt blocked out all view. The cranes had lifted the fuselage ten feet above the lake's surface when a thought struck him and he turned and gazed at Pitt questioningly.

"I see no provisions for a makeshift barge. How do you expect to carry the wreckage to shore?"

Pitt grinned. "This is where we send for a sky hook, Admiral." He gestured at Giordino. "Okay, signal Dumbo."

Within two minutes, like some great pterodactyl flushed from its Mesozoic nest, an ungainly structured helicopter soared over the treetops, its two big rotors pounding the thin mountain air with peculiar-sounding thumps.

The pilot hovered the giant helicopter above the moored cranes. Two hooks gradually unreeled from the gaping belly and were rapidly attached to the hoist cradles by the derrick crews. Then the pilot took up the strain of the full weight and the connectors from the crane cables slackened and were released. The Dumbo clawed at the air, its turbines struggling under the massive load. Very tenderly, as if maneuvering a cargo of fragile crystal, the pilot eased Vixen 03 toward shore.

Pitt and the others turned their backs as a cloud of spray, kicked up by the rotor blades, swirled in from the lake. Giordino, ignoring the gusting wetness, moved to where the pilot could plainly see him, motioning with his hands while directing the lowering operation over the earphone transmitter.

Five minutes was all it took for the Dumbo to release its load and disappear again over the trees. Then they all stood there staring, no one making a move for the wreckage. Steiger murmured a command to his Air Force detail and they smartly marched to the truck and began unloading the coffins, setting them on the ground in an orderly row. One of Pitt's men produced a ladder and propped it against the exposed rear of the upper cargo deck. Pitt remained silent and indicated with his hand that Admiral Bass be the first to enter the aircraft.

Once inside, Bass made his way around the canisters to the control-cabin doorway. He stood immobile for several seconds, looking pale and very ill.

"Are you all right, sir?" Pitt asked, coming up behind him.

The voice that answered was remote and far away. "I can't seem to bring myself to look at them."

"It would serve no purpose," said Pitt gently.

Bass leaned heavily against the bulkhead, the agony in his chest growing. "A minute to get my bearings. Then I'll take stock of the warheads."

Steiger approached Pitt, gingerly stepping around the canisters as though he were afraid to touch them. "Whenever you give the word I'll bring my men on board to recover the remains of the crew."

"Might as well begin with our unexplained guest." Pitt tilted his head at a jumble of loose canisters. "You'll find him strapped to the floor about ten feet to your right."

Steiger searched in the area Pitt instructed and shrugged, his facial expression blank. "I don't find anything."

"You're practically standing on top of him," Pitt said.

"What gives, for Christ's sake?" Steiger demanded. "I'm telling you there's nothing here."

"You must be blind." Pitt pushed Steiger aside and looked down. The straps were still attached to the cargo tie-down rings but the body in the old khaki uniform had vanished Pitt stared dumbly at the space on the floor while his mind stumbled to grasp the reality of the missing remains. He knelt and picked up the rotting straps. They had been cut.

Steiger's eyes reflected doubt. "That water was like ice the day you dived. Perhaps your mind saw something . . ." His voice trailed off but the implication was clear.

Pitt rose to his feet. "He was here," he said, expecting no further argument and receiving none.

"Could he have washed out the aft opening during the lift operation?" Steiger offered lamely.

"Not possible. The divers who swam beside the wreck to the surface would have reported any debris falling free."

Steiger started to say something, but suddenly his eyes turned uncomprehending at a strangled gasping sound that emitted from the forward end of the compartment. "What in God's name is that?"

Pitt wasted no time in answering. He knew.

He found Admiral Bass lying on the wet floor, fighting for breath, his skin bathed in cold sweat. The unbearable severity of the pain contorted his face into a tormented mask.

"His heart!" Pitt called out to Steiger. "Find Giordino and tell him to get that helicopter back here."

Pitt began tearing the clothing away from the admiral's neck and chest. Bass reached up and grasped Pitt's wrist. "The . . . the warheads," he rasped.

"Rest easy. We'll soon have you on your way to a hospital."

"The warheads . . ." Bass repeated.

"All safe in their canisters," Pitt reassured him.

"No . . . no . . . you don't understand." His voice was a hoarse whisper now. "The canisters . . . I counted them . . . twenty-eight."

Bass's words were becoming barely audible, and Pitt had to place his ear at the tremoring lips.

Giordino rushed up carrying several blankets. "Steiger gave me the word," he said tensely. "How is he?"

"Still hanging in there," Pitt said. He released the vise-like grip from his wrist and gently squeezed Bass's hand. "I'll see to it, Admiral. That's a promise."

Bass blinked his dull eyes and nodded in understanding.

Pitt and Giordino had covered him and cushioned his head with the blankets when Steiger reappeared, followed by two airmen carrying a stretcher. Only then did Pitt rise to his feet and step aside. The helicopter had already returned and landed when they carried the still-conscious Bass from Vixen 03.

Steiger took Pitt's arm. "What was he trying to tell you?"

"His inventory of the warhead canisters," Pitt answered. "He counted twenty-eight."

"I pray the old guy makes it," Steiger said. "At least he had the satisfaction of knowing the monstrosities were retrieved. Now all that's left is to dump them in the ocean. End of horror story."

"No, I'm afraid it's only the beginning."

"You're talking in riddles."

"According to Admiral Bass, Vixen 03 did not depart Buckley Field carrying twenty-eight warheads filled with the Quick Death agent."

Steiger sensed an icy dread in Pitt's tone. "But his inventory . . . the count came to twenty-eight."

"He should have tallied thirty-six," Pitt said ominously. "Eight warheads are missing."

4

NO RETURN TICKET

42

Washington, D.C.—December 1988

The National Underwater and Marine Agency building, a tubular structure sheeted in green reflective glass, rose thirty stories above an East Washington hill.

On the top floor Admiral James Sandecker sat behind an immense desk made from a refinished hatch cover salvaged from a Confederate blockade runner in Albemarle Sound. His private line buzzed.

"Sandecker."

"Pitt here, sir."

Sandecker pushed a switch on a small console that activated a holographic TV camera. Pitt's lifelike image materialized in three-dimensional depth and color in the middle of the office.

"Raise the camera from your end," said Sandecker. "You've chopped off your head."

Through the miracle of satellite holography Pitt's face seemed to grow from his shoulders, and his projected self, including voice and gestures, became identical to the original. The major difference, which never ceased to amuse Sandecker, was that he could pass a hand through the image because it was totally lacking in matter.

"That better?" asked Pitt.

"At least you're whole now." Sandecker wasted no more words. "What's the latest on Walter Bass?"

Pitt looked tired as he sat on a folding chair beneath a large pine tree, his ebony hair tossed by a stiff breeze.

"The heart specialist at the Fitzsimons Army Hospital in Denver reports his condition as stable. If he survives the next forty-eight hours, his chances for recovery look good.

As soon as he's strong enough for the trip, they're going to transfer him to Bethesda Naval Hospital."

"What about the warheads?"

"We trucked them to a rail siding in Leadville," Pitt answered slowly. "Colonel Steiger volunteered to arrange shipment to Pier Six in San Francisco."

"Tell Steiger we're grateful for his cooperation. I've ordered our Pacific Coast research ship to be standing by. Instructions were given to the skipper to dump the warheads off the continental shelf in ten thousand feet of water." Sandecker hesitated at posing the next question. "Did you locate the missing eight?"

Pitt's negative expression answered him even before the image spoke.

"No luck, Admiral. A thorough search of the lake bed failed to turn up a trace."

Sandecker read the frustration on Pitt's face. "I fear the time has come to inform the Pentagon."

"Do you honestly think that a wise course?"

"What other options do we have?" Sandecker came back. "We don't have the means at our disposal for a large-scale investigation."

"All we need is a lead," Pitt said, pressing on. "Odds favor the warheads' being stored somewhere, gathering dust. It's even possible the thieves don't know what they really have on their hands."

"I'll accept that," Sandecker said. "But who would want them in the first place? Christ, they weigh nearly a ton each, and they're easily recognizable in exterior appearance as obsolete naval shells."

"The answer will also lead us to the murderer of Loren Smith's father."

"No corpus delicti, no crime," Sandecker said.

"I know what I saw," Pitt said evenly.

"It won't alter present circumstances. The dilemma staring us all in the face is how to get a tag on those lost warheads and do it before someone gets it in his head to play demolition expert."

Suddenly the exhaustion seemed to drop from Pitt. "Something you just said jogged a thought. Give me five days to flush out the warheads. If I turn up nothing, then it's your ball game."

Sandecker smiled tightly at Pitt's sudden show of intensity. "This happens to be my ball game, any way you look at it," he said sharply. "As the senior government official involved in this mess, it became my unwanted responsibility the day you hijacked a NUMA aircraft and underwater camera system."

Pitt stared back across the room but remained discreetly silent.

Sandecker left Pitt stewing for a moment while he rubbed his eyes. Then he said, "All right, against my better judgment I'll take the gamble."

"You'll go along, then?"

Sandecker caved in. "You've got five days, Pitt. But heaven help us if you come up empty-handed."

He hit the switch to the holograph and Pitt's image faded and disappeared.

43

It was just before sunset when Maxine Raferty turned from her clothesline and spied Pitt walking up the road. She continued her chore, pinning up the last of her husband's shirts before waving a greeting.

"Mr. Pitt, how nice to see you."

"Mrs. Raferty."

"Loren with you up to the cabin?"

"No, she had to remain in Washington." Pitt looked around the yard. "Is Lee at home?"

"In the house, fixing the kitchen sink." A brisk breeze was sweeping down the mountains from the west and Maxine thought it odd that Pitt was carrying his Windbreaker over his right hand and arm. "Just go on in."

Lee Raferty was sitting at the kitchen table, filing burrs from a length of plumbing pipe. He looked up as Pitt entered.

"Mr. Pitt. Hey, sit down; you're just in time. I was about to open a bottle of my private stock of grape squeezin's."

Pitt pulled up a chair. "You make wine as well as beer?"

"Gotta be self-sufficient up here in the high country," Lee said, grinning, and pointing a cigar stub at the pipe. "Take this. Cost me a fortune to get a plumber up here from Leadville. Cheaper to do it myself. Leaky gasket. Any kid could fix it."

Raferty laid the rusty pipe on an old newspaper, rose from the table, and produced two glasses and a ceramic jug from under a cupboard.

"I wanted to talk with you," Pitt said.

"Sure thing." Lee poured the glasses to their brims. "Hey, what do you think about all that commotion up at the lake? I hear tell they found an old airplane. Could it be the one you was askin' about?"

"Yes," Pitt answered, sipping from the wineglass, which he held in his left hand. He was mildly surprised to find the wine quite smooth. "That's part of the reason I'm here. I was hoping you might enlighten me as to why you murdered Charlie Smith."

The only reaction was the slight lift of one gray eyebrow. "Me . . . murder old Charlie? What on earth are you talking about?"

"A falling-out of partners who thought they'd discovered a pot of gold deep in a mountain lake."

He stared at Pitt and tilted his head questioningly. "You're talking like a crazy man."

"The last thing you expected was a stranger appearing on your doorstep asking questions about a lost airplane. You'd already made a mistake by not disposing of the oxygen tank and nose gear. I pay homage to you and your wife's theatrical talents. I swallowed your country-bumpkin act with all the gullibility of a tourist. After I left, you covered my every move, and when you saw me dive in the lake, you were dead certain I had discovered the aircraft and Charlie Smith's bones. At that point you made an irreversible blunder: you panicked and removed Charlie, in all probability burying his bones deep in the mountains. If you'd left him strapped to that sunken cargo floor, the sheriff would have been hard pressed to tie you to a three-year-old murder."

"You'll pay hell proving anything," Lee said, calmly relighting his cigar stub, "without a body."

"Not in a court of law," Pitt said casually. "Innocent until proven guilty, but the story is a worn classic. Kill thy neighbor for profit; there's your title. Suppose we begin at chapter one with an eccentric inventor named Charlie Smith who was testing his latest brainstorm, an automatic fishing-pole caster. On one cast the sinkers took the hook deep and it snagged on an object. Charlie, an experienced angler, thought he had hooked a submerged log and expertly worked the line until the tension gave and it pulled free. But he felt a drag; something was surfacing with the hook. And then he saw it: an aircraft oxygen tank. Its mounts had torn loose, eroded over the years of submersion, and Charlie's tugs were all the tank needed to break away and rise to the lake's surface.

"The practical course would have been to call the sheriff. Unluckily for Charlie, he was the curious sort. He had to prove to himself there was a plane down there, so he scrounged a rope and grappling iron and began dragging the lake bottom. On one pass he must have caught and yanked up the shattered nose gear, which must have broken out of its housing. Suspicions confirmed, Charlie then became greedy and sniffed the sweet smell of treasure. So instead of playing Honest John Citizen and reporting his discovery, he headed straight for Lee Raferty."

"Why would Charlie come to me?"

"A retired Navy man, a deep-water diver; you were made to order. I venture to guess the diving equipment and air compressor you and Charlie scrounged are sitting in your garage right now. A hundred-and-forty-foot dive must have been child's play for a man of your experience, wearing hard-hat gear. The strange cargo in the aircraft stirred the juices of your imagination. What did you expect to find inside the canisters? Old atomic bombs, perhaps? I can only envision the backbreaking work it took for two men nearing seventy to dive in frigid waters and wrench weights of two thousand pounds from the lake depths to shore. I give you both credit for guts. I can only hope I'm in half the physical shape when I reach your age."

"Not so tough." Lee smiled; he seemed to have no fear of Pitt at all. "Once Charlie devised a small explosive charge to enlarge the already cracked opening on the fuselage, it was a simple matter for me to attach a cable to a canister while he towed it to shore with the four-wheel-drive."

"Where there's a will," Pitt said. "What then, Lee? Once the canister was removed, it was obvious to an ex-Navy man and a former demolitions expert that you were looking at a prize that could have only warmed the cockles of an old battleship admiral's heart. But what was the value at today's prices? What was the demand for an outdated naval shell, except for scrap?"

Lee Raferty casually resumed filing the rough edges of the pipe. "Pretty slick guesswork, Mr. Pitt. I admit it. Not one hundred percent, mind you, but a passing grade. You underestimated a pair of foxy veterans, though. Hell, we knew them things in the canisters weren't armor-piercing projectiles the minute we laid eyes on one. Took Charlie all of ten minutes to peg it as a poison-gas carrier."

Pitt was stunned. Two old men had made fools of them all. "How?" he asked tersely.

"Outwardly it looked like standard naval ordnance, but we saw it was rigged the same as a star shell. You know the kind: after reaching a preset altitude, a parachute is released while a small explosive charge splits the head, igniting a wad of phosphorus. Except this devil was set to unleash a bundle of tiny bomblets filled with lethal gas instead."

"Charlie figured they contained gas merely by looking at it?"

"He discovered the parachute-escape-hatch cover. That gave him his first clue. Then he came around front, dismantled the head, disconnected the charge, and peeked inside."

"Dear God!" Pitt murmured in near despair. "Charlie opened the warhead?"

"So what's the big deal? Charlie was a master at demolitions."

Pitt took a deep breath and pitched the obvious question. "What did you do with the warheads?"

"The way I saw it, it was finders, keepers."

"Where are they?" Pitt demanded.

"We sold them."

"You what?" he gasped. "To whom?"

"The Phalanx Arms Corporation, in Newark, New Jersey. They buy and sell weapons on an international front. I contacted the vice-president, a screwy sort of duck, looks more like a hardware peddler than a death merchant. Name's Orville Mapes. Anyway, he flew out to Colorado, checked over the projectile, and offered us five thousand bucks for every one we could ship to his warehouse. No questions asked."

"I can guess the rest," Pitt said. "It occurred to Charlie that if those shells were detonated, he would be responsible for thousands, possibly hundreds of thousands of deaths. You were more callous, Lee. The money meant more to you than conscience. You two argued, then fought, and Charlie lost. You hid his body in the sunken aircraft. Then you set off a few sticks of dynamite, tossed a boot and his thumb in the debris, and cried all the way to his funeral."

Raferty displayed no reaction to Pitt's accusation. His mellow eyes never left his pipe. His hands slowly, placidly filed away at the threaded ends. He was far too nonchalant, Pitt thought. Raferty wasn't acting like a man about to be turned in for murder. The look of a cornered rat was nowhere apparent.

"A shame Charlie didn't see things my way." Raferty shrugged almost sadly. "Contrary to what you may think, Mr. Pitt, I am not a greedy man. I did not attempt to sell off the projectiles in one swoop. You might say I looked upon them as a sort of savings account. When Max and I needed a few dollars, I'd make a one-at-a-time withdrawal, you might say, and call Mapes. He'd send a truck to pick up the merchandise and pay me in cash. A clean-cut, nontaxable transaction."

"I'd like to hear how you murdered Charlie Smith."

"Sorry to disappoint you, Mr. Pitt, but I don't have it in me to take a human life." Raferty leaned forward and his wrinkled face seemed to leer. "Max is the stronger one. She handles the killing. Shot old Charlie in the heart as neat as can be."

"Maxine?" The shock that swelled within Pitt did not come so much from the sudden disclosure as it did from the realization that he had committed a sad mistake.

"Throw a dime in the air at twenty paces and Max will make change," Raferty continued, nodding over Pitt's shoulder. "Let Mr. Pitt know you're there, honey."

Two metallic clinking sounds answered Raferty, followed by a gentle thud.

"The cartridge striking the floor should tell you Max's old lever-action Winchester is loaded and cocked," said Raferty. "Any doubts?"

Pitt braced both feet squarely on the floor and flexed his hand under the Windbreaker jacket. "Nice try, Lee."

"Then see for yourself. But I warn you—no sudden moves."

Pitt gradually turned to face Maxine Raferty, whose kindly blue eyes were staring over the sights of a repeating rifle. The barrel was pointed, rock steady, at Pitt's head.

"Sorry, Mr. Pitt," she said sadly. "But Lee and I ain't of a mind to spend our few remaining years in jail."

"Another murder on your hands won't save you," said Pitt. He tightened his leg muscles as he gauged the distance between himself and Maxine. It was five feet. "I brought my own witnesses."

"Did you see anybody, honey?" asked Lee.

Maxine shook her head. "He came up the road alone. I kept watch after he entered the house. No one followed him."

"I figured as much," Lee Raferty said, and sighed. "You've been playing a bluffing hand, Mr. Pitt. If you had any solid evidence against Maxine and me, you'd have brought the sheriff."

"Oh, but I did." Pitt smiled and appeared to relax. "He's sitting in a car about half a mile away, with two deputies hanging on our every word."

Raferty tensed. "Damn you, you're lying!"

"He taped a transmitter to my chest," Pitt said, his left hand loosening the top button of his shirt. "Right here, under my—"

Maxine had dipped the rifle no more than a fraction of an inch as Pitt launched himself sideways and pulled the trigger of the Colt automatic he held under the folds of his jacket.

The Winchester and the Colt seemed to explode at the same instant.

Al Giordino and Abe Steiger had arrived minutes before Pitt and taken up a prone position beneath a stand of blue-spruce trees. Through field glasses Steiger observed Maxine hanging out the wash. "Any sign of the husband?" asked Giordino.

"Must be in the house." The glasses angled slightly in Steiger's hands. "Pitt is approaching her now."

"That Colt forty-five must stick out like a third arm."

"He's got his Windbreaker draped over it." Steiger bent a branch out of the way to clear his field of vision. "Pitt's going inside the house now."

"Time to move closer," said Giordino. He was in the act of raising up on his knees when Steiger's trunklike arm pinned him back down.

"Hold it! The old broad is hanging back to see if he was followed."

They stayed quiet and motionless for several minutes while Maxine walked around the yard, her eyes probing the surrounding trees. She took a final look up the road and lumbered around a corner of the house and out of Steiger's view.

"Give me time to make my way around back before you move on the front door," said Steiger.

Giordino nodded. "Watch out for bears."

Steiger threw him a tight grin and slipped off into a small ravine. He was still a good fifty yards short of his goal when he heard the shots.

Giordino had been marking time when the roar echoed through the windows of the house. He leaped to his feet and sprinted down a small hill, hurdling a lean-to fence into the yard. At that moment, Maxine Raferty burst backward through the front door like an out-of-control Patton tank, tumbled down the porch steps, and crashed to the ground. Giordino halted in his tracks, surprised by the sight of her bloodstained dress. He stood rooted as the elderly woman scrambled back to her feet as agilely as a gymnast. Not until it was too late did Giordino notice what looked like a battered rifle clutched in her hand.

Maxine, ready to charge back in the house, spotted Giordino standing dumbly in the yard. She gripped the Winchester awkwardly, with one hand under the breech, the other over the barrel, and snapped off a shot from the hip.

The force of the bullet spun Giordino through the air in a half turn and smashed him to the grass, his left thigh exploding in a spray of red through the cloth of his pants.

To Pitt, everything had seemed to grind into slow motion. The muzzle of the Winchester flashed in his face. At first he thought he had been hit, but when he collided with the floor, he found himself still able to move his limbs and body. Maxine's shot had nicked his ear while his bullet smashed the stock on her Winchester, ricocheting into an antique kerosene lamp, shattering its glass shade.

Lee Raferty growled like an animal and swung the pipe. It caught Pitt on the shoulder and grazed his skull. Pitt grunted in pain and swung around, fighting off blackness and trying desperately to clear his fogging vision. He aimed the Colt at the blurred figure he knew to be Lee.

Maxine brought her rifle barrel down on the Colt, pounding it from Pitt's fingers into the fireplace.

Maxine hastily labored to recock the mangled gun as Lee advanced, swinging the plumbing pipe. Pitt raised his left arm to fend off the blow and was surprised not to hear the bone snap. He lashed out with his feet and caught Lee on the knees, spilling the scarecrow-bodied man on top of him.

"Shoot, dammit!" Lee yelled to his wife. "Shoot!"

"I can't!" she shrieked back. "You're in my line of fire."

Lee dropped the pipe and violently fought to disentangle himself, but Pitt locked him around the neck with the good right arm and hung on. Maxine danced around the room, excitedly pointing the Winchester, frantically trying for a safe shot. Pitt held on and kept Lee turned in front as a shield while struggling to regain his feet. Then Lee abruptly twisted, kneed Pitt in the groin, and broke free.

Through the burning haze of agony Pitt managed to grab the kerosene lamp and hurl it at Maxine, catching her across the chest. She screamed as the glass splintered into fragments, slicing her dress and penetrating one immense sagging breast. Then Pitt thrust his weight upward and charged, hitting her harder than he had ever hit anyone in his life. For a woman of advanced age, Maxine was hard, but she was no match against Pitt's brutal onslaught. She soared backward with such force that she flew through the front door of the house and vanished.

"You bastard!" Lee screamed. He threw himself into the fireplace, snatched the Colt from among the ashes, and swung to face Pitt.

A window suddenly disintegrated and Abe Steiger tumbled into the kitchen, collapsing the table beneath him. Lee spun, giving Pitt the instant he needed to snatch the pipe on the floor. A dazed Steiger never forgot the sickening sound of the pipe's crushing the bone of Lee Raferty's temple.

Giordino sat on the ground, his eyes staring numbly at his punctured leg. He looked up at Maxine, not fully grasping what had happened. Then his mouth went slack and he watched helplessly as she deliberately ejected the spent shell and recocked the rifle. Maxine took careful aim at his chest and curled her finger around the trigger.

The blast was deafening and the slug tore the breastbone away, catapulting gore and marrow in a grisly pile at Giordino's outstretched feet. Maxine stood inert for almost three seconds before she folded limply to the yard in a fat, grotesque heap, her blood spilling out between her breasts and staining the grass.

Pitt leaned against a porch railing, his hand wielding the Colt, barrel poised in the recoil position. He lowered the gun and walked stiffly toward Giordino. Steiger came out to look, paled, and threw up into a flowerbed.

Giordino's eyes were locked on a gleaming white bit of cartilage as Pitt knelt beside him. "You . . . you blew that sweet little old lady's chest off?" Giordino asked.

"Yes," Pitt replied, feeling none too proud of himself.

"Thank God," Giordino murmured, pointing. "I thought that thing on the ground belonged to me."

44

"You fool!" Thomas Machita shouted across the desk. "You bloody fool!"

Colonel Randolph Jumana sat and regarded Machita's outburst with controlled indulgence. "I had the very best of reasons for issuing those orders."

"Who gave you the authority to attack that village and slaughter fellow blacks?"

"You overlook basic facts, Major." Jumana removed a pair of horn-rimmed reading glasses and stroked one side of his flattened nose. "During General Lusana's absence I am in command of the AAR. I am simply carrying out his directives."

"By switching attacks from military targets to civilian villages?" Machita snapped angrily. "By terrorizing our brothers and sisters whose only crime is working as underpaid civil servants for the South Africans?"

"The strategy, Major, is to drive a wedge between the whites and the blacks. Any of our people who hire out to the government must be labeled as traitors."

"Black members of the Defense Forces, yes," Machita argued. "But you can't gain support by indiscriminately murdering schoolteachers, mailmen, and road laborers."

Jumana's face went cold and impersonal. "If killing a hundred children would advance our ultimate victory over the whites by one hour, I would not hesitate to give the order for execution."

Machita was swept by a wave of abhorrence. "You're talking butchery!"

"There is an old Western World saying," Jumana said flatly. " 'The end justifies the means.' "

Machita stared at the obese colonel and his flesh crawled. "When General Lusana hears of this, he will expel you from the AAR."

Jumana smiled. "Too late. My campaign to spread fear and havoc throughout South Africa is irreversible." Jumana managed to look even more sinister. "General Lusana is an outsider. He will never be fully accepted by the tribes of the interior, nor by the black leaders of the cities, as one of their own. I guarantee he will never sit in the Prime Minister's office in Cape Town."

"You're talking treason."

"On the other hand," Jumana continued, "you were born in Liberia before your parents immigrated to the United States. Your skin is as black as mine. Your blood has not been fouled by mixed sexual intercourse with whites, as has most American blacks'. It might not be a bad idea, Machita, for you to consider a change of allegiance."

Machita replied coldly. "You swore the same oath as I when we enlisted in the AAR, to uphold the principles set down by Hiram Lusana. What you're proposing sickens me. I want no part of it. Rest assured, Colonel, your treachery will be exposed to General Lusana within the hour."

Without another word, Machita turned and stormed from Jumana's office, slamming the door with a loud crack.

Seconds later, Jumana's aide knocked and entered. "The major seems upset."

"A small difference of opinion," said Jumana without emotion. "A shame his motives are misdirected." He motioned outside. "Quickly, take two of my bodyguards and go to the communications wing. You should find Major Machita about to transmit a message to the general, in Washington. Stop the transmission and arrest him."

"Arrest the major?" The aide was astonished. "On what charge?"

Jumana thought a moment. "Passing secrets to the enemy. That should be sufficient to lock him in a basement cell until he can be tried and shot."

Hiram Lusana stood in the entrance to the House of Representatives library and searched until he spied Frederick Daggat. The congressman was sitting at a long mahogany table, taking notes from a large leatherbound book.

"I hope I'm not interrupting," said Lusana. "But your message sounded urgent and your secretary said I might find you here."

"Sit down," Daggat said with no sign of friendliness. Lusana pulled up a chair and waited.

"Have you read the late-edition morning paper?" asked Daggat, again looking at the book.

"No, I've been lobbying with Senator Moore, of Ohio. He seemed most receptive to our cause after I explained the aims of the AAR."

"Apparently the senator missed the news, too."

"What are you talking about?"

Daggat reached into his breast pocket and handed a folded news clipping to Lusana. "Here, my friend. Read it and weep."

TAZAREEN, South Africa (UPI)—At least 165 black inhabitants of the village of Tazareen in the province of Transvaal were killed in a seemingly senseless slaughter by African Army of Revolution insurgents in a dawn raid, South African Defence officials report.

An army officer at the scene said the raid was carried out by an estimated 200 AAR guerrillas who swept into the village, shooting anything moving and chopping and hacking with bush knives.

"Forty-six women and children were murdered, some children still in their beds clutching dolls," one stunned investigator said as he pointed to the burned remains of the once prosperous village. "Militarily, it was terrible waste, an act of pure animalistic savagery."

One girl about four years of age was found with her throat slit. Pregnant women were found with large bruises on their abdomens, indicating they had been stomped to death.

Defence Ministry officials were hard pressed to speculate on what provoked the attack. All the victims were civilians. The nearest military installation is 12 miles away.

Until now, the African Army of Revolution, led by American expatriate Hiram Jones, who now calls himself Hiram Lusana, has fought a strict military war, attacking only South African Defence Forces and facilities.

Barbaric assaults by other insurgent groups have been commonplace along South Africa's northern borders. Defense leaders find this new pattern most puzzling.

The only previous type of massacre involving the

AAR occurred during the Fawkes farm raid in Umkono, Natal, in which 32 were killed.

It is known that Hiram Jones-Lusana is currently in Washington soliciting support for the AAR.

Lusana could not accept the article's impact until he had read it through four times. Finally he looked up, shaken, and opened his palms in a gesture of amazement.

"This is not my doing," he said.

Daggat looked up from the book. "I believe you, Hiram. I am quite aware that gross stupidity is not one of your virtues. However, as commanding officer, you are responsible for the conduct of your troops."

"Jumana!" Lusana blurted as full realization dawned on him. "You're mistaken, Congressman, I *am* stupid. Tom Machita tried to warn me of Jumana's renegade leanings, but I refused to listen."

"The heavyset colonel weighted down with medals," said Daggat. "I remember him from your cocktail party. A leader of a prominent tribe, I believe you said."

Lusana nodded. "A 'favorite son' of the Srona tribe. He spent over eight years in South African prisons before I arranged his escape. He has strong support throughout Transvaal province. Politically, I thought it an expedient move to name him my second-in-command."

"As with too many Africans who are suddenly thrust into a position of power, he apparently conjured up fantasies of grandeur."

Lusana stood and leaned wearily against a shelf of books. "The idiot," he muttered, almost to himself. "Can't he understand that he's destroying the very cause he's fighting for?"

Daggat rose and put his hand on Lusana's shoulder. "I suggest you catch the first flight back to Mozambique, Hiram, and regain control of your movement. Issue news releases denying the AAR's involvement in the massacre. Blame it on the other insurgent groups, if you have to, but get out from under and put your house in order. I'll do what I can to soften adverse reaction at this end."

Lusana extended his hand. "Thank you, Congressman. I'm grateful for all you've done."

Daggat shook his hand warmly.

"And your subcommittee. How will they vote now?" Lusana said.

Daggat smiled confidently. "Three to two in favor of aid to the AAR, providing you offer a convincing performance in front of the news cameras when you deny any involvement with the Tazareen massacre."

Colonel Joris Zeegler had taken over the basement of a schoolhouse ten miles from the boundary separating Natal province and Mozambique. While class continued on the top two floors, Zeegler and several ranking officers of the Defence Forces studied aerial maps and a scale mock-up of the AAR headquarters, not twenty-five miles away, across the border.

Zeegler squinted through a wisp of smoke curling from the cigarette that dangled in his mouth and tapped a pointer on a miniature building in the center of the mock-up.

"The former university-administration building," he said, "is used by Lusana as his nerve center. A Chinese-supplied communications network, field-staff offices, intelligence section, indoctrination rooms—they're all housed there. They've gone too bloody far this time. Destroy it and everyone in it and you cut off the head of the AAR."

"Begging your pardon, sir"—this from a big red-faced captain with a bushy mustache—"but it was my understanding that Lusana was in America."

"Quite correct. He's in Washington this very minute, on his hands and knees, begging the Yanks for financial support."

"Then what bloody good is cutting off the serpent's head if the brain lies elsewhere? Why not wait until he returns and bag the head bugger as well?"

Zeegler gave him a cold, condescending stare. "Your metaphor needs refining, Captain. However, to answer your question . . . it will not be practical to await Lusana's return. Our intelligence sources have confirmed that Colonel Randolph Jumana has engineered a mutiny within the ranks of the AAR."

Surprised looks were exchanged among the officers clustered around the model. It was the first they'd heard of Lusana's ouster.

"Now is the time to strike," he went on. "By brutally murdering helpless women and children at Tazareen, Jumana has thrown open the door for retaliation. An across-the-border raid on AAR headquarters has been approved by the Prime Minister. The usual diplomatic protests from

Third World countries are to be expected, of course. A formality, nothing more."

A tough-looking customer with the rank of major and dressed in camouflage fatigues raised his hand. Zeegler acknowledged him.

"Your intelligence report also mentions the presence of Vietnamese advisers and possibly a few Chinese observers. Surely our government will suffer repercussions if we snuff the bastards."

"Accidents happen," Zeegler said. "If a foreign national by chance stumbles into your line of fire, do not lose sleep if a stray bullet sends him straightaway to Buddhaland. They have no business being in Africa. Defence Minister De Vaal is aware of the likelihood and has consented to let that particular problem rest on his shoulders."

Zeegler turned his attention back to the mock-up.

"Now, gentlemen, for the final phase of the attack. We have decided to take a page from the AAR handbook on the policing of a battlefield." He smiled without humor. "Except we intend to go them one better."

Thomas Machita shivered in his cell. He couldn't remember when he had felt so cold. The temperature of the African interior had run its normal course, from ninety degrees the previous afternoon to a frosty thirty in the hours prior to dawn.

Jumana's goons had dragged Machita from the radio room before he could send a message of warning to Lusana in Washington. They savagely pulverized his face before stripping away his clothes and throwing him in a damp little cell in the building's basement. One eye was swollen shut; a deep gash above the other eyebrow had coagulated during the night, and he had vision after wiping away the clotted blood. His lips were swollen and two teeth were missing, courtesy of a well-aimed rifle butt. He shifted his position on a filthy pile of dried leaves, gasping at the pain that stabbed his cracked ribs.

Machita lay in dark frustration, gazing vacantly at the concrete walls of his prison as the new day's light filtered through a small barred window above his head. The cell was no more than a cube, five by five by five feet, and barely allowed enough room for Machita to lie down, provided he raised his knees. The low arched door to the basement hall was three-inch-thick mahogany and had no latch or handle on the inside.

He heard voices through the window and painfully pulled himself to a stooped position and looked out. The window faced the camp's parade ground at eye level. Elite commando sections were lining up for roll call and inspection. Across the way, mess-hall roof vents emitted shimmering waves of heat as the cooks stoked their stoves to life. A company of recruits from Angola and Zimbabwe crawled sleepily from their tents at the prodding of their veteran section leaders.

It began like another ordinary day of political indoctrination and combat training, but this day was to be far different.

His eyes aimed intently at his watch, Joris Zeegler spoke softly into a field radio. "Tonic One?"

"Tonic One in position, sir," a voice crackled over the receiver.

"Tonic Two?"

"Ready to fire, Colonel."

"Ten seconds and counting," said Zeegler. "Five, four, three, two . . ."

The formation of commandos on the parade ground dropped to the ground in concert as though by command. Machita could not believe that two hundred men had died almost instantly as a salvo of gunfire erupted from the dense bush surrounding the perimeter of the camp. He jammed his face against the bars, unmindful of his pain, twisting his head to see better through his one functioning eye. The firing increased in intensity as confused AAR soldiers began a hopeless counterattack against their unseen enemy.

He could distinguish the cracking sounds of the AAR's Chinese CK-88 automatic rifles from the Israeli-manufactured Felo guns used by the South African Defence Forces. The Felo gun emitted a barking noise as it shotgunned swarms of deadly razor-sharp disks capable of severing an eight-inch tree trunk with one burst.

Machita realized the South Africans had crossed the border in a lightning raid to avenge Tazareen. "Damn you, Jumana!" he shouted in helpless rage. "You brought this upon us."

Bodies were dropping everywhere in frenzied contortions. So many littered the parade ground it was impossible to walk from one side to the other without stepping on torn flesh. A Defence Forces helicopter swooped over the main dormitory, where a company of men had taken cover. A bulky packet dropped from the aircraft's cargo door and landed on the roof. Seconds later the building fragmented in a thunderous explosion of brick and dust.

Still the South African ground forces had not shown their positions. They were wiping out the main core of the AAR without the slightest risk to themselves. Brilliant planning and execution had paid the whites rich dividends.

The green and brown of the helicopter's camouflage blurred into Machita's view for an instant, disappearing above the headquarters building housing his cell.

He braced his pain-wracked body against the inevitable explosion. The concussion was two, three times what he expected. The breath was pounded from his lungs as if by a jackhammer. Then the ceiling of his cell closed down on him and his tiny world went black.

"They're coming in now, sir," said a sergeant, saluting smartly.

Pieter De Vaal acknowledged the message with a methodical wave of his swagger stick. "Then I think we should extend them the courtesy of greeting, don't you?"

"Yes, sir." The sergeant opened the car door and stood aside as De Vaal unlimbered himself from the blackness of the backseat, meticulously straightened his tailored uniform, and began walking toward the grass landing pad.

They both stood there for a minute and screwed up their eyes as the bright glare of the helicopter's landing lights cut the evening darkness. Then the gust from the approaching rotor blades forced them to clamp their hands to their caps and turn away as small pebbles blown from the pad pelted their backs.

With perfect precision the Defence Forces copters hovered in sequence until all twelve were aligned. Then, on order from the squadron commander, they eased gracefully to the ground as one unit and the lights blinked out. Zeegler emerged from the lead craft and trotted over to De Vaal.

"How did it go?" the Defence Minister asked.

Zeegler's grin was barely visible in the darkness. "One

for the history books, Minister. An incredible exploit. There are no other words to describe it."

"Casualties?"

"Four wounded, none seriously."

"And the rebels?"

Zeegler paused for effect. "The body count tallied at twenty-three hundred and ten. At least another two hundred lie buried in the rubble of the destroyed buildings. No more than a handful could have escaped into the bush."

"Good God!" De Vaal was shocked. "Are you serious?"

"I checked the body count twice."

"In our wildest expectations we conceived no more than a few hundred rebel dead."

"A windfall," said Zeegler. "The camp was lined up for inspection. It was what the Americans would call a turkey shoot. Colonel Randolph Jumana was cut down by the first salvo."

"Jumana was an idiot," De Vaal snapped. "His days were numbered. Thomas Machita—there's the cagey one. Machita is the only bastard in the AAR who could fill Lusana's boots."

"We identified several officers on Lusana's staff, including Colonel Duc Phon Lo, his Vietnamese military adviser, but Machita's body did not turn up. I believe I'm safe in saying his remains are buried under tons of debris." Zeegler paused and stared De Vaal in the eyes. "In view of our success, Herr Minister, it might be wise to scratch Operation Wild Rose."

"Why not quit while we're ahead—is that it?"

Zeegler silently nodded.

"I am a pessimist, Colonel. It may take months, perhaps years, for the AAR to recover, but recover they will." De Vaal seemed to sink into a private reverie. Then he shook it off. "So long as South Africa lives under the threat of black rule, we have no option but to use any method available to survive. Wild Rose will take place as planned."

"I'll feel better when Lusana falls in our net."

De Vaal threw Zeegler an off-kilter grin. "You haven't heard?"

"Sir?"

"Hiram Lusana won't be coming back to Africa, ever."

Machita had no way of telling when he had recrossed the threshold of consciousness. He could see nothing but darkness. Then the pain began multiplying in his nerve endings and he groaned involuntarily. His ears recorded the sound, but nothing else registered.

He tried to raise his head and a yellowish ball appeared above and to his left. Slowly the strange object came into focus and formed a frame of reference. He was looking at a full moon.

He struggled to a sitting position with his back crammed against a cold, bare wall. In the light that sifted through the wreckage he could see that the floor above had dropped only two feet before becoming wedged between the narrow walls of his cell.

After a brief rest to collect his strength, Machita began pushing away the rubble. His hands discovered a short length of board and he used it to pry away the topside flooring until at last he forced an opening large enough to crawl through. Cautiously he peered over the edge into the chill night air. Nothing stirred. He bent his knees and shoved his body upward until his hands touched the grass of the parade ground. A sudden heave and he was free.

Machita took a deep breath and looked around. It was then that he saw the miracle of his salvation. The wall of the administration building facing the parade field had caved inward, collapsing the first floor, which had effectively shielded his cell from falling debris and the deadly wrath of the South Africans.

No one greeted Machita as he staggered to his feet, because there was no one in sight. The moon illuminated an eerie, barren landscape. Every facility, every building, had been leveled. The field was empty; the bodies of the dead were gone.

It was as though the African Army of Revolution had never existed.

45

"I wish I could help you, but I don't really see how."

Lee Raferty had been right, Pitt reflected. Orville Mapes did look more like a hardware peddler than a weapons dealer. Raferty was wrong on one count, though: Mapes was no longer a vice-president; he had moved up to president and chairman of the board of the Phalanx Arms Corporation. Pitt stared back into the gray eyes of the stubby little man.

"A check of your inventory records would be helpful."

"I do not open my records for a stranger who wanders in from the street. My customers would not look kindly upon a supplier who failed to keep their transactions confidential."

"The law requires you to list your arms sales with the Defense Department, so what's the big secret?"

"Are you with Defense, Mr. Pitt?" asked Mapes.

"Indirectly."

"Then whom do you represent?"

"Sorry, I can't say."

Mapes shook his head irritably and rose. "I'm a busy man. I have no time for games. You can find your own way out."

Pitt remained in his chair. "Sit down, Mr. Mapes . . . please."

Mapes found himself looking into a pair of green eyes that were as hard as jade. He hesitated, and considered challenging the command, then slowly did as he was asked.

Pitt nodded at the telephone. "So we both know where we stand, I suggest you call General Elmer Grosfield."

Mapes made a nettled face. "The Chief Inspector of Foreign Arms Shipments and I seldom see eye to eye."

"I take it he frowns on classified weapons being sold to unfriendly nations."

Mapes shrugged. "The general is a narrow-minded man." Mapes leaned back in his chair and stared speculatively at Pitt. "What, may I ask, is your connection with Grosfield?"

"Let's just say he respects my judgment more than he does yours."

"Do I detect a veiled threat, Mr. Pitt? If I don't play ball, you cry foul to Grosfield—is that it?"

"My request is simple," said Pitt. "A check of the whereabouts of the naval shells you bought from Lee Raferty in Colorado."

"I don't have to show you a damn thing, mister," Mapes replied stubbornly. "Not without a logical explanation or proper identification, or, for that matter, a court order."

"And if General Grosfield makes the request?"

"In that case I might be persuaded to string along."

Pitt nodded at the phone again. "I'll give you his private number . . ."

"I have it," Mapes said, fishing through a small box. He found the slotted index card he was looking for and held it up. "Not that I don't trust you, Mr. Pitt. But if you don't mind, I prefer using a number from my own file."

"Suit yourself," said Pitt.

Mapes lifted the receiver, inserted the card in the automatic-dialer phone, and pressed the code button. "It's after twelve o'clock," he said. "Grosfield is probably out to lunch."

Pitt shook his head. "The general is a brown-bagger. He eats at his desk."

"I always figured him for a cheapass," Mapes grunted.

Pitt smiled, hoping Mapes couldn't read the anxiety behind his eyes.

Abe Steiger rubbed the sweat from his palms on his pants legs and picked up the phone on the third ring, taking a bite from a banana before he spoke.

"General Grosfield here," he mumbled.

"General, this is Orville Mapes, of Phalanx Arms."

"Mapes, where are you? You sound like you're talking from the bottom of a barrel."

"You sound muffled and distant, too, General."

"You caught me in the middle of a peanut-butter sandwich. I like them thick with gobs of mayonnaise. What's on your mind, Mapes?"

"Sorry to interrupt your lunch, but do you know a Mr. Dirk Pitt?"

Steiger forced a pause and took a deep breath before answering. "Pitt. Yes, I know Pitt. He's an investigator for the Senate Armed Forces Committee."

"His credentials are right up there, then."

"They don't go any higher," said Steiger, as though talking with a mouthful. "Why do you ask?"

"He's sitting in front of me, demanding to inspect my inventory records."

"I wondered when he'd get around to you civilians." Steiger took another bite from the banana. "Pitt is heading up the Stanton probe."

"The Stanton probe? I never heard of it."

"I'm not surprised. They're not advertising. Some do-good senator got it in his head that stockpiles of nerve-gas weapons are hidden under the Army's carpet. So he launched a probe to find them." Steiger wolfed down the last of the banana and tossed the peel in one of General Grosfield's desk drawers. "Pitt and his investigators didn't turn up so much as a pellet. Now he's after you surplus boys."

"What do you suggest?"

"What I suggest," Steiger blurted, "is that you give the bastard what he wants. If you have any gas canisters stashed in your warehouses, give them to him and save yourself a carload of grief. The Stanton Committee is not out to prosecute anybody. They only want to make damned sure some Third World dictator doesn't lay his hands on the wrong kind of weapons."

"Thanks for the advice, General," Mapes said. Then, "Mayonnaise, you say? I prefer peanut butter with onions, myself."

"To each his own, Mr. Mapes. Good-bye."

Steiger hung up the phone and let out a deep, satisfied sigh. Then he wiped the receiver with his handkerchief and exited into the hall. He was just in the act of closing the door to the general's office when a captain in Army green walked around a corner. The captain's eyes grew mildly suspicious at the sight of Steiger.

"Excuse me, Colonel, but if you were looking for General Grosfield, he's out to lunch."

Steiger straightened and offered the captain his best "I outrank you" stare and said, "I don't know the general. This jungle of concrete threw my sense of direction out of balance. I'm looking for the Army Accident and Safety

Department. Got lost and poked my head in this office to ask directions."

The captain seemed noticeably relieved at avoiding an embarrassing situation. "Oh hell, I get lost ten times a day myself. You'll find Accident and Safety one floor down. Just take the elevator around the next corner to your right."

"Thank you, Captain."

"My pleasure, sir."

In the elevator Steiger smiled devilishly to himself as he wondered what General Grosfield would think when he found the banana peel in his desk.

Unlike most security guards who wear ill-fitting uniforms with waist belts sagged by heavy revolvers, Mapes's people looked more like fashionably attired combat troops as imagined by the editors of *Gentlemen's Quarterly* magazine. Two of them stood smartly at the gate to the Phalanx warehouse grounds in neatly tailored field fatigues with the latest in assault rifles slung over their shoulders.

Mapes slowed his Rolls-Royce convertible and lifted both hands from the steering wheel in an apparent greeting. The guard nodded and waved to his partner, who pulled open the gate from the inside.

"I assume that was a signal of some kind," said Pitt.

"Pardon?"

"The hands-in-the-air routine."

"Ah yes," Mapes said. "If you had been holding a concealed gun on me, my hands would have remained on the wheel. A normal gesture. Then, as we were waved through and your attention was lulled by the guard's opening the gate, his teammate would have discreetly stepped behind the car and blown your head off."

"I'm glad you remembered to raise your hands."

"You're most observant, Mr. Pitt," said Mapes. "However, you force me to issue a new signal to the gate guards."

"I'm crushed you don't trust me to keep your secret."

Mapes did not reply to Pitt's sarcasm. He kept his eyes on a narrow asphalt road that passed between seemingly endless rows of Quonset huts. After about a mile they came to an open field crammed with heavily armored tanks in various states of rust and disrepair. A small army of mechanics was busily crawling over ten of the massive vehicles that had been parked in formation beside the road.

"How many acres do you have?" Pitt asked.

"Five thousand," Mapes replied. "You're looking at the world's sixth-largest army in terms of equipment. Phalanx Arms also ranks seventh as an air force."

Mapes turned the car onto a dirt road that paralleled several bunkers set into a hillside, and stopped in front of one marked ARSENAL 6. He slid from behind the wheel and pulled a single key from his pocket, inserted it in a large brass lock, and pulled the catch free. Then he swung open a pair of steel doors and flipped on the light switch.

Inside the cavelike bunker, thousands of ammunition cases and crates containing a vast variety of shell sizes lay stacked in a tunnel that seemed to stretch into infinity. Pitt had never seen so much potential destruction heaped in one place.

Mapes motioned toward a golf cart. "No need to raise blisters walking. This storage area runs underground for nearly two miles."

The arsenal was cold and the hum from the electric cart seemed to hang in the damp air. Mapes turned into a side tunnel and slowed down. He held a map up to the light and studied it. "Beginning here and ending about a hundred yards down is the last store of sixteen-inch naval shells in the world. They're obsolete because only battleships can use them, and there is not a single operational battleship left. The gas shells I bought from Raferty should be stacked in an area near the middle."

"I see no sign of their canisters," said Pitt.

Mapes shrugged. "Business is business. Stainless-steel canisters are worth money. I sold them to a chemical company."

"Your supply seems endless. It might take hours to dig them out."

"No," replied Mapes. "The gas shells were assigned to Lot Six." He stepped from the cart and walked amid the sea of projectiles for about fifty paces and then pointed. "Yes, here they are." He carefully stepped through a narrow access and stopped.

Pitt remained in the main aisle, but even under the dull glow of the overhead lights he could detect a blank expression on Mapes's face.

"Problem?"

Mapes paused, shaking his head. "I don't understand it. I find only four. There should be eight."

Pitt stiffened. "They must be around somewhere."

"You start looking from the other end, beginning at Lot Thirty," Mapes ordered. "I'll go back to Lot One and began there."

After forty minutes they met in the middle. Mapes's eyes reflected a bewildered look. He held out his hands in a helpless gesture.

"Nothing."

"Dammit, Mapes!" Pitt shouted, his voice echoing off the concrete walls. "You must have sold them!"

"No!" he protested. "They were a bad buy. I miscalculated. Every government I pitched was afraid to be the first to use gas since Vietnam."

"Okay, four down, four to go," Pitt said, pulling his emotions back under control. "Where do we go from here?"

Mapes seemed to lose his train of thought for a moment. "The inventory . . . we'll check inventory records against sales."

Mapes used a call phone at the tunnel entrance to alert his office. When he and Pitt got back, the Phalanx Arms accountant had laid out the records on his desk. Mapes flipped through the ledgered pages swiftly. It took him less than ten minutes to find the answer.

"I was wrong," he said quietly.

Pitt remained silent, waiting, his hands clasped.

"The missing gas shells were sold."

Pitt was still silent, but there was murder in his eyes.

"A mistake," Mapes said thinly. "The arsenal crew took the shells from the wrong lot number. The original shipping order called for the removal of forty pieces of heavy naval ordnance from Lot Sixteen. I can only assume that the first digit, the one, did not emerge on the shipping crew's carbon copy, and they simply read it as Lot Six."

"I think it appropriate to say, Mapes, that you run a sloppy ship." Pitt's fingers bit into the flesh of his hands. "What name is on the purchase order?"

"I'm afraid there were three orders filled during the same month."

God, Pitt thought, why is it nothing ever comes easy? "I'll take a list of the buyers."

"I hope you appreciate my position," said Mapes. The clipped business tone was back. "If my customers got wind of the fact I disclosed their arms sales . . . I think you understand why this matter must remain confidential."

"Frankly, Mapes, I'd like to stuff you in one of your own cannons and pull the lanyard. Now give me that list before I yank the Attorney General and Congress down around your ears."

A faint pallor clouded Mapes's face. He took up a pen and wrote the names of the buyers on a pad. Then he tore off the paper and handed it to Pitt.

One shell had been ordered by the British Imperial War Museum, in London. Two had gone to the Veterans of Foreign Wars, Dayton City Post 9974, Oklahoma. The remaining thirty-seven were purchased by an agent representing the African Army of Revolution. No address was given.

Pitt slipped the paper into his pocket and rose to his feet. "I'll send a team of men to remove the other gas shells in the tunnel," he said coldly. He detested Mapes, detested everything the fat little death merchant stood for. Pitt couldn't bring himself to leave without one final shot.

"Mapes?"

"Yes?"

A thousand insults swirled in Pitt's mind, but he could not sort out any one in particular. Finally, as Mapes's expectant expression turned to puzzlement, Pitt spoke.

"How many men did your merchandise kill and maim last year, and the year before that?"

"I do not concern myself with what others do with my goods," Mapes said offhandedly.

"If one of those gas shells went off, you'd be responsible for perhaps millions of deaths."

"Millions, Mr. Pitt?" Mapes's eyes hardened. "To me the term is merely a statistic."

46

Steiger set the Spook F-140 jet fighter down lightly on the airstrip at Sheppard Air Force Base, outside Wichita Falls, Texas. After checking in with the flight-operations officer, he signed out a car from the base motor pool and drove north across the Red River into Oklahoma. He turned onto State Highway Fifty-three and pulled over to the side of the road; he felt a sudden urge to relieve himself. Though it was a few minutes past one in the afternoon, no car, no sign of life, was visible for miles.

Steiger could not remember seeing such flat and desolate farm country. The wind-swept landscape was barren except for a distant shed and an abandoned hay rake. It was a depressing sight. If someone had placed a gun in Steiger's hand, he'd have been tempted to shoot himself out of sheer melancholy. He zipped up his fly and returned to the car.

Soon a water tower appeared beside the arrow-straight road and grew larger through the windshield. Then a small town with precious few trees materialized and he passed a sign welcoming him to Dayton City, Queen City of the Wheat Belt. He pulled into a dingy old gas station that still sported glass tanks above its pumps.

An elderly man in mechanic's coveralls emerged from a grease pit and shuffled up to the passenger window. "Can I help ya?"

"I'm looking for VFW Post Ninety-nine seventy-four," said Steiger.

"If yer speakin' at the luncheon, yer late," admonished the old man.

"I'm here on other business," Steiger said, smiling.

The Oklahoman was unimpressed. He took an oily rag from his pocket and wiped his equally oily hands. "Go to the stop sign in the middle of town and turn left. Ya can't miss it."

Steiger followed the instructions and pulled into the gravel parking lot of a building strikingly modern compared to others in the town. Several cars were leaving the area, trailing clouds of red dust behind their bumpers. The luncheon was over, Steiger surmised. He entered and stood for a moment at the edge of a large room with a hardwood floor. The dishes on several tables still bore the wreckage of fried chicken. A group of three men noticed his presence and waved. A tall, gangly individual about fifty years of age and at least six feet five inches tall separated from the rest and sauntered over to Steiger. He had a ruddy face and short-clipped shiny hair parted down the middle. He offered his hand.

"Good afternoon, Colonel. What brings you to Dayton City?"

"I'm looking for the post commander, a Mr. Billy Lovell."

"I'm Billy Lovell. What can I do for you?"

"How do you do," said Steiger politely. "My name is Steiger, Abe Steiger. I've come from Washington on a rather urgent matter."

Lovell stared at Steiger, his eyes friendly but speculative. "You're putting me on, Colonel. I suppose you're going to tell me a top-secret Russian spy satellite came down in a field somewhere near town."

Steiger gave a casual tilt of his head. "Nothing that dramatic. I'm looking for a couple of naval shells your post purchased from Phalanx Arms."

"Oh, them two duds?"

"Duds?"

"Yeah, we were going to blow 'em up during the Veterans Day picnic. Set 'em on an old tractor and popped away all afternoon, but they didn't go off. We tried to get Phalanx to replace 'em." Lovell shook his head sadly. "They refused. Claimed all sales was final."

A chilling thought passed through Steiger's mind. "Perhaps they're not the self-detonating type of ordnance."

"Nope." Lovell shook his head. "Phalanx guaranteed they was live battleship shells."

"Do you still have them?"

"Sure, right outside. You passed 'em coming in."

Lovell led Steiger outside. The two shells bordered the entrance to the post. They were painted white, and welded to their sides were chains that stretched along the walkway.

Steiger sucked in his breath. The tips of the shells were

rounded. They were two of the missing gas shells. His knees suddenly turned to rubber, and he had to sit down on the steps. Lovell stared questioningly at Steiger's dazed expression.

"Somethin' wrong?"

"You shot at these things?" Steiger asked incredulously.

"Pumped close to a hundred rounds at 'em. Nicked the heads some, but that's all."

"It's a miracle . . ." Steiger murmured.

"A what?"

"Those are not explosive shells," Steiger explained. "They're gas shells. Their firing mechanisms will not self-activate until the parachutes are released. Your bullets had no effect because unlike ordinary explosive projectiles, they had not been preset to detonate."

"Whooee!" gasped Lovell. "You mean them things has poison gas in 'em?"

Steiger merely nodded.

"My Gawd, we might have wiped out half the county."

"And then some," Steiger muttered under his breath. He rose from the steps. "I'd like to borrow your john and a telephone, in that order."

"Sure, you come along. The john is down the hall to your left and there's a phone in my office." Lovell stopped and his eyes turned canny. "If we give you them shells . . . well, I was wonderin' . . ."

"I promise you and your post will receive ten sixteen-inch shells in prime explosive condition, enough to give your next Veterans Day picnic a super bang."

Lovell grinned from ear to ear. "You're on, Colonel."

In the rest room Steiger ran cold water over his face. The eyes that stared back in the mirror were red and tired, but they also radiated hope. He had successfully tracked down two of the Quick Death warheads. He could only pray that Pitt was as fortunate.

Steiger picked up the phone in Lovell's office and asked the operator to put through a collect long-distance call.

Pitt was asleep on a couch in his NUMA office when his secretary, Zerri Pochinsky, leaned over and gently shook him awake. Her long fawn-colored hair hung down, framing a face that was warm and pretty and full of merry admiration.

"You've got a visitor and two calls," she said in a soft Southern drawl.

Pitt pushed aside the cobwebs and sat up. "The calls?" he said.

"Congresswoman Smith," Zerri answered with a trace of acidity, "and Colonel Steiger on long distance."

"And the visitor?"

"Says his name is Sam Jackson. He doesn't have an appointment but he insists that it's important."

Pitt began to pull his sleep-fogged mind to even keel. "I'll take Steiger's call first. Tell Loren I'll call her back, and send in Jackson as soon as I'm off the phone."

Zerri nodded. "The colonel is on line three."

He walked unsteadily to the desk and punched one of the blinking buttons. "Abe?"

"Greetings from sunny Oklahoma."

"How'd it go?"

"Paydirt," said Steiger. "Scratch two warheads."

"Nice work," Pitt said, smiling for the first time in days. "Any problems?"

"None. I'll stand by until a crew arrives to pick them up."

"I've got a NUMA Catlin loaded with a forklift sitting at Dulles. Where can they set down?"

"One second."

Pitt could hear muffled voices as Steiger conversed with someone at the other end of the line.

"Okay," Steiger said. "The post commander says there is a small private airfield about eight hundred yards long a mile south of town."

"Twice what a Catlin requires," Pitt said.

"Any luck at your end?"

"The curator at the British Imperial War Museum said the shell they purchased from Phalanx for a World War Two naval exhibit is definitely armor piercing."

"Leaving the African Army of Revolution holding the other two QD warheads."

"Thereby hangs a tale," Pitt said.

"What earthly purpose are heavy naval shells in the African jungle?"

"Our riddle for the day," said Pitt, rubbing his reddened eyes. "At least we're temporarily blessed with the fact that they're no longer in our backyard."

"Where do we go from here?" asked Steiger. "We

can't very well tell a pack of terrorists they've got to give back the most horrendous weapon of all time."

"The first item on the agenda," said Pitt, "is to pinpoint the warheads. On that score Admiral Sandecker has persuaded an old Navy buddy at the National Security Agency to do some digging."

"Sounds touchy. Those guys are no dummies. They might ask some embarrassing questions."

"Not likely," said Pitt confidently. "The admiral came up with a classic cover story. I almost bought it myself."

47

It was a difficult choice. Dale Jarvis wavered between the Dutch apple pie and the calorie-laden lemon meringue. Throwing diet to the winds, he took both and set them on his tray along with a cup of tea. Then he paid the girl at the computer register and sat at a table along one wall of the spacious cafeteria in the NSA headquarters complex at Fort Meade, Maryland.

"One of these days you're going to bust your gut."

Jarvis paused and looked up into the solemn face of Jack Ravenfoot, head of the agency's domestic division. Ravenfoot was all muscle and bone, the only full-blooded Cheyenne in Washington who had a Phi Beta Kappa key from Yale and held the retired rank of commodore.

"I'd rather consume fattening, savory goodies than that salted buffalo jerky and boiled prairie gopher you call food."

Ravenfoot stared up at the ceiling. "Come to think of it, I haven't had prairie gopher—good prairie gopher, that is—since the victory celebration after Little Big Horn."

"You guys really know how to stick it to a paleface where it hurts," Jarvis said, grinning. "Pull up a chair."

Ravenfoot remained standing. "No thanks. I've got a meeting in five minutes. While I've got you, John Gossard, in the Africa Section, mentioned that you had a handle on some far-out project dealing with battleships."

Jarvis slowly chewed a piece of the apple pie. "Battleship, singular. What's on your mind?"

"An old friend from my Navy days, James Sandecker—"

"The director of NUMA?" Jarvis said, interrupting.

"The same. He asked me to track down a particular load of old sixteen-inch naval shells."

"And you thought of me."

"Battleships mounted sixteen-inch guns," said Ravenfoot. "I should know. I was executive officer aboard the *New Jersey* during the Vietnam orgy."

"Any idea what Sandecker wants them for?" asked Jarvis.

"He claims a team of his scientists want to drop them on Pacific coral formations."

Jarvis halted between bites. "He what?"

"They're conducting seismological tests. It seems armor-piercing shells dropped from a plane at two thousand feet on coral make a rumble nearly identical to an earthquake!"

"I should think ground explosives would achieve the same purpose."

Ravenfoot shrugged. "I can't argue the point. I'm no seismologist."

Jarvis dug into the lemon meringue. "I see nothing of interest to the evaluation section or, for that matter, a sinister design to the admiral's request. Where does Sandecker figure these special shells are stored?"

"The AAR has them."

Jarvis took a sip of his tea and patted his mouth with a napkin. "Why deal with the AAR when old naval ordnance can be picked up at most any surplus-arms dealer?"

"An experimental type developed near the end of the Korean war and never fired in anger. Sandecker says they work far better than the standard projectile." Ravenfoot leaned on the backrest of a chair. "I checked with Gossard on the AAR involvement. He thinks Sandecker is mistaken. The guerrillas need those shells like a high jumper needs gallstones—his exact words. It's his guess that the shells NUMA wants are rusting in a naval depot somewhere."

"And if the AAR actually possessed the shells, how would Sandecker deal with them?"

"Make them a trade, I suppose, or buy the shells at an inflated price. After all, it's only taxpayer money."

Jarvis sat back and poked his fork at the meringue. He wasn't hungry anymore. "I'd like to talk to Sandecker. Do you mind?"

"Be my guest. You'd probably do better working through his special-projects director, though. He's the guy who's heading up the search."

"What's his name?"

"Dirk Pitt."

"The fellow who raised the *Titanic* a few months back?"

"The same." Ravenfoot held up his wristwatch and noted the time. "I have to run along. If you get a lead on those shells, I'd appreciate a call. Jim Sandecker is an old friend. I still owe him a favor or two."

"Count on it."

Jarvis sat for several minutes after Ravenfoot left, poking his fork idly at the pie. Then he rose and walked back to his office, lost in thought.

Barbara Gore knew the instant her boss stepped through the door that his intuition was working overtime. She had seen that haunted look of deep concentration too many times not to recognize it. Without waiting to be asked, she picked up her pad and pencil and followed Jarvis into his private office. Then she sat down, crossed her magnificent legs, and waited patiently.

He stayed on his feet and stared at the wall. Then he turned slowly and his eyes came back in focus. "Call Gossard and set up a meeting with his Africa Section staff, and tell him I'd like another look at the Operation Wild Rose folder."

"You've changed your mind? There may be something to it after all?"

He didn't answer immediately. "Maybe, just maybe."

"Anything else?"

"Yes, ask the ID department to send up whatever they have on Admiral James Sandecker and a Dirk Pitt."

"Aren't they with NUMA?"

Jarvis nodded.

Barbara gave him a questioning look. "Surely you don't think there is a connection."

"Too early to tell," said Jarvis thoughtfully. "You might say that I'm picking up loose threads to see if they run to the same spool."

48

Frederick Daggat and Felicia Collins were waiting in the limousine when Loren came through the portico of the Capitol. They watched as she gracefully skipped down the steps, her cinnamon curls trailing in a light breeze. She wore a persimmon pantsuit with double-buttoned blazer and vest. A long gray silk scarf curled around her neck. Her briefcase was covered with the same material as the suit.

Daggat's chauffeur opened the door for her. She slipped beside Felicia as Daggat gallantly took one of the jump seats. "You look lovely, Loren," Daggat said familiarly—too familiarly. "It was obvious the minds of my male colleagues were elsewhere when you stood up on the House floor in that outfit."

"Being a woman has its advantages during debate," she said coolly. "You look stylish, Felicia."

A strange look flashed over Felicia's face. The last thing she expected from Loren was a compliment. She smoothed the skirt of her creamy white jersey dress and avoided Loren's eyes.

"It's good of you to see us," she said quietly.

"Did I have a choice?" Loren's face was a mask of resentment. "I'm afraid to ask what you demand of me this time."

Daggat raised the window behind the chauffeur. "The vote comes up tomorrow on whether or not to grant aid to the African Army of Revolution."

"So you two poked your heads above the slime to see if I was still in the fold," Loren said bitterly.

"You refuse to understand," said Felicia. "There is nothing personal in this. Frederick and I do not stand to gain financially. Our only reward is the advancement of our race."

Loren stared at her. "So you sink to blackmail to further your great moral cause."

"If it means saving countless thousands of lives, yes."
Daggat spoke as though he were lecturing a child. "Each
day the war continues brings a hundred deaths. The
blacks will eventually win in South Africa. A foregone
conclusion. It is the manner in which they win that is
important. Hiram Lusana is not a murderous psychopath
like Idi Amin was. He has assured me that when he becomes Prime Minister, the only major change he seeks is
equal rights for South Africa's black people. All democratic principles the present government was founded
upon will remain in effect."

"How can you be fool enough to accept the word of
a criminal?" asked Loren.

"Hiram Lusana grew up in one of the worst slums in
the nation," Daggat continued patiently. "His father deserted his mother and nine children when he was eight. I
don't expect you to understand what it's like to pimp for
your own sisters in order to put food on the table, Congresswoman Smith. I don't expect you even to imagine
living in a fifth-floor tenement with newspapers stuffed in
the cracks to keep out blowing snow, with overflowing
toilets because there is no water, with an army of rats
waiting to scavenge when the sun goes down. If crime is
your only means to exist, then you embrace it with open
arms. Yes, Lusana was a criminal. But when his opportunity came to rise above the filth, he snatched it and
turned his energies toward fighting the very circumstances
that cursed him."

"Then why play God in Africa?" Loren said defiantly.
"Why doesn't he fight to improve conditions for blacks
in his own country?"

"Because Hiram fervently believes our race must have
a firm base to rise from. The Jews look with pride toward Israel; you Anglo-Saxons have a rich British heri-
tage. Our homeland, on the other hand, is still struggling
to emerge from a primitive society. It's no secret the
blacks who have taken over most of Africa have made
an unholy mess of it. Hiram Lusana is our one hope to
steer the black race in the right direction. He is our Moses
and South Africa is our Promised Land."

"Aren't you overly optimistic?"

Daggat looked at her. "Optimistic?"

"According to the latest military reports from South

Africa, their Defence Forces crossed into Mozambique and destroyed the AAR and its headquarters."

"I read the same reports," said Daggat, "and nothing has changed. A temporary setback, perhaps; nothing more. Hiram Lusana is still alive. He will raise a new army, and I intend to do all in my power to aid him."

"Amen, brother," Felicia added.

The three of them were too wrapped up in their own thoughts to notice a car pulling in front of the limousine and then slowing down. At the next stoplight the driver swung the car to the curb and leaped out. Before Daggat's chauffeur could react, the man ran up to the limousine, jerked open the right rear door, and climbed in.

Daggat's mouth dropped open in surprise. Felicia froze, her mouth tensed. Only Loren seemed mildly puzzled.

"Who the hell are you?" Daggat demanded. Over the stranger's shoulder he saw the chauffeur reach into the glove compartment for a gun.

"How unobservant of you not to recognize me from my pictures," the man said, laughing.

Felicia tugged at Daggat's sleeve. "It's him," she whispered.

"Him who?" shouted Daggat, visibly upset.

"Pitt. My name is Dirk Pitt."

Loren looked at Pitt intently. She had not seen him for several days and she scarcely associated this man with the one who had made love to her. His eyes were ringed from lack of sleep and his chin was stubbled with beard. There were creases in his face she had never noticed before, creases of stress and exhaustion. She reached over and squeezed his hand.

"Where did you come from?" Loren asked.

"Coincidence," Pitt replied. "I was coming to see you and happened to be passing by the Capitol steps when I noticed you entering this car. As I drove alongside, I spotted Congressman Daggat in the back."

The chauffeur had lowered the window behind him and was holding a small revolver inches from the back of Pitt's head. Daggat relaxed noticeably. He felt in control again.

"Perhaps it's time we met, Mr. Pitt." He made a slight wave of his hand. The chauffeur nodded and lowered the gun.

"My very thoughts," said Pitt, smiling. "In fact, it saves me a trip to your office."

"You wanted to see me?"

"Yes, I've decided to order some reprints." Pitt produced a small stack of photographs and fanned them in one hand. "I've seen better results, of course. But then, these weren't exactly shot under ideal studio conditions."

Loren knotted one hand against her mouth. "You know about those awful pictures? I tried to keep you out of it."

"Let me see," Pitt said, as if Loren hadn't spoken. He began dropping the photographs in Daggat's lap one by one. "I'll take a dozen of these, and five of those—"

"I do not appreciate your pathetic attempt at humor," Daggat said, interrupting him.

Pitt gave him an innocent look. "I thought as long as you were in the dirty-picture-taking business, you wouldn't mind serving your clients—or should I say 'models.' Naturally, I expect a discount."

"What's your game, Mr. Pitt?" asked Felicia.

"Game?" Pitt looked amused. "There is no game."

"He can politically ruin your father and me," said Loren. "As long as he holds the negatives of the photographs, he can call the shots."

"Come now," Pitt said, smiling at her. "Congressman Daggat is about to retire from the blackmail profession. He has no talent for it anyway. He wouldn't last ten minutes against a tried and true professional."

"Like yourself?" said Daggat menacingly.

"No, like my father. I believe you know of him. Senator George Pitt. When I explained your little operation, he jokingly asked for a set of photos as a memento. You see, he's never seen his fair-haired boy in action before."

"You're insane," Felicia hissed.

"You told your father?" Daggat murmured. He looked slightly dazed. "I don't believe you."

"The moment of truth," Pitt said, the smile still tugging the corners of his mouth. "Does the name Sam Jackson ring a bell with you?"

Daggat sucked in his breath. "He talked. The bastard talked."

"Sang like a superstar. Hates your guts, by the way. Sam can't wait to testify against you at the House Ethics Committee hearing."

A trace of fear edged Daggat's voice. "You wouldn't dare expose those pictures to an investigation."

"What in hell have I got to lose?" Pitt said. "My father is getting ready to retire next year anyway. Take my case: once those photos are distributed, I'll probably have to beat half the secretaries in town off with a club."

"You egotistical pig," Felicia said. "You don't care about what happens to Loren."

"I care," Pitt said softly. "Being a woman, she'll suffer embarrassment, but that will be a small price to pay so our friend Daggat here can spend a few years making license plates in the slammer. When he gets paroled, he'll need a new vocation, since his party will want no part of him."

Daggat flushed and leaned threateningly toward Pitt. "Bullshit!" he raged.

Pitt fixed Daggat with a stare that would have frozen a shark. "Congress frowns on scum who pull gutter tactics to pass legislation. There was a time not too many years ago when your scheme might have worked, Congressman, but these days there are enough honest people on Capitol Hill who would boot your ass from the city limits if they got wind of this."

Daggat relaxed. He was beaten and he knew it. "What do you want me to do?"

"Destroy the negatives."

"That's all?"

Pitt nodded.

Daggat's face took on a leery expression. "No pound of flesh, Mr. Pitt?"

"We don't all swim in the same sewer, Congressman. I think Loren will agree it's best for all concerned to drop the whole affair." Pitt opened the door and helped Loren out. "Oh, one more thing: I have Sam Jackson's sworn statement of your dealings with him. I trust it will not be necessary to blow the whistle on further shakedowns by you and your girl friend. If I find you've crossed me, I'll come down hard on you, mister. That's a promise."

Pitt slammed the door and leaned in the chauffeur's window. "Okay, pal, move it."

The two of them stood and watched the limousine until it disappeared in the traffic. Then Loren stood on tiptoe and kissed Pitt's prickly cheek.

"What's that for?" he asked, grinning with pleasure.

"A reward for bailing me out of a nasty situation."

"Pitt to the rescue. I always was a pushover for congresswomen in distress." He kissed her on the lips, ignoring the curious stares of passersby. "And that's your reward for playing noble."

"Playing noble?"

"You should have told me about the photographs. I could have saved you many a sleepless night."

"I thought I could handle it," she said, avoiding his eyes. "Women should be able to stand alone."

He put his arm around her and led her to his car. "There are times when even a dedicated feminist needs a chauvinist to lean on."

As Loren slid into the passenger seat, Pitt noticed a small slip of paper under one of his windshield wipers. At first he thought it was only an advertising flyer and was about to throw it away, but curiosity won out and he glanced at it. The message was written in a precise hand.

DEAR MR. PITT,
I would be most grateful if you would call this number (555-5971) at your earliest convenience.
                              Thank you, DALE JARVIS

Instinctively Pitt looked up and down the crowded sidewalk, trying vainly to make the mysterious messenger. It was a hopeless chore. There were nearly eighty people within a hundred-yard radius; any one might have slipped the paper onto his car while he was confronting Daggat.

"Do you know a Dale Jarvis?" he asked Loren.

She thought a moment. "Can't say the name is familiar. Why?"

"It appears," Pitt said pensively, "that he left me a love note."

49

The chilly winter air seeped through the seams of the truck bed and stabbed Lusana's skin. He was lying on his stomach, his hands and legs tightly bound to his sides. The metal ribs of the floor jarred his head with every bump the stiffly sprung truck took from the road. Lusana's senses were hardly functioning. The hood over his head closed out all light and left him disoriented, and the loss of circulation had turned his body numb.

His last memory was of the smiling face of the flight captain in the first-class hospitality bar at the airport. The few lucid thoughts he had had since then ended on the same image.

"I'm Captain Mutaapo," the tall, slender pilot had said. He was a balding middle-aged black man, but his smile made his face youthful. He wore the dark-green uniform of BEZA-Mozambique Airlines, with an abundance of gold braid entwining the lower sleeves. "A representative from my government has requested me to ensure a safe and secure flight for you, Mr. Lusana."

"Precautions were necessary for entering the United States," Lusana had said, "but I seriously doubt I am in any danger on a departing flight surrounded by American tourists."

"Nonetheless, sir, you are my responsibility, as well as the one hundred and fifty other passengers. I must ask if you foresee any problems that may endanger lives."

"None, Captain, I assure you."

"Good." Mutaapo's teeth flashed. "Let's drink to a smooth and comfortable flight. What will be your pleasure, sir?"

"A martini, straight up with a twist, thank you."

Stupidity, Lusana thought as the truck rumbled over a railroad crossing. Too late it dawned on him that commercial-airline pilots cannot take alcohol twenty-four hours before a flight. Too late he realized that his drink

had been drugged. The bogus flight captain's smile seemed
frozen in time before it slowly clouded and dissolved into
nothingness.

Lusana could not measure the hours or the days. He
had no way of knowing that he was kept in a constant
state of stupor by frequent injections of a mild sedative.
Unfamiliar faces appeared and reappeared as the hood
was temporarily removed, their features floating in an
ethereal haze before blackness closed in once more.

The truck braked to a halt and he heard muffled
voices. Then the driver shifted gears and moved forward,
stopping again in less than a mile.

Lusana heard the rear doors open and he felt two
pairs of hands pick him up roughly and carry his numbed
body up some kind of ramp. Strange sounds came out of
the darkness. The blast of a distant air horn. Metallic
clanging, as though steel doors were being opened and
slammed shut. He also detected the smells of fresh paint
and oil.

He was unceremoniously dumped on another hard
floor and left there as his bearers faded out of earshot.
The next thing he sensed was the rope's being cut from
his body. Then the hood was removed. The only light
came from a small incandescent red bulb on one wall.

For nearly a full minute Lusana lay there motionless
while the circulation slowly awakened his agonized limbs.
He screwed up his eyes and squinted. It appeared to him
that he was on the bridge of a ship. The red glow from
above revealed a helm and large console dotted with
multicolored lights that reflected off a long row of square
windows embedded in three of four gray walls.

Above Lusana, still holding the hood in his hand, was
a huge mass of a man. Looking like a distorted giant, from
Lusana's prone position on the deck, the man stared down
from a kindly face and smiled. Lusana was not taken in.
He well knew that most hardened killers flashed angelic
expressions before slitting their victims' throats. And yet
the face on this man seemed strangely innocent of bloodthirsty intent. Instead, he exuded a detached sort of curiosity.

"You are Hiram Lusana." The deep bass voice echoed
against the steel bulkheads.

"I am," Lusana answered hoarsely. His voice sounded
odd to him. He had not used it in nearly four days.

"You don't know how much I've looked forward to meeting you," the giant said.

"Who are you?"

"Does the name Fawkes mean anything to you?"

"Should it?" Lusana said, determined to resist.

"Aye, it's a terrible thing when you forget the names of the people you've murdered."

A realization mushroomed within Lusana. "Fawkes . . . the raid on the Fawkes farm, in Natal."

"My wife and children cut down. My house burned. You even slaughtered my workers. Whole families with the same skin as yours."

"Fawkes . . . you're Fawkes," Lusana repeated, his drugged mind fighting to grasp a bearing.

"I'm satisfied the filthy business was done by the AAR," said Fawkes, a subtle hardening in his voice. "They were your men; you gave the orders."

"I was not responsible." The fog was lifting from Lusana's head and he was coming back on balance, inwardly at least. His arms and legs would not respond to command. "I'm sorry for what happened to your family. A tragic bloodletting that had no rhyme or reason. But you will have to look elsewhere to place the blame. My men were innocent."

"Aye, a denial was to be expected."

"What do you intend to do with me?" Lusana asked, his eyes without fear.

Fawkes looked out the bridge windows. It was pitch dark outside and a light mist coated the glass. There was a strange kind of sadness in his eyes.

He turned to Lusana. "We're going to take a little trip, you and I, a trip with no return ticket."

50

The taxi passed through a back gate of the Washington National Airport at precisely nine thirty P.M. and dropped Jarvis behind a solitary hangar that sat on a seldom-used end of the field. Except for a faint glow of light through the dusty glass of a side door, the giant building seemed bleak and cavernous. He pushed open the door and was mildly surprised not to hear it creak. The well-oiled hinges pivoted without a whisper.

The yawning interior was brilliantly illuminated by overhead fluorescent lighting. A venerable old Ford tri-motor aircraft sat like a huge goose in the center of the concrete floor, its wings protectively reaching out over several antique automobiles in various stages of restoration. Jarvis walked over to a car that seemed no more than a pile of rusted iron. A pair of feet protruded from beneath the radiator.

"You are Mr. Pitt?" Jarvis inquired.

"And you are Mr. Jarvis?"

"Yes."

Pitt rolled from under the car and sat up. "I see you found my humble abode all right."

Jarvis hesitated, taking in Pitt's greasy coveralls and disheveled appearance. "You live here?"

"I have an apartment upstairs," Pitt said, pointing to a glass-enclosed level above the hangar floor.

"You have a nice collection," said Jarvis, gesturing at the relics. "What is the one over there with the black fenders and silver coach work?"

"A 1936 Maybach-Zeppelin town car," Pitt answered.

"And the one you're working on?"

"A 1912 Renault open-drive landaulette."

"Seems a bit the worse for wear," said Jarvis, wiping a finger through a layer of rust.

Pitt smiled patiently. "She doesn't really look all that

253

bad when you consider she's been immersed in the sea for seventy years."

Jarvis understood immediately. "From the *Titanic?*"

"Yes. I was allowed to keep her after the salvage project. Sort of a prize for services rendered, so to speak."

Pitt led the way up a flight of stairs to his apartment. Jarvis entered and his professional eye routinely traveled over the unusual furnishings. The occupant was a well-traveled man, he surmised, judging from the nautical objects decorating the interior. Copper divers' helmets from another age. Mariners' compasses, wooden helms, ships' bells, even old nails and bottles, all neatly labeled with the names of famous ships from which Pitt had salvaged them. It was like looking into a museum of a man's life.

Jarvis sank into a leather sofa at Pitt's invitation. He looked his host directly in the eyes. "Do you know me, Mr. Pitt?"

"No."

"Yet you had no qualms about seeing me."

"Who can resist intrigue?" Pitt said, grinning. "It's not every day I find a note on my windshield with a phone number that turns out to be the National Security Agency."

"You guessed, of course, that you were being followed."

Pitt reclined in a leather chair and propped his feet on an ottoman. "Let's sack the wordplay, Mr. Jarvis, and get to the point. What's your sport?"

"Sport?"

"Your interest in me."

"Okay, Mr. Pitt," said Jarvis. "Cards on the table. What is the real purpose behind NUMA's search for a special type of heavy naval shell?"

"Sure you wouldn't like a drink?" Pitt countered.

"No thanks," Jarvis answered, appraising Pitt's casual stall.

"If you know we're in the market, then you know why."

"Seismological tests on coral formations?"

Pitt nodded.

Jarvis stretched his arms out on the sofa's backrest. "When do you have the tests scheduled?"

"The last two weeks of March next year."

"I see." Jarvis gave Pitt a benign, fatherly look and then lunged for the heart. "I've talked to four seismologists, two from your own agency. They do not subscribe to your idea of dropping sixteen-inch naval shells from an airplane. In fact, they found it downright ludicrous. I was also informed that there are no seismographic tests scheduled by NUMA in the Pacific. In short, Mr. Pitt, your clever little dodge won't hold water."

Pitt closed his eyes in thought. He could lie, or simply offer no comment. No, he reasoned, his alternatives had narrowed down to zero. There was virtually no hope that he and Steiger and Sandecker could negotiate a quick return of the QD warheads from the AAR. They had carried the search as far as their limited resources could take them. The time had come, he decided, to call in the professionals.

He opened his eyes and stared at Jarvis. "If it were within my power to place in the palm of your hand a plague organism that could kill without interruption for three hundred years, what would you do with it?"

Pitt's question caught Jarvis off guard. "I don't know what you're driving at."

"The question stands," said Pitt.

"Is it a weapon?"

Pitt nodded.

An uneasy feeling gripped Jarvis. "I know of no such weapon. Chemical and biological arms were effectively and unconditionally banned by every member of the United Nations ten years ago."

"Please answer the question," Pitt said.

"Turn it over to our government, I suppose."

"Are you certain that's the correct course?"

"Good God, man, what do you want? The case is purely hypothetical."

"Such a weapon must be destroyed," said Pitt. His green eyes seemed to burn into the back of Jarvis's brain.

There was a short silence. Then Jarvis said, "Does one truly exist?"

"It does."

The pieces were falling into place, and for the first time in all the years he could remember, Jarvis wished he hadn't been so damned efficient. He looked at Pitt and smiled thinly.

"I'll have that drink now," he said quietly. "And then I think you and I should exchange some very disturbing news."

It was past midnight when Phil Sawyer stopped the car in front of Loren's apartment building. He was what most women thought a handsome man, with a solid face and a neatly styled mass of prematurely gray hair.

Loren flashed a provocative expression at him. "Would you like to open my apartment door for me? The lock always seems to stick."

He smiled. "How can I refuse?"

They got out of the car and strolled through the garden entrance in silence. The sidewalk was wet and reflected the glow from the streetlights. Loren nestled against his body as the cold drizzle attacked their hair and clothes. The doorman greeted them and held the elevator open. At her door she fished in her purse and handed Sawyer the key. He turned the lock and they entered.

"Fix yourself a drink," she said, shaking out her damp hair. "I'll be back in a minute."

Loren slipped into the bedroom and Sawyer went over to a small portable bar and poured himself a cognac. He was on his second when Loren came back into the room. She was wearing pajamas with a silvery-gray wrap top and pants that were lace edged. As she came through the doorway, the light from the bedroom silhouetted her lithe figure through the vaporous nylon. The combination of the pajamas, her cinnamon hair, and her violet eyes suddenly made Sawyer feel like a confused adolescent.

"You look ravishing," he managed to say.

"Thank you." She poured a Galliano for herself and sat down next to him on the couch. "It was a lovely dinner, Phil."

"My pleasure."

She moved closer and lightly caressed his hand. "You seem different tonight. I've never known you to be so relaxed. Not once did you mention the President."

"Six weeks and three days from now the new President-elect takes the oath and my eight-year battle with the gentlemen and ladies of the news media comes to an end. God, I never thought I would feel good about being part of a lame-duck administration."

"What are your plans after the inauguration?"

"My boss has the right idea. As soon as he turns over the reins of office, he's sailing a forty-foot ketch to the South Pacific, where he says he's going to drink and screw himself to death." Sawyer lowered his glass and stared into Loren's eyes. "Now, me, I prefer the Caribbean, particularly for a honeymoon."

An edge of anticipation began to form inside Loren. "Anyone special in mind?"

Sawyer set down their glasses and took Loren's hands in his. "Congresswoman Smith," he said with mock seriousness. "I respectfully implore you to cast your vote in favor of marriage to Phil Sawyer."

Loren's eyes grew somber and thoughtful. Though she'd been sure this moment would eventually come, she was still uncertain of her answer. Sawyer misread Loren's hesitancy.

"I know what's going through your mind," he said gently. "You're wondering what life would be like with an unemployed presidential press secretary, right? Well, rest your fears. I have it on good authority the party leaders want me to run for senator from my home state in the next election."

"In that case," she said resolutely, "the ayes have it."

Sawyer did not see the uneasiness in Loren's eyes. He took her head in his hands and gently kissed her on the lips. The room seemed to blur and the female scent that emanated from her body closed over him. He felt strangely at peace as he buried his face in her breasts.

Afterward, when Sawyer lay spent and asleep, Loren's tears stained the pillow. She had tried desperately, with all her soul. She had loved hard; even forcing the expected animal sounds from her throat. But nothing worked. Throughout their violent lovemaking she found herself comparing Sawyer to Pitt. There was no way of logically explaining the difference. They both felt the same inside her, and yet Pitt turned her into a savage, demanding animal, whereas Sawyer left her empty and unfulfilled.

She pressed the pillow against her face to muffle the sobs. "Damn you, Dirk Pitt," she said silently. "Damn you to hell!"

"I'm not sure whose story comes off the craziest," Pitt said, "yours or mine."

Jarvis shrugged. Who can say. The horror is that it's

just possible your Quick Death warheads and my Operation Wild Rose might prove a match."

"An attack on a major coastal city with a battleship by South African blacks posing as terrorists of the AAR. It's lunacy."

"Wrong," said Jarvis. "The plan smacks of genius. A few bombs placed here or there, or another skyjacking, would hardly move an entire nation to see red. But an old battleship with flags flying, raining explosives on a helpless population, that's sensationalism at its best."

"What city?"

"None was specified. That part of the plan remains a mystery."

"Fortunately, the prime ingredient is missing."

"A battleship," Jarvis said.

"You said they've all been removed from active status."

"The last one was sold for scrap months ago. All the rest are nonoperational memorials."

Pitt stared off into space for a moment. "I recall seeing a capital ship docked on an inlet in Chesapeake Bay only a few weeks ago."

"More than likely a heavy-missile cruiser," said Jarvis.

"No, I'm certain it had three massive gun turrets," Pitt said firmly. "I was on a flight to Savannah and the plane flew right over it before turning south."

Jarvis remained unconvinced. "I have no reason to doubt the accuracy of my information; however, in the interest of security, I'll have your sighting checked out."

"There is something else," Pitt said, rising from the chair and searching a row of encyclopedias on a bookshelf. He pulled out a black-bound volume and flipped the pages.

"Did you trigger another memory?" asked Jarvis.

"Operation Wild Rose," answered Pitt.

"What about it?"

"The name. Can it stand for anything?"

"Code names seldom have an ulterior meaning," said Jarvis. "It might give them away."

"I'll bet you a vintage bottle of wine this one does."

Pitt held out the book. The pages were open at a map. Jarvis slipped on his reading glasses and took a cursory glance at it.

"All right, so Iowa is the Hawkeye State. So what?"

Pitt pointed to a spot halfway down the right-hand

page. "The state flower of Iowa," he said softly, "is the wild rose."

The color abruptly washed from Jarvis's face. "But the battleship *Iowa* was scrapped."

"Scraped, or *sold* for scrap?" said Pitt. "There is a big difference."

A series of worry lines grew on Jarvis's forehead.

Pitt looked at Jarvis and let the worry lengthen. "If I were you, I'd run a check on all shipyards located on the western Chesapeake shoreline of Maryland."

"Your phone." It was more a command than a request.

Pitt silently pointed to one on an end table.

Jarvis dialed a number. Then, as he waited for an answer, he looked at Pitt. "Do you have a car that isn't an antique?"

"I have a NUMA car parked outside."

"I came in a taxi," said Jarvis. "Will you do the honors?"

"Give me a minute to clean up," Pitt replied.

When Pitt emerged from the bathroom, Jarvis was waiting at the door. "You were right," he said evenly. "As of yesterday, the battleship *Iowa* was docked at the Forbes Marine Scrap and Salvage Yard, in Maryland."

"I know the facility," said Pitt. "It's a few miles below the bay entrance to the Patuxent River."

51

As Pitt drove through the rain, Jarvis seemed mesmerized by the flailing windshield wipers. Finally his eyes focused and he made a casual gesture at the road ahead. "I make the next town to be Lexington Park."

"Another four miles," Pitt said without turning.

"There is an all-night gas station on the outskirts," Jarvis continued. "Pull up at the pay phone."

Minutes later the headlights picked out the Lexington Park city-limits sign. In less than a mile, around a sweeping curve, a brightly lit service station beckoned through the soggy night. Pitt turned in the driveway and parked beside an outside phone booth.

The station attendant sat warm and dry inside the office, his feet propped up on an old oil-burning stove. He put down his magazine and for two or three minutes watched Pitt and Jarvis suspiciously through water-streaked windows. Then, satisfied they weren't acting like holdup men, he returned to his reading. The pay phone's light blinked out and Jarvis hurriedly ducked back into the passenger seat.

"Any late word?" Pitt asked.

Jarvis nodded. "My staff has uncovered a piece of discouraging information."

"Bad news and dismal weather go hand in hand," Pitt said.

"The *Iowa* was stricken from Navy rolls and auctioned as surplus. The winning bidder was an outfit called the Walvis Bay Investment Corporation."

"I've never heard of it."

"The corporation is a financial front for the African Army of Revolution."

Pitt gave a slight twist of the wheel to avoid a deep puddle in the road. "Is it possible Lusana pulled the rug from under the South African Defence Ministry's pipe dreams by outbidding them for the ship?"

"I doubt it." Jarvis shivered from the damp cold and held his hands over the dashboard's defroster vents. "I'm convinced the South African Defence Ministry bought the *Iowa*, handling the transaction under the guise of Walvis Bay Investment."

"You don't think Lusana is wise?"

"He has no way of knowing," said Jarvis. "It's common policy to keep the bidders' names confidential upon request."

"Christ," Pitt muttered, "the sale of the warheads by Phalanx Arms to the AAR . . ."

"With a little more digging," Jarvis said, his voice strained, "I'm afraid we'll find that Lusana and the AAR had nothing to do with that deal either."

"That's the Forbes shipyard dead ahead," Pitt said.

The high chain-link fence enclosing the shipyard met and began paralleling the road. At the main gate Pitt braked to a stop in front of a cable that stretched across the entrance. Nothing of the ship could be seen through the falling rain. Even the huge derricks were lost in the blackness. The guard was at Pitt's door almost before he rolled the window down.

"May I help you, gentlemen?" he asked courteously.

Jarvis leaned across Pitt and displayed his credentials. "We'd like to confirm the *Iowa*'s presence in the shipyard."

"You can take it from me, sir, she's down at the dock. Been there refitting close to six months."

Pitt and Jarvis exchanged worried looks at the word "refitting."

"My orders are to admit no one without a pass or proper authority from company officials," the guard continued. "I'm afraid you'll have to wait until morning to take a tour of the ship."

Jarvis's face flushed with anger. But before he could launch an official tirade, another car pulled up and a man wearing a dinner jacket emerged.

"Problems, O'Shea?" he said.

"These gentlemen want to enter the yard," answered the guard, "but they don't have passes."

Jarvis swung out of the car and met the stranger halfway. "My name is Jarvis, director of the National Security Agency. My friend is Dirk Pitt; he's with NUMA. It's a matter of highest priority that we inspect the *Iowa*."

"At three o'clock in the morning?" muttered the confused man, studying Jarvis's identification under the floodlights. Then he turned to the guard.

"They're okay; let them through." He faced Jarvis again. "The way to the dock is a bit tricky. I'd better come along. By the way, I'm Metz, Lou Metz, superintendent of the shipyard."

Metz went back to his car and said something to a woman sitting on the passenger side. "My wife," he explained, hunching into Pitt's backseat. "Tonight is our anniversary. We were on our way home from celebrating and I happened to drop by the yard to pick up some blueprints."

O'Shea unhooked the barrier cable and dropped it to the wet ground. He motioned to Pitt to hold while he leaned in the window. "If you see that bus driver, Mr. Metz, ask him what's delaying his departure."

Metz looked puzzled. "Bus driver?"

"Came through about seven o'clock this evening carrying a load of about seventy black guys. They were headed for the *Iowa*."

"You let them through?" Metz asked incredulously.

"They all had proper passes, including the driver of the truck, who followed them in."

"Fawkes!" Metz snapped angrily. "What's that crazy Scott up to now?"

Pitt shifted into drive and steered the car into the yard. "Who's Fawkes?" he asked.

"Captain Patrick McKenzie Fawkes," Metz said. "Royal Navy retired. He made no secret of the fact that some black terrorist bunch hired him to refit the ship. The man is nuttier than a cashew factory."

Jarvis turned and faced Metz. "How so?"

"Fawkes has driven me and my crew up the bulkheads giving the entire vessel a major face-lift. He's made us strip her down next to nothing and replace half the superstructure with wood."

"The *Iowa* was never designed to float like a cork," said Pitt. "If her buoyancy and gravity centers are drastically altered, she could capsize in a heavy storm."

"Tell me about it," Metz grunted. "I've argued with that stubborn bastard for months. I might as well have farted at a hurricane for all the good it did me. He even demanded we remove two perfectly good General Elec-

tric geared turbine engines and seal their shafts." He
paused and tapped Pitt on the shoulder. "Turn right at the
next pile of steel plating and then swing a left at the
derrick's rail tracks."

The temperature had dropped and the rain was becoming an icy sheet. Two large boxlike shadows materialized
under the headlights. "The bus and truck," announced
Pitt. He parked the car but left the motor running and
the lights on.

"No sign of the drivers," said Jarvis.

Pitt took a flashlight from the car's door pocket and
got out. Jarvis followed, but Metz hurried off into the
night without saying a word. Pitt aimed the beam
through the bus windows and into the back of the truck.
They were both empty.

Pitt and Jarvis skirted the deserted vehicles and found
Metz standing stock still, hands clenched at his sides. His
evening jacket was soaked and his hair plastered to his
scalp. He looked like a resurrected drowning victim.

"The *Iowa?*" Jarvis asked.

Metz spastically waved his arms at the dark. "Shagged
ass."

"Shagged . . . what?"

"That damned Scot has sailed her away!"

"Jesus, are you sure?"

Metz's face and his voice were alive with a desperate
kind of urgency. "I don't misplace battleships. This is
where she's been moored during the refit." Suddenly he
spotted something and ran over to the edge of the dock.
"My God, look at that! The mooring lines are still tied
to the dock bollards. The crazy idiots cast off their lines
from the ship. It's as though they never intend to moor
her again."

Jarvis leaned over and stared down at where the heavy
lines disappeared into the inky water. "My fault. Criminal
negligence not to have believed the handwriting on the
wall."

"We still can't be certain they're actually going through
with an attack," Pitt said.

Jarvis shook his head. "They're going to do it; you can
count on that." Tiredly, he rested his weight against a
piling. "If only they'd given us a date and a target."

"The date was there all the time," said Pitt.

Jarvis looked at him questioningly and waited.

"You said the idea behind the attack was to motivate sympathy for the South African whites and provoke American anger against the black revolutionaries," Pitt continued. "What more perfect day than today?"

"It is now five minutes past twelve on Wednesday morning." Jarvis's voice was tense. "I make nothing eventful out of that."

"The originators of Operation Wild Rose have a superb sense of timing," said Pitt in a dry, ironic tone. "Today is also December the seventh, the anniversary of Pearl Harbor."

"You said the idea behind the attack was to provide
equality for the Sigma Alphas," Stinger said, and provoke
Ainsidian anger against the black resurrectionists," Bill
continued. "What more perfect day than today?"

"It's now five minutes past twelve on Wednesday
morning," Harris voice was tense. "Eight minutes into a fateful one of that.

"It's beginning," of Operation Wild Rose. "Two aspects
sense of Junina," said Bill in a dry, weak tone. "Today is
also December the twenty, the anniversary of Pearl Harbor.

5

THE IOWA

52

Pretoria, South Africa—
December 7, 1988

Pieter De Vaal sat alone and read a book in his office at the Defence Ministry. It was early evening and the summer light filtered through the arched windows. A soft rap came at the door.

De Vaal spoke without looking up from his reading. "Yes?"

Zeegler entered. "We've been alerted that Fawkes has launched the operation."

De Vaal's face showed no trace of interest as he laid aside the book and handed Zeegler a piece of paper. "See that the communications officer on duty personally sends this message to the American State Department."

It is my duty to warn your government of an impending attack on your shore by African Army of Revolution terrorists under the command of Captain Patrick Fawkes, Royal Navy retired. I deeply regret any inadvertent rôle my cabinet has played in this grave infamy.

ERIC KOERTSMANN
Prime Minister

"You have admitted guilt in the name of our Prime Minister, who is totally ignorant of Operation Wild Rose," said an astonished Zeegler. "May I ask why?"

De Vaal clasped his hands in front of him and peered at Zeegler. "I see no reason to discuss the details."

269

"Then may I ask why you have thrown Fawkes to the wolves?"

The Minister went back to his book with a dismissive gesture. "See to it that the message is sent. Your questions will be answered at the appropriate moment."

"We promised Fawkes to attempt his rescue," Zeegler persisted.

De Vaal sighed with impatience. "Fawkes knew he was a dead man the instant he accepted command of the raid."

"If he survives and talks to the American authorities, his confession would prove disastrous to our government."

"Rest easy, Colonel," De Vaal said with a crooked smile. "Fawkes will not live to talk."

"You seem quite certain, Minister."

"I am," De Vaal said calmly. "I am indeed."

Deep inside the bowels of the *Iowa* a figure dressed in greasy coveralls and a heavy wool jacket stepped from a passageway into what had been the ship's sick bay. He closed the door behind him and was enveloped in a smothering blackness. He aimed the flashlight and played its beam about the gutted room. Several of the bulkheads had been cut away and it seemed as though he was standing in an immense cavern.

Satisfied he was quite alone, he knelt on the deck and removed a small gun from inside his jacket. Then he attached a silencer to the end of the barrel and inserted a twenty-shot clip into the handgrip.

He pointed the 27.5 Hocker-Rodine automatic into the darkness and squeezed the trigger. An almost indistinguishable *piff* was followed by two faint thuds as the bullet ricocheted off unseen bulkheads.

Pleased with the results, he taped the gun to his right calf. After a few steps to make sure it was comfortably snug, Emma switched off the flashlight, slipped back into the passageway, and made his way toward the ship's engine room.

53

Carl Swedborg, skipper of the fishing trawler *Molly Bender*, rapped the barometer with his knuckles, regarded it stoically for a moment, then walked over to the chart table and picked up a cup of coffee. His mind visualizing the river ahead, he sipped at the coffee and gazed at the ice that was building on the deck. He hated miserable wet nights. The dampness seeped into his seventy-year-old bones and tortured his joints. He should have retired a decade past, but with his wife gone and his children scattered around the country, Swedborg could not bear to sit around an empty house. As long as he could find a berth as skipper he would stay on water until they buried him in it.

"At least visibility is a quarter of a mile," he said absently.

"I've seen worse, much worse." This from Brian Donegal, a tall, shaggy-haired Irish immigrant who stood at the helm. "Better we have rotten weather going out than coming in."

"Agreed," said Swedborg dryly. He shivered and buttoned the top button of his mackinaw. "Mind your helm and keep wide aport of the Ragged Point channel buoy."

"Don't you fret, Skipper. Me faithful Belfast nose can sniff channel markers like a bloodhound, it can."

Donegal's blarney seldom failed to raise a smile from Swedborg. The skipper's lips involuntarily curled upward and he spoke in a stern tone that was patently fake. "I prefer you use your eyes."

The *Molly Bender* swung around Ragged Point and continued her course downriver, passing an occasional lighted channel buoy that came and went like a street-light beside a rain-soaked boulevard intersection. The shore lights glowed dully through the thickening sleet.

"Somebody coming up the channel," announced Donegal.

Swedborg picked up a pair of binoculars and looked beyond the bows. "The lead ship carries three white lights. That means a tug with her tow astern. Too murky to distinguish her outline. Must be a long tow, though. I make out the two white thirty-two-point lights on the last vessel in line about three hundred yards astern the tug."

"We're on a collision course, Skipper. Her mast lights are in line with our bow."

"What is the bastard doing on our side of the river?" Swedborg wondered out loud. "Doesn't the damn fool know that two boats approaching each other should keep to their starboard side of the channel? He's hogging our lane."

"We can maneuver easier than he can," said Donegal. "Better we alert him and pass starboard to starboard."

"All right, Donegal. Swing to port and give two blasts of the whistle to signal our intentions."

There was no answering blast. The strange tug's lights, it seemed to Swedborg, were approaching far more rapidly than he had any right to expect, far more rapidly than any tug he'd ever seen with a fleet of barges in tow. He was horrified as he watched the other vessel turn toward the *Molly Bender*'s altered course.

"Give the fool four short whistle blasts!" Swedborg shouted.

It was the Inland Waterway danger signal—sounded when the course of an opposing vessel or its intentions were not understood. Two of Swedborg's crew, roused from sleep by the whistle shrieks, groggily entered the wheelhouse, instantly snapped to sudden astonishment by the nearness of the strange vessel's running lights. Clearly, she wasn't acting like a tug in tow.

In the few remaining seconds Swedborg snatched a bullhorn and shouted into the night. "Ahoy! Turn hard aport!"

He might as well have shouted at a ghost. No voice replied; no return whistle blast came through the icy dark. The lights bore down relentlessly upon the helpless *Molly Bender*.

Realizing collision was inevitable, Swedborg braced himself by clutching the lower frame of the window. Fighting to the last, Donegal frantically reversed engines and twisted the wheel back to starboard.

The last thing any of them saw was a monstrous gray bow looming through the sleet high above the wheelhouse, a massive steel wedge bearing the numeral 61.

Then the little fishing trawler was crushed to pieces and swallowed by the icy water of the river.

Pitt stopped the car in front of the White House gate. Jarvis was halfway out when he turned and looked back at Pitt. "Thank you for your assistance," he said sincerely.

"What now?" asked Pitt.

"I have the distasteful duty of booting the President and the Joint Chiefs of Staff out of their beds," Jarvis said with a tired smile.

"What can I do to help?"

"Nothing. You've done more than your share. It's up to the Defense Department to carry the ball from here."

"The Quick Death warheads," said Pitt. "Do I have your assurance they will be destroyed when the ship is located and taken into custody?"

"I can only try. Beyond that, I promise nothing."

"That's not good enough," said Pitt.

Jarvis was too tired to argue. He shrugged listlessly, as though he no longer gave a damn. "Sorry, but that's the way it is." Then he slammed the door, showed his pass to the guard at the gate, and was gone.

Pitt turned the car around and swung onto Vermont Avenue. A couple of miles on he spotted an all-night coffee shop and slipped into a parking stall. After ordering a cup of coffee from a yawning waitress, he found the pay phone and made two calls. Then he downed the coffee, paid, and left.

54

Heidi Milligan met Pitt when he entered Bethesda Naval Hospital. Her blond hair was half hidden under a scarf, and despite the weariness around her eyes, she looked vibrant and strangely youthful.

"How is Admiral Bass?" Pitt asked her.

She gave him a strained look. "Walt is hanging in there. He's tough; he'll pull through."

Pitt didn't believe a word of it. Heidi was clinging to a slowly parting thread of hope and putting up a valiant front. He put his arm around her waist and led her gently down the corridor.

"Can he talk to me?"

She nodded. "The doctors aren't keen on the idea, but Walt insisted after I gave him your message."

"I wouldn't have intruded if it wasn't important," Pitt said.

She looked up into his eyes. "I understand."

They came to the door and Heidi opened it. She motioned Pitt toward the admiral's bed.

Pitt hated hospitals. The sickening sweet smell of ether, the depressing atmosphere, the businesslike attitude of the doctors and nurses, always got to him. He had made up his mind long ago: when his time came, he would die in his own bed, at home.

His resolve was further braced by his first look at the admiral since Colorado. The waxen paleness of the old man's face seemed to blend with the pillow, and his rasping breathing came in unison with the respirator's hiss. Tubes ran into his arms and under the sheets, supplying sustenance and draining his body wastes. His once-muscular body looked withered.

A doctor stepped forward and touched Pitt on the arm. "I doubt if he has the strength to speak."

Bass's head rolled slightly in Pitt's direction and he

made a feeble gesture with one hand. "Come closer, Dirk," he muttered hoarsely.

The doctor gave a shrug of surrender. "I'll stay close, just in case." Then he stepped into the hall and closed the door.

Pitt pulled a chair up to the bed and bent over Bass's ear. "The Quick Death projectile," Pitt said. "How does it operate during its trajectory?"

"Centrifugal force . . . rifling."

"I understand," Pitt replied in a hushed tone. "The spiral rifling inside the bore of the gun rotates the shell and sets up a centrifugal force."

"Activates a generator . . . in turn activates a small radar altimeter."

"You must mean a barometric altimeter."

"No . . . barometric won't work," Bass whispered. "Heavy naval shell has high velocity with a flat trajectory . . . too low for accurate barometric reading . . . must use radar to bounce signal from ground."

"It doesn't seem possible a radar altimeter can survive the high g-forces when the gun is fired," Pitt said.

Bass forced a faint smile. "Designed the package myself. Take my word for it . . . the instrument survives the initial surge when the power charge is detonated."

The admiral closed his eyes and lay still, exhausted by his efforts. Heidi moved forward and put her hand on Pitt's shoulder.

"Perhaps you should come back in the afternoon."

Pitt shook his head. "By then it will be too late."

"You'll kill him," Heidi said, her eyes welling with tears, her expression angry.

Bass's hand inched across the sheets and weakly gripped Pitt's wrist. His eyes fluttered open. "Just needed a minute to catch my breath. . . . Don't go . . . that's an order."

Heidi read the tortured look of compassion in Pitt's eyes and she reluctantly backed away. Pitt leaned toward the admiral again.

"What happens next?"

"After the shell passes its zenith and begins the flight to earth, the altimeter's omnidirectional indicator begins signaling the decrease in altitude. . . ."

Bass's voice trailed off and Pitt waited patiently.

"At fifteen hundred feet a parachute is released. Slows the shell's descent and activates a small explosive device."

"Fifteen hundred feet, parachute opens," Pitt repeated.

"At one thousand feet, device detonates and splits head of projectile; releases a cluster mass of bomblets containing the Quick Death organism."

Pitt sat back and considered the admiral's description of the projectile's operation. He looked into the waning eyes.

"The time element, Admiral. How much time between the parachute's ejection and the QD dispersal?"

"Too long ago . . . can't remember."

"Please try," Pitt implored.

Bass was clearly sinking. He fought to bring his brain into gear, but its cells responded sluggishly. Then the tension lines in his face relaxed and he whispered, "I think . . . not sure . . . thirty seconds . . . rate of descent about eighteen feet per second . . ."

"Thirty seconds?" Pitt said, seeking verification.

Bass's hand released Pitt's wrist and fell back on the bed. His eyes closed and he drifted into coma.

55

The only damage to the *Iowa* after she slashed through the *Molly Bender* was a few scrapes to the paint on her bows. Fawkes had not noticed the slightest bump. He could have averted the tragedy if he had spun the wheel hard to port, but it would have meant swerving the battleship from the deep part of the channel and running her aground.

He needed every inch he could squeeze between the riverbed and the *Iowa*'s hull. The months of gutting thousands of tons of nonessential steel had raised the ship from a wartime operational draft of thirty-eight feet to a few inches less than twenty-two, giving Fawkes a razor-thin margin. Already the great whirling screws were churning up bottom mud that dirtied the *Iowa*'s wake for miles.

Fawkes's countless trips up and down the river in the dark, sounding every foot, marking each channel buoy, each shoal, were paying off. Through the diminishing sleet he made out the lighted mid-channel buoy off St. Clements Island, and a minute or two later his ears picked up its sepulchral tolling bell as if it were an old friend. He wiped his sweating hands one at a time on his sleeves. The trickiest part of the run was coming up.

Ever since slipping the moorings, Fawkes had worried about the danger of Kettle Bottom Shoals, a six-mile section of the river mazed with a network of shallow sand-bars that could grip the *Iowa*'s keel and hold her helpless miles from her goal.

He lifted one hand from the helm and picked up a microphone. "I want a continuous depth reading."

"Understood, Captain," a voice scratched back over a speaker.

Three decks below, two of Fawkes's black crewmen took turns calling up the depths as they appeared on the

279

modified Fathometer. They gave their readings in feet instead of the usual fathoms.

"Twenty-six feet . . . twenty-five . . . twenty-four-five."

Kettle Bottom Shoals was beginning to make its presence known and Fawkes's hamlike hands clenched the spokes of the helm as though they were glued to them.

Down in the engine room Emma made a show of helping the pitifully small crew who were somehow running the huge ship. All were bathed in sweat as they struggled to handle duties that normally took five times their number. The removal of two engines had helped, but there was still far too much to do, particularly when they considered their dual role as engineers and, when the time came, gunners.

Not one to become mired in physical labor, Emma made himself useful by passing around gallon jugs of water. In that steaming hell no one seemed to take notice of his unfamiliar face; they were only too grateful to gulp down the liquid that replaced the body fluids running from their pores in streams.

They worked blind, never knowing what was happening on the other side of the hull's steel plates, never remotely aware of where the ship was taking them. All Fawkes had told them when they boarded was that they were going on a short practice run to shake down the old engines and fire a few rounds from the main guns. They assumed they were heading out of the bay and into the Atlantic. That's why they were stunned when the ship suddenly gave a shudder and the hull began creaking in protest beneath their feet.

The *Iowa* had rammed a shoal. The suction of the mud had drastically cut her speed, but she was still making way. "Full ahead" came down on the telegraph from the bridge. The two massive shafts increased their mighty revolutions as the engines threw their 106,000 horsepower into the task.

The faces of the men in the engine room mirrored confusion and bewilderment. They had thought they were in deep water.

Charles Shaba, the chief engineer, hailed the bridge. "Captain, have we run aground?"

"Aye, laddie, we've nudged an uncharted bar," Fawkes's

voice boomed back. "Keep pouring it on till we've sailed past."

Shaba did not share Fawkes's optimism. The ship felt as if she were barely maintaining headway. The deck plates beneath his feet vibrated as the engines strained in their mountings. Then, slowly, he sensed their beat smoothing somewhat, as though the screws were biting into new water. A minute later, Fawkes shouted down from the bridge.

"Tell your boys we're free. We're back in deep water!"

The engine crew tackled their respective duties again, their faces wearing relieved smiles. One oiler began a popular chant and soon they all took it up in chorus with the hum from the great turbines.

Emma did not join in. Only he knew the truth behind the *Iowa*'s strange voyage. In a few hours the men around him would be dead. They might have been reprieved if the *Iowa*'s flat bottom had remained firmly stuck in the shoal's mud. But it was not to be.

Fawkes was the lucky one, he thought. Damned lucky. So far.

voice became thick. "Keep pushing it on till we've reached
port."

Shala did not share Fawkes's optimism. The ship felt
as if she were barely maintaining headway. The deck
plates beneath her feet vibrated as the engines strained to
their capacities. Then, slowly, he sensed their feel
somehow somewhat as though the screens were rising
into view. A quarter-view, Fawkes shouted down
from the bridge.

"Tell your tong we're free. We're back in clear water!"
The engine crew rattled their repetitions, unflagging.
Deep below, pitched, pale-red smoke. One pilot began a
deeper-throated road along slow as each began to choke with
the fume from the great turbine.

Lanna did not join in. Only he knew that if he failed
the lords's strange voyage, in a few hours the most
august he would be dead. They might have been im-
proved if the lever. But before he remained fairly
naked in the diced shard that it was not to be.

Fawkes was the lucky one, he thought. Damned lucky.

56

The President sat at the end of a long conference table in the emergency executive offices three hundred feet beneath the White House and stared Dale Jarvis squarely in the eye. "I don't have to tell you, Dale, the last thing I need is a crisis during the last few days of my administration, especially a crisis that can't wait until morning."

Jarvis felt the tingling fingers of nervousness. The President was noted for his volcanic temper. Jarvis had been present on more than one occasion when the famous mustache, a delight of political cartoonists, fairly bristled with wrath. With little to lose, except his job, Jarvis counterattacked.

"I am not in the custom of interrupting your sleep, sir, nor the martial dreams of the Joint Chiefs, unless I have a damned good reason."

Defense Secretary Timothy March sucked in his breath. "I think what Dale means—"

"What I mean," Jarvis said, "is that somewhere out in Chesapeake Bay there are a bunch of nuts loose with a biological weapon that could conceivably exterminate every living creature in a major city and keep on exterminating for God knows how many generations."

General Curtis Higgins, Chairman of the Joint Chiefs, gave Jarvis a doubting look. "I know of no weapon with that killing power. Besides, the gas weapons in our arsenal were neutralized and destroyed years ago."

"That's the bullshit we give the public," Jarvis snapped back. "But everyone in this room knows better. The truth is the Army has never stopped developing and stockpiling chemical-biological weapons."

"Settle down, Dale." The President's lips were stretched in a grin beneath the mustache. He took a perverse sort of pleasure whenever his subordinates took to fighting among themselves. Casually, in a move to relieve the tense atmosphere, he leaned back in his chair and draped

283

one leg over the armrest. "For the moment, I suggest we take Dale's warning as gospel." He turned to Admiral Joseph Kemper, the chief of Naval Operations. "Joe, since this appears to be a naval raid, it falls in your bailiwick."

Kemper hardly fit the image of a military leader. Portly and white haired, he could have easily been hired as a department-store floorwalker. He looked thoughtfully at the notes he had scribbled during Jarvis's briefing.

"There are two facts that bear out Mr. Jarvis's warning. First, the battleship *Iowa* was sold to Walvis Bay Investment. And as of yesterday, our satellite pictures showed it docked at the Forbes shipyard."

"And its current status?" asked the President.

Kemper did not answer but pressed a button on the table in front of him and rose from his chair. The wood paneling against the far wall slid apart, revealing an eight-by-ten-foot projection screen. Kemper picked up a telephone and said tersely, "Begin."

A high-resolution TV picture taken high above the earth flashed on the screen. The clarity and color were far superior to anything transmitted to an ordinary home set. The satellite camera penetrated the early-morning darkness and cloud cover as though they did not exist, projecting a view of the eastern Chesapeake Bay shoreline so clear it looked as if it came off a picture postcard. Kemper moved to the screen and made a circular motion with the pencil he used for a pointer.

"Here we see the entrance to the Patuxent River and the basin just inside Drum Point to the north and Hog Point to the south." The pencil held steady for a moment. "These small lines are the docks at the Forbes yard. . . . A point for Mr. Jarvis. As you can see, Mr. President, there is no sign of the *Iowa*."

On Kemper's command the cameras began sweeping toward the upper end of the bay. Freighters, fishing boats, and a missile frigate passed by in parade, but nothing resembling the massive outlines of a battleship. Cambridge on the right of the screen; soon, the Naval Academy at Annapolis on the left; the toll bridge below Sandy Point; and then up the Patapsco River to Baltimore.

"What lies south?" the President asked.

"Except for Norfolk, no city of any size for three hundred miles."

"Come now, gentlemen. Not even Merlin and Houdini together could make a battleship disappear."

Before anyone could comment, a White House aide entered the conference room and laid a paper at the President's elbow.

"Just in from the State Department," the President said, scanning the print. "A communiqué from Prime Minister Koertsmann, of South Africa. He urgently warns us of an imminent attack on the United States mainland by the AAR and apologizes for any indirect involvement by his cabinet."

"It doesn't figure that Koertsmann would suggest an involvement with his enemy," March said. "I should think he'd categorically deny any connection."

"Probably hedging his bets," ventured Jarvis. "Koertsmann must suspect Operation Wild Rose has fallen into our hands."

The President kept gazing at the wording on the paper as if unwilling to accept the frightening truth.

"It looks," he said solemnly, "as if all hell is about to break loose."

The bridge had been his only miscalculation. The *Iowa*'s superstructure was too high to pass under the one man-made obstacle that stood between Fawkes and his target. The vertical clearance was three feet lower than he'd reckoned.

He heard, rather than saw, the plywood gun-director housing being torn off the forward gun-control platform as it smashed into the overhead span of the bridge.

Howard McDonald slammed on his brakes and skidded to a sideways stop, toppling stacked crates of milk bottles in his delivery van. To McDonald, who was crossing the Harry W. Nice Memorial Toll Bridge to begin his regular milk route, it appeared that an airplane had crashed through the supporting girders almost on top of his truck. He sat there for a few moments in shock, his headlights illuminating a huge pile of debris blocking the two narrow north- and southbound lanes. Fearfully, he stepped from the van and approached, expecting to find mangled pieces of human anatomy embedded in the wreckage.

Instead, all he discovered were splintered sheets of

gray-painted wood. His initial reaction was to stare at a
low overcast sky, but all he saw was a red aircraft-
obstruction light flashing atop the main span. Then Mc-
Donald walked over to the railing and peered down.

Except for what seemed to be the running lights of a
string of vessels disappearing around Mathias Point, to the
north, the channel was empty.

57

Pitt, Steiger, and Admiral Sandecker stood around a drafting table in Pitt's hangar at the Washington National Airport and examined a large-scale map of the area's waterways. "Fawkes did a radical facelift on the *Iowa* for a damned good reason," Pitt was saying. "Sixteen feet. That's how much he raised her waterline."

"You certain you have an accurate figure?" Sandecker asked. "That leaves a draft of only twenty-two feet." He shook his head. "It doesn't seem credible."

"I got it from the man who should know," answered Pitt. "While Dale Jarvis was on the phone to NSA headquarters, I questioned Metz, the shipyard boss. He swore to the measurements."

"But for what purpose?" said Steiger. "By removing all the guns and replacing them with wooden dummies, the ship is totally useless."

"Number-two turret and all its fire-control equipment is still in place," Pitt said. "According to Metz, the *Iowa* can lob a salvo of two-thousand-pound shells twenty miles into a rain barrel."

Sandecker concentrated his attention on lighting a large cigar. Satisfied that it was properly stoked, he blew a cloud of blue smoke at the ceiling and rapped the map with his knuckles. "Your plan is crazy, Dirk. We're meddling in a conflict way over our heads."

"We can't sit here and piss and moan," said Pitt. "The President will be persuaded by the Pentagon strategists either to blow the *Iowa* out of the water, more likely than not spreading the QD to the winds, or to send out a boarding party to capture the gas shells, with the idea of incorporating them into the Army's arsenal."

"But what good is a plague organism that can't be controlled?" asked Steiger.

"You can bet every biologist in the country will be funded to search for an antidote," Pitt replied. "If one

287

makes a breakthrough, then someday, somewhere, a general or an admiral may panic and give the order for its dispersal. Me, I don't want to grow old knowing I had an opportunity to save countless lives but failed to act."

"Pretty speech," said Sandecker. "I'm in total agreement, but the three of us are hardly in a position to compete with the Defense Department in a race to recover the two remaining QD warheads."

"If we could sneak a man on board the *Iowa* first, a man who could disarm the firing mechanism of the projectiles and dump the organism pellets over the side into the water . . ." Pitt let his thought linger.

"And you are that man?" ventured Sandecker.

"Of us three, I'm the best qualified."

"Aren't you forgetting me, mister?" Steiger said acidly.

"If all else fails, we'll need a good man at the controls of the helicopter. Sorry, Abe, but I can't fly one, so you're elected."

"Since you put it that way," replied Steiger with a wry smile, "how can I refuse?"

"The trick is to ferret out the *Iowa* before the boys at Defense," said Sandecker. "Not a likely event, since they have the advantage of satellite reconnaissance."

"What if we know exactly where the *Iowa* is headed?" Pitt said, grinning.

"How?" grunted a skeptical Steiger.

"The draft was the giveaway," answered Pitt. "There's only one waterway within Fawkes's steaming distance that would require a draft of no more than twenty-two feet."

Sandecker and Steiger stood silent and expressionless, waiting for Pitt to unravel the knot.

"The Capital," Pitt said with a certain finality. "Fawkes is going to run the *Iowa* up the Potomac River and hit Washington."

Fawkes's arms ached and the sweat of intense concentration rolled down his weathered face and trickled into his beard. But for his arm movements, he might have been cast in bronze. He was desperately tired. He had stood at the helm of the *Iowa* for nearly ten hours, wresting the mighty ship through channels she was never designed to enter. The palms of his hands were seeded with broken blisters, but he did not care. He was in the homestretch of his impossible journey. The long, lethal guns of number-two turret were already within range of Pennsylvania Avenue.

He called for flank speed on the telegraph, and the vibration from deep belowdecks increased. Like an old warhorse at the sound of the bugle, the *Iowa* dug her screws into the muddy river and charged up the narrows beside Cornwallis Neck on the Maryland bank.

The *Iowa* looked like something not of this world; rather, it looked like a mammoth smoke-breathing monster erupting from the depths of hell. She forged ahead faster, sweeping past the channel buoys that fell back toward the first tendrils of dawn. It was as if she had a heart and soul and somehow, knew this was her final voyage, knew she was about to die, the last of the fighting battleships.

Fawkes stared in fascination at the glow from the lights of Washington looming twenty miles ahead. The Marine base at Quantico fell behind the stern as the *Iowa*'s irresistible mass hurtled around Hallowing Point and sped past Gunston Cove. Only one bend remained before her bows entered the straight channel ending on the edge of the golf course at East Potomac Park.

"Twenty-three feet," the depth reader's voice droned over the speaker. "Twenty-three . . . twenty-two-five . . ."

The ship dashed by the next channel buoy, her eighteen-foot five-bladed outboard propellers flailing at the bottom silt, her bow throwing sheets of white foam as she plowed against the five-knot current.

"Twenty-two feet, Captain." The voice had a tone of urgency. "Twenty-two, holding . . . holding . . . Oh God, twenty-one-five!"

Then she struck the rising riverbed like a hammer into a pillow. The impact seemed a sensation more known than felt as the bows bored into the mud. The engines continued to hum and the screws went on thrashing, but the *Iowa* lay still.

She had come to rest below the sloping grounds of Mount Vernon.

58

"I didn't believe it possible," said Admiral Joseph Kemper as he gazed in admiration at the *Iowa*'s image on the viewing screen. "Sailing a steel fortress ninety miles up a narrow, meandering river in the dead of night is a remarkable feat of seamanship."

The President looked pensive. He massaged his temples. "What do we know about this fellow Fawkes?"

Kemper nodded to an aide, who passed a blue folder to the President.

"The British Admiralty obliged my request for Captain Fawkes's service record. Mr. Jarvis has added an addendum from NSA files."

The President slipped on a pair of reading glasses and opened the folder. After a few minutes he peered over the horn-rims at Kemper. "A damn fine record. Whoever picked him for the job knew his onions. But why would a man of his reputable background suddenly involve himself with such a bizarre venture?"

Jarvis shook his head. "The best guess is that the massacre of his wife and children by terrorists pushed him off the deep end."

The President mulled over Jarvis's words and turned to the Joint Chiefs. "Gentlemen, I'm open for proposals."

General Higgins took the cue and pushed back his chair and stepped to the screen. "Our staff planners have programmed a number of alternatives, all based on the assumption that the *Iowa* is carrying a deadly biological agent. First, we can call up a squadron of Air Force F-one-twenty Specter jets to blast the *Iowa* with Copperhead missiles. The attack would coincide with supporting firepower by Army units on shore."

"Too uncertain," said the President. "If the destruction is not immediate and total, you may well disperse the Quick Death agent."

"Second," Higgins continued, "we send in a team of

Navy SEALs to board the *Iowa* from the water and secure the stern section, which contains a helicopter landing pad. Then Marine assault troops can land and seize the
ship." Higgins paused, waiting for comments.

"And if the ship was battened down"—this from Kemper—"how would the Marines gain entry?"

Jarvis fielded the question. "According to the shipyard
people, most of the *Iowa*'s armor and superstructure were
replaced with wood. The Marines could blast through
to the ship's interior, providing, of course, Fawkes's men
hadn't cut them down while they were landing."

"If all else fails," said Higgins, "our final alternative is
to finish the job with a low-yield nuclear missile."

For nearly a minute no one in the room spoke, each
man unwilling to air the unthinkable consequences to the
general's last proposal. Finally, as he knew he must, the
President took the initiative.

"It seems to me a small neutron bomb would be a more
practical out."

"Radioactivity alone won't kill the QD agent," said Jarvis.

"Also," Kemper injected, "I doubt if the lethal rays could
penetrate the turret. They're nearly airtight when buttoned
up."

The President looked at Higgins. "I must assume your
people have weighed the terrible possibilities."

Higgins solemnly nodded. "It comes down to the age-old
choice of sacrificing a few to save many."

"What do you call a few?"

"Fifty to seventy-five thousand dead. Perhaps twice that
number injured. The small communities closest to the *Iowa*
and the congested sector of Alexandria would be the hard-
est hit. Washington proper would receive minor damage."

"How soon before the Marines can go in?" asked the
President.

"They are boarding helicopters at the staging area this
very minute," answered General Guilford, the Marine com-
mandant. "And the SEALs are already on their way
downriver in a Coast Guard patrol boat."

"Three combat units of ten men each," added Kemper.

A muted buzzer sounded on the phone beside General
Higgins's chair. Kemper leaned over and answered it, listened, and replaced the receiver. He looked up at Higgins,
who had remained standing by the viewing screen.

"Communications teams have set up cameras on the southern bluffs above the *Iowa*," he said. "They'll be transmitting pictures in a few seconds."

Almost before Kemper had finished speaking, the aerial image from the satellite cameras faded into blackness and was replaced by a shot of the *Iowa* that filled the screen with the ship's superstructure.

The President slowly poured himself a cup of coffee but did not drink it. He stared at the *Iowa*, his mind churning in search of a decision that only he could make. At last he sighed and addressed himself to General Higgins.

"We go with the SEALs and Marines. If they fail, whistle up the Specter jets and order your forces on shore to open fire with everything they've got."

"And the nuclear strike?" asked Higgins.

The President shook his head. "I cannot carry the burden of ordering mass murders of my own countrymen, regardless of the circumstances."

"We have another half hour before sunrise," said Kemper softly. "Captain Fawkes must have daylight to sight his guns. All radar-operated and automatic-fire control systems were removed from the *Iowa* before she was decommissioned. He cannot possess any degree of accuracy unless he has a spotter in or near the target area who can report the range and accuracy of the *Iowa*'s fire by radio."

"Could be the spotter is sitting on a rooftop across the street," the President said, sipping at the coffee.

"I wouldn't be surprised," replied Kemper. "However, he won't be on the air for long. We have computerized triangulation monitors set up that can pinpoint his location within seconds."

The President sighed. "Then that about covers it for the moment, gentlemen."

"One more prospect, Mr. President, that I left for last," said Higgins.

"Shoot."

"The Quick Death projectiles. Should we capture them intact, I suggest they be analyzed by Defense Department laboratories—"

"They must be destroyed!" Jarvis cut in. "No weapon that ghastly is worth saving."

"I fear a more immediate problem has just cropped up," said Timothy March.

Every eye whipped back to the viewer at the sound of

March's voice. Kemper swiftly snatched the phone and shouted into it. "Pull back your lens to the rear and above the *Iowa*'s stern!"

Unseen hands dutifully did as they were told and the battleship's outline grew smaller as the camera increased the image area. A set of aircraft-navigation lights approaching upriver immediately gripped everyone's attention.

"What do you make of it?" demanded the President.

"A helicopter," Higgins replied angrily. "Some damned civilian must have gotten curious and taken it into his head to buzz the ship."

The men left their chairs and clustered around the screen, watching helplessly as the intruding craft beat its way toward the grounded battleship. The observers tensed, their eyes betraying helpless frustration.

"If Fawkes panics and opens fire before our forces are in position," said Kemper tonelessly, "a lot of people are going to get hurt."

The *Iowa* lay dead in the middle of the Potomac, her engines quiet, the telegraph turned to "all stop." Fawkes looked about him with guarded optimism. The crew was unlike any he'd ever commanded. Several of its members looked to be mere boys, and all were dressed in the camouflage jungle uniforms popularized by the AAR. And, except for the efficient manner in which they carried out their assigned duties, there was nothing about them that remotely suggested South African naval personnel.

Charles Shaba's job as chief engineer was terminated by the idle engines, and according to his orders, he now became the gunnery officer. When he climbed to the bridge, he found Fawkes leaning over a small radio set. He threw a smart salute.

"Pardon me, Cap'n, but can we talk?"

Fawkes turned around and placed a loglike arm on Shaba's shoulder. "What's on your mind?" he said, smiling.

Pleased to catch the captain in a good mood, Shaba stood at attention and shot the question that was burning in the minds of the crew. "Sir, where in hell are we?"

"The Aberdeen proving grounds. Are you familiar with it, lad?"

"No, sir."

"It's a sprawling piece of land where the Americans test their weapons."

"I thought . . . that is, the men thought we were going to sea."

Fawkes looked out the window. "No, lad, the Yanks have kindly allowed us to hold gunnery practice on their target grounds."

"But how do we get out of here?" Shaba asked. "The ship is stuck on the bottom." ·

Fawkes gave him a fatherly expression. "Don't fret. We'll float her off at high tide as easy as you please. You'll see."

Shaba looked noticeably relieved. "The men will be glad to hear that, Cap'n."

"Good, lad." Fawkes patted him on the back. "Now get back to your station and see to the loading of the guns."

Shaba saluted and left. Fawkes watched the young black man fade into the darkness beyond the passageway, and for the first time he felt a great wave of sorrow for what he was about to do.

His reverie was diverted by the sound of an aircraft. He looked into the brightening sky and saw the blinking multicolored lights of a helicopter flying upriver from the east. He grabbed a pair of night glasses and aimed them at the craft as it passed overhead. The letters NUMA were vaguely distinguishable through the lenses.

National Underwater and Marine Agency, Fawkes translated silently. No danger there. Probably returning to the Capital from some oceanographic expedition. He nodded at his reflection in the glass, a feeling of security growing within him.

He replaced the binoculars on the bridge counter and turned his attention once again to the radio. He held the headset to one ear and pressed the microphone button.

"Black Angus One calling Black Angus Two. Over."

A slurred, unmistakably Southern drawl answered almost immediately. "Hey man, we don't need all that coded jive. You're comin' in cool as a White Christmas."

"I'd appreciate economy of speech," snapped Fawkes.

"As long as the bread I signed for is good, you're the boss, boss."

"Ready, target range?"

"Yeah, movin' into position now."

"Good." Fawkes glanced at his watch. "Five minutes and ten seconds till Hogmanay."

"Hog . . . what?"

"Scots for a smashing New Year's Eve."

Fawkes clicked off the mike and noted thankfully that the NUMA helicopter had continued on its leisurely course toward Washington and disappeared beyond the bluffs upriver.

At almost the same instant, Steiger altered the controls and banked the Minerva M-88 helicopter in a wide, sweeping turn over the Maryland countryside. He kept low, shaving the tops of the leafless trees, dodging an occasional water tower, grimacing at the words that came over his earphones.

"They're beginning to get nasty," he said casually. "General Somebody-or-other claims he's going to shoot us down if we don't get the hell out of the area."

"Acknowledge," said Pitt. "And tell him you're complying."

"Who should I say we are?"

Pitt thought a moment. "Tell him the truth. We're a NUMA copter on special assignment."

Steiger shrugged and began talking into his microphone.

"Old General Whosit bought it," said Steiger. He angled his head toward Pitt. "You'd better get ready. I judge it about eight minutes to the drop."

Pitt unclasped his seat belt and waited until Sandecker did the same, then moved into the helicopter's small cargo compartment. "Do it right the first time," Pitt said into Steiger's ear, "or you'll make an ugly red mess on the side of the *Iowa*."

"You're looking at a neatness nut," Steiger said with a diluted smile. "All you have to do is hang tight and leave the driving to old Abe. If you have to drop early, I'll make damn sure you've got a nice cushion of deep water under your ass."

"I'm counting on it."

"We'll come around and swing in from the west to cloak our outline against whatever darkness is left." Steiger's eyes never strayed from the windshield. "I'm flicking off the navigation lights now. Good luck!"

Pitt squeezed Steiger's arm, stepped into the cargo section of the Minerva, and closed the cockpit door. The compartment was ice cold. The loading hatch was open and the wintry morning air whistled into what seemed a vibrating aluminum tomb. Sandecker held the harness out to him and he strapped it on.

The admiral started to say something and then hesitated. At last, his cast-iron features taut with suppressed emotion, he said, "I'll expect you for breakfast."

"Make my eggs scrambled," Pitt said.

Then he stepped into the frigid dawn.

Lieutenant Alan Fergus, leader of the SEAL combat units, zipped up his wet suit and cursed the vagaries of the high command. Not more than an hour ago he'd been rudely awakened from a dead sleep and hurriedly briefed on what he regarded as the dumbest exercise ever to come his way during seven years in the Navy. He pulled on his rubber hood and tucked his ears under the lining. Then he approached a tall, burly man who sat slouched in a nonregulation director's chair. His feet were propped on the bridge railing and he peered intently down the Potomac.

"What's it all about?" asked Fergus.

Lieutenant Commander Oscar Kiebel, the dour skipper of the Coast Guard patrol boat that was ferrying Fergus and his men, twisted the corners of his mouth in an expression of distaste and shrugged. "I'm as confused as you."

"Do you believe that bullshit about a battleship?"

"No," Kiebel said in a rumbling voice. "I've seen four-thousand-ton destroyers cruise upriver to the Washington Navy Yard, but a fifty-thousand-ton battleship? No way."

"Board and secure the stern for Marine helicopter-assault teams," Fergus said irritably. "Those orders are sheer crap, if you want my opinion."

"I'm not any happier about this outing than you," said Kiebel. "I take my picnics as they come." He grinned. "Maybe it's a surprise party with booze and wild women."

"At seven o'clock in the morning, neither holds much interest. Not out in the open, at any rate."

"We'll know soon. Two more miles till we round Sheridan Point. Then our objectives should be within—" Suddenly Kiebel broke off and cocked his head, listening. "You hear that?"

Fergus cupped his ears and turned, facing the patrol boat's wake. "Sounds like a helicopter."

"Coming like a bat out of hell without lights," Kiebel added.

"My God!" Fergus exclaimed. "The Marines have jumped the gun. They're going in ahead of schedule."

An instant later every head on the patrol boat turned upward as a helicopter roared past at two hundred feet, a dim shadow against a gray sky. All were so engrossed in the mysterious, darkened craft they didn't notice the vague shape trailing below and slightly to the rear of the copter until it swept over the decks and carried away the radio antennae.

"What in hell was that?" blurted Kiebel in genuine astonishment.

Pitt would have been only too glad to supply the answer if he'd had the time. Strapped in the harness, dangling under the NUMA helicopter only thirty feet above the river, he barely managed to extend his legs forward as he crashed into the patrol boat's antennae. His feet took most of the shock, and fortunately—damned fortunately—none of the wiring had entangled his body, sectioning him like a lettuce slicer. As it was, he would carry a nice welt across his buttocks where a piece of thin tubing had made brief contact.

The rising sun cooperated by hiding behind a low range of dark clouds, its filtered light obscuring any detail of the surrounding countryside. The air was keen, barbed with the energy of its chill, a polar frigidity that stabbed through Pitt's heavy clothing. His eyes were watering like faucets and his cheeks and forehead smarted with the intensity of overloaded pincushions.

Pitt was on a ride no amusement park in the country could equal. The Potomac was a blur as he soared over its lazy current at nearly two hundred miles an hour. Trees edging the banks hurtled by like cars on a Los Angeles freeway. He looked skyward and made out a small pale oval against the black doorway of the helicopter and recognized it as the anxious face of Admiral Sandecker.

He felt a sideways motion as Steiger banked the craft around a wide bend in the river. The long umbilical cable that held him to a winch in the cargo compartment arched in the opposite direction, swinging him outward, like the end child in a playground game of crack the whip. The momentum twisted him sideways and he found himself looking at the grounds of Mount Vernon. Then the cable straightened and the huge mass of the *Iowa* swung into view, her forward guns trained ominously upstream.

Overhead, Steiger eased back on the throttle and slowed the flight of the helicopter. Pitt felt the harness straps pressing into his chest at the deceleration and braced himself for the drop. The superstructure of the ship filled up the windshield in front of the control cabin when Steiger gently eased the helicopter into a hovering position above the starboard side of the ship, behind the main bridge.

"Too fast! Too fast!" Steiger muttered over and over, fearful that Pitt would be swinging ahead of the hovering helicopter like a weight on the bottom of a pendulum.

Steiger's fears were justified. Pitt was indeed pitching forward on an uncontrollable course, high above the main deck, where he'd planned to land. Narrowly missing an empty five-inch-gun turret, he came to the end of his arc. It was now or never. He made his decision and hit the quick-release buckle and dropped clear of the harness.

From the doorway of the helicopter Sandecker's eyes strained in the early-morning gloom, his insides knotted, his breath halted, as Pitt's huddled figure fell behind the forward superstructure and vanished. Then the *Iowa* was gone, too, as Steiger snapped the helicopter into a steep angle, the rotor blades biting the air, dipping over the forested shore and out of sight. As soon as the craft leveled, Sandecker released his safety strap and made his way back into the cockpit.

"Is he away?" Steiger asked anxiously.

"Yes, he's down," answered Sandecker.

"In one piece?"

"We can but hope," Sandecker said, so quietly that Steiger hardly heard him above the roar of the engine. "That's all any of us has left."

59

Fawkes was not overly concerned with the helicopter so long as it continued on its way. He did not see a human form drop out of the twilight, as his attention was directed to the boat that was approaching downriver at high speed. There was no doubt in his mind that it was a welcoming committee, courtesy of the United States government. He spoke into a microphone.

"Mr. Shaba."

"Sir?" Shaba's voice crackled back.

"Please see to it the machine-gun crews man their stations and prepare to repel boarders." Repel boarders. My God, Fawkes thought. When was the last time a captain of a capital ship gave that command?

"Is this a drill, sir?"

"No, Mr. Shaba, this is no drill. I fear American extremists who support the enemies of our country may attempt to take the ship. You will instruct your men to fire at any person, vessel, or aircraft that endangers the welfare of this ship and her crew. Your men may begin by driving off a terrorist boat that is approaching from the west."

"Aye, Captain." The radio could not hide the excitement in Shaba's voice.

Fawkes felt a growing urge to order his unsuspecting crew off the *Iowa,* but he could not bring himself to admit he was murdering sixty-eight innocent men, men who had been deceived into believing they were serving a country that treated them little better than cattle. Fawkes had a method of casting off any cold tentacles of guilt. He forced an image of a burned-out farm and the charred bodies of his wife and children into his mind and his resolve for the task at hand quickly hardened.

He picked up the mike again. "Main battery."

"Main battery ready, Captain."

"Single fire on commnd." He glanced once more at his computations on the chart beside him. "Range, twenty-three thousand nine hundred yards. Target bearing, oh-one-four degrees."

Fawkes stared hypnotically at the three sixty-eight-foot guns stretching out of the number-two main-battery turret, each barrel and its mechanism weighing 134 tons, obediently lifting its herculean muzzle to an elevation of fifteen degrees. Then they stopped, waiting for the command to unleash their awesome power. Fawkes paused, took a deep breath, and pushed the "transmit" button.

"Are you in position, Angus Two?"

"Say the word, man," replied the spotter.

"Mr. Shaba?"

"Standing by to fire, sir."

This was it. The journey that had begun on a farm in Natal had relentlessly run its course to this moment. Fawkes stepped outside to the bridge wing and raised the AAR battle flag on a makeshift staff. Then he returned to the control room and spoke the fateful words.

"You may fire, Mr. Shaba."

To the men on the Coast Guard patrol boat it was as if they had sailed into a holocaust. Though only one gun of the triple battery had fired directly over the *Iowa*'s bow, the blast created a path of turbulence and a great arm of incandescent gas that reached out and engulfed the small craft. Most of the men standing were knocked to the deck. The ones facing the *Iowa* at the moment of discharge actually had their hair singed and were blinded for the next several moments by the flash.

Almost before the effects of the muzzle blast had dissipated, Lieutenant Commander Kiebel had taken the helm and thrown the boat in a sharply cut *S* turn. Then the windshield across the bridge shattered and fell away. For a fraction of a second he thought he was being attacked by wasps. He could feel the hum as they flew past his cheeks and hair. Only after his right arm was jerked from the wheel and he looked down to see an evenly spaced set of reddening holes through his jacket sleeve did it dawn on him what was happening.

"Get your men over the side!" he yelled at Fergus. "The bastards are shooting at us!"

He didn't have to repeat the message. Instantly, Fergus scrambled across the deck, ordering and in some cases physically shoving his men into the dubious safety of the river. Miraculously, Kiebel was the only one who had been hit. Alone in broad view on the bridge, he stood as though on a stage in the eyes of the *Iowa*'s gunners.

Kiebel brought the boat so close alongside the *Iowa*'s hull that the sideboard bumpers were crushed against the vast wall of steel and torn off. It was a wise move; the gunners above could not depress their sights low enough to do more than shoot away part of the patrol boat's radar mast. Then Kiebel broke into open water, the bullet splashes falling fifty feet to starboard, attesting to the bad aim of his startled adversaries. The gap between them widened. He stole a quick glance aft and was relieved to see that Fergus and his men were gone.

He had run interference for the SEALs. It was their ball game now. Gratefully, Kiebel turned over the helm to his first officer and watched dourly as a chief petty officer broke open a first-aid kit and started cutting away the blood-soaked sleeve of his jacket.

"Son of a bitch," Kiebel muttered.

"Sorry, sir, you'll just have to grit your teeth and bear it."

"That's easy for you to say," snorted Kiebel. "You didn't lay out two hundred bucks for the coat."

Jogging his way across the pedestrian walk of the Arlington Memorial Bridge, Donald Fisk, an inspector with the Bureau of Customs, gasped out the crisp city air in wispy clouds of vapor.

He was on the return leg, passing around the Lincoln Memorial, his thoughts trailing from nowhere to nowhere from the boredom of the exercise, when a strange sound brought him to a halt. As it became louder, it reminded him of the roar of a speeding freight train. Then it turned into a screaming *whoosh*, and suddenly a massive crater appeared in the middle of Twenty-third Street, followed by a thunderous clap and a shower of dirt and asphalt.

Standing rigidly still after the explosion, Fisk was amazed to find he was untouched. The projectile had passed over him and struck the street at an angle, spraying its destructive force ahead of its trajectory.

A hundred yards away, a man driving a delivery truck had his windshield blown inward. He managed to stop the truck and stagger from the cab, his face sliced to hamburger.

Dazed, he held his hands in front of him and screamed, "I can't see! Help me! Someone please help me!"

Fisk shook off the cold shivers of shock and ran toward the stricken driver. The early-morning traffic rush was still an hour away and the street was empty. He wondered how he could call the police and an ambulance. The only other vehicle he saw was a street sweeper calmly whisking its way up Independence Avenue as though nothing had happened.

"Angus Two," Fawkes called. "Report effect of fire."

"Man, you sure tore up the street."

"Keep your remarks to a minimum," said Fawkes irritably. "Your transmission is no doubt being pinpointed."

"I read, big man. Your cock shot is seventy-five yards short and one hundred eighty yards to the left."

"You heard, Mr. Shaba."

"Adjusting, Captain."

"Fire as you bear, Mr. Shaba."

"Aye, sir."

Buried in the seventeen-hundred-ton steel turret, black South African gunners sweated and loaded the gaping breeches, shouting and cursing in tune with the clanging hoist machinery, while five decks below, the magazine crew sent up the shells and the silk bags containing the powder. First the conical-nosed twenty-seven-hundred-pound armor-piercing projectile was shoved into the breech's throat by a power rammer, followed by the powder charge, weighing six hundred pounds. Next the huge downswing carrier breech was twisted shut, providing a gas-tight seal. Then, on command, the great gun spat its devastating vehemence and recoiled four feet into its steel lair.

Fourteen miles away, Donald Fisk was attending the injured truck driver as the incoming freight thundered down from the sky and smashed into the Lincoln Memorial. In one thousandth of a second the hollow ballistic cone on the projectile disintegrated as it crashed into the white marble. Then the heavy slug of hardened steel behind punched its way deep into the memorial and exploded.

To Fisk it seemed the thirty-six Doric columns peeled outward like the petals of a flower before crumbling to the manicured landscape. Then the roof and inner walls collapsed as great chunks of marble bounced down the steps like children's wooden blocks and a violent burst of white dust spiraled heavenward.

As the rumble of the explosion trailed off across Washington, Fisk slowly rose to his feet in numbed bewilderment.

"What happened?" shouted the blinded truck driver. "For God's sake, tell me what's happening!"

"Don't panic," said Fisk. "There's been another explosion."

The driver grimaced and clenched his teeth in agony. Nearly thirty splinters of glass had buried themselves in his face. One eye was filled with congealing blood; the other was gone, sliced through to the retina.

Fisk took off his sweatshirt and pressed it in the driver's hands. "Twist, tear, or bite it if you must to stand the pain, but keep your hands away from your face. I'm going to leave you for a few moments." He paused as his ears caught the distant sound of approaching sirens. "The police are coming. An ambulance will be right behind them."

The truck driver nodded and sat on the curb, wadding the shirt in a ball and squeezing the cloth until his knuckles turned ivory. Fisk ran across the traffic circle, strangely ill at ease without something to cover his naked chest. Dodging the jagged chunks of marble that littered the memorial's stairway, he trotted up to what had once been the doorway facing the mall's reflecting pool.

Suddenly he stiffened, and stopped in astonishment.

There, amid the vast pile of rubble and the settling dust, the figure of Abraham Lincoln sat virtually unscathed. The walls and roof of the structure had somehow parted as they crumbled, crashing around, but not upon, the nineteen-foot statue.

Unmarred and unchipped, the hauntingly melancholy face of Lincoln still gazed downward solemnly, into infinity.

60

General Higgins slammed the phone receiver into its
cradle. It was his first show of temper. "We missed the
spotter," he said bitterly. "Our monitor units zeroed his
location, but he'd flown the coop by the time our nearest
patrol arrived."

"Obviously a mobile unit," said Timothy March. "With
three out of four cars on the road carrying a CB radio,
identifying the bastard will be next to impossible."

"Our special-forces team and the city police are setting
up roadblocks at key intersections around the Capitol
area," said Higgins. "If we can keep the spotter out of
visual contact of his targets, he won't be able to report
range corrections to the ship. Then Fawkes will be firing
blind."

The President's eyes were locked on the viewing screen,
staring sadly at the enlarged satellite picture of the de-
molished Lincoln Memorial. "Shrewd planning on their
part," he muttered. "A few dead would mean little more
than a newspaper headline to most Americans. But destroy a revered national monument and you touch everyone. Rest assured, gentlemen, by this evening a lot of
mad Americans are going to seek a way to vent their anger."

"If the next shell contains the QD . . ." Jarvis's voice
trailed off.

"It's like playing Russian roulette," March said. "Two
shells fired. That means the odds are down to two out
of thirty-six."

Higgins looked across the table at Admiral Kemper.
"What do you figure as the *Iowa*'s rate of fire?"

"The time span between shells one and two was four
minutes, ten seconds," Kemper answered. "Slow by half
compared to former wartime efficiency, but respectable in
view of forty-year-old obsolete equipment and a skeleton
crew."

307

"What puzzles me," said March, "is why Fawkes is only using the turret's center gun. He seems to be making no attempt to operate the other two."

"He's going by the book," said Kemper. "Conserving his strength by firing one shell at a time for effect. He got lucky on the second shot and found his target. Next time he gets the range you can bet he'll uncork all three barrels."

The phone in front of Higgins buzzed. He picked it up, listened for a moment, his expression grim. "The third round is on its way."

The satellite camera pulled back to show a two-mile radius around the White House. Everyone's eyes roamed over the bird's-eye view of the city, fearful that this projectile held the Quick Death organism while at the same time trying to guess which landmark was the target. Then came a geysering explosion that pulverized a fifty-foot section of sidewalk and two trees on the north side of Constitution Avenue.

"He's going for the National Archives building," the President said, a bitter edge to his voice. "Fawkes is trying to destroy the Declaration of Independence and the Constitution."

"I urge you, Mr. President, to order a nuclear strike on the *Iowa* at once." Higgins's normally reddish coloring had turned to gray.

The President looked like one hunted. His shoulders were hunched as though he were cold. "No," he said with finality.

Higgins dropped his hands to his side and sat heavily in his chair. Kemper tapped the table with a pencil, quietly mulling something over.

"There is another solution," he said slowly, deliberately. "We knock out the *Iowa*'s number-two turret."

"Knock out the turret?" Higgins said, a skeptical look in his eyes.

"Some of the F-one-twenty Specters are carrying Satan penetration missiles," explained Kemper. "Am I right, General Sayre?"

Air Force chief General Miles Sayre nodded in agreement. "Each aircraft is armed with four Satans, primed to gouge their way through three yards of concrete."

"I see your point," said Higgins. "But the accuracy? Miss, and you might unleash the QD."

"It can be done," said Sayre, a usually taciturn man. "As

soon as the pilots fire the missiles, they switch guidance control to the ground troops. Your people, General Higgins, are close enough to the *Iowa* to lay a Satan within a two-foot diameter."

Higgins snatched the phone and stared at the President. "If Fawkes maintains his firing schedule, we have less than two minutes."

"Go for it," the President said without hesitation.

While Higgins gave instructions to the forces deployed around the *Iowa*, Kemper consulted a file on the ship's construction.

"That turret is protected with steel-armor plating seven to seventeen inches thick," said Kemper. "We may not destroy it, but we'll sure as hell stun the crew."

"The SEALs," said the President. "Can they be warned of our intentions?"

Kemper looked grim. "We would if we could, but there has been no radio contact with them since they took to the water."

Fergus could not make contact, because the radio had been shot out of his hands by a machine gun deployed on the *Iowa*'s citadel. A bullet had neatly amputated the middle finger of his left hand before biting through the transmitter and his right palm. The backup radio was also gone, strapped to the belt of a team leader who took a hit in the chest and now floated lifelessly somewhere downriver.

Fergus had lost six men out of his original party of thirty while boarding the *Iowa*. They had climbed the sides after shooting and then looping small lines from crossbows across the ship's stern. These were attached to nylon ladders, which in turn were pulled up to the bulwarks. The SEALs were met with a scathing fire when they reached the main deck. Individually and in small teams they began pouring a return fire at the ship's defenders.

Fergus became cut off from his command and was pinned down behind the fantail mounting where the aircraft crane had once stood. Frustration overrode the pain in his wounded hands. Time was running out. His orders were to secure the landing pad before the South Africans could open fire. He shouted a curse as the burst from the third blast rumbled down the river channel.

Above the bluffs he could see the Marine helicopters hovering, waiting impatiently for his signal to land. Warily he poked his head around the crane mount and peered forward. The guns perched behind steel-armor plating atop the main bridge temporarily ignored Fergus and concentrated on his men, who had moved forward without him.

Cradling his automatic weapon in one arm, Fergus sprang to his feet and sprinted across the open deck, laying down a curtain fire. He'd nearly made it to cover beneath the aft turret when Fawkes's men repaid his attention, and a bullet tore through the calf of his left leg.

He stumbled a few steps, fell, and rolled under the bulk of the dummy turret. The new wound felt as though it were burning every nerve ending in his leg. He lay on the deck, listening to the gunfire forward, soaking up the pain as two Specter jets screamed out of the morning sun and expelled their lethal cargo.

If it weren't for the dull ache that clutched every inch of his body, Pitt would have sworn he was dead. Almost regretfully, he pushed the gray from his mind and forced his eyes opened.

Then he ran his hands over his legs and body. The worst he discovered, besides a horde of bruises, were two, possibly three cracked ribs. He probed his head and sighed gratefully when his fingers came back free of blood. The wooden splinters he found embedded in his right shoulder puzzled him.

He pushed himself to a sitting position and then rolled to his hands and knees. All muscles were responding to command. So far, so good. He took a deep breath and wove to his feet, no less elated at the accomplishment than if he'd climbed Mount Everest. A patch of daylight spilled through a jagged hole several feet away and he stumbled toward it.

His mind slowly began to hit on six of eight cylinders and analyzed why he hadn't been crushed to oatmeal when he smashed into the side of the ship's superstructure. The quarter-inch plywood panels installed to replace the steel bulkheads had broken his impact. He'd barreled through one outer partition like a cannonball and made a healthy dent in a second before coming to rest in a passageway outside the officers' wardroom. So much for the mysterious slivers.

Through the haze he recalled a great booming sound

and vibration. The sixteen-inch guns, he figured. But how often had they fired? How long had he been out? Sounds of small-arms fire rattled from outside. Who was fighting whom? He dismissed the thoughts almost as they occurred: they really didn't matter. He had his own problems to solve.

He moved twenty feet down the passageway, stopped, and pulled a flashlight from one pocket and a folded paper containing the *Iowa*'s deck plans from another. It took him nearly two full minutes to pinpoint his exact location. Looking at the maze that made up the internal arrangement of a battleship was like looking at a cutaway view of a skyscraper lying on its side.

Tracking out a path to the forward shell magazines, he moved soundlessly along the passageway. He had covered but a short distance when the ship rocked under a barrage of solid blows. Dust accumulated during the *Iowa*'s long years in mothballs erupted in smothering clouds. Pitt flung out his arms to maintain his balance, lurched, and grabbed the frame of a door that had opportunely swung open. He stood there choking back the dust while the tremors subsided.

He almost missed it, would have missed it if an indefinable curiosity hadn't tugged at his mind. Not a curiosity, really; rather an incongruity caught within his peripheral vision. He beamed the flashlight on a brown shoe—an expensive, handcrafted brown shoe—and saw it was attached to the leg of a black man stylishly attired in a business suit with vest. His hands were tied wide apart by ropes wrapped to overhead pipes.

61

Hiram Lusana could not distinguish the features of the man standing in the doorway of his prison. He looked large, but not as large as Fawkes. That was all Lusana could tell; the flashlight in the stranger's hands blinded him.

"I take it you lost the ship's popularity contest," came a voice that sounded more friendly than hostile.

The dark form behind the light moved closer and Lusana felt his bonds being loosened. "Where are you taking me?"

"Nowhere. But if you value social security in your old age, I suggest you get the hell off this boat before it's blown to pieces."

"Who are you?"

"Not that it matters, the name's Pitt."

"Are you part of Captain Fawkes's crew?"

"No, I'm free-lance."

"I don't understand."

Pitt untied Lusana's left hand and started on the other without answering.

"You are an American," said Lusana, more confused than ever. "Have you taken the ship from the South Africans?"

"We're working on it," said Pitt, sorely wishing he'd brought along a knife.

"Then you don't know who I am."

"Should I?"

"My name is Hiram Lusana. I am the leader of the African Army of Revolution."

Pitt finished with the last knot and stood back, aiming the light at Lusana's face. "Yes, I see that now. What's your involvement? I thought this was a South African show."

"I was kidnapped boarding an airplane back to Africa." Lusana gently pushed the light aside. Then a thought flooded his mind. "You know about Operation Wild Rose?" he asked.

"Only since last night. My government, however, was aware of it months ago."

"Impossible," said Lusana.

"Suit yourself." Pitt turned and started for the doorway. "Like I said, you better jump ship before the party gets out of hand."

Lusana hesitated, but only for a second. "Wait!"

Pitt turned. "Sorry, I can't spare the time."

"Please hear me out." Lusana moved closer. "If your government and the news media discover my presence here, they will have no choice but to overlook the truth and hold me responsible."

"So?"

"Let me prove my innocence in this ugly affair. Tell me what I can do to help."

Pitt read the sincerity in Lusana's eyes. He pulled an old Colt, .45 automatic from his belt and passed it to the black man. "Take this and cover my ass. I need both hands to hold the flashlight and read a diagram."

Somewhat taken aback, Lusana accepted the gun. "You'd trust me with this?"

"Sure," Pitt said offhandedly. "What would you gain by shooting a total stranger in the back?"

And then he motioned for Lusana to follow and quickly darted down the passageway toward the forward part of the ship.

Turret number two had survived the onslaught from the Satan missiles. Her steel plating was gouged and sprung in eight places but never penetrated. The port-outside gun barrel was severely fractured at the recoil base of the turret.

Dazed, Fawkes saw all this through the shattered remains of the glass in the bridge windows. Magically, he was untouched. He had been standing behind one of the few remaining steel bulkheads when the Satans had unerringly zeroed in on number-two turret. He snatched the microphone.

"Shaba, this is the captain. Do you hear me?"

The only reply was a faint ripple of static.

"Shaba!" Fawkes shouted. "Speak up, man. Report your damage."

The speaker crackled to life. "Cap'n Fawkes?"

The voice was unfamiliar. "Aye, this is the captain. Where is Shaba?"

"Below in the magazine, sir. The hoist, she's broken. He went to fix it."

"Who is this?"

"Obasi, Cap'n. Daniel Obasi." The voice had an adolescent pitch.

"Did Shaba leave you in charge?"

"Yes sir," Obasi said proudly.

"How old are you, son?"

There was a harsh, coughing sound. "Sorry, Cap'n. The smoke, she's real bad." More coughing. "Seventeen."

Good Lord, Fawkes thought. De Vaal was to have sent him experienced men, not boys whose names and faces he had yet to see in daylight. He was in command of a crew who were completely unknown to him. Seventeen. A mere seventeen years old. The thought sickened him. Was it worth it? God, was his personal revenge worth the terrible price?

Steeling his determination, Fawkes said, "Are you able to operate the guns?"

"I think so. All three are loaded and breeched tight. The men don't look too good, though. Concussion, I think. Most of them are bleedin' through the ears."

"Where are you now, Obasi?"

"In the turret officer's booth, sir. It's awful hot down here. I don't know if the men can take much more. Some are still out. One or two may be dead. No way of tellin'; I guess the ones that's dead are the ones bleedin' through the mouth."

Fawkes squeezed the microphone handle, his face filled with indecision. When the ship went, as he knew it surely must, he wanted to be standing on the bridge, the last battleship captain to die at his station. The silence over the radiophone became heavy with torment. Ever so slightly the curtain lifted and Fawkes glimpsed the terrible dimension of his actions.

"I'm coming down."

"The outside deck hatch is jammed tight, sir. You'll have to come up from the magazines."

"Thank you, Obasi. Stand by." Fawkes paused to remove his old Royal Navy cap and wipe the sweat and grime oozing from the pores of his forehead. He gazed through the splintered windows and studied the river. The cold mists rose along the shallows and reminded him of the Scottish lochs on just such a morning. Scotland: it seemed a thousand years since he'd seen Aberdeen.

He replaced the cap and spoke into the microphone again. "Angus Two, come in, please."

"Gotcha, big Angus One."

"Range?"

"Eighty yards short but right on the money. Just compensate for elevation and you got her, man."

"Your job is finished, Angus Two. Take care."

"Too late. I think the dudes in the khaki suits are about to take me away. So long, man. It's been a heavy date."

Fawkes stared at the receiving end of the microphone, wanting to speak words of appreciation to the man he'd never met, to thank him for jeopardizing his life even if it was for a price. Whoever Angus Two was, it would be a long time before he could spend the money placed in a foreign bank account by the South African Defence Ministry.

"A street sweeper," snorted Higgins. "Fawkes's spotter drove a goddamned city street sweeper. The city police are booking him now."

"That explains how he moved through the roadblocks without arousing suspicion," said March.

The President seemed not to hear. His attention was trained on the *Iowa*. He could clearly make out small forms in black wet suits darting from cover to cover, pausing only to fire their weapons before moving ever closer to the machine guns that dwindled their numbers. The President counted ten inert SEALs sprawled on the decks.

"Can't we do something to help those men?"

Higgins gave a helpless shrug. "If we open up from shore, we'd probably kill more SEALs than we'd save. I'm afraid there is little we can do for the moment."

"Why not send in the Marine assault teams?"

"Those copters are sitting ducks once they land on the *Iowa*'s aft deck. They each carry fifty troops. It would be mass slaughter. We'd accomplish nothing."

"I agree with the general," said Kemper. "The Satans bought us a breather. Number-two turret appears to be knocked out. We can afford to give the SEALs more time to clear the decks of terrorist opposition."

The President sat back and stared at the men surrounding him. "Then we wait—is that what you're saying? We wait and watch while men die in living color before our eyes on that damned TV screen?"

"Yes, sir," Higgins answered. "We wait."

62

Consulting his diagram of the ship while on the run, Pitt unerringly led Lusana down a series of darkened passages and alleyways, past dank empty rooms, until he finally paused at a bulkhead door. Then he wadded the diagram in a ball and tossed it to the deck. Lusana stopped obediently and waited for an explanation.

"Where are we?" he asked.

"Outside the projectile-storage area," Pitt answered. He leaned his weight against the door, which grudgingly creaked three quarters open. Pitt peered into a dimly lit room and listened. They both heard men shouting against the metallic clash of heavy machinery, the rattle of chains, and the hum of electric motors. The sounds seemed to come from above. Cautiously, Pitt stepped over the sill.

The tall armor-piercing shells were neatly stacked on their bases around the hoist tube, their conical heads gleaming menacingly under two yellow light bulbs. Pitt eased past the shells and looked upward.

On the deck overhead two black men were leaning in the hoist-tube access doors and hammering and cursing at the elevator cradle. The explosions that rocked the ship had jammed the mechanism. Pitt pulled back from the opening and began examining the shells. There was a total of thirty-one, and only one shell had a rounded head.

The second QD warhead was not present.

Pitt took a tool kit from his belt and handed the flashlight to Lusana. "Hold this steady while I operate."

"What are you going to do?"

"Deactivate a shell."

"If I am to be blown to smithereens," said Lusana, "may I know why?"

"No!" Pitt snapped. He hunched down and motioned for the light. His hands circled the cone of the shell as lightly as those of a safecracker fingering a tumbler dial. Locating the locking screws, he carefully undid them with a screwdriver. The threads were frozen with age and they fought his every twist. Time, Pitt thought desperately; he needed time before Fawkes's crew repaired the hoist and returned to the projectile-storage compartment.

Suddenly, unexpectedly, the last of the screws sheared off and the nose cone came loose in his hands. Tenderly, as though it were a sleeping baby, he set it aside and looked inside the warhead.

Then Pitt began to disconnect the explosive charge that was set to split the warhead and release the cluster of bomblets containing the QD organism. There was nothing tricky or particularly hazardous about the procedure. Working on the theory that too much concentration makes the hands tremble, Pitt idly whistled under his breath, thankful that Lusana wasn't plying him with questions.

Pitt cut the wires leading to the radar altimeter and removed the explosive detonator. He paused for a moment and took a small money sack from his coat pocket. Lusana was mildly amused to see that the lettering on the soiled canvas read WHEATON SECURITY BANK.

"I've never admitted this to a soul," Lusana said, "but I once robbed an armored truck."

"Then you should feel right at home," replied Pitt. He lifted the QD bomblets from the warhead and gently deposited them in the money bag.

"Damned clever smuggling method," Lusana said, smiling tightly. "Heroin, or diamonds?"

"I'd be interested in knowing that myself," Patrick Fawkes said as he ducked under the door frame into the compartment.

63

Lusana's first reflex was to shoot Fawkes. He spun around in a firing crouch and threw up the Colt, confident he couldn't miss such a massive target, dead certain the captain had the split-second advantage of a first shot.

Lusana barely caught himself in time. Fawkes's hands were empty. He was unarmed.

Slowly lowering the Colt, Lusana looked down at Pitt to see how the other man was taking the situation. As far as he could see, Pitt gave not the slightest reaction. He continued loading the sack as if the intrusion had never occurred.

"Have I the honor of addressing Patrick McKenzie Fawkes?" Pitt finally said without looking up.

"Aye, I'm Fawkes." He moved closer, his expression one of curiosity. "What goes on here?"

"Excuse me for not rising," Pitt said casually, "but I'm deactivating a poison gas warhead."

Perhaps five seconds passed as Lusana and Fawkes digested Pitt's brief explanation, staring at each other blankly and then back down at Pitt.

"You're daft!" Fawkes blurted.

Pitt held up one of the bomblets. "Does this look like your everyday explosive charge?"

"No, it does not," Fawkes admitted.

"Is it some sort of nerve gas?" Lusana asked.

"Worse," Pitt answered. "A plague organism with an ungodly potency. Two shells containing the deadly organism were mixed in with the shipment sent by the arms supplier."

There was the stunned silence of incredulity. Fawkes hunkered down and examined the shell and the bomblet in Pitt's hand. Lusana bent over and stared, too, not sure what he was supposed to be looking at.

The skepticism slowly faded from Fawkes's eyes. "I believe you," he said. "I've seen enough gas shells to recognize one." Then he gazed questioningly into Pitt's face. "Mind telling me who you are and how you came to be here?"

"After we find and deactivate the other shell," Pitt said, brushing him off. "Do you have another projectile-storage area?"

Fawkes shook his head. "Except for the three shells we've fired, all of which were of the armor-piercing variety, this is the lot—" He broke off as the realization struck him. "The turret! All guns are loaded and the breeches locked. The other plague projectile must be inside one of the three barrels."

"You fool!" Lusana shouted. "You murdering fool!"

The agony in Fawkes's eyes was apparent. "It's not too late. The guns will not fire except by my order."

"Captain, you and I will find and neutralize the other warhead," Pitt ordered. "Mr. Lusana, if you will be so kind as to drop this over the side." He handed Lusana the sack bulging with the QD bomblets.

"Me?" Lusana gasped. "I don't have the vaguest idea how to get out of this floating coffin. I'll need a guide."

"Keep making your way topside," Pitt said confidently. "Eventually you'll hit daylight. Then throw the sack in the deepest part of the river."

Lusana was about to leave when Fawkes placed a great paw on his shoulder. "We'll settle our business later."

Lusana stared back steadily. "I look forward to it."

And then the leader of the African Army of Revolution melted into the darkness like a shadow.

At two thousand feet Steiger made a slight adjustment in pitch and the Minerva dipped over the Jefferson Memorial and crossed the Tidal Basin on a course along Independence Avenue.

"It's crowded up here," he said, motioning to a bevy of Army helicopters hovering from one end of the Capitol mall to the other like a swarm of mad bees.

Sandecker nodded and said, "Better keep your distance. They're liable to shoot first and ask questions later."

"How long since the *Iowa*'s last shot?"

"Nearly eighteen minutes."

"Maybe that's the end of it, then," said Steiger.

"We won't land until we're sure," Sandecker replied. "How's the fuel?"

"Enough for nearly four more hours' flying time."

Sandecker twisted in his seat to relieve his aching buttocks. "Stay as close as you dare to the National Archives building. If the *Iowa* cuts loose again, you can bet that's the target."

"I wonder how Pitt made out?"

Sandecker put up an unworried front. "He knows the score. Pitt is the least of our problems." He turned away and looked out a side window so Steiger couldn't see the lines of worry that creased his face.

"I should have been the one to go in," said Steiger. "This is strictly a military show. A civilian has no business risking his life attempting a job he wasn't trained for."

"And you were, I suppose."

"You must admit my credentials outweigh Pitt's."

Sandecker found himself smiling. "Care to bet?"

Steiger caught the admiral's cagey tone. "What are you implying?"

"You've been had, Colonel, pure and simple."

"Had?"

"Pitt carries the rank of major in the Air Force."

Steiger looked over at Sandecker, his eyes squinting. "Are you going to tell me he can fly?"

"Just about every aircraft built, including this helicopter."

"But he claimed—"

"I know what he claimed."

Steiger looked lost. "And you sat back and said nothing?"

"You have a wife and children. Me, I'm too old. Dirk was the logical man to go."

The tenseness went out of Steiger's body and he sagged into his seat. "He better make it," he murmured under his breath. "By God, he better make it."

Pitt would have gladly given the last penny in his savings account to be anyplace but climbing a pitchblack stairway deep inside a ship that at any second might turn into an inferno. His brow was clammy and cold with sweat, as though he were running a fever. Suddenly Fawkes stopped and Pitt ran into him like a blind man against an oak tree.

"Please remain where you stand, gentlemen." The voice came from the lightless landing several steps above.

"You cannot see me, but I can see enough of you both to strike your hearts with a bullet."

"This is the captain," Fawkes snapped angrily.

"Ah, Captain Fawkes himself. How convenient. I was beginning to fear I had missed connections. You were not on the bridge, as I supposed."

"Identify yourself!" Fawkes demanded.

"The name is Emma. Not very masculine, I admit, but it serves the purpose."

"Stop this foolishness and let us pass." Fawkes made a move up two steps when the Hocker-Rodine hissed and a bullet zinged past his neck. He froze in midstep. "Good God, man, what is it you want?"

"I admire a no-nonsense approach, Captain." Emma paused, and then said, "I've been ordered to kill you."

Slowly, unnoticed by Fawkes and, he hoped, by the man on the landing, Pitt slipped down to his stomach on the steps, shielded by the shadowy bulk of the captain. Then, fractionally, he began slithering up the stairs like a snake.

"Ordered, you say," said Fawkes. "By whom?"

"My employer does not matter."

"Then why all the prattle, damn you. Why not shoot me in the chest and be done with it?"

"I do not operate without purpose, Captain Fawkes. You have been deceived. I think you should know that."

"Deceived?" Fawkes thundered. "Your foggy words tell me nothing."

An alarm began to sound in the back of Emma's mind, an alarm honed by a dozen years of cat-and-mouse existence. He stood there silently, not answering the captain's question, his senses probing for a sound or a movement.

"What about the man behind me?" asked Fawkes. "He has no hand in this. No need to murder an innocent bystander."

"Rest easy, Captain," said Emma. "My fee is for only one life. Yours."

With agonizing slowness, Pitt raised his head until he was eye level with the landing. He could see Emma now. Not in detail—the light was too dim for that—but he could make out the pale blur of a face and the outline of a figure.

Pitt didn't wait to see more. He could only guess Emma would blast Fawkes in the gut during the middle of a sentence, after lulling him with idle conversation. An old but effective trick. He dug the balls of his feet into the steps, took a breath, and lunged, going for a vicious impact with Emma's legs, his hands clawing for the gun.

The silencer flashed in Pitt's face, and a stabbing pain slammed the right side of his head as he grabbed for Emma's arm. After the haze of sudden shock he swam into unconsciousness and began falling, falling. It seemed to take forever before the abysmal void swallowed him and there was nothing.

64

Goaded on by Pitt's flying tackle, Fawkes charged up the steps like a maddened rhino and threw his great weight against the bodies of both men. Pitt went limp and fell off to one side. Emma struggled to bring the gun to bear, but Fawkes slapped it away as though it were a toy in a child's hands. Then Emma went for Fawkes's crotch, clutched his cock and balls, and squeezed ruthlessly.

It was the wrong move. The captain roared like thunder and reacted by swinging both his massive fists from over his head down upon Emma's upturned face, crushing cartilage and tearing skin. Astoundingly, Emma maintained the pressure.

Though his groin felt as if it were bursting in white-hot agony, Fawkes was wise enough not to try knocking away the hands that held him like a vise. Calmly, purposefully, like a man who knew exactly what he intended to do, he gripped Emma's head and began pounding it into the metal deck landing with every ounce of strength in his tree-trunk arms. Mercifully, the pressure eased, but shrouded in his pain-lashed rage, he kept smashing away until the back of Emma's skull turned to pulp. When his fury was finally spent, he rolled over and gently massaged his groin, cursing.

After a minute or two he rose stiffly to his feet, took the coat collars of the two inert men, and dragged them up the stairway. One more short flight, a few yards down a passageway, and he came to a cargo-loading door in the upper starboard side of the *Iowa*'s hull. He cracked the door enough to let in daylight and examined Pitt's wound.

The bullet had scored Pitt's left temple, causing, at worst, Fawkes figured, a nasty gash and a concussion. Then he checked Emma. What skin that was visible through the mask of blood on the assassin's face was turning blue. Fawkes went through his pockets and found only a spare clip for the Hocker-Rodine pistol. Strapped around a heavy woolen sweater was an inflatable life vest.

"A nonswimmer, hey?" Fawkes said, smiling. "I don't guess you'll be needing this anymore."

He removed the vest from Emma and tied it around Pitt. Reaching into his own coat pocket, Fawkes took out a small notebook and made several notations with the stub of a pencil. Next he took his eelskin tobacco pouch, emptied the contents, inserted the notebook, and tucked the packet snugly under Pitt's shirt. The cord to the CO_2 bottle was yanked and the vest hissed as it inflated.

Returning to Emma, Fawkes grabbed the corpse by the front of the sweater and pulled it toward the open hatch. The weight was too much for the angle of Fawkes's grip and the sweater slipped over Emma's head. Something around Emma's upper torso caught Fawkes's eye. It was a nylon binding that tightly circled the chest. Entranced, Fawkes undid a tiny clasp and the nylon fell away, releasing two small rosebud-tipped mounds.

For a moment Fawkes stood petrified.

"Holy Mother of Christ!" he murmured in awe.

Emma had indeed been a woman.

Dale Jarvis pointed at the viewing screen. "There, just below the second gun turret, on the side of the hull."

"What do you make of it?" asked the President.

"Someone has opened the forward loading hatch," answered Kemper. He turned to General Higgins. "Better alert your men to the possibility that the crew may attempt an escape."

"They won't get ten feet past the shoreline," said Higgins. They watched as the hatch was thrown back to its stops and a monster of a man stepped to the threshold and threw out what looked like a body. The form hit the water with a splash and disappeared. Soon he returned with another body, but this time he lowered it on a line to the leisurely flowing current—almost tenderly, it seemed to the men in the conference room—until the inert figure bobbed and floated free of the ship. Then the line was cast away and the doors closed.

Kemper motioned to an aide. "Contact the Coast Guard and have them pick up that man drifting in the river."

"What was that little performance all about?" The President's question echoed the thoughts of the men at the table.

"The hell of it is," Kemper said quietly, "we may never know."

After what seemed like ages, Hiram Lusana found a doorway that exited to the main deck. He stumbled outside, bone chilled in his thin business suit, clutching the sack of bomblets in both hands. His sudden emergence into daylight blinded him and he paused to get his bearings.

He found himself standing beneath the aft fire-control bridge, forward of the number-three gun turret. Small-arms fire whistled about the ship, but his mind was intent on disposing of the Quick Death bomblets, and he was oblivious of it. The river beckoned and he began sprinting toward the bulwarks edging the outer limits of the deck. He still had twenty feet to go when a man in a black rubber wet suit rose from the shadows of the turret and aimed a gun at him.

Lieutenant Alan Fergus no longer felt the burning pain from the hole in his leg, no longer felt the agony from seeing his combat teams cut to pieces. His whole body was quivering with hatred for the men responsible. It did not matter that the man in his sights wore a business suit instead of a uniform, or that he appeared to be unarmed. Fergus saw only a man who in his mind was murdering his friends.

Lusana halted abruptly and stared at Fergus. He had never before seen such cold malignity on a man's face. They looked into each other's eyes from no more than twelve feet, trying to exchange thoughts in that brief instant. No word passed between them, only a strange kind of understanding. Time seemed to pause and all sounds diminished into a blurred background.

Hiram Lusana knew his fight to rise above the filth of his childhood had culminated in this time and place. He had come to realize he could not be the leader of a people who would never fully accept him as one of their own. His path became clear. He could do far more for the oppressed of Africa by becoming a martyr to their cause.

Lusana accepted the invitation of death. He threw Fergus a silent smile of forgiveness and then leaped toward the bulwarks.

Fergus pulled the trigger and sprayed a pattern of automatic fire. The sudden impact of three bullets in his side pitched Lusana forward in a shuddered dance that pounded the breath from his lungs. Miraculously, he stayed on his feet and staggered drunkenly on.

Fergus fired again.

Lusana fell to his knees, still struggling toward the edge of the deck. Fergus watched in detached admiration, vaguely wondering what drove the incongruously dressed black man to ignore at least a dozen bullets in his body.

With brown eyes glazed with shock, and with a determination known only to a man who could never quit, Lusana crawled across the deck, holding the canvas sack against his stomach, leaving an ever-widening trail of crimson behind him.

The bulwarks were only three feet away. He fought closer despite the blackness beginning to cloud his vision and the blood streaming from the corners of his mouth. Summoning an inner strength born of final desperation, he threw the sack.

It hung on the bulwark for an instant that seemed frozen in time, teetered, and then fell into the river. Lusana's face sank to the deck and he passed the gate into oblivion.

The interior of the massive gun housing reeked of sweat and blood and the pungent odors of powder and heated oil. Most of the crew were still in shock, their eyes glazed, unknowing, dulled with confusion and fear; the rest were lying amid the machinery in unnatural poses, blood trickling from their ears and mouths. A charnel house, Fawkes thought, a damn charnel house. God, I'm no better than the butchers who slaughtered my family.

He peered down the center elevator tube to the magazines and saw Charles Shaba hammering away with a sledge on a shell cradle that had become wedged ten feet below the turret deck. The interlock doors, designed to prevent accidental breech failure from communicating explosive flash to the magazines, were jammed open, and to Fawkes it was like looking into a bottomless pit. Then the black void seemed to fuzz and he suddenly realized the problem. The air was too foul to breathe. Those who survived the concussion caused by the Satan missile were dropping from lack of oxygen.

"Open the outside hatch!" he roared. "Get some fresh air in here!"

"She's buckled, Captain," a voice rasped on the other side of the turret. "Jammed tight."

"The ventilators! Why aren't they operating?"

"Blown circuits," another man said, coughing. "The only air we've got is what's coming up through the magazine tubes."

In the choking haze and gloom Fawkes could barely make out the form of the man who spoke. "Find me something to pry the hatch open. We've got to make a path for crossventilation."

He made his way around the bodies and over the huge gun mechanism to the hatch that opened to the main deck. Looking at its seven-inch-thick wall of hard steel, Fawkes could well appreciate what he was up against. The only points in his favor were the shattered locking prongs and the inch of daylight showing at the top where the hatch had been blown inward.

Someone tapped his shoulder and he turned. It was Shaba.

"I heard you down in the magazine tube, Captain. I thought you might need this." He handed Fawkes a heavy steel bar four feet long and two inches thick.

Fawkes wasted no words of appreciation. He wedged the bar into the opening to the outside and pulled. His face flushed with the effort and his great arms trembled, but the hatch would not budge.

The obstinacy of the hatch came as no surprise to Fawkes. It was an age-old Scottish adage that nothing fell to a man's lot on the first try. He closed his eyes and sucked in great breaths, hyperventilating. Every cell in his body focused on kindling the strength locked within his immense body. Shaba watched, fascinated. He had never seen such a demonstration of sheer concentration. Fawkes reinserted the bar, paused a few seconds more, and finally began to heave. It looked to Shaba as though the captain had turned to stone; there was no obvious hint of effort, no tenseness of the muscles. The sweat began to pop from Fawkes's forehead and the tendons of his neck bulged and tautened, every muscle turned rock hard with strain; then, slowly, incredibly, the hatch shrieked as steel scraped against steel.

Shaba could not believe that such brute force existed; he could not know of the secret that drove Fawkes far above and beyond his normal energies. Another inch of light appeared between the hatch and the turret armor. Then, three inches . . . six . . . and abruptly the mangled steel twisted from its broken hinges and dropped to the deck with a great metallic echo.

Almost immediately, the stench and smoke were driven outside and replaced with cool, damp air from below. Fawkes stood aside and tossed the bar through the hatch, his clothes soaked through with sweat, his torso shuddering as he caught his breath and his pounding heart slowed to normal.

"Clear the breeches and secure the guns," he ordered.

Shaba looked blank. "We've lost hydraulic pressure to the power rammer. It can't be reversed to remove the shells."

"Damn the rammer," Fawkes snorted. "Do it by hand."

Shaba said nothing in reply. He had no time. A gun barrel poked through the open hatch and a hail of bullets ricocheted throughout the armored chamber. The burst whistled past Fawkes's side.

Shaba was not as lucky. Four bullets entered his neck almost simultaneously. He sank to his knees, his eyes staring uncomprehendingly at Fawkes, his mouth moving but expelling no words, only a gush of red that rivered down his chest.

Fawkes stood by helplessly and watched Shaba die. Then a rage swelled inside him and he whirled and grabbed a gun muzzle. The heat from the barrel seared the flesh from his hands but he was far beyond any sensation of pain. Fawkes gave a great pull, and the SEAL outside, stubbornly refusing to let go of his weapon, catapulted past the narrow aperture and landed inside, his index finger still locked on the trigger.

There is no fear in a man who knows with certainty he is about to die. Fawkes did not possess that certainty. His face was white with fear, fear that he would be killed before the Quick Death shell inside one of the three guns could be deactivated.

"You bloody fool!" he grunted as the SEAL kicked him in the stomach. "The guns . . . inside the guns . . . a plague . . ."

The SEAL twisted violently and slashed out with his free hand to Fawkes's jaw. Fighting to keep the muzzle away from his body, Fawkes could do nothing but absorb the blow. His strength was draining away when he lurched backward and fell partially through the hatch opening, try- ing with one last mighty effort to yank the gun from the

SEAL's grasp. Instead, the flesh came away from his palms and fingers and he lost his grip. The SEAL jumped sideways and lowered the gun, aiming it with agonizing deliberation at Fawkes's stomach.

Daniel Obasi, the young boy sitting in the turret officer's firing booth, watched in numbed horror as the SEAL's finger tightened on the trigger. He tried to yell, to distract the killer in the black wet suit, but his throat was dry as sand and a mere whisper rasped through his lips. Out of sheer desperation, in what he prayed was his one hope of saving his captain's life, Obasi pushed the red "fire" button.

65

There was no way to reverse the process, no way to halt the firing sequence. The powder charges detonated and two projectiles spit out of the center and starboard muzzles, but inside the port barrel the warhead jammed tight at the fracture caused by the Satan missiles, trapped the exploding gases at its base, and blocked them from escaping.

A new gun might have withstood the tremendous blowback and the staggering pressures but the tired, rusty old breech had seen its day, and it shattered and burst. In a microsecond a volcanic eruption of flame compressed within the turret, flashed down the magazine elevator tubes, and set off the powder sacks stored far below.

The *Iowa* blew her guts out.

Patrick Fawkes, in the fleeting instant he was blasted through the outside hatch, saw the utter waste, the terrible stupidity, of his actions. He reached out to his beloved Myrna to beg her forgiveness as he smashed against the unyielding deck and was crushed to pulp.

The armor-piercing shell from the starboard barrel reached its zenith and hurtled downward through the limestone dome of the National Archives building. By freakish chance it fell past the twenty-one tiers of books and records, crashed through the granite floor of the exhibition hall less than ten feet from the glass case containing the Declaration of Independence, and came to rest with half its length embedded in the concrete floor of the subbasement.

Shell number two was a dud.

Not so number three.

Activated by its tiny generator, the radar altimeter inside the Quick Death package began beaming signals to the ground and recording its downward trajectory. Lower and lower the warhead dropped until at fifteen hundred feet an electrical impulse popped the parachute release and an umbrella of fluorescent-orange silk blossomed against the blue sky. Amazingly, the thirty-plus-year-old material took the sudden strain without splitting at the seams.

Far below the streets of Washington, the President and his advisers sat motionlessly in their chairs, their eyes blinking as they followed the relentless descent of the projectile. At first, like passengers on the *Titanic* who refused to believe the huge ocean liner was sinking, they sat entranced, their minds unable to grasp the true scope of the events before them, feebly optimistic that somehow the mechanism inside the warhead would fail, causing it to fall harmlessly onto the grass of the mall.

Then, with a frightening momentum, they all began to feel the tightening pincers of despair.

A light breeze sprang up from the north and nudged the parachute toward the Smithsonian Institution buildings. Soldiers who had blocked off the streets around the Lincoln Memorial and the National Archives building and crowds of government employees caught in the morning traffic gazed sheeplike as a forest of hands pointed skyward.

Around the conference table the air was still with tension, a growing anxiety that reached insufferable proportions. Jarvis could watch no more. He placed his head in his hands. "Finished," he said, his voice hoarse. "We're finished."

"Isn't there something that can be done?" asked the President, his eyes locked on the floating object on the viewing screen.

Higgins shrugged in defeat. "Shooting that monster out of the sky would only disperse the bacteria. Beyond that, I'm afraid we can do nothing."

Jarvis saw a flash of realization flood the President's eyes, a sickening realization that they had come to the end of the road. The impossible could not happen, could not be accepted, but there it was. Death for millions was only seconds and a few hundred feet away.

So intently were they watching the scene that they did not notice the speck in the distance growing larger. Admiral Kemper was the first to distinguish it; he seldom missed a thing. He rose out of his chair and peered as though his eyes were laser beams. The others finally saw it too as the speck enlarged into a helicopter coming straight on the warhead.

"What in God's name . . ." Higgins muttered.

"It looks like the same crazy bastard who buzzed the *Iowa*," announced Kemper.

"This time we'll blast his ass," Higgins said, reaching for his communications phone.

The low sun bounced off the helicopter's canopy, making a bright momentary glint on the viewing screen. The craft grew, and soon, large black letters could be seen on its side.

"NUMA," said Kemper. "That's one of the National Underwater and Marine Agency copters."

Jarvis's hands fell from his face and he looked up as if suddenly awakening from a deep sleep. "You did say 'NUMA.' "

"See for yourself," Kemper said, pointing.

Jarvis looked. Then, like a man demented, he knocked over his chair and stretched across the table, slapping the phone out of Higgins's hand. "No!" he shouted.

Higgins looked stunned.

"Leave well enough alone!" Jarvis snapped. "The pilot knows what he's doing."

All that Jarvis was certain of was that Dirk Pitt was behind the drama being played out over the capital city. A NUMA helicopter and Pitt. The two had to be connected. A tiny glimmer of hope flickered within Jarvis as he watched the gap narrow between aircraft and warhead.

The Minerva bored in on the bright-orange parachute like a bull charging a matador's cape. It was going to be a tight race. Steiger and Sandecker had overestimated the trajectory of the Quick Death warhead and were hovering near the National Archives building when they saw the chute open early, a quarter of a mile short of their position. Precious time was lost while Steiger feverishly swung the aircraft on a closing course in a desperate gamble conceived by Pitt a few hours previously.

"Twelve seconds gone," Sandecker announced impassively from the cabin door.

Eighteen seconds to detonation, Steiger thought to himself.

"Ready on the hook and winch," said Sandecker.

Steiger shook his head. "Too risky. One pass is all we'll get. Must take it through the shrouds bow-on."

"You'll foul the rotor blades."

"The only shot we've got," Steiger replied.

Sandecker did not argue the point. He hurriedly dropped into the copilot's seat and strapped himself in.

The warhead was looming through the windshield. Steiger noted that it was painted regulation Navy blue. He pushed in the throttles to the twin turboshaft engines and at the same time pulled the pitch-control column back. The Minerva's forward speed was cut so abruptly that both men winced as they were thrown against their safety harnesses.

"Six seconds," said Sandecker.

The shadow of the huge parachute was falling over the helicopter when Steiger flipped the craft on its starboard side. The violent maneuver sent the pointed bow of the Minerva knifing between the shroud lines. Orange silk collapsed and covered the windshield, blotting out the sun. Three of the lines caught and wrapped around the rotor shaft before the tired old material gave way and shredded. The rest entwined around the fuselage and jerked the Minerva to a near stop as they tautened and took up the strain of the heavy projectile.

"Two seconds," Sandecker rasped through clenched teeth.

The Minerva was being pulled downward by the weight of the shell. Steiger returned the craft to an upright position with the pitch-control column, yanked the throttles back against their stops, and pulled up on the collective-pitch lever in a blur of hand movements.

The twin engines struggled under the load. Sandecker had stopped counting. Time had run out. The altimeter needle was quivering at one thousand feet. Sandecker leaned out an open window and stared past the flapping silk at the warhead dangling beneath the fuselage expecting to see an explosion.

The Minerva's rotor blades slapped the air, causing a thumping sound that could be heard for miles above the sea of enthralled faces turned to the sky. Parachute, projectile, and helicopter hung together, suspended. Sandecker darted his attention back to the altimeter. It hadn't budged. A sheen of sweat glistened on his brow.

Ten seconds passed, which to Sandecker seemed ten years. Steiger, absorbed in his task, battled the controls. The admiral could do little but sit there. It was the first time he could remember feeling totally useless.

"Lift, damn you, lift," Steiger said, pleading with the Minerva.

Sandecker watched the altimeter as though mesmerized. It seemed to him the needle made a fractional tic above the one-thousand-foot mark. Was it wishful thinking, or had the instrument really registered an upward reading? Then, slowly, almost infinitesimally, the needle appeared to move.

"Climbing," he reported. His voice had a tremor in it.

Steiger did not answer.

The rate of ascent began to increase. Sandecker remained quiet until he was sure his eyes weren't playing tricks on his brain. There was no more cause for uncertainty. The needle was slowly sweeping past the next indication.

66

The relief of the men in the emergency executive offices was impossible to describe. If polled, they would have unanimously agreed they had never seen any sight half so wonderful in their lives. Even dour General Higgins was grinning the widest grin on record. The suffocating cloud of doom had been suddenly swept away, and they began cheering as the Minerva dragged its deadly cargo toward a safe altitude.

The President sagged in his chair and allowed himself the pleasure of lighting a cigar. He nodded down the table at Jarvis through a haze of smoke.

"It would appear, Dale, that you are clairvoyant."

"A calculated guess, Mr. President," said Jarvis.

Admiral Kemper lifted his phone. "Put me in communication with that NUMA chopper!" he ordered.

"We haven't weathered the storm yet," said Higgins. "Those people up there can't fly around forever."

"We are in voice contact." A crisp announcement came out of the speakers beside the viewing screen.

Kemper spoke into his desk phone while keeping both eyes locked on the progress of the Minerva. "This is Admiral Joseph Kemper of the Joint Chiefs, NUMA copter; please identify yourself."

A voice replied so calmly and clearly it could have come from across the room.

"Jim Sandecker, Joe. What's on your mind?"

The President sat up in his chair. "The director of NUMA?"

Kemper nodded. "You know damn well what's on my mind!" he snapped into the receiver.

"Ah yes, the Quick Death warhead. I assume you're aware of its potential."

"I am."

"And you want to know what I'm going to do with it."

"The thought *had* occurred to me."

"As soon as we reach five thousand feet," said San-decker, "the pilot, Colonel Abe Steiger, and I are going to make a beeline for the sea and drop the son of a bitch as far from shore as our fuel will carry us."

"How far do you reckon?" asked Kemper.

There was a pause as Sandecker consulted with Steiger. "Approximately six hundred miles due east of the Dela-ware coastline."

"How secure is the projectile?"

"Seems snug enough. Might help if we didn't have to rely on instruments and could enjoy the scenery."

"Come again?"

"The parachute canopy is snagged across our wind-shield. We can only look straight down."

"Can we assist you?" asked Kemper.

"Yes," replied Sandecker. "By notifying all military and commercial flight traffic to stay clear of our path to the sea."

"Consider it done," Kemper said. "I'll also arrange to have a rescue vessel standing by near your estimated splashdown point."

"Negative, Joe. Colonel Steiger and I appreciate the gesture, but it would be a foolish waste of men's lives. You understand."

Kemper did not answer immediately. His eyes took on a look of deep sorrow. Then he said, "Understood. Kem-per out."

"Is there no way they can be saved?" Jarvis asked.

Kemper shook his head. "The sad truth is that Admiral Sandecker and Colonel Steiger are committing suicide. When the helicopter runs out of fuel and drops toward the sea, the projectile goes with it. When they both reach one thousand feet, the warhead disperses the Quick Death organism. The rest goes without saying."

"But surely they can cut away the canopy and fly a safe distance before ditching," Jarvis persisted.

"I see Admiral Kemper's point," said Higgins. "The answer is on the viewing screen. The parachute is the heli-copter's death shroud. The lines are woven around the base of the rotor and overhang the side opposite the cargo door. Even if the craft were hovering in a stationary position, it would be impossible for a man to climb out on that stream-lined fairing far enough to reach the lines with a knife."

"Could they bail out of the helicopter before it goes down?" Jarvis inquired.

General Sayre shook his head. "Unlike conventional aircraft, whirlybirds do not have automatic control systems. They must be flown manually every second. If the crew were to ditch, the craft would fall on top of them."

"The same principle applies to a midair pickup," said Kemper. "We might snatch one of the men, but not both."

"There is nothing we can do?" There was a faint catch in Jarvis's voice.

The President gazed forlornly at the lacquered tabletop for several moments. At last he said, "Just pray that they carry that vile abhorrence safely past our shores."

"And if they make it?"

"Then we sit helplessly by and watch two brave men die."

The icy water jabbed Pitt back to consciousness. The first minute, eyes blinking back the bright daylight, his mind tried to fathom his condition, to make sense out of why he was floating in a cold, dirty river. Then the pain began to bloom and his head felt like the receiving end of a carpenter's nail.

He felt a vibration in the water, heard a muffled popping sound, and soon a Coast Guard patrol boat slid out of the rising sun and idled in his direction. Two men in wet suits dropped over the side and expertly fitted Pitt into a hoist rig. The signal was given and he was gently hauled on board.

"A bit early in the morning for a swim," said a huge bear of a man with his arm in a sling. "Or are you practicing for the English Channel?"

Pitt looked around and saw the shattered glass and shredded wood on the boat's bridge. "Where did you come from? The battle of Midway?"

The bear grinned and replied, "We were headed for our dock when we were ordered back to pick you out of the drink. I'm Kiebel, Oscar Kiebel, commander of what was once the cleanest boat on the Inland Waterway."

"Dirk Pitt. I'm with NUMA."

Kiebel's eyes narrowed. "How did you come to be on the battleship?"

Pitt looked up at the boat's broken rigging. "I believe I owe you a new radio aerial."

"That was you?"

"Sorry about the hit and run, but there was no time to fill out an accident report."

Kiebel motioned toward a doorway. "Better come inside and get a bandage on your head. It looks as though you took a nasty crack."

It was then that Pitt saw a great pall of smoke rising around a bend in the Potomac. "The *Iowa*," he said. "What of the *Iowa?*"

"She blew herself up."

Pitt leaned heavily against the railing.

Kiebel gently put his good arm around Pitt as one of his men brought up a blanket. "Better take it easy and lie down. A doctor will be waiting when we dock."

"It doesn't matter," Pitt said. "Not anymore."

Kiebel steered him into the pilothouse and found Pitt a steaming cup of coffee. "Sorry there's no booze on board. Regulations and all that. A bit early for a shot anyway." Then he turned and spoke through an open doorway to his communications officer. "What's the latest on that helicopter?"

"She's over Chesapeake Bay, sir."

Pitt looked up. "What helicopter is that?"

"Why, one of yours," Kiebel said. "Damnedest thing. A shell from the *Iowa*'s final salvo came down in a parachute and this idiot in a NUMA chopper nabbed it on the fly."

"Thank God!" Pitt said as the full implication hit him. "A radio. I need to borrow your radio."

Kiebel hesitated. He could read the urgency in Pitt's eyes. "Allowing civilians to use military communications gear is hardly kosher. . . ."

Pitt held up a hand and cut him off. The feeling was returning to his cold-numbed skin and he sensed something pressing into his stomach under the shirt. His face went blank as he removed a small packet and stared at it speculatively.

"Now where in hell did that come from?"

Steiger warily regarded the temperature gauge as the needle crept toward the red. The Atlantic coastline was still sixty miles away, and the last thing he wanted was a seized turbine bearing.

The call light on the radio blinked on and the admiral

pressed the "transmit" button. "This is Sandecker. Go ahead."

"I'm ready for those scrambled eggs," Pitt said, his voice crackling over the headphones.

"Dirk!" Sandecker blurted. "Are you all right?"

"A trifle shopworn but still kicking."

"The other warhead?" Steiger asked anxiously.

"Disarmed," Pitt answered.

"And the Quick Death agent?"

Pitt's tone betrayed no uncertainty. "Flushed down the drain."

Pitt could be only reasonably sure Hiram Lusana had disposed of the bomblets in the river, but he was not about to suggest to Steiger and the admiral that it was possible their efforts had been in vain.

Sandecker briefed Pitt on the grappling of the parachute and explained that the outlook was grim. Pitt listened without interrupting. When the admiral had finished, Pitt posed only one question.

"How long can you stay in the air?"

"I can stretch the fuel for another two, maybe two and a half hours," replied Steiger. "My immediate problem is the engines. They're running rough and getting hot under the collar."

"Sounds like the parachute's canopy is partially blocking the intake chambers."

"I'm open for brilliant ideas. Got any?"

"It so happens I do," Pitt responded. "Keep your ears up. I'll be back in touch two hours from now. In the meantime, dump every ounce you can. Seats, tools, any piece of the ship you can pry loose to lighten your weight. Do whatever has to be done, but claw the air till you hear from me. Pitt out."

He switched off the microphone and turned to Lieutenant Commander Kiebel. "I must get ashore as quickly as possible."

"We'll be dockside in eight minutes."

"I'll need transportation," said Pitt.

"I still don't know how you fit into this mess," said Kiebel. "For all I know, I should place you under arrest."

"This is no time to play vigilante games," snapped Pitt. "Christ, do I have to do everything myself?" He bent over the radio operator. "Patch me in to NUMA headquarters and the Stransky Instrument Company, in that order."

"A little free with my men and equipment, aren't you, mister?"

Pitt didn't doubt for a second that if Kiebel had had two good arms, he'd have mashed him to the deck. "What do I have to do to get your cooperation?"

Kiebel fixed his cork-brown eyes on Pitt with a murderous stare; then, slowly, they took on a twinkle as his mouth etched into a smile. "Say 'please.' "

Pitt complied, and exactly twelve minutes later he was in a Coast Guard helicopter, racing back to Washington.

67

The two hours came and went with agonizing slowness for Steiger and Sandecker. They had crossed the Delaware shoreline at Slaughter Beach and were now five hundred miles out over the Atlantic. The weather remained relatively calm, and the few thunderclouds obligingly floated free of their flight path.

Everything that wasn't bolted down, and some things that were, had been jettisoned out the cargo door. Sandecker estimated he had dumped in the neighborhood of four hundred pounds. That and the weight loss from the diminishing fuel had kept the protesting engines from overheating as they struggled to keep the overladen Minerva aloft.

Sandecker was lying with his back against the cockpit bulkhead. He had removed every seat except Steiger's. The physical efforts of the past two hours had exhausted him. His lungs heaved and his arms and legs were stiff with muscle fatigue.

"Any word . . . anything from Pitt?"

Steiger shook his head without taking his eyes off the instruments. "Dead silence," he said. "But then, what can we expect? The man isn't a card-carrying miracle worker."

"I've known him to pull off what others thought impossible."

"I know a pathetic attempt to instill false hope when I hear one." Steiger tilted his head toward the panel clock. "Two hours, eight minutes since the last contact. I guess he's written us off."

Sandecker was too exhausted to argue. As if through a heavy mist, he reached over, pulled a headset down over his ears, and closed his eyes. A gentle peace was settling over him when a loud voice abruptly blasted him to full wakefulness.

"Hey, Baldy, you fly like you screw."

"Giordino!" Steiger rasped.

Sandecker punched the "transmit" button. "Al, where are you calling from?"

"About a half mile back and two hundred feet below you."

Sandecker and Steiger exchanged stunned looks.

"You're supposed to be in the hospital," Sandecker said dumbly.

"Pitt arranged my parole."

"Where *is* Pitt?" Steiger demanded.

"Looking up your ass, Abe," Pitt replied. "I'm at the controls of Giordino's CatlinM–two hundred."

"You're late," said Steiger.

"Sorry, these things take time. How's your fuel?"

"Sopping the bottom of the tank," answered Steiger. "I might squeeze another eighteen or twenty minutes if I'm lucky."

"A Norwegian cruise liner is standing by sixty miles, bearing two-seven-zero degrees. Her captain has cleared all passengers from the sun deck for your arrival. You should make it—"

"Are you crazy?" Steiger cut in. "Cruise ship, sun deck—what are you ranting about?"

Pitt continued quite unruffled. "As soon as we cut away the projectile, head for the cruise ship. You can't miss her."

"How I'll envy you guys," said Giordino. "Sitting around the poolside deck, sipping mai tais."

"Sipping mai tais!" repeated an awed Steiger. "My God, they're both crazy!"

Pitt turned to Giordino, ensconced in the copilot's seat, and nodded toward the plaster cast covering one leg. "You sure you can work the controls wearing that thing?"

"The only function it won't let me perform," said Giordino, giving the cast a light thump, "is scratching an itch from within."

"It's yours, then."

Pitt lifted his hands from the control column, climbed out of the seat, and moved back into the Catlin's cargo section. Intense cold whistled in from the open hatch. A light-skinned man with Nordic features and dressed in multicolored skiing togs was huddled over a long black rectangular object that was mounted on a heavy-legged tripod. Dr. Paul Weir was clearly not cut out to scramble around drafty airplanes in the dead of winter.

"We're in position," Pitt said.

"Almost ready," Weir replied through lips that were turning blue. "I'm hooking up the cooling tubes. If we don't have water circulating around the head and power supply, the unit will barbecue its anatomy."

"Somehow I expected a more exotic piece of equipment," said Pitt.

"Large-frame argon lasers are not spawned for science-fiction movies, Mr. Pitt." Dr. Weir went on talking as he made a final check of the wiring connector. "They are designed to emit a coherent beam of light for any number of practical applications."

"Has it the punch to do the job?"

Weir shrugged. "Eighteen watts concentrated in a tiny beam that releases a mere two kilowatts of energy doesn't sound like much, but I promise you it's ample."

"How close do you want us to the projectile?"

"The beam divergence makes it necessary to be as near as possible. Less than fifty feet."

Pitt pressed his mike button. "Al?"

"Come in."

"Close to within forty feet of the projectile."

"At that range we'll be buffeted by turbulence from the copter's rotor."

"Can't be helped."

Weir flicked the laser's main switch.

"Do you read me, Abe?" Pitt asked.

"I'm listening."

"The idea is for Giordino to maneuver close enough so we can sever the shroud lines attached to the projectile with a laser beam."

"So that's the angle," Sandecker said.

"That's the angle, Admiral." Pitt's voice was soft, almost casual. "We're moving into position now. Steady on course. Keep whatever fingers you have free crossed and let's do it."

Giordino eased the controls with the precision of a watchmaker and slipped the Catlin beside and slightly below the Minerva. He began to feel the chopping wind currents on the control surfaces and his hands tightened about the yoke. Back in the cargo section the violent shaking rattled everything that wasn't tied down. Pitt alternated his gaze between the projectile and Weir.

The head physicist from Stransky Instruments bent over

the laser head. He showed no signs of fear or anxiety. If anything, he seemed to be enjoying himself.

"I don't see any beam," said Pitt. "Is it working?"

"Sorry to shatter your conceptions," answered Weir, "but the argon laser beam is invisible."

"How can you zero it in?"

"With this thirty-dollar telescopic rifle sight." He patted the round tube, which had been hastily screwed to the laser. "It won't win me the Nobel Prize, but it should suffice."

Pitt lay on his stomach and crawled until his head was past the threshold of the open hatch. The blasting cold tore at his head bandage, causing one end of the gauze to flap like a flag in a hurricane. The projectile was hanging below the helicopter, trailing at a slight angle toward the tail rotor. Staring at it, Pitt found it difficult to believe a universe of agony and death could be crammed into so small a package.

"Closer," Weir shouted. "I need another ten feet."

"Move in ten feet," Pitt said over the microphone.

"Any closer and we can use a pair of scissors," Giordino muttered. If he was tense with anxiety, he didn't show it. His face displayed the expression of one who was half dozing. Only the burning eyes gave any hint of the concentration required for precision flying. The sweat felt like it was exploding inside his cast and the nerve endings in his leg screamed at the irritation.

Pitt could make out something now—a blackening color in the twisted shroud lines above the projectile. The invisible beam had locked in and was melting the nylon strands. How many were there? he wondered; perhaps as many as fifty.

"She's overheating!" Two words and a skipped heartbeat. "Too cold in here with that hatch open," Weir yelled. "The coolant tubes have frozen up."

Weir's eyes returned to the telescopic sight. Pitt could see several lines parting, their charred ends snapping horizontally and lashing out in the airstream. The acrid smell of burning insulation began to invade the cabin.

"The tube won't take much more," said Weir.

Another half-dozen shroud lines burned free, but the rest remained taut and undamaged. Weir suddenly straightened up and tore off his smoldering gloves.

"God, I'm sorry!" he shouted. "The tube is gone!"

The Quick Death projectile still hung ominously beneath the Minerva.

Thirty seconds dragged by while Pitt lay there, staring at the deadly projectile swinging through the sky. There was no expression on his face, just a peculiar preoccupation. Then he broke the silence.

"We've lost the laser," he announced without elaboration.

"Damn, damn, damn!" Steiger snarled. "Where did our luck go?" His voice was almost savage in bitterness and frustration.

"So now?" Admiral Sandecker asked calmly.

"You break off and put that turkey in a dive," Pitt answered.

"A what?"

"The last card in the deck. Head into a dive. When you build up sufficient g-forces, pull up. Maybe Abe's luck will change and your unwanted passenger will drop free."

"It'll be sticky," said Steiger. "I'll have to do it on instruments. I can't see shit with the canopy covering the windshield."

"We'll stay with you," Giordino said.

"Don't come too close or you'll catch our cold," Steiger replied. He eased the helicopter clear of the chase plane. "Let's pray this baby isn't constipated." Then he pushed the control stick forward.

The Minerva tipped over and down on a seventy-degree angle. Sandecker braced his feet against the base of Steiger's seat and clawed for a handhold. To the men watching in rapt fascination from the Catlin, the helicopter's nose pointed straight at the sea.

"Ease your angle of descent," said Pitt. "The projectile is beginning to trail back toward your tail rotor."

"I read you," said Steiger, his words tense and strained. "It's like jumping off a building with your eyes closed."

"You're looking good," Pitt said reassuringly. "Not too fast. Pass seven g-factors and you lose your rotor blades."

"Wouldn't think of it."

Four thousand feet.

Giordino did not attempt to match Steiger foot for foot. He lagged behind, keeping the Catlin in a shallow banking dive, corkscrewing down behind the Minerva. Dr. Weir, his job finished, groped toward the warmth of the control cabin.

The sharp tilt to the helicopter's cabin floor made Admiral Sandecker feel as though he were standing with his back against a wall. Steiger's eyes danced from the altimeter to the air-speed indicator to the gauge showing the artificial horizon and back again.

Three thousand feet.

Pitt could see that the canopy of the parachute was flapping dangerously near the twirling rotor, but he remained silent. Steiger had enough on his mind, he reasoned, without hearing another dire warning. He watched as the sea rushed up to meet the Minerva.

Steiger began to experience a mounting vibration. The wind noise was picking up as his speed increased. For a fleeting second he considered holding the stick in position and ending the torment. But then, for the first time that day, he thought of his wife and children, and his desire to see them again stoked a fierce determination to live.

"Abe, now!" Pitt's command boomed over his earphones. "Pull out."

Steiger hauled back on the stick.

Two thousand feet.

The Minerva shuddered from the tremendous gravitational drag that attacked every rivet of her structure. She hung poised as the projectile, reacting to the force like a weight at the end of a giant pendulum, arched outward. The surviving shroud lines that had withstood the laser's beam tautened like banjo strings. In twos and threes they began to fray.

Just as the Quick Death projectile looked as though it was going to whip back and smash the helicopter, it tore free and dropped away.

"She's gone!" shouted Pitt.

Steiger was too drained to reply. Fighting the blackness framing his vision from the sudden pull-out, Sandecker struggled to his knees and shook Steiger by the shoulder.

"Make for that cruise ship," he said in a very tired and very relieved voice.

Pitt did not watch the Minerva as it veered off and headed toward safety. He watched the projectile until its blue skin blended against the blue of the rolling water and faded from sight.

Designed for a descent rate of eighteen feet per second, the projectile hurtled past one thousand feet without blowing off its warhead. The detonation mechanism lagged until it was too late. At nearly three hundred sixty feet per second the biological organism, carrying its threat of agony and mass extinction, plunged into the waiting arms of the abysmal sea.

Pitt was still watching when the tiny white scar from the splash was closed over by the relentless swells.

There is something heartsickening about seeing a proud ship die. The President felt deeply moved, his eyes centered on the billowing pillars of smoke rolling from the *Iowa* as the fireboats edged close to the inferno in a futile effort to extinguish the flames.

He sat with Timothy March and Dale Jarvis, the Joint Chiefs having returned to their respective offices in the Pentagon to begin launching the expected investigations, dictating the expected reports, and issuing the expected directives. In a few hours the shock would wear off and the news media would start shouting for blood, anyone's blood.

The President had settled on a course of action. The public outcry had to be softened. Nothing would be gained by proclaiming the raid as another day of infamy. The pieces were to be swept under the carpet of confusion as delicately as possible.

"Word has just come in that Admiral Bass has died at Bethesda Naval Hospital," Jarvis announced softly.

"He must have been a strong man to have carried the terrible burden of the Quick Death's secret all these years," said the President.

"That's the end of it, then," March murmured.

"There is still Rongelo Island," said Jarvis.

"Yes," the President said, nodding wearily, "there is still that."

"We cannot allow any trace of the organism to remain."

The President looked at Jarvis. "What do you propose?"

"Erase the island from the map," Jarvis replied.

"Impossible," said March. "The Soviets would raise holy hell if we set off a bomb. The moratorium on above-ground nuclear tests has been respected by both nations for two decades."

A thin smile touched Jarvis's lips. "The Chinese have yet to sign the pact."

"So?"

"So we take a page from Operation Wild Rose," explained Jarvis. "We send one of our missile-carrying subs as close as we dare to the Chinese mainland, then order it to launch a nuclear warhead at Rongelo Island."

March and the President exchanged thoughtful glances. Then they turned to Jarvis, waiting for the rest of it.

"As long as American preparations for a test are non-existent and none of our surface ships or aircraft are within two thousand miles of the blast area, there is no tangible evidence the Russians can use to build a case against us. On the other hand, their spy satellites cannot help but record the missile trajectory as originating from Chinese territory."

"We might pull it off if we played shadylike," said March, warming to the scheme. "The Chinese would, of course, deny any involvement. And after the usual nasty accusations from the Kremlin, our own State Department, and the other outraged nations, condemning Peking, the episode would die and be mostly forgotten inside two weeks."

The President stared into space as he battled with his conscience. For the first time in nearly eight years he felt the total vulnerability of his office. The armor of power was filled with hairline cracks that could burst apart when struck by the unanticipated.

At last, with the exertion of a man twice his age, he rose from his chair.

"I pray to God," he said, his eyes filled with sadness, "I am the last man in history who willfully orders a nuclear strike."

Then he turned and slowly made his way toward the elevator that would take him up to the White House.

FOOL'S MATE

Umkono, South Africa—
January 1989

The heat from the early-morning sun made itself felt as two men gently slipped the cradle ropes through their hands and lowered the wooden box to the floor of the grave. Then the ropes were pulled free, making a soft rustling sound as they snaked around the sharp, unsanded edges of the coffin.

"Sure you don't want me to fill it in?" asked an ebony-skinned gravedigger as he coiled the rope around a sinewy shoulder.

"Thanks, I'll take care of it," Pitt said, holding out several South African rand notes.

"No pay," said the gravedigger. "The captain was a friend. I could dig a hundred graves and never repay the kindness he rained upon my family when he was alive."

Pitt nodded in understanding. "I'll borrow your shovel."

The digger obliged, shook Pitt's hand vigorously, and flashed an enormous smile. Then with a wave he set foot over a narrow path that led from the cemetery to the village.

Pitt looked around. The landscape was lush but harsh. Steam from the damp undergrowth wisped above the plants as the sun rose higher in the sky. He rubbed a sleeve over his sweat-soaked forehead and stretched out under a mimosa tree, studying its blossoming yellow fluffy balls and long white thorns and listening to the honking of hornbills in the distance. Then he turned his attention back to the large granite stone sitting at the head of the grave site.

HERE LIE THE
FAMILY FAWKES

Patrick McKenzie
Myrna Clarissa
Patrick McKenzie, Jr.
Jennifer Louise

Joined together for
all eternity
1988

A prophetic man, the captain, Pitt thought. The stone
had been carved in its entirety months before Fawkes's
death on board the *Iowa*. He brushed away a vagrant ant
and dozed for the next two hours. He was awakened by the
sound of a car.

The uniformed driver, a sergeant, braked the Bentley,
slipped from behind the wheel, and opened the rear door.
Colonel Joris Zeegler stepped out, followed by Defence
Minister Pieter De Vaal.

"Seems peaceful enough," said De Vaal.

"This sector has been quiet since the Fawkes massacre," Zeegler replied. "I believe the grave is this way,
sir."

Pitt rose to his feet and brushed himself off as they
approached. "It was good of you gentlemen to come so
far," he said, extending his hand.

"No great effort, I assure you," De Vaal said arrogantly.
He ignored Pitt's outstretched hand and sat irreverently on
the Fawkes headstone. "By coincidence, Colonel Zeegler
had arranged an inspection tour of Northern Natal Province. A short detour, a brief stop-off in the schedule. No
harm done."

"This won't take long," said Pitt, casually checking his
dark glasses for smudges. "Did you know Captain
Fawkes?"

"I appreciate the fact your rather strange request to
meet me in a rural cemetery came down from high sources
in your government, but I want it understood that I'm here
out of courtesy, not to answer questions."

"Understood," Pitt said.

"Yes, I once met Captain Fawkes." De Vaal gazed into

space. "Back in October, I believe it was. Soon after his family were murdered. I expressed my condolences on behalf of the Defence Ministry."

"Did he accept your offer to command the raid on Washington?"

De Vaal didn't bat an eye. "Pure rot. The man was mentally unbalanced by the death of his wife and children. He planned and conducted the raid entirely on his own."

"Did he?"

"My position and rank do not have to tolerate rudeness." De Vaal came to his feet. "Good day, Mr. Pitt."

Pitt let him walk nearly twenty feet before he said, "Operation Wild Rose, Minister. Our intelligence people knew about it almost from the beginning."

De Vaal stopped in midstride, turned, and looked at Pitt. "They knew?" He walked back until he was standing face to face with the man from NUMA. "They knew about Wild Rose?"

"That shouldn't surprise *you*, of all people," Pitt said affably. "After all, it was you who leaked it to them."

De Vaal's haughty composure cracked and he looked to Zeegler for support. The colonel's eyes were unblinking and his face was as hard as stone. "Preposterous," De Vaal said. "You're making a wild accusation based on the wind."

"I admit to a few holes in the net," said Pitt. "But I came into the game late. A neat scheme, and whatever the outcome, you won, Minister. The plan was never meant to succeed. Blaming the AAR for the raid in order to drum up sympathy for the South African white minority was a smoke screen. The real purpose was to embarrass and topple Prime Minister Koertsmann's party so the Defence Ministry could have an excuse for stepping in with a new military government headed by none other than Pieter De Vaal."

"Why are you doing this?" De Vaal said savagely. "What do you hope to gain?"

"I don't like to see traitors prosper," Pitt retorted. "Incidentally, how much did you and Emma salt away? Three, four, five million dollars?"

"You're chasing shadows, Pitt. Colonel Zeegler, here, can tell you. Emma was a paid agent for the AAR."

"Emma sold doctored reports from your Defence Ministry files to any black revolutionary sucker enough to pay for them and split the take with you. A most lucrative side venture, De Vaal."

"I do not have to stand here and listen to his garbage," the Minister hissed. He nodded at Zeegler and gestured toward the waiting Bentley.

Zeegler did not move. "I'm sorry, Minister, but I think Mr. Pitt should be heard out."

De Vaal was nearly choking with rage. "You have served me for ten years, Joris. You well know I punish insubordination to the extreme."

"I'm aware of that, sir, but I think we should stay, particularly in light of the circumstances." Zeegler pointed toward a black man who was threading his way between the gravestones. He wore a grim, determined face and was dressed in the uniform of the AAR. A long, curved Moroccan knife was gripped loosely in one hand.

"The fourth actor in the drama," said Pitt. "Permit me to introduce Thomas Machita, the new leader of the African Army of Revolution."

Though the Minister's entourage carried no weapons, Zeegler stood unconcerned. De Vaal spun and shouted to his chauffeur while gesturing wildly at Machita. "Sergeant! Shoot him! For God's sake, shoot him!"

The sergeant looked through De Vaal, as though the Minister were transparent. De Vaal turned to Zeegler, his eyes sick with a mounting fear. "Joris, what goes on?"

Zeegler did not answer; his face was an emotionless void.

Pitt pointed into the open grave. "It was Captain Fawkes who blew the whistle on your shifty act. He may have been unhinged by the death of his family and blinded by revenge, but it struck him that he had been horribly and pitifully duped when you sent Emma to kill him. A necessary part of your plan. Captured alive, he might have revealed your direct involvement. Also, you couldn't take the chance he could somehow become wise that it was you who masterminded the attack on his farm."

"No!" The word scratched from De Vaal's throat.

"Captain Patrick McKenzie Fawkes was the only man in South Africa who could pull off Wild Rose. You ordered the murders of his wife and children knowing a grief-stricken man would seek retribution. The massacre was a stroke of cunning. Even your own people at the

Ministry were at a loss to connect the raiders with any known insurgent organization. It never dawned on them their boss sneaked in a team of black mercenaries from Angola."

De Vaal's eyes registered stunned desperation. "How is it possible you know all this?"

"Like any good intelligence officer, Colonel Zeegler kept investigating until he ran down the truth," Pitt said. "Also, as do most sea captains, Fawkes kept a log. I was there when Emma tried to kill him. Fawkes saved my life before the ship blew up. But not before inserting his log, along with a few added notes about you, into a watertight tobacco pouch and slipping it under my shirt. The pages made damned interesting reading, especially to the President and the director of the NSA.

"By the way," Pitt continued, "that phony message you sent implicating Prime Minister Koertsmann was never really taken at face value. The White House was satisfied that Operation Wild Rose was conceived and conducted behind his back. Thus, your oily scheme to take over your own government was blown to dust. In the end Fawkes did you in, even if it was posthumously. The other details were supplied by Major Machita, who agreed to bury the hatchet with Colonel Zeegler long enough to put you away. As to my presence, I asked for and received the role of master of ceremonies because of my debt to Captain Fawkes."

De Vaal stared at Pitt, his features set in defeat. Then he turned to Zeegler. "Joris, you arranged for my betrayal?"

"No man stands with a traitor."

"If ever a man deserved to die, De Vaal, it is you," said Machita. The hatred seemed to seep from his pores.

De Vaal ignored Machita. "You cannot simply execute a man of my station. The law demands a trial."

"It is Prime Minister Koertsmann's wish that there be no scandal." Zeegler spoke without looking his chief in the eye. "He suggested you die in the line of duty."

"That would make me a martyr." A tiny degree of confidence restored De Vaal's composure. "Can you see me as a martyr?"

"No, sir. That's why he agreed to my proposal that you turn up missing. Better you become a forgotten mystery than a national hero."

Too late, De Vaal caught the glint of steel as Machita's knife arched up between his groin and navel. The Defence Minister's eyes bulged in shock. He tried to speak; his mouth moved slackly, but the only sound that came was an animallike gasp. A red stain spread across his uniform.

Machita kept his hand on the knife's handle, watching death as it closed about De Vaal. Then, as the body sagged, Machita gave it a push backward, and De Vaal fell into the open grave. The three men walked to the edge and stood looking down as streams of dirt trickled and dropped on the figure sprawled below.

"A fitting rest for his kind," Machita muttered.

Zeegler's face was pale. He was hardened to seeing battlefield dead, but this was quite another thing. "I'll have the driver fill in the grave."

Pitt shook his head. "No need. Fawkes made one final request in his log. I promised myself I'd see to it."

"As you wish." Zeegler turned to leave. Machita looked as if he were going to say something, thought better of it, and started toward the underbrush surrounding the cemetery.

"Hold on," said Pitt. "Neither of you can afford to waste this opportunity."

"Opportunity?" Zeegler said.

"After acting together to destroy a mutual cancer, it would be stupid not to stand face to face and discuss your differences."

"A waste of words," Zeegler said contemptuously. "Thomas Machita only speaks with violence."

"Like all Westerners, Mr. Pitt, you are naive to our battle," Machita said, his face stoic. "Talk cannot change what is meant to be. The racist South African government will fall to blacks in time."

"You will pay dearly before your flag flies over Cape Town," said Zeegler.

"Fool's mate," said Pitt. "You're both playing a fool's-mate gambit."

Zeegler looked at him. "Perhaps in your eyes, Mr. Pitt. But to us it goes to a depth no outsider can fathom."

The colonel continued to his car and Machita faded into the jungle.

The truce was over. The chasm was too wide to be crossed.

A wave of impotency mixed with anger swept Pitt.

"What will it all matter a thousand years from now?" he shouted after them.

He picked up the shovel and in a slow tempo began scooping dirt into the grave. He could not bring himself to look at De Vaal. Soon he heard the splatter of dirt on dirt and he knew no one would ever see the Defence Minister again.

When he was finished and the mound was neatly shaped, he opened a box that lay on the grass beside the headstone and removed four flowering plants. These he carefully embedded in the soil at the corners of the Fawkes burial plot. Then he straightened and stepped back.

"Rest well, Captain Fawkes. May you not be judged too harshly."

Feeling neither remorse nor sadness but rather a kind of contentment, Pitt placed the empty box under one arm and the shovel over his shoulder and set a course for the village of Umkono.

Behind him, the four bougainvillea plants arched their blossoms toward the African sun.

OMEGA

South Pacific—January 1989

Rongelo Island—actually a tiny atoll, an island in name only—was a solitary fragment of land floating in isolation on 160,000 square miles of Pacific. Its mass rose only six feet above the glitter of the ocean, so low it was impossible to see from ten miles away. Driven by wind and tide, the waves burst on the fragile reef surrounding the narrow strand of bone-white beach, and then closed ranks on the other side, marching on for hundreds of miles before making the next landfall.

The island was barren except for a few rotting coconut palms that had been battered to stumps by typhoon waves. In the middle of its highest point the skeletons of Dr. Vetterly and his assistants, turned bleached and porous over the years, lay on the jagged coral, the empty eye sockets of their skulls turned skyward, as though waiting for deliverance.

At sunset the thunderclouds behind Rongelo caught the diminishing rays of light and glowed a flaring gold as the missile dropped silently from space, the thunder of its passage through the atmosphere left far behind.

Suddenly a blue-white blaze lighted the sea for hundreds of miles, and a great fireball swallowed the atoll. In less than a second the fiery mass erupted and swelled like a monstrous spastic bubble. The blinding colors on its surface melted from orange to pink and finally to deep purple. The shock wave lashed across the water like a lightning bolt, flattening the rolling swells.

Then the fireball released its hold on the surface and boiled toward the sky, digesting millions of tons of coral before spitting it out in a swirling geyser of steam and rubble. The mass inflated to a diameter of five miles, and in less than a minute the inferno reached an altitude of 115,000 feet. There it hung, gradually cooling into an immense dark cloud that slowly drifted to the north.

Rongelo Island had disappeared. All that remained was a depression three hundred feet deep and two miles across. Quickly the sea rushed in and covered any trace of the gaping wound. The sun was tinted an eerie yellow-green as it stole below the horizon.

The Quick Death organism had ceased to be.